THE
HOPE
WE
KEEP

THE LOST LIGHT SERIES BOOK THREE

KYLA STONE

Est. 2000
Paper Moon
PRESS

The Hope We Keep

This book is a work of fiction. Any references to historical events, real people, or
real places are used fictitiously. Other names, characters, places, and events are
products of the author's imagination, and any resemblances to actual events or
places or persons, living or dead, is entirely coincidental.

Printed in the United States of America

Cover design by Christian Bentulan

Book formatting by Vellum

First Printed in 2023

ISBN: 978-1-945410-97-0

❦ Created with Vellum

PREFACE

This novel takes place in the Upper Peninsula of Michigan. While most of the locations are real, a few creative liberties have been taken by the author for the sake of the story.

1

SHILOH EASTON
DAY SIXTY-TWO

A twig cracked behind her.

Thirteen-year-old Shiloh Easton spun and reached for her crossbow. Pulse thudding in her ears, she scanned the woods from left to right, right to left, searching for threats.

Deep shadows blanketed the woods. Late afternoon sunlight spilled in panels through the leafy canopy, trees tall as sentinels surrounding her, towering pines and dense green balsam firs.

Ahead of her, the deer trail angled to the right and disappeared around the bend. Deer hooves left fresh imprints in the damp earth.

The hairs on the back of her neck prickled. It was a feeling more than anything else. Something—or someone—was out there. Following her. Watching her.

Planting her feet, she nestled the crossbow's butt stock against her shoulder, her cheek pressed to the stock, lining up her dominant eye with the sight. She tightened her grip, index finger balanced on the trigger guard, the sleek fiberglass bolt ready to fly.

Black squirrels rustled in the leaf litter scattered across the forest floor. Robins and sparrows twittered from the branches of a great spreading oak. She inhaled the comforting scents of the forest—rich soil, wet leaf litter, and pine sap.

Her mouth had gone bone-dry. She had a hydration bottle with a filter in her pack, but she didn't reach for it. The stock of the crossbow dug into her shoulder. Beads of sweat trickled down the back of her neck.

Movement out of the left corner of her eye. Her heart kicked against her ribs. She shifted the crossbow to the left, squinting as she examined the shadows, the way the light played across the birch, maple, and ash trees. Deeper shadows pooled beneath the rhododendrons dripping with pink flowers.

The shiny leaves of the blackberry bushes five yards to her right trembled as if something large had brushed past moments ago.

Fear knotted in her throat; she fought it back. Shiloh held her breath and strained her ears, steadying her breathing the way Eli had taught her.

It was the deer she was tracking, or a black bear. Or a raccoon.

Maybe it was nothing. It didn't feel like nothing.

There. Ten yards to her southeast, a shadow lurked among deeper shadows. Was the shadow denser than the others? It appeared to deepen, shifting in a manner contrary to nature. The contours of the forest seemed to bend into the shape of a crouched human figure.

Perhaps it was a hunter trailing a deer, like her, or her wild imagination playing tricks on her. Or maybe it was a monster, a windigo lying in wait. According to Ojibwe legend, the windigo was a malevolent, flesh-eating spirit roaming the woods in search of humans to devour, body and soul.

She was distinctly aware of her aloneness in the Hiawatha National Forest, which consisted of almost nine hundred thousand acres of rolling hills, flat plains, wetlands, and winding rivers and streams, a vast wilderness tucked into Michigan's Upper Peninsula along the vast and rugged shoreline of Lake Superior.

The radio was clipped to the belt at her hip, but it only crackled with static. Without realizing it, she'd wandered out of range in pursuit of her prey.

The closest help was several miles away in Munising, population two thousand or so, the closest town to the famed Pictured Rocks National Lakeshore. She was on her own.

She'd spent the day searching for deer, but deer had grown scarce close to town. Everyone and their brothers, cousins, mothers, and in-laws were traipsing the woods in Alger County, hunting for white-tailed deer, elk, cottontail rabbit, feral pig, ruffled grouse, and even weasels and coyotes—whatever meat they could find.

Her stomach growled loudly. She flinched at the sudden noise.

The dense shadow lurking within the trees didn't flicker in response, didn't move. Her ragged breath was the only sound. She forced herself to stay calm. She was just skittish, her nerves on edge, jumpy. But then, everyone was jumpy these days.

Two months ago, brilliant auroras had lit up the heavens as a series of powerful super-flares erupted from the surface of the sun. As massive bursts of radiation struck the Earth's magnetosphere, power grids were destroyed, transformers overloaded, and power lines burst into flames. Induced currents burned out satellite circuit boards, obliterating GPS, telephone, internet, television, banking networks, and high-frequency communication systems.

In a matter of days, the infrastructure of half the world was annihilated.

Everything was ripping apart at the seams.

The daylight glinting through the trees began to change, turning golden as the shadows lengthened, stretching long fingers across the leaf litter. The first hint of coolness kissed the back of her neck. She had a few hours before sundown; it was past time to head back.

Studying the quivering shadows, she couldn't shake the disconcerting feeling that something out here which did not belong—an evil she couldn't see or name, lurked in secret places, prowling and skulking in the shadows, biding its time.

That she was the hunted, not the hunter.

The sound came again. Leaves crackled off to her left. A shuffling noise as something moved furtively across the forest floor.

The birds had gone silent. A hush fell across the forest. Sound dimmed but for her blood whooshing in her ears. Despite the heat, a cold sweat broke out on her forehead.

Her pulse leaped against her throat. Her finger slipped from the trigger guard of her crossbow to the trigger. Every instinct screamed at her to run, to flee.

She didn't. Resolute, she took a quiet step closer. She moved stealthily, heel to toe, squinting to decipher the indistinct shape of the thing hidden in the trees, the crossbow held up and ready.

Mosquitoes landed on her bare skin. Black flies buzzed incessantly in her face. She didn't dare swipe them away.

Another step closer and—

A burst of movement. With a flurry of wings, a wild turkey darted from the underbrush. She caught a flash of brown and white feathers and iridescent plumage. Ten feet in front of her, the ungainly bird screeched as it scurried across the deer trail, headed for the deeper thickets of witch hazel and chokeberry.

Shiloh recovered in an instant. Finger on the trigger, she swung to the right, sighted the turkey, and released the fiberglass bolt.

The bolt flew true. It buried itself in the turkey's feathered chest. The bird let out a startled squawk of pain and flopped onto its side, its scrawny neck and head writhing in the dirt.

Sheer relief flooded her veins. Shiloh hastened to its side, dropped to her knees with the crossbow beside her, and swiftly put the creature out of its misery. "And here I thought you were the windigo come to life. Stupid me."

Unslinging her backpack, she wrenched the bolt from the carcass and tossed the dead bird into the canvas bag she'd brought, then stuffed it into the pack and slung it over her shoulder. "Thanks for dinner—"

Behind her came the heavy crack of a twig underfoot.

Shiloh spun, reaching for the crossbow. Too late.

A shadow loomed over her. Before she could react, someone seized her from behind, grasped her arms, and hauled her off of her feet. A large calloused hand clamped over her mouth and nose. Her right arm was wrenched painfully behind her back.

Fear pierced her like a fishhook. For an instant, she froze. Then Eli's training kicked in. She fought like a wildcat, wriggling, scratching, screaming, the sound muffled by his meaty fingers. The hand completely covered her nose; she couldn't breathe.

Clawing frantically at her attacker's hand, she grabbed the little finger and yanked down as hard as she could; the bone snapped. Flinging her head back, her skull connected with his face. Bone crunched.

He growled in rage. His grip on her face loosened, but not enough.

Writhing in his grasp, her lungs bursting, she managed to half-turn and jabbed the point of her elbow at his eye. With a curse, the attacker's hand slipped from her mouth. She forced her jaw open and bit down on the webbed skin between his thumb and pointer finger. Warm, coppery blood squirted onto her tongue.

She wriggled from his grasp and fell to her feet. Whirling, she struck at his throat with the heel of her palm. He made an enraged choking sound as she kneed him in the groin.

Before she could hit him again, her attacker swung at her with a huge fist. He punched her in the side. Pain exploded through her ribs. White spots danced in front of her vision.

He hit her again in the solar plexus, slamming her to the ground and knocking the breath from her chest. Her lungs convulsed and spasmed. Eternal airless seconds passed.

He stood half-bent over her, breathing heavily, clutching at his injured hand. He was tall and muscular, with sloped shoulders and a broad, ruddy, sweat-streaked face. The stink of something foul and unwashed emanated from his pores.

He leered at her with bloodshot eyes. "You little slut! You'll pay for that!"

Frantic thoughts spun inside her head: *Mexico City, Mexico; Managua, Nicaragua; Panama City, Panama.* She forced herself to stay present, to fight as hard and as fast as she could. Scrambling to her hands and feet, she skittered backward, desperate to get away from him.

He grimaced, revealing brownish-yellow teeth in advanced decay, the gums red and swollen as he stared in shock at his bloody hand. "You bit me, you stupid little—"

"Touch me again and I'll kick your balls into your throat!" Fury mingled with the fear churning in her gut. The crossbow lay beneath the beech tree ten feet away. She wouldn't reach it before he did. It was unloaded, basically worthless.

The bolt that had shot the turkey was nestled in the pine needles next to her feet, half-buried. He hadn't noticed it.

"You're a brave one. Too bad you still have to die." Straightening, he stalked toward her, drawing a knife. "You're worth too much dead, Shiloh."

Her pulse thundered in her ears. Frantic thoughts stuttered through her brain: How the hell did he know her name? Why was she worth money dead? No time to worry about that now.

On her hands and knees, she seized the bolt in one hand; in the other, she clawed up a handful of dirt.

Her attacker bent low to seize her by the neck. Shiloh hurled the dirt into his face. Simultaneously, she lunged upward and stabbed the bolt into his groin, shoving it in as deep as she could. She twisted and yanked violently.

The man jerked back with a howl. The bolt was torn from her fingers. She lost her balance and fell back onto her butt. Her chest heaved with panic and adrenaline.

With both hands, he gripped the quivering bolt where it jutted from his pelvis, shrieking in agony. Bright red arterial blood pulsed from the wound.

She'd hit his femoral artery. It had slowed him. But he could still kill her before he bled out.

With a roar, he came at her.

Leaping to her feet, Shiloh ran. She sprinted to the crossbow and grabbed it as she raced into the woods. Terror vibrated inside her skin and thrummed through her teeth.

Barreling through the forest, she tripped on a root. Stumbling to her feet, she ran on. Branches slapped her face. Thorns scratched her arms and legs. Her surroundings a blur, she craned her neck to check her six, convinced danger was nipping at her heels, death in hot pursuit.

There was nothing behind her. That didn't mean he wasn't chasing her, didn't mean she was safe.

Finally, she reached M-28, bursting out of the woods a quarter-mile north of the trailhead. Racing to the hidden spot where she'd stashed Eli's bike inside the tree line, she unlocked the padlock, seized the handlebars with trembling fingers, and yanked it out to the road, weeds catching in the spokes.

Shiloh rode toward home like a bat out of hell.

The heat of mid-July beat down on her head and shoulders, hot even as the sun sank below the tops of the trees. There were no vehicles on the road except the abandoned ones. Grass and weeds grew tall around fenders and bumpers, vines creeping from the forest and ensnaring tires as if Mother Nature was bent on reclaiming the earth, one car at a time.

Her heart still thumped in her chest like a jackrabbit. Her ribs ached from being punched, but other than that, she was unharmed.

The attack hadn't been random. He'd stalked her through the woods. He'd known her name. Someone had paid to have her killed. But why? And what did it mean?

Pumping her legs like pistons, her palms sweaty on the handlebars, Shiloh rounded the curve on M-28, glimpsing the welcome sign to the hamlet of Christmas outside Munising.

There was something on the side of the road, something that did not belong.

She slammed the brakes. The tires squealed, leaving skid marks across the pavement, nearly hurtling her over the handle-bars. The bike came to a halt in the center of the road.

She thought this day couldn't get worse, but it could. Things could always get worse.

On the left side of the road, something hung from the top of the telephone pole. The figure slowly rotated, as if pushed by an unseen hand. It didn't seem real, like a Halloween decoration or a scarecrow staked in a cornfield.

Drawn by some ghastly compulsion, Shiloh drew closer, taking in the gruesome details: unkempt nut-brown hair, the pale rubbery skin of the face, the ripped and tattered shirt that was once white. A noose was wrapped around the throat. The head lolled to the side, the chin resting on the top of the shoulder as if the dead man were simply dreaming.

Flies buzzed in dense clouds around the corpse. A puddle of dried blood stained the dirt along the shoulder of the road. As she approached, carrion birds flapped their wings and squawked belligerently at her, as if these death-eaters had more right to this place than she did.

Shiloh shuddered. A dead body strung up in such a grisly display was meant to be found, meant to instill horror, to strike fear into the hearts of those who beheld it.

Something was coming—something worse than anything they'd faced before.

2

LENA EASTON
DAY SIXTY-THREE

L ena Easton shielded her eyes with her hand against the blistering sun. The humid air was stifling. Sweat dampened her temples, her underarms, and the small of her back. Even in jean shorts and a tank top, her long chestnut hair yanked back in a ponytail, she was melting.

The heat agitated the crowd. People jostled against her, pressing forward like a larger organism, beating to a drum of quiet desperation that grew louder with every passing second.

The scent of sour sweat filled her nostrils. Elbows bumped into her; someone stepped on her heel. She tried to retreat but there was no room, no give. Someone shoved against her back.

She checked to ensure Shiloh was right at her shoulder, afraid of losing her in the teeming crowd. Her chest constricted at the thought of the attack in the woods yesterday. She'd nearly lost her niece; she was determined to keep Shiloh within sight at all times.

"This is a bad idea," she said under her breath. "We should go."

A couple of hundred people had gathered in the Munising High School parking lot. At the front of the crowd, a FEMA emergency resupply semi-truck was parked, where it had been unloaded through the gym's side doors. Two Guardsmen stood sentry at the school's front doors to keep potential thieves out of the gymnasium, but from what Lena could see, most if not all of the supplies had already been distributed.

Four National Guardsmen surrounded the semi-truck, their body language stiff, shoulders back, feet planted, their expressions grim, bordering on hostility as they kept the crowd back. They didn't point their M4s at anyone but carried their weapons low and ready. Everything about them telegraphed aggression.

Shiloh warily scanned the crowd. "We have to get the antibiotics."

Lena wanted topical and oral antibiotics, steroids, antihistamines, and other meds to help the community and ease the backlog of patients at the local hospital. She wasn't here for insulin, though she'd gladly take diabetic supplies if FEMA offered them.

Before they could move, a man in glasses stepped onto a makeshift podium in front of the truck. Even though it was ninety degrees and humid, he wore a dark blue jacket with FEMA emblazoned in white on the back.

Below him, the undersheriff, Jackson Cross, attempted to calm the crowd, along with his deputies, Devon Harris and Jim Hart, and police officer Ramon Moreno. Next to Munising Police Chief Sarah McCallister, Sheriff Underwood stood with hunched shoulders near the front of the truck, a recalcitrant expression on his face.

Jackson met her gaze over the crowd and gave a rueful shake of his head. Her heart sank; she wouldn't be getting the antibiotics she'd hoped for.

"Where's our food?" someone shouted.

"Feed our kids!"

"We've been waiting for hours!"

They weren't wrong. Lena's stomach grumbled. Her legs were rubbery, muscles aching from standing for three hours. The FEMA emergency delivery had arrived hours late. She had snacks in her pack, homemade granola bars wrapped in aluminum foil, but she didn't touch them.

Her anxiety rising, Lena's gaze swept the crowd again. Some folks looked like they hadn't eaten in a week. Their faces had thinned; some were already gaunt, their clothes wrinkled and unwashed. Everyone looked haggard, bedraggled, worn down.

The fear of the coming devastation held a destructive power all its own, an invisible force clawing into people's hearts and minds, sinking talons deep into their brains. It was making everybody crazy.

Luckily, the U.P. was rural, where people could hunt, fish, and grow gardens, but complete forced self-reliance without access to stores, gas stations, or pharmacies was proving an incredible hardship—for even the most prepared.

"Look." Shiloh angled her chin at the right side of the seventy-foot-long semi-truck. Several punctures were scattered across the aluminum side panel. "Bullet holes."

"They must've been ambushed on the road."

"Explains the guards being all jittery."

Lena repressed a shudder. "Yeah, it does."

"Thank you for your patience!" the FEMA representative said into the megaphone. In his mid-thirties, he was short and slim, his blond hair was mussed, and there were deep bags of exhaustion beneath his eyes, his black-framed glasses skewed. He introduced himself as Milton Sanders.

"What're we supposed to feed our kids?" someone yelled.

"My mom's about to die of heart failure! We need those meds!"

"We understand; we're working on it, I promise." His voice was high and squeaky with stress. "We'll relay information to your sheriff as we have it."

"Where the hell are the rest of the supplies you promised?" a middle-aged woman shouted.

Another woman pushed to the front of the line. Lena recognized Dana Lutz, a tough, brazen woman in her forties who always seemed to find herself in the middle of town drama.

"You're lying!" She had no megaphone but didn't need one. Her throaty voice carried over the apprehensive rustling of the crowd. "You promised us supplies and meds and you've got nothing left! You only brought enough for a hundred people. What about the rest of us?"

"Ma'am, step back, please," Sanders said. "This is an orderly proceeding—"

"I was here early. I overheard you telling the sheriff you weren't coming back. Raiders attacked FEMA shipments on the highways. The roads up from Detroit and Chicago are far too dangerous. Isn't that what you said? That FEMA has zero supplies left anyway, at least, not for us regular people. It's all been siphoned away by the rich."

Lena stiffened.

Shiloh said, "Oh, hell no."

For a tense moment, the crowd was absolutely silent. Then a cacophony of panicked shouting broke out.

"Give me my blood thinners!"

"We need heart meds!"

"My mother has cancer!"

"I don't have a thyroid. I need meds to live!"

"I paid taxes! Where the hell is FEMA when we need it?"

"You've got no right!"

Sanders shouted useless platitudes into the megaphone, waving an arm in a futile attempt to regain the attention and trust of the crowd. That wasn't gonna happen.

The crowd's outrage hummed through her veins and vibrated in her chest. The solar flares weren't FEMA's fault, but the government could've handled this catastrophe far better than they had so far.

By refusing to make preparations, through their hubris and stupidity, the world's leaders had hurled everyone headlong into destruction. Their house of cards held together with lies, duct tape, and delusion had utterly collapsed.

The whole planet was suffering for it.

"Time to go," Lena said. "Stay right by my side."

"I'm not a little kid," Shiloh said.

"People are desperate. They're doing things they never would've done before, not in a million years. Survival is a powerful motivator."

They were both thinking about the man who'd attacked Shiloh in the woods, not to mention the dead body strung from a telephone pole. Neither of those acts had been motivated by survival but by something far more insidious. It terrified Lena to her core.

Shiloh scowled. With her oil-black hair and eyes like two bits of coal in her elfin face, she looked so much like Eli. The ancient arrowhead tied to a piece of rawhide string woven into her braid glinted in the sunlight. The girl was sharp as a blade, one hundred pounds of spit and fire—as fierce and stubborn as her father, too.

Lena said, "We have to be careful."

"Okay, okay," Shiloh muttered. "Fine."

Before they could move, an altercation broke out along the fringe of the crowd. People screamed insults. Two men shoved each other, the second man falling back and knocking over a middle-aged woman and an elderly man. A dozen people surged into the fight, their voices rising and fists flailing.

Sheriff Underwood stepped onto the platform and seized the megaphone from the FEMA agent. Brad Underwood was an imposing black man in his fifties with ramrod posture, a clean-shaven jaw, and hard eyes. He was used to getting his way.

The sheriff shouted, "Everyone remain calm! Panicking won't change anything!"

Underwood continued to speak, but his words didn't calm anyone. The crowd grew more agitated, surging toward the FEMA truck, shouting and making demands no one could meet, let alone the impotent FEMA agent.

Tense, Lena scanned the crowd again, her nerves raw. People were balanced on the razor's edge of civility. A sort of madness had overtaken them, a hive mind of anger, fear, and desperation.

She took hold of Shiloh's arm, and they backed up, pushing

through the masses toward the rear of the parking lot. The crowd thinned as they reached the perimeter of the cracked asphalt. She hadn't realized she'd been holding her breath until they broke into the open air.

Something hard poked the small of her back.

Lena spun, instinctively reaching for her pistol.

3

LENA EASTON
DAY SIXTY-THREE

Lena kept her hand on the butt of her pistol. "It's you."

Astrid Cross leaned heavily on her cane to support her scarred legs. A tall, striking woman, her porcelain skin was unlined, and her blonde hair fell silkily to her broad shoulders. Her pale blue eyes met Lena's with an implacable expression.

She tried to restrain her dislike and failed. She didn't know what she'd done to get on Astrid's bad side, but somehow she had. Astrid had disclosed Lena's insulin stash to a couple of meth heads, who'd attacked Lena and Shiloh at their old house. "I guess they're letting the patients out of the asylum."

Astrid grinned. "Oh honey, I'm the one running the asylum." Her smile contorted into a grimace, perspiration dotting her forehead from the effort of holding herself upright with her cane. It was obvious that she was in considerable pain.

A pang of pity hit Lena, despite what Astrid had done and whom she'd dated. Bad men took advantage of women all the time. It didn't mean Astrid had known what Cyrus Lee was or what he had done.

Lena repressed a shudder. "How did you get here?"

"I'd think you were concerned for my welfare, but somehow I doubt it." She waved a hand vaguely behind her. "My father hired a pimply teenager to drive me around. We hid the car off a side road since the locals have sticky fingers. A few months without creature comforts and you can't leave your house without the threat of getting hijacked."

"You still have fuel," Lena said it as a statement, not a question. She wasn't surprised. Horatio Cross and his daughter always found a way to survive, like cockroaches.

Astrid shrugged. "Sure. But we're rationing, of course. Father is looking into procuring us some horses. Jackson will help with that." She shifted her attention to Shiloh. "You're Lily Easton's girl."

Shiloh watched Astrid cautiously as if she wasn't sure what to make of her yet. "Yeah."

"We grew up together, though you wouldn't know it by the way your aunt treats me. You'd think she was born with a silver spoon in her mouth and not the other way around. The Eastons were always like that."

"Always so pleasant to see you too, Astrid," Lena said.

Astrid ignored Lena and kept her attention on Shiloh. "I heard you were attacked in the woods and defended yourself. I'm impressed."

Shiloh shrugged as though it was no big thing. It was a big thing. Lena repressed a shudder at the thought of Shiloh alone in the woods fighting for her life. It both terrified and enraged her. Shiloh could have been killed or kidnapped, vanishing without a trace.

The attack wasn't random, which meant it could happen again. Someone wanted her dead. Lena suspected that whoever had killed Lily all those years ago was tying up loose ends. And Shiloh was a huge loose end.

"He had it coming," Shiloh said. "I'm only sorry I didn't kick his balls into his throat."

"Next time." Astrid hesitated. "I've heard you know how to use that crossbow better than most men."

"I can shoot anything I aim at."

"I bet you could teach some of the girls. I volunteer at the homeless youth shelter, you know. It's overflowing right now. If you ever want to show up, we could use your help."

Shiloh flushed from the praise. "Sure."

"My brother may have put down Walter Boone and Cyrus Lee Jefferson, but we're surrounded by wolves. Only way to survive is if the sheep have teeth."

Shiloh went rigid at the mention of Boone. "I have teeth. And I'm no sheep."

"Oh, I can see that."

Astrid watched Shiloh in a way that unsettled Lena though she couldn't put her finger on why. Her gaze was intense and penetrating; she examined Shiloh like a bug under a microscope.

"We're leaving," Lena said. "This place is a powder keg ready to blow."

"Lena," Astrid said, with her eyes still on Shiloh. "You're looking...healthy."

"No thanks to you."

"I'm sure I have no idea what you mean."

"I'm sure," Lena said stiffly. She had no wish to confront Astrid here and now. Astrid would never admit it anyway; she thrived on the drama. Playing into her games only gave her more ammunition.

Astrid smiled. A beautiful smile, shiny and sharp. "Say hi to my brother for me."

Lena and Shiloh walked parallel to the crowd toward the rear of the parking lot where they'd locked their bikes, bumping past people to gain distance from Astrid. Within a few seconds, they'd left her behind.

To their left, people shouted at the FEMA rep, the tension like the ozone buzz before a storm broke out. A rock struck the side of the semi-truck, then another.

At the front of the crowd, Devon and Moreno waded into the melee as the National Guardsmen pushed back, shouting orders, attempting to regain order.

Fear knotted in Lena's gut. "Let's go."

As she turned away, something snagged her gaze. A woman stood at the rear of the crowd, weeping with shoulder-shaking sobs. In her mid-forties, she wore a rusty orange tank top and cut-off shorts that sagged from her hips. Her curly blonde hair clung in damp, sweaty ringlets to her furrowed forehead.

A young boy of about eight stood close beside her. The boy held a non-working Gameboy in one limp hand, his gaze dull, his eyes glazed.

"Lena." Shiloh halted midstride and pointed at a familiar, tell-tale bulge beneath the boy's *Avengers* T-shirt on his lower right side. A clear tube looped below the hem of his shirt, barely visible, but she knew what it was: an infusion set, canula, and pump.

Lena's throat thickened. They needed to leave before a full-on riot broke out. She didn't leave. Instead, she took a step closer.

"Ma'am?" she asked. "Is your son Type 1?"

The woman looked at Lena with frantic eyes. Mutely, she nodded. Her fingers dug into her son's shoulder as if she was afraid he might disappear if she let go.

"How much insulin do you have left?"

"We ran out this morning. What are we going to do?" the woman mumbled in a half-daze. "What will we do now?"

"Let's talk. Follow me." Lena gestured for her to follow them away from the crowd to a set of picnic tables near the middle school wing. Pine needles littered the ground and carpeted the tops of the picnic tables. Overgrown grass scratched at Lena's legs.

The woman sank onto the closest bench. The boy slumped next to his mother. A fringe of blond curls encircled his head like a halo. He stared off at something in the middle distance, his face pale, his eyes glassy. Lena bent and felt his forehead—his skin was hot and dry, his breathing shallow. He was likely hyperglycemic.

The woman brushed her hair from her drawn face. "I'm Traci Tilton. This is Keagan. We're from Detroit. We were on vacation here when the power went out for good. We didn't have the fuel to get home, and the gas stations were closed...when the reports came in of the rioting in Detroit, the owners of the Northwoods Inn let us stay. We're doing our part. I'm helping with the cleaning, even with my fibromyalgia, while my husband Curt cooks. He's a lawyer by trade, but there's no need for lawyers now..." Her voice trailed off, and she blinked rapidly, her fists clenched in her lap as if she were holding onto her sanity for dear life.

"Tim and Lori Brooks are good people. You're lucky."

Traci nodded. "Yes, yes, we are. We didn't tell anyone that Keagan was diabetic. My husband wanted to, but I had this worry...this fear that they'd kick us out if they knew. They'd see us as a liability."

"You're not a liability. Neither is your son."

"We've come to every FEMA supply drop. We took the supplies they doled out, but it's been one insulin vial at a time, only a few test strips, a couple of infusion sets, sensors, and reservoirs, and no batteries for the glucose meter. We've been reusing the reservoirs, but the infusion sets and sensors have to be replaced every seven days. We never have enough.

"This time, FEMA came two weeks later than they were supposed to. We were afraid they wouldn't come at all. I've been rationing as much as I can, being so careful with his carbs, but look at him. I—I don't know what to do. We checked every pharmacy we could. We went to the hospital. Everyone is out. They've been out for weeks."

Compassion welled inside Lena. She knew this mother's fear, knew it as intimately as she knew herself. She looked at the boy, conflicted, her heart torn.

She didn't know these people. It wasn't as if they were friends, lifelong neighbors, or kids she'd grown up with. She had no tie to them, no fealty. They were strangers, outsiders, trolls as Shiloh loved to call them, which meant downstaters from south of the bridge.

The boy was just a kid, in third grade maybe, small for his age and too thin.

Mentally, she counted her insulin vials. Between her long and short-acting stash, she had twenty-two months. Twenty-two months in a world that had gone dark. There was no electricity, no GPS, and no banks or stock markets. Nor was there any manufacturing or semblance of a supply chain.

To surrender an ounce of insulin was to knowingly shorten her life.

And yet, it was in her nature to give to others. She was a caretaker, a nurturer. A finder of the lost. She wanted to believe the federal government wouldn't entirely abandon its citizens; congress would obtain critical meds manufactured in the southern hemisphere and disperse them throughout the country. There had to be a way.

If she hoarded her meds now, this boy would die within a week or two. That was a certainty.

It was dangerous to share her insulin. If she gave some to the boy, the mother would be right back begging for more as soon as it ran out. Worse, they might tell someone else about Lena's stash, someone who might be willing to steal it.

"Mom, I'm thirsty," Keagan mumbled.

"I know, honey." Traci pulled a filtered water bottle from her backpack and handed it to Keagan as she glanced at Lena with brows furrowed in worry. "He's thirsty all the time."

It was another symptom of hyperglycemia, or high blood sugar. Lena nodded in resignation, her mind made up. She wasn't going to tell them how much she had or where she kept it. Even still, she knew the risk she was taking.

"I think I can help you," she said cautiously.

Shiloh's eyes widened with horror. She stared at Lena like she'd grown two heads. "No way. Don't even think about it."

Traci glanced from Shiloh to Lena in confusion. "What does she mean?"

Shiloh scrunched up her nose. "Eli wouldn't like this."

Lena's heart contracted at the thought of Eli Pope. "He's not in charge of me. I am."

Shiloh huffed in disapproval, but Lena didn't care. There were things she could live with and things she couldn't. Watching an innocent boy die from the disease that plagued her wasn't one of them, not when she could do something about it.

Lena turned to Traci and Keagan and offered the boy a warm smile. "I know where there is a small amount left. Go back to the Inn, and I'll meet you there."

Once they'd departed, Shiloh whirled on Lena. "This is a terrible idea."

"If we don't keep our humanity, then what's the point?" Lena asked.

Shiloh rolled her eyes. "Life, Lena. We're *alive*. The whole point of survival, remember?"

Lena said, "Not the whole point."

4

ELI POPE
DAY SIXTY-THREE

E li Pope slapped at his arm and left a smear of blood on his palm. Black flies buzzed around his face, biting his exposed flesh, tormenting him.

Dusk slanted low over the trees. The dense windless air was sticky and hot, thick with clouds of mosquitos. He inhaled the stench of decomposition and fought his gag reflex.

He stood with several deputies and police officers, gazing up at the corpse swinging from a telephone pole along the shoulder of M-28, four miles northwest of Munising.

The scene had been secured, taped off, and photographed. The victim had been shot in the face at close range with a small caliber pistol and then gutted and hung for dramatic effect. The gruesome sight was overkill but extremely effective.

His stomach clenched in horror and revulsion—and rage.

He hated that Shiloh had discovered the grisly scene. He hated it more that some scumbag had stalked her in the woods. Yesterday, he and Jackson had hiked to the scene of the attack and tracked the scumbag a mile to a ravine, where he'd apparently fainted from blood loss, tumbled down the incline, and struck his head on a boulder.

He was very dead. Technically, Shiloh hadn't killed him; she didn't need that on her conscience. Jackson had arrested the perp years ago for assault. They feared that the attack on Shiloh had been a hit. There was only one person who'd hire a hitman to murder a teenage girl—Lily Easton's killer.

The killer was still out there, hiding in plain sight.

Fresh fury flared through him. His hands flexed into fists at his sides. He wanted to strangle someone. He'd fight the whole world to protect her.

He felt wary eyes on him. His presence was far from welcome; the cops stared at him with suspicion and hostility, wondering what the hell he was doing here.

Jackson cleared his throat. "In case I haven't mentioned it, I've deputized Eli Pope."

A startled gasp rose from several of the officers. They knew he wasn't a killer; that didn't mean years of negative emotions died overnight. They didn't trust him.

That was fine. He didn't trust them, either.

Eli watched Jackson. His spine was straight and his gaze resolute. His tousled, dirty-blond hair fell across his forehead. He had one hand resting on the service pistol attached to his belt.

They were no longer enemies; they weren't friends, either. Once, he'd loved this man like a brother. Once, he'd plotted to kill him. It was complicated. Everything about his relationship with Jackson was complicated.

Jackson stared down his team. "Truth be told, I deputized him months ago when we assaulted Boone's cabin and rescued Shiloh Easton. Need I remind you that he went undercover for us, infiltrating Sawyer's criminal organization, risking his life to uncover a serial killer? Eli was a Ranger, a tier-one operator. He has hostage rescue training and expertise in intelligence gathering, counterintelligence, counter-sniper teams, and terrorism investigations. His unit worked protection for generals, ambassadors, and state department politicians in war zones from Serbia to Iraq. Anyone else with equal experience and skills, please come forward and say your piece."

No one spoke. The cops and deputies stared at Eli in sullen, disgruntled silence. It was one thing to stage a mission to rescue a guy but quite another to work with him side by side, to trust him to have your back in a fight.

Jim Hart was the first to capitulate. A former Marine, the long-time Munising cop was in his fifties, balding, and sported a hefty gut, but he was tough and kept himself in decent fighting shape. "If you trust him, then I'm good."

Cicadas buzzed in the grass. Shadows lengthened, and gnats swirled like little tornadoes.

The others nodded grudgingly. They were reluctant, but they were on board. That was what mattered.

Moreno slapped at a mosquito and pointed up at the slowly twisting corpse. "Truth be told, that right there scares the daylights out of me. We're fighting bad guys with one hand tied behind our backs. If Eli can help us catch whoever did that, then I'm in."

Devon Harris gave him a genuine smile. "Welcome to the team, Eli."

Eli gave her a grateful nod. One of the newer deputies, Devon was in her mid-twenties, short and fit, with long black braids spilling down her back. Her brown skin crinkled around her eyes when she smiled.

Devon was tough and brave. She'd saved Lena and Shiloh at the lighthouse. Of Jackson's team, Eli trusted her the most.

"Glad to get that housekeeping out of the way." Jackson turned to Eli. "Is it him?"

"It's him," Eli said. "This is Sykes' handiwork."

"You're certain?"

"Yes. He wants us to know he hasn't left the Upper Peninsula and that he's still around. Instilling fear is his M.O. It's what he does, how he controls both enemies and allies alike."

"Who is this joker?" Phil Nash asked. He was a rookie and had been a kid during the Hells Angels' reign of terror. He was green as hell, but he showed up, which was more than most people these days.

Jackson's mouth twisted like he'd tasted something unpalatable. "Darius Sykes is the former leader of a violent Hells Angels chapter. He murdered not only his rivals but also their families, including children. He's infamous for stringing corpses along the highway in a grotesque warning to those who might consider crossing him in the future.

"Ten years ago, he went on a murder spree and killed six members of a rival gang. They were shot, gutted, and then hung from telephone poles along M-28, every twenty miles between Wakefield and Sault Ste. Marie. Sykes is ruthless and brutal."

Ugly memories seared Eli's mind. He'd spent eight years in a cage, buried alive in Alger Correctional Facility with its concrete walls, barred windows, and cramped, hot cells.

Sykes had killed at least seven men in prison. He'd beaten and maimed a dozen more. He'd been accused of rape, intimidation, and coercion. It was all part of his manipulative games, his entertainment.

The day Eli had been released from prison after his case was overturned on a technicality, Sykes attempted to assassinate him. He'd beaten Sykes in prison because he had the element of surprise. He'd also severely wounded Sykes' two best men—a grievous insult Sykes would not ignore.

He hadn't forgotten Sykes' last words: *I will come for you. I will find everyone you love, and I will hunt them down and slit their throats in front of you, one by one.*

A former tier-one operator with the 75th Ranger Regiment, Eli had never feared men like Sykes. He did now. Now, he had everything to lose.

His thoughts strayed to the lighthouse. He wanted to be there, with Lena and Shiloh—anywhere but here staring at Sykes' hideous handiwork.

For years, he had tried to push thoughts of Lena out of his head and failed miserably. The vanilla scent of her chestnut hair, her kind smile, how her cobalt blue eyes crinkled when she laughed. How she used to look at him as if he was something special, as if he was worthy.

That was the man he wanted to be, that he was determined to become.

He doubted Lena would have him, not the way he longed for, but he would accept what he did have: her friendship. He treasured whatever she could give him, would love her from afar, would lay down his life to protect this woman and his daughter.

He pressed his lips into a thin line. The clear and present danger that Sykes posed threatened everything he held dear.

Shiloh still didn't know she was his daughter. The thought of telling her turned his bowels to water. What if he wasn't good enough? What if he didn't have what it took to be a father? What if she hated him?

He pushed his troubled thoughts from his mind and focused on the task at hand. One thing at a time.

"Do we know the identity of the victim?" Alexis Chilton pushed her oversized, black-framed glasses up the bridge of her nose. In her late twenties, her strawberry-blonde hair was shaved on the sides with the rest tied in a messy bun. She was a tech genius, or she had been before half the world's tech died.

"That's a Hells Angel tattoo." Moreno pointed at the tattoo of a helmeted skull with wings like blades on the dead guy's right bicep. "The victim is Marcus Delaney. He's the snitch who turned on Sykes and got him rolled up. Five consecutive life sentences, I think it was."

Eli said, "Sykes is getting revenge."

Jackson raked a hand through his unruly hair. A five o'clock shadow stubbled his square jaw, shadows smudging his eyes. "We haven't heard anything regarding the escaped convicts for three weeks. It's like they've vanished into thin air. We hoped they'd gone north, escaped across the International Bridge to Canada, or west to Wisconsin, or even south, down where there's more people, more supplies, more victims."

"He's still here," Eli said. "He's been gathering his strength. He will only strike from a position of power. Likely, he's growing his forces with members of Hells Angels who ran with him, stealing supplies, weapons, you name it. He's found a hidey-hole to hole up in, consolidate, take stock of his men, and gather not only resources for himself and his men but also intel to plan his next step. By now, they'll have stolen enough weapons to be well-armed. He may be a psychopath, but he's far from stupid. He's the leader. They followed him in prison, and they'll follow him outside, too. You've got a group of thirty to forty violent convicts out for vengeance. They're lurking like wolves in the woods, watching and waiting, ready to strike when they see an opportunity."

Hart adjusted his gun belt and swiped a hand over his reddened, sweating face. "We've had a drastic increase in reports of theft, robberies, and break-ins. Delta and Schoolcraft counties reported several home invasions in the last two weeks where the whole place was wrecked, things broken and smashed, not just stolen. High-end homes, mostly summer residences whose owners live elsewhere. No one injured yet."

"Could be him," Eli said. "Too little intel to know for certain."

Jackson looked at the scene again and shook his head. "Let's get the vic down. Then we'll track down this sicko before he can do any more damage. We're establishing a task force, deputizing more volunteers. We need more men. We need to beef up patrols and set up additional checkpoints. Boots on the ground, knocking on doors to find witnesses."

"Hell's bells," Moreno moaned as he wiped the sweat from his brow with a damp handkerchief. His left leg dragged slightly as if he was favoring a bum knee. "Damn, but it's hot as the devil's crack out here."

"Speaking of devils," McCallister said as she stared up at the corpse with a frown. "Seems like a lot of devils for a small town."

"There are devils everywhere," Eli retorted. "Always have been. People didn't want to see it. Now they don't have a choice."

The police chief shook her head. "This is a small community, rural. We have good people here."

"That's true," Jackson said. "But people can be driven to all kinds of madness when they're desperate, do things they'd never do otherwise, never thought themselves capable of doing."

"They were always capable," Eli said.

"What?" McCallister asked.

Eli said, "What people do in a crisis reveals who they really are. Their true selves stripped of society, of mandates and rules, of social artifice. It's easy to be a decent human being when you're comfortable, your needs are met, and everything is going your way. It's another thing when all hell breaks loose. When people take off the mask and show you who they truly are, believe what they show you."

Devon looked shaken but nodded grimly. McCallister pursed her lips as if she disagreed. Eli didn't care what she thought of him so long as she did her job.

He looked at Jackson. "There's a difference between seeing the good in others and not being honest with yourself about who they are."

To his credit, Jackson did not drop his gaze. "Duly noted."

Eli turned on his heel and headed back to where he'd parked his ATV.

"Where are you going?" Devon called after him.

The cops didn't need him for this part of the investigation. He longed to be somewhere else. His chest contracted as he spoke the word: "Home."

5

JACKSON CROSS
DAY SIXTY-FOUR

Astrid grimaced. "I didn't do it, whatever it is."

"No one's accusing you of anything." Jackson struggled to remain calm, though he felt anything but. His sister's mere presence could rile him. "We just want to talk."

Astrid sat astride a dun-colored mare named Cinnamon, currently the property of the Alger County Sheriff's Office. Devon rode a white mare named Marshmallow, while Jackson rode beside his sister on a black gelding named Midnight.

The Horseshoe Falls Stable outside of Munising stabled fifteen horses used for tourist horseback rides along the popular trails of Pine Marten Run Trail and Grand Island Trail. With tourist season over for good, the owners offered their horses for rent in trade for goods and services.

The Munising Police department had taken three horses, and the sheriff's office had borrowed four. Sourcing enough hay in winter would be an issue, but for now, the horses grazed freely in yards, fields, and meadows.

A team of volunteers had been formed to cut and gather some of the overgrown grasses to store them for winter to feed the horses. Another team worked to collect the manure to use for composting and fertilizer for the neighborhood gardens cropping up everywhere.

Astrid leaned forward and patted her mare's sweaty neck. She murmured into the horse's ear, which flicked toward Astrid as if listening intently. Jackson had never seen her so at ease with herself or others. She was a natural on horseback, moving easily with the horse's cadence.

Jackson, however, couldn't wait to return to solid ground. The saddle jostled beneath him; he felt about to slide off at any moment. Sitting stiffly, he bumped along with every jolt of his horse's gait. The horse flicked his ears and snorted in annoyance.

Astrid flicked the reins, gazing straight ahead. Tall at five-eleven, broad-shouldered and sturdy, she was a strong, athletic beauty, their family's Scandinavian descent apparent in her ice-blue eyes and white-blonde hair. "I wondered when you'd want to have a chat."

"It's been a busy few weeks," Devon said.

"You're going to ask how I could not have known that Cyrus Lee was a killer."

"Not in so many words," Devon said.

"You and your lurid curiosity, just like everyone else." Her lip curled in derision. "Everyone used to look at me with pity; now they glare at me with suspicion. *How could she not know?* They all think they'd be smart enough, intuitive enough, and discerning enough to distinguish the wolves from the sheep. But they're all sheep, and they're as stupid and self-deluded as everyone else."

"We aren't assuming anything," Devon said. "We're here to listen to your side of the story."

"Cyrus Lee Jefferson is dead. What does it matter?"

"Tying up loose ends," Devon said easily. "So we can close out the case."

"I thought the case was closed."

"It is," Jackson said. "We're dotting our i's and crossing our t's. It's unlikely, but in the event this case ever goes before the DA, I want to be sure we did everything by the book."

"There is no book anymore," Astrid said.

"There is." Jackson couldn't take notes on horseback without toppling to the ground, so he used the recording app on his phone. Even without the internet or cell towers, phones proved to be useful gadgets. He dreaded the day the battery died or a circuit shorted.

He asked Astrid a series of questions to which he already knew the answers. She answered dutifully, sounding bored. "He never laid a hand on me. He never raised his voice. He was a perfect gentleman."

Devon raised her brows in disbelief.

"He was," Astrid insisted. "He was shy, subservient, and compliant. Spineless. Did everything I asked of him, asked how high when I said jump."

"Don't blame yourself," Jackson said. "Serial killers like Cyrus Lee are skilled at camouflage."

"He saw me as the perfect mark. And I was, wasn't I?" Her voice was laced with bitterness. "Poor little crippled girl couldn't do any better than a killer. That's what they're all thinking." She shot a hard look at Jackson. "I hate them all."

No one spoke for a minute. The horses snorted, their hooves thudding against the packed dirt. A red-tailed hawk took flight from an oak tree whose branches spread over the trail like gnarled fingers.

Compassion swelled in his chest, surprising him. No one could call her stupid. She was astute, especially when it came to the human condition; she knew how the town saw her, and she hated it. He couldn't blame her.

"Did you know he was in bed with Sawyer, dealing drugs?" Jackson asked.

Astrid pursed her pretty lips. "No. I had no idea. Of course, I would have told you had I known." She fluttered her eyelashes at him, the picture of innocence.

He wasn't sure if he believed her, but he had zero evidence to the contrary. The thought of a drug dealer embedded with Sawyer eating dinner at his table and setting foot in his home made his skin crawl. He wasn't just a drug dealer but a serial killer. If she had known, if she'd said something...so many lives might have been saved.

"Did you ever see any evidence?" Devon asked. "One of the necklaces? Any other keepsake he might have kept from the killings?"

"I had no reason to go into that dilapidated shed, let alone dig out the tackle box. Everything else in the house was normal. I mean, he rented it from his grandmother, so she could have entered it anytime she wanted. I went there occasionally, but his house was small and smelled like a musty old lady. Plus, he had to load up the wheelchair, and it was too much work. Mostly he just stayed at my house."

She gave Jackson an accusatory look. "Our house, I mean, which is where he got insider access to missing persons' cases. Not from me, but from you."

Jackson had no defense. Guilt wormed inside him. For a long moment, no one spoke.

His horse kept ducking his head to munch on the grass growing along the trail. Jackson jerked on the reins to no avail. Black flies buzzed around them, the horses swishing their tails constantly to try and brush them away.

"It's still hard to believe that Cyrus Lee killed Lily," Astrid said.

Jackson kept his gaze straight ahead. Only he and Devon knew the truth, and it needed to stay that way, especially after the attack on Shiloh. He was certain the man who'd assaulted her had been hired by Lily's real killer.

The killer feared that the girl might remember her past and was growing desperate to tie up loose ends. As the only witness to her mother's murder, Shiloh's very existence posed a threat; she wouldn't be safe until the perpetrator was caught.

"And to think, you put your best friend away for it. Damn, but that must leave a mark."

He gritted his teeth at the fresh wave of shame washing through him. Astrid always did like to rub in his humiliations.

"At least you can stop pining for her now."

Jackson clenched the reins and refused to respond. Astrid was needling him for the hell of it. The best reaction was no reaction.

"I never knew what you saw in her. That girl was a lost cause from the get-go."

Back in high school, Lily and Astrid had been rivals, queen bees who were catty and competitive. It made little sense to cling to resentments for decades, but Astrid collected offenses and perceived slights like prized possessions: nursing them, breeding anger, resentment, and bitterness.

Where there was no insult intended, Astrid would manufacture one. She was the kind of person who set fire to things simply to see what happened next.

Astrid offered him a pitying smile. "Let it go, dear brother."

"I'm working on it," he said evenly.

"Are we done here?"

Reluctantly, Jackson nodded. They hadn't gotten much that they didn't already know. Still, it was a box to check off.

"When are you coming home?" Astrid asked.

"You know I moved out. I'm not coming back."

Astrid pouted. It did nothing to diminish her good looks. "Mom misses you. So do I."

She continually surprised him. Was it another manipulative move to make him feel guilty, or a genuine admission? He never knew with her. "Look, Astrid, I—"

"I'm keeping the horse."

"The horse is the property of the department—"

Astrid ignored him as she clucked to her mount. She increased her speed to a trot and swiftly pulled away from them, her back straight and her white-blonde hair streaming in the wind behind her, the sunlight haloing her head like a crown.

"Where are you going?" he called after her.

Her laugh echoed in the deep woods. "Wherever I want!"

Jackson watched her go with a sense of utter relief. "At least it's over. I need to get off this damn horse before I can't move for a week."

He had a million things on his to-do list. Sykes and his ex-convicts were a dangerous threat looming over the county. And despite what he'd said to Astrid, he couldn't let Lily's case go, not while he drew breath, and not while the killer presented a threat to Shiloh.

Jackson had to solve the case. He wouldn't let go, not even if it killed him. And it just might.

"I feel sorry for her," Devon said.

"If you knew her, you wouldn't." Guilt pricked him. She was his sister; he both loved and resented her in equal measure. He sighed and rubbed his thickly stubbled jaw. He hadn't shaved in two weeks.

"What's wrong, Boss?"

"It's complicated. Family is supposed to be everything. I owe them."

Devon cocked her head as if faintly disappointed in him. "No, Boss, you don't."

He wanted to believe her, to snap his fingers and be free of his dutiful obligations, his shame, the love he still felt for them despite everything they'd done.

Like so much in life, that was a thing easier said than done.

Jackson's radio crackled. Moreno's gravelly voice came through: "Cross, we've got two more dead bodies."

6

JACKSON CROSS
DAY SIXTY-FOUR

"It's bad," Moreno said. "I'm telling you."

Jackson stood with Devon on the blistering sidewalk and stared up the porch steps at the red brick, ranch-style house. Heavy striped curtains covered the windows. Like most yards, the grass grew two feet high, weeds choked the sidewalk, and thorns of overgrown rose bushes snagged their ankles and shins.

Ramon Moreno's bronze skin had taken on an ashen hue; he looked like he might vomit. A Munising police officer, Moreno liked to act tough and sarcastic, but underneath all his bluster, he had a soft heart.

Moreno scratched nervously at his beard. "Neighbors heard a gunshot around 3:30 p.m. this afternoon."

Jackson scanned the street. Folks were boarding up windows, installing chain-link fencing to protect their properties, and bent over hoes and shovels, breaking up grassy areas to plant backyard gardens.

Some sat sweating in camping chairs in front of their garages, soaking their bare feet in buckets of water to cool their bodies. Without air conditioning the humidity was oppressive, with the threat of heatstroke a real danger.

He caught several people greedily eyeing their electric bikes.

Upon their arrival, Devon and Jackson had secured their bikes to the lamp post at the end of the cul-de-sac with bike chains. There were precious few fuel reserves. What they had left, they saved for emergencies.

For the last several weeks, deputies and police officers had traveled via horseback or electric bicycles, which they charged each night with the solar-powered generator at the sheriff's office. They'd bought six electric bikes off Fred Combs, the misanthrope who owned the auto body shop off of Adams Trail. The grumpy old man was a genius with mechanics and a sucker for vodka.

Jackson entered the house first with Devon behind him, his service pistol drawn, though Moreno had already cleared the house. He carried a Glock 17 on his gun belt with a round chambered, along with handcuffs, a tactical flashlight, two 17-round magazines in a pouch, and a backup pistol in an ankle holster.

The door hung open. The smell hit him first; the rancid stink of something dead struck him in the face like a punch. The interior of the house was dark and stifling.

Wiping the sweat from his brow, he covered his nose with his handkerchief and strode through the living room. Devon made a retching noise, covering her mouth with her hand.

"Keep it together, Harris," she chided herself.

"You okay?" Jackson asked her.

She nodded, but she didn't look okay. They both felt it, the wrongness of this place. A bad thing had happened here.

Moreno entered behind them. He moved haltingly as if he dreaded every step. "The neighbor, Mrs. Lauren Cola, came to the station to report it. She hadn't seen the daughter, named Finley, or the father, Justin Martz, in three days, and the last time she did see them she said the girl was looking sickly."

"That seems to be going around," Jackson muttered.

In the shadowed kitchen, dust filmed the countertops and the barren shelves. There was no food anywhere, not in the cabinets, the pantry, or the unplugged fridge. The occupants of the house had drunk the olive oil and balsamic vinegar and eaten the salt from the shakers.

Jackson's gut tied in knots. It shouldn't be like this. Things shouldn't be like this.

Moreno seemed to read his thoughts. "The neighbor said they were real private, kept to themselves. The father wouldn't ask for help, ever. Not even for some sugar or an egg."

Devon grimaced. "People would have done something, even with their cupboards getting scarce. We have gardens. Scavenging teams that donate a percentage of supplies to the food pantry. The FEMA emergency deliveries. We're all getting tired of fish, but we've got the lake, all these rivers. At least we've got that."

"They were starving in plain sight," Jackson said.

"Not just them," Moreno said. "Everyone's getting skinny if not outright gaunt. Hell, I've lost twenty pounds. Not that I didn't need to lose some chub, but a lot of people can't afford to lose anymore, fish or no fish. Everybody's trying to garden, but it's not enough. You know a whole bowl full of lettuce, cucumbers, tomatoes, and onions is like two hundred calories? It's not enough."

"No arguments there," Devon said.

They went down the hall, the walls papered with family photos, a smiling single dad with a beaming little girl of about six or seven.

They entered the first bedroom. The door creaked open. The smell worsened.

Pictures of unicorns and ponies decorated the pink walls. The curtains were festooned with purple polka dots. Tucked beneath the purple comforter curled the shape of a little girl. A spray of reddish-brown curls spread across the pink satin pillow.

Beside him, Devon stiffened. She didn't make a sound; she didn't need to. The same horror washed through him, invisible but toxic.

Moreno spoke in an almost reverent voice. Cops were tough, but kids did everyone in. "According to the neighbor, the little girl had a heart defect. She'd gotten extremely weak without eating.

Her heart must've failed in her sleep or she got dizzy and slipped and fell, lost consciousness, and never woke up. There's not a mark on her."

"And the father?" Devon asked, her voice strained.

"There's a mark on him," Moreno said. "He's in his room, sitting in a chair by the window. He ate his shotgun. He was probably so wracked with grief at losing her, life wasn't worth living, so he took the avenue he saw left to him. He wanted to be with his daughter."

Jackson felt sickened. The burden he carried weighed more by the day, a heaviness deep in his bones. The tragic image of the little girl dead in her bed and her dead father, distraught at his inability to protect her, refused to vacate his head. It never would.

How could he stop tragedies like this from happening again and again across his county, the state, the entire country? He did not know. His helplessness threatened to overwhelm him.

"I hope they're both in a better place than here," Devon said, her words laced with sadness and anger.

Jackson placed a comforting hand on her shoulder. She was trembling. "There's nothing more we can do for them."

They fled the dark oppressive house. The screen door squeaked on its hinges as it slapped shut behind Moreno. Jackson gulped fresh air. He felt the probing, curious gazes of the neighbors on his back.

A loud thud came from behind him. Moreno let out a muffled curse. Jackson spun in time to see the burly cop trip, stumble down the porch steps, and land hard on his rear end.

Jackson raised an eyebrow. "You've never been a ballerina, but stairs are too much for you now?"

"Go to hell." Moreno tried to stand, winced, and grasped the handrail to steady him. He looked genuinely pained.

"Are you okay?" Devon asked.

"Dandy," Moreno wheezed. "Never better. Let's throw an all-night party. I volunteer as tribute."

Devon crossed her arms over her chest. "I noticed you've been limping."

Moreno had been moving strangely the last few days. "What's wrong with you? Stub your toe in the dark or something? You're shuffling around like an old lady."

Moreno grimaced. "It's nothing."

"Doesn't look like nothing."

Moreno's eyes darted to the side, refusing to meet Devon's gaze. "It's just a little cut on my shin, a bit of an infection. No big deal."

Devon frowned, concerned. "Show me."

Moreno muttered a disgruntled curse, but he obeyed. He sank onto the porch steps and rolled up his pants leg, revealing his lower left leg, which was swollen to twice its normal size. A savage six-inch cut sliced his leg open halfway up his shin. Pus and blood oozed from the laceration, and reddish veins spidered across his flesh. It was infected.

"What the hell did you do?" Jackson asked.

"I got it chasing down a carjacker and saving two babies strapped into their car seats before their minivan pitched over a ravine. Even got a kiss of thanks from their pretty momma."

Devon narrowed her eyes. "This is no time for playing stupid games."

Moreno sighed. "Play stupid games, win stupid prizes."

Devon and Jackson stared him down.

"You two have zero sense of humor. Anyone tell you that?"

"All the time," Jackson said.

Finally, he relented. "Whatever. Fine. It's stupid, okay? Last week, I was walking a scene, going through Eddie Auburn's woodshop out on M-28 outside Christmas. He'd claimed a bunch of stuff was missing. Boards and plywood were lying around everywhere as were big hunks of aluminum paneling. It was dark as sin in there with no power. I slipped and fell. That's it, just a dumb accident. I'm fine."

"Like hell," Devon said. "You need medical care for that, Moreno."

Moreno scoffed. "I'm not a wuss running to a doctor every time I get a paper cut. Ignore it, and it eventually goes away. That's how I deal with things, how I always deal with things. It all works out in the end, man. No big deal."

Jackson struggled to rein in his frustration. "Damn it, Moreno! I'm with Devon on this. Things aren't like they used to be. We can't throw endless antibiotics at an infection. You could lose your leg or worse. You can die from gangrene."

Moreno's skin turned ashen as if this was the first time he'd considered such a possibility. "Really? I could lose my leg?"

Devon threw up her hands in exasperation. "Yes, you idiot!"

"Truth be told, I knew it wasn't good, but other people need the medical supplies more than I do. I didn't want to take anything that should be going to save a kid's life, you know?"

Devon's features softened, and she squeezed his shoulder. "We get it. But your health matters too, Ramon. And if you go down, who's going to protect those kids from the bad guys?"

Moreno nodded soberly. "I get the message, loud and clear."

Jackson's radio crackled. Alexis Chilton's voice was threaded with static. "Where are you guys? You're supposed to be at the sheriff's office for the big press conference, remember?"

Jackson hadn't forgotten but finding the dead kid had driven the press conference right out of his head. He despised committees, endless meetings, and pointless press conferences.

Sheriff Underwood was extremely fond of the sound of his own voice. After the near-riot debacle with FEMA yesterday, Underwood was desperate for some good PR. Alger County residents were restless, edgy, upset, and vulnerable. Underwood thought he could placate them, or at the very least, keep them from tarring and feathering the sheriff's office.

"On our way." He clipped the radio to his belt. "Underwood wants the sheriff's office and the police department present. Have Nash secure the scene. We'll take care of the bodies afterward."

Jackson pulled Moreno to his feet. He gritted his teeth as he put weight on the infected leg. He could hobble on it, but barely.

"The hospital has a five-day waiting list," Devon said. "Go to Lena first. She'll get that nasty wound cleaned, disinfected, and bandaged. You should go now."

Moreno shook his head, stubborn as ever. "After the press conference. Underwood will have my hide if I don't go."

"He'll have my hide if I let you die," Jackson grumbled.

Moreno flashed him a mischievous grin and winked at Devon. "Then I guess I won't die. Not yet, at any rate."

7

JACKSON CROSS
DAY SIXTY-FOUR

J ackson grimaced as he scanned the growing crowd milling in front of the sheriff's office. People crammed the overgrown lawn and poured into the street.

This was a press conference, but there were no press, media, TV, or internet. Whoever showed up got the news, which was then spread by word of mouth.

A dozen deputies and police officers ranged on either side of Sheriff Underwood, who stood before a wood podium and spoke into a megaphone. The crowd was loud, unruly, and angry. They needed someone to blame for their misery.

At that moment, Sheriff Underwood was that person.

After the battle on Sawyer's yacht and the death of Cyrus Lee Jefferson, Underwood had given a brief press conference. He cared more about polls and popularity than solving cases, especially when the credit belonged elsewhere. But he'd finally succumbed to the pressure.

Blow by blow, he gave the people a detailed account of the hunt and apprehension of Cyrus Lee. He left out several pertinent details: that law enforcement had barely escaped the burning yacht with their lives, and that the serial killer had been left to Sawyer's brutal vengeance.

Jackson had been forced to choose between the law and saving the lives of the men and women under his command. He'd saved his people.

Raising his voice over the disgruntled crowd, Underwood nearly shouted as he read from a handwritten statement: "The investigation led our fine law enforcement officers to the residence of Cyrus Lee Jefferson where a toolbox was discovered in the shed that contained the matching halves of the necklaces found on the victims buried in the woods behind Walter Boone's shed, Cyrus Lee Jefferson's partner-in-crime." The sheriff read off a list of the known victims' names, "...Summer Tabasaw, Elice McNeely, Lily Easton."

The crowd let out an audible gasp at the mention of Lily. Underwood had waited too long to give the official statement; rumors had run rampant for three weeks. Most folks knew that he'd been unmasked as the serial killer.

Jackson and Devon had decided not to release the fact that Cyrus Lee had an alibi for the night of Lily Easton's murder, hoping the real killer would relax their guard, believing someone else had again taken the fall for their crime.

"Unfortunately, in the process of apprehending the suspect, he resisted arrest and was killed," Underwood boomed. "Let's congratulate the Alger County Sheriff's Office task force, in conjunction with the Munising Police Department. A citizen volunteer and two officers perished in the mission. One officer, Jim Hart, was wounded but has recovered fully. We have completed the investigation and—"

"You lied to us!" someone in the crowd shouted.

"The killer could've murdered our daughters in their beds!" yelled Pam Broskey.

"Quiet!" Underwood said. "The real Broken Heart serial killer has been identified and stopped. That's what is important here—"

"No thanks to you!" shouted a middle-aged accountant named Marty James.

"You told us there was no killer!"

"How could you have been so wrong?"

"You failed us, Sheriff!"

Sheriff Underwood's usual bluster vanished. Sweat trickled down his temples, and his brown skin went ashen. His eyes bulged, and his hands waved frantically as if he could rein in the tide turning against him. "Now listen here! Settle down or we'll be forced to arrest you for disturbing the peace!"

Devon and Jackson exchanged guarded but incredulous glances. Moreno rolled his eyes skyward. Hart looked bored. Nash gaped at Underwood like he was watching a man implode before his eyes.

Devon elbowed Jackson in his ribs and jutted her chin at a man striding toward the podium. "Isn't that your father?"

Horatio Cross walked up to the sheriff and took the megaphone from him midsentence. Underwood was too shocked to fight back.

Horatio brought the megaphone to his mouth. "Ladies and gentlemen! Your attention for one minute, please." His voice was measured, clear, and commanded respect. He'd served this county as sheriff for eighteen years; he'd wielded power with every glance, with every word, and echoes of that power continued to hold sway over the townspeople.

They quieted, even if impatiently, waiting for what he would say.

"Sheriff Cross," Johannes Heikkinen, a grizzled Finnish fisherman, said with deference.

Horatio smiled. A network of tiny wrinkles laced the skin around his eyes, which were so blue they reflected the light from the battery-operated lanterns. "You know I gave up that hat years ago, Johannes, but I believe I did a damn fine job keeping Alger County safe, and I believe you would agree with that assessment."

A murmur of agreement rippled through the crowd. Not everyone, but enough.

"Maybe we could have forgiven Sheriff Underwood for failing to catch Walter Boone, the man who stalked and kidnapped our young girls, our sisters and daughters, the criminal who stole Ruby Carpenter. Some of you recall that a certain law enforcement officer insisted that another predator hunted among us. He was dismissed and ridiculed by Sheriff Underwood. It is due to Underwood's incompetence that not one, but two predators lived among us for so long. And now another dead body has been found, a corpse shot and hung. We will not put up with excuses any longer. We cannot afford to. We've reached a crisis point, not just in Alger County, but the country, the entire world. We need strength and courage to act now more than ever."

"Hear, hear!" Dana Lutz shouted.

"The man we need right now is not a coward who cowers behind his office and title when the going gets tough. The leader we need is morally fearless. The hero of the hour caught not only Boone but the serial killer Cyrus Lee Jefferson. That man is my son, Jackson Cross."

People looked at each other in confusion, unsure where Horatio was headed. Horatio made a gesture toward Underwood, who stewed in silence. Grey-faced, he looked like a man whose dog had just died. "Underwood agrees, don't you?"

The crowd rumbled, their boisterous voices melding in a raucous roar. Horatio must have paid off several people to rile up the rest of the crowd, to control the narrative to achieve his desired outcome, whatever that was.

"There are protocols," Chief McCallister said. "The sheriff is an elected position—"

"Hey," Johannes said, his voice getting lost in the uproar. "This isn't a legal proceeding! You can't just take the law into your own hands!"

"Shut up, old man!" a man yelled back.

Visible tension hummed through the crowd. Some cheered, and others jeered, as the crowd grew more agitated. A few looked at their neighbors in consternation and dismay.

This wasn't right. This shouldn't be happening.

Jackson shook his head, chagrined. They were right. A sheriff in Michigan could be lawfully removed by a special election or by order of the governor for due cause. Even if the citizens were furious, which they were, many would see this as a *coup d'état*, which wasn't far from the truth.

Things couldn't go down like this. This was acting far outside the law. Once you took the law into your own hands, you surrendered the right to claim the title of law enforcement, apocalypse or not.

Jackson needed to stop this.

As he headed toward the stage, Horatio leaned in and whispered something in Sheriff Underwood's ear. Underwood's shoulders drooped. His body deflated.

Horatio handed him the megaphone. Underwood cleared his throat. "I'm proud of my years serving Alger County. I hereby resign my position as sheriff, effective immediately."

Horatio jutted his chin at the police chief. Chief McCallister walked to the podium, took Underwood's arm, and led him off the left of the stage. Underwood departed like a man who had no fight left in him, fleeing like a beaten dog with his tail between his legs.

The crowd seemed to pause, holding its collective breath in shock.

Horatio turned to Jackson and gestured for him, a radiant smile plastered across his face. "Due to Underwood's resignation, we have a new acting sheriff, until an election can be held. Come on up, Jackson Cross!"

Jackson watched it happen as if from a great distance. The noise drummed through his brain. He couldn't escape the feeling that his father had planned this. Horatio had dirt on Underwood and had used it to force Underwood's hand.

By forcing Underwood's resignation, Jackson became sheriff by default, without the stink of a coup hanging over his head. It was the only explanation that made sense.

Moreno leaned forward, gesturing at him. "Get your scrawny butt up on that stage before there's a riot."

Nerves knotted his stomach, but he didn't let it show. He hadn't wanted this, hadn't asked for it, but he wouldn't reject the promotion. He didn't have a choice, even if he wanted one.

The people needed a leader. Without an acting superintendent, with a governor who was MIA, that leader had defaulted to the sheriff.

Jackson straightened his shoulders and strode up to the podium. His heart thrashed in his chest. He didn't know whether to be horrified or elated.

He met Horatio's proud gaze as he handed Jackson the megaphone. His father nodded in approval, smiling graciously at his son. Jackson tried to remember the last time his father had shown him such kindness, such validation, but he could not.

"Thank you for your confidence in me," he said to the people. "As the situation worsens, there will be more who turn to crime and law-breaking to survive. We will stand for justice, no matter what governments may fall. Things are difficult and they'll only get harder. I can't promise you ease or comfort, but I promise you I'll do my best. I promise I won't give up on this county, on us."

The throng broke into uproarious applause. Folks clapping, smiling, and whooping as if he was some sort of celebrity. Unease slithered through his gut; he forced himself to project confidence instead.

They wouldn't feel such enthusiasm for long. Trouble lay ahead for all of them, trouble and hard times.

"What about the dead body you found?" Dana Lutz asked loudly. "The one strung up like a Christmas decoration on M-28?"

"We will find the perpetrators," Jackson said. "We're stronger together, and I have faith that we'll figure out a way forward."

He lowered the megaphone and searched the dozens of upturned faces until he found the singular face he sought. Eli Pope stood aloof at the back of the crowd. His black hair and black eyes were distinctive, the slash of his cheekbones revealing his Ojibwe heritage.

He stood tall and straight, broad-shouldered with powerful,

ropy muscles bulging beneath his gray T-shirt. His flinty eyes bore down on Jackson with absolute focus.

They had history, he and Eli—decades of blood, both good and bad, between them. Jackson had both betrayed Eli and then saved his life. Eli had sworn to kill him and yet had come to Jackson's aid when it was needed, even going undercover to catch a killer.

They weren't friends, but they'd graduated from enemies to something else, a grudging respect.

Motionless, his hardened features unflinching, Eli met his gaze. For a moment, they stared across the crowd at each other. Much as he'd tried not to, Jackson had sought Eli's approval his entire life, like he'd sought his father's.

Finally, Eli gave an almost imperceptible nod.

Something like relief flushed through him. Maybe someday, they could regain the friendship they'd once shared. Jackson could hope.

He turned his attention to the people before him. His people. He sensed their misery, their exhaustion, and their fear. The constant low terror affected everyone. He could see it in their strained faces, their slumped postures, their vacant smiles: the numbness and depression, the anxiety and despair.

They expected him to save them. He knew no salvation was coming.

8

LENA EASTON
DAY SIXTY-FIVE

"You've got to be kidding me." Lena stood in the ER waiting room of Munising Memorial Hospital. The air smelled not of antiseptic but of blood and vomit. Frustration and anger flared through her. "Tell me you're joking."

"I wish I was." Dr. Kathleen Baldwin stared at her with regret in her eyes. "It's a terrible joke, and nobody gets the punchline."

Lena fisted her hands on her hips. "People need you. You can't close the hospital. That's not an option."

Dr. Baldwin wiped her forehead with a handkerchief that had seen better days. In her mid-fifties, her gray-streaked brown hair was tied in a straggly bun at the back of her neck. Her smudged glasses slipped down her nose, her skin gray with fatigue. She smoothed the wrinkles in her lab coat like that might make a difference.

Behind her, two security guards carried rifles slung across their chests. They guarded the doors to the ER to keep out desperate family members willing to break in, to do anything to help their dying loved ones.

Lena frowned. "Who are those guards?"

"Hired security. We've had...altercations...between distraught patients and irate family members and the nurses. One husband

49

attacked a doctor when he couldn't perform the surgery his wife needed."

"Those aren't security guards. They're Sawyer's enforcers."

"And?" Dr. Green snapped. "We're doing what we have to do, like everyone else. I don't see the sheriff's office volunteering manpower for guard duty, Their hands are full. Do you see any National Guard coming to our aid?"

The sounds of crying and moaning filtered through the closed double doors of the ER. The waiting room was filled to capacity and then some. Dozens of patients slumped in chairs and on the floor or stood against the walls.

A small girl had a deep, phlegmy cough that sounded like bronchitis. A father and mother waited with a preteen with a broken arm. A mother in stained pajamas cradled a baby wrapped in a thin blanket, crooning softly as the baby wailed and wailed.

Appalled, Lena gestured at the waiting patients. "How can you turn these people away?"

Dr. Baldwin cleared her throat. "We have no choice. The hospital is using battery and solar-operated portable light towers. We have no power to run the equipment we need to keep people alive: respiratory ventilators, EKG machines, ultrasound machines, x-ray machines, CAT scans machines, anesthesia machines, and patient monitors. The only meds we have left are common Tylenol and Advil. We can't do anything—"

Lena scoffed. "There's always something."

The doctor's expression hardened. She was losing patience. "I'm speaking with you as a courtesy, Lena. Life support machines were turned off two weeks ago—ventilators, everything. Every doctor and nurse has gone above and beyond. Our staff members are people, too. I have worked around the clock, seven days a week, for well over two months. We lost another pediatrician and two nurses yesterday. They're quitting so they can try to feed *their* families. I can't do it anymore. We can't. We've become a morgue, not a hospital."

"What are people supposed to do when they get hurt or sick? When there's a medical emergency—"

"The township superintendents have decided to consolidate resources. I know it doesn't feel like it, but this is the best option. It truly is. The UP Health System in Marquette still has fuel for its generator. They have power, they have anesthesia and can conduct surgeries, as can War Memorial Hospital in the Soo. We don't. Neither does Helen Newberry Joy Hospital in Newberry or Bay Mills, Schoolcraft Memorial, or any of the others. Separated like this, we've run out of supplies, but by maintaining just the two hospitals in Marquette and the Soo, we can still help people."

"You're going to Marquette," Lena said dully.

"Yes." Guilt flickered in her tired eyes. She pursed her lips as if pushing that guilt down somewhere deep. "Those of us on staff who wish to do so are departing tomorrow morning. Someone from the Marquette County municipal office will pick us up in a couple of vans they've converted to biofuel, along with security to protect us on the trip."

The horror of it sank in slowly. No hospitals within reach. There'd been no ambulances running for a while, but if you could make it into town and endured the days-long line, you could still be seen by a doctor, and could still get some treatment.

And now?

Lena's chest constricted. It was hard to breathe. "And how are patients supposed to get there without fuel or vehicles? It's too far. How is that mother with cancer who has two kids going to get there? Or a grandpa with a broken leg?"

Dr. Green blanched. "Look, I didn't say it was perfect, but it's all we can do."

"How many?" Lena asked. "How many doctors are leaving?"

"As far as I know, all of them."

Lena blinked. "What?"

"They've offered housing for our families and food, shelter, and hot showers, in a secure neighborhood. It's a good deal." She raised her brows. "Perhaps they could use a good paramedic. I'm sure they could use you and your dog in search-and-rescue. I could put in a word for you."

"No. I'm not leaving. I—" For half a second, she hesitated, torn by the temptation. If she could take Shiloh and Eli with her...but would Eli leave? She didn't know. Would Jackson? He wouldn't. Neither could she. For better or worse, this was home. "I'm needed here."

Dr. Baldwin gave a curt nod. "Understandable. We must do what we feel we need to do."

Before Lena could argue, a woman came up behind Dr. Baldwin. It was the county medical examiner, Dr. Venla Virtanen.

Lena turned to her. "Please tell me you're staying."

Dr. Virtanen was a stout Finnish woman in her fifties with short white-blonde hair. Instead of a lab coat, she wore PPE over slacks and a sweater. Jackson had spoken of her with respect. She was dedicated and good at her job.

The ME shook her head. "My daughter and her family are in Paradise. I haven't heard from her since the skies lit on fire. She could be dead or alive. My responsibility is to her. The administrators of War Memorial offered me a position and will give us a house. The Soo Locks generate electricity but not only for the hospital; there are also some houses and businesses that have power. I can do more good there than here."

Lena stared at her, stricken. How would Jackson solve murder cases without a medical examiner? The odds were staggering and grew more impossible with every setback.

There was nothing Lena could say or do to change their minds. Though she was incensed, the rational part of her brain understood that medical professionals had families to take care of as much as anyone. Dr. Baldwin and Dr. Virtanen had the decency to look remorseful, but sorry didn't change a thing.

"Do—do the hospitals in Marquette or the Soo have insulin?" Lena managed to ask.

Dr. Green shook her head. "I'm sorry, but no. As far as I know, everyone is out everywhere, at least in the Midwest."

Lena thought she was prepared for Dr. Green's answer, but it still struck her like a blow to the solar plexus. She thought of little Keagan Tilton with a pang in her chest.

In the ER, a nurse frantically called a code. Dr. Baldwin backed away. "I need to get back to work. We will do our best to provide comfort to those we can before we leave. Take care, Lena."

The doctors turned on their heels and headed toward the ER doors. The security guards opened the doors, watching warily to make sure the sick and dying in the waiting room didn't make a run for it.

Dr. Virtanen looked over her shoulder with regret in her expression. Then she was gone.

Defeated, Lena walked back through the cramped waiting room. Outside, dozens more people made a straggly line along the sidewalk, limping, bandaged, and feverish: an exhausted mother with twin preschoolers, a father holding the hand of a pale-faced, chemo-bald child, an older man with his arm in a cast, and a woman pushing an elderly woman in a wheelchair, probably her mother.

Several people waiting in line had lain on the sidewalk, either sleeping or dead. No one had come for them. Lena's heart ached in compassion and horror. She wanted to save them all.

Moreno was waiting for her in the parking lot. He leaned against the door frame of a Honda Odyssey and stared morosely at the pus oozing from his bandaged leg. "What are we gonna do now?"

Frustration, worry, and trepidation swirled in her stomach. She was no stand-in for an actual doctor or surgeon, but she wasn't worthless, either. There were things she could do for mild cases, for fevers and infections, to ease pain. She could help Moreno and others like him.

"I'm going to get you taken care of, Moreno. I'm bringing you to the lighthouse. I can't promise anything, but I'll do my best." She glanced back at the hospital, at the line of sick and wounded who hadn't made it through the ER doors and never would. "I'm going to start a clinic. I'm going to help these people."

Moreno looked at her in concern. "You can't save everyone, Lena."

Lena set her jaw. "I'm gonna damn well try."

9

LENA EASTON
DAY SIXTY-SEVEN

Shiloh's cry woke Lena from a dead sleep.

Lena leaped to her feet, grabbed the M&P she kept loaded on the nightstand, and moved through the liquid shadows to the hallway, padding toward Shiloh's bedroom, pistol held low at her side.

It was likely a nightmare, but Lena took no chances.

Bear had been snoring like a freight train on the rug at the foot of her bed, but he awakened when she arose. He lumbered to his feet, his paws clicking across the wood floor as he followed her out of the bedroom.

His thick cinnamon fur was rumpled. He yawned, his jowls pulling back to reveal his impressive jaws, drool glistening on his muzzle. The one-hundred-and-fifty-pound Newfoundland was a giant teddy bear—with teeth.

Shiloh cried out again. Lena quickened her step.

The girl often bedded down in a sleeping bag in the lantern room topping the lighthouse tower, but sometimes she wanted the comfort of a warm bed and a soft pillow. This was one of those nights.

Lena entered her room, scanning the darkness, the white sheet fluttering over the window, and the empty corners—no threats—then rushed to the bed, setting the pistol on the nightstand next to Shiloh's knife. Her crossbow leaned against the bed.

Shiloh sat bolt upright, whimpering, the sheets kicked off, her hands balled into fists like she could fight off the demons that invaded her dreams and stalked her nightmares. Tears streaming down her cheeks, she let out a keening wail of grief and fear that tore Lena's heart into pieces.

"Oh, honey." Lena sat on the edge of the bed and gathered her niece into her arms. Trembling, Shiloh sank into her embrace and wept. Lena held her tenderly, offering a safe harbor, an anchor in her sea of sorrow.

"I'm here," she whispered into Shiloh's tangled hair. "I'm right here."

Lena and Bear stayed with Shiloh for an hour, until the nightmare's grip released her, and the tension in her body eventually went slack as she drifted back to sleep. Lena tucked her beneath the sheets and smoothed her sweat-dampened hair back from her face.

Bear leaped onto the bed, the mattress sagging beneath his weight, and squeezed his considerable bulk between Shiloh and the wall. Flopping down, he rested his big head on his paws, the length of his furry body pressed against hers. Shiloh gave a soft moan and rolled against him, her hands tangling in his fur, gradually quieting as though she sensed his vigilant presence even in sleep, watching over her.

Lena scratched his favorite spot behind his ears. "Chase the nightmares away, Bear. Keep her safe."

Bear looked up at her with his doleful brown eyes. Intelligent and sensitive, he could sense his humans' pain and seemed to instinctively understand that Shiloh needed him. He wouldn't leave her side tonight. She was incredibly brave and resilient, but she was just a kid. She'd endured more than any person should ever have to endure.

Lena stood but remained by the bed. She studied Shiloh in the dim light from the sweeping beacon flaring through the window, diffused by the damp sheet they'd strung over the windows to cool the air inside at night.

In her mind's eye, she saw all the dead girls in their shallow graves, the missing girls and boys and mothers and fathers and siblings she had searched for over the years, she and Bear.

She saw Ruby, a sixteen-year-old girl shattered by trauma, her heart a pulsing maw of hurt. She saw her murdered sister, Lily, a ghost begging for her killer to be found. And she saw Elice McNeely, stolen from her life and buried in the woods like so much trash.

They were all there, lined up one after another, all different, but in some ways all the same. Girls who had gone missing in their own lives, all searching for something, and then searched for, utterly lost to themselves and others as if they'd slipped through a crack in the center of the universe.

A powerful dread took hold of her, the likes of which she'd never experienced. She felt it out there, that faceless threat, an unknown enemy barreling toward them.

It wasn't a single enemy that could be defeated but something much larger, uncontrollable, a tsunami of destruction looming over them all. They could do nothing to stop it, prevent it, or even hold it at bay.

How did you face such an incomprehensible thing? How did you live through unthinkable moments? Her unceasing fear for Shiloh felt like an incredible weight pressing down on her.

She looked down at Shiloh. She would bear it all for the sake of the people she loved. That's what people did—they endured.

The cottage ticked and creaked within the quiet. The sheet tacked to the window billowed as a gust of wind blew across the lake and filtered through the six-inch gap between the sill and the partially opened window, which they'd nailed in place for security reasons.

For thousands of years, Egyptians had hung damp linens in windows and doorways to cool their homes through evaporation. Every evening, she and Shiloh dipped sheets in buckets of lake water, wrung them out, and hung them inside the windows with nails. The softly undulating white sheets reminded her of funeral shrouds.

Sleep eluded her, so she padded through the silent rooms and made her way out to the front porch, her nightgown swishing around her shins. Outside, she breathed in the stillness, the quiet peace.

The cool night breeze caressed her exposed skin. Constellations of stars wheeled overhead. Waves gently lapped the shoreline as the lighthouse beacon swept back and forth, casting the yard and the beach beyond in an eerie, almost otherworldly glow.

The beacon reminded her that their fuel for the diesel generator was running low. While gasoline was out almost everywhere, there was still a bit of diesel around, though folks with boats and trucks had stored what diesel fuel they could. Soon, they would need to switch the light source to a kerosene or oil lantern, using the Fresnel lens prism to disperse the beam.

There were still boats trading goods up and down the Superior coastline that needed the beacon to avoid the dangerous shoals and rocks close to shore.

She wished Eli were here. The thought came unbidden, but it was no less true. In some ways, she had never felt so lonely, had never been so acutely aware of the hole in her heart that Eli had left behind. It was a hole no one else had been able to fill.

She closed her eyes and breathed deeply. It comforted her to know he was out here, somewhere on the property. He was physically close, and yet a chasm separated them, a canyon she both desired and feared to cross.

As if she'd conjured Eli into existence, a figure approached from the east, from the wooded tree line, his tall and sinewy shape limned by starlight. He had conducted another perimeter check. Even in the middle of the night, he was alert and watchful.

Eli halted a few feet from the porch and looked up at her. His rifle was slung across his chest, his pistol tucked into his belt. She couldn't read his expression in the darkness. "You're up late."

Against her will, her stomach fluttered. "You're one to talk."

"Touché." He jutted his chin at the porch. "May I?"

"Of course." She made room for him to stand on the porch beside her. "Shiloh had a nightmare."

He went still. "Is she okay?"

"Okay is such a useless, insubstantial word, but yeah. She's strong and she's brave and she's going to make it." Lena slanted her gaze at him in the dark. "She's like her father."

Eli didn't respond. He stared into the yard, into the darkness. He seemed pensive tonight, more anxious than usual.

"Is something wrong?"

"Everything is wrong."

Now that was the naked, unvarnished truth. Lena hesitated. "Jackson said the man who tried to kill Shiloh is dead."

"He is."

"Whoever sent him might try again."

"It's possible."

"Jackson thinks the person behind it is whoever killed Lily. That exposing Cyrus Lee spooked them, and now they're trying to ensure that Shiloh will never remember what happened that night."

"We'll keep her close. We won't give him another chance to come after her."

"The body that Shiloh found. Jackson said Sykes did it."

"He's here. If he finds out about you, he'll come after you and Shiloh, and use you to hurt me. It's what he does. I won't let him hurt you."

She sucked in a steadying breath. The threats seemed all-consuming, overwhelming. They were being attacked from every side.

"I'm afraid," she whispered into the night.

"Me too," Eli said simply.

The thing she'd learned about fear was how it clarified things. Everything unimportant stripped away: your insecurities, your mistakes, rules and expectations.

Nothing else mattered. Fear solidified whom you trusted and whom you didn't. It distilled life into its most elemental part: protecting the people you loved.

"It's good to be scared," Eli said. "The second you're not scared, you're dead. Fear can't be eradicated but it can be used. It can be controlled and channeled into defending yourself, and others. Doing what you need to do."

Lena's lips twitched. "Like telling Shiloh the truth?"

Eli gave a grunt. After a moment, he gave a resigned sigh. "Yes, I will. I promise."

"She doesn't bite, you know."

"Have you met her?" Eli asked, incredulous.

"Touché." Lena chuckled, then grew serious. "We'll keep her safe. We have to keep her safe."

"We will," Eli said.

They stood together in comfortable silence, watching the bright white beam of the beacon ripple across the black waves in a mesmerizing play of light and dark.

The stars were like diamonds tossed across the velvet of the sky. Millions and millions of stars, bright and dense, layers upon layers. The Milky Way a scattered arc above their heads.

You could see so clearly without the distracting haze of civilization.

There were so many dangers in the world but right here, right now, she felt safe. Safe, and somehow, for the moment, content. She was aware of the heat of Eli's body beside her, his broad shoulder nearly brushing hers, the strength radiating from his every movement. He seemed unusually tense.

She bit her lower lip, thinking of all the times they'd watched the stars together, as kids, as love-struck teens, as young adults filled with dreams. They'd kissed beneath these same stars, danced on the beach, bathed in the same moonlight.

Her stomach flip-flopped. Maybe he was thinking of the same things.

"Lena, I—"

A shriek echoed across the water. The sound originated from the woods beyond the reach of the lighthouse beacon. It sounded like a woman screaming, perhaps several women screaming.

Alarmed, Lena tensed.

"Coyotes," Eli said. "A pack of coyotes."

They listened to the staccato of yips, the long mournful howls, the high-pitched baying. Barks and yelps broke the stillness, cutting off even the incessant chirring of the insects. By the sound of them, the coyotes were traveling together somewhere to the east, deep in the woods, hunting for prey.

Lena shivered and wrapped her arms around her ribs. They stood and listened to nature in her wild ferocity. After several minutes, the howls faded as the pack drifted further away.

Lena glanced up at Eli. The silvered starlight reflected off the sharp planes of his face. His expression was hard, his mouth flat. She knew that look. "What were you going to say?"

Eli shrugged. "Nothing."

She started to say something but pursed her lips and held her tongue. They both had secrets they'd kept for years. It was difficult to say what needed to be said, especially between people who'd known each other so long and carried the baggage they did.

He was in pain. It hurt her to see it, as if his pain was her own. And when Eli was in pain, he pushed everyone away, including her.

He'd closed himself off. It was a solid wall between them which seemed impossible to breach.

It was an old dance, one she was intimately familiar with. A younger version of herself had been hurt, had let him push her away; she hadn't been stubborn or strong enough to stare pain in the face without flinching.

But she wasn't that girl anymore. He was no longer the boy who'd hurt her.

"You can talk to me," she said. "About anything. I'm right here."

Eli said, "I know."

He stepped off the porch and retreated into the night. Once again, Lena found herself watching Eli Pope leave with her heart in tatters.

10

JACKSON CROSS
DAY SIXTY-EIGHT

Jackson stood on the top deck of his family's mansion beside Horatio. He gripped the railing and took in the spectacular view of the limestone bluffs and the vastness of Lake Superior.

The surface of the immense lake rippled like aluminum foil, reflecting the cobalt blue of the sky studded with cottony clouds. The native Ojibwe people called the lake *Gichigamiing*—the "great water."

Over thousands of years, fierce winds had sheared off treetops and foliage, the cliffs taking on shapes like the prows of great ships jutting into the lake. Powerful waves carved coves and caverns and inlets out of the multi-colored limestone.

Behind him loomed the palatial house of his childhood, a mansion of stone and cedar designed to resemble a grand Tahoe Lodge—which as a kid had felt more like a prison.

The property had been passed down through generational wealth. The Cross grandparents and great-grandparents were timber barons, exploiting the land and water, stripping the Upper Peninsula of its great trees and leaving enormous graveyards of ravaged tree stumps in their wake.

Jackson had wanted none of it. He'd made his own way. Now

he was home and did not want to be, but he was compelled to return, seeking answers from his father, baffled by his need, and yet he could not seem to stay away.

He had just come from Munising Hospital. The hospital had closed its doors, leaving hundreds of sick, wounded, and desperate people seeking answers he couldn't give them. He was furious, frustrated, and helpless.

"You did something to make Underwood step down," he said to his father. "He didn't resign on his own."

Horatio gazed at Jackson with an impenetrable expression. Tall and slender in his mid-sixties, his silvery hair brushed back from his high forehead, Horatio Cross had the air of a distinguished gentleman. As the powerful former sheriff of Alger County, he was wealthy and well-connected, and he was accustomed to giving orders, controlling and manipulating everyone around him, including his family.

Horatio slapped him on the back. "You've humiliated Underwood twice now, first with Boone and then with Cyrus Lee Jefferson—"

Jackson stiffened, gritting his teeth. "That wasn't my intention—"

Horatio spoke over him. "Underwood proved to the entire county that he isn't fit to be a dog catcher. I only gave you what you deserved. I've always looked out for you, made sure you lived up to your full potential. You're a Cross, after all."

His father's chest puffed with pride as if Jackson's successes were his triumphs, as if Jackson only succeeded because of his bloodline. The accolades were due to Horatio, and Horatio alone.

His father beamed at him, proud in a way he'd never been before, not when Jackson had graduated top of his class, not when he'd served his first day as a deputy, and not when he was promoted to undersheriff.

Jackson shifted uneasily, struggling to hide the tangled thicket of emotions pricking his insides like thorns. "What will happen to Underwood now?"

Horatio shot him a scornful look, the way he used to when Jackson was a kid, like he was a squirming bug beneath a magnifying glass. Jackson had wilted beneath his father's unrelenting disapproval. "Forget about him and look forward, Jackson. Only look forward. What's behind you is a distraction, a snare to trip you. Don't let yourself fall."

The words were innocuous enough, yet they sounded faintly like a threat. Something sour-sick churned in his gut. How hard he'd tried to measure up, to make his father proud, to earn a look of satisfaction that Horatio had so readily bestowed upon Jackson's brother and sister.

Somehow, no matter what he did, he was never enough.

Horatio's teeth flashed, too white, too bright. "You're a Cross. Don't forget where you came from and to whom you owe your allegiance."

That dark unsettled sensation took root and grew. His father expected a quid pro quo. Jackson owed him. Horatio believed he had handed Jackson the promotion on a silver platter. That favor needed to be repaid a hundred times over; you were never square with a man like Horatio Cross.

He kept his shoulders straight and tried to ignore the insult, the needling guilt-trip he'd heard all his life. "I'm going to do my job. No special perks. I'm not going to turn a blind eye to anything."

Horatio made a dismissive gesture and spun on his heel, headed for the deck stairs. When Horatio was done with a conversation, it was done. At the edge of the deck, Horatio paused and glanced over his shoulder, his eyes hard. "Don't start to think you're the kind of man we both know you're not."

Then he was gone.

Jackson gripped the railing with whitened knuckles. A hawk soared high above the bluffs on columns of wind. Below him, the lake sparkled bright and hard as a diamond.

Childhood memories bristled with fear, shame, disappointment—and longing. The pathetic fact he couldn't escape: the

unwanted boy inside him still yearned for that love, that acceptance, that warm bright circle of his father's withheld affection.

He could not simply switch off his sense of duty to his family.

Love was the anchor chained to his neck that would drown
him. Or was it obligation, or guilt? He feared he could no longer
tell one from the other. That was the problem.

11

SHILOH EASTON
DAY SIXTY-NINE

"It's official." Shiloh groaned, sank back on her heels, and hurled her spade at the nearest rain containment barrel in disgust. "I hate gardening."

"What? Why?" Ruby Carpenter asked. "I love gardens."

Ruby knelt across from Shiloh, dutifully weeding her section of the garden, her flame-red hair pulled back in a ponytail beneath a straw hat with a wide brim to protect her fragile skin from the sun.

They'd been weeding the stupid garden for two excruciating hours. Last week, they'd built a fence to keep out pests. Little good it was doing.

Bear watched them work from his comfortable spot in the shade cast from the cottage, plopped on his belly with his paws stretched out, panting merrily. He lay next to Shiloh's crossbow, pistol, and knife as if he were guarding her battle weapons.

Shiloh scowled at Ruby. "That's because you have a green thumb. My thumb is black, blacker than black, blacker than coal. The tomato plants keep getting bug infestations, the dumb rabbits dig underneath the wire netting to devour whatever lettuce I manage to get sprouted, and weeds are growing more than the potatoes!"

"It's not that hard."

"Say that again and I'll make a necklace of your teeth."

Ruby gave her a reproachful look. She had the patience of the saints, damn her. Not Shiloh. She'd rather be hunting things. And skinning the bad guys alive.

"Whatever. Lena says we can't break for lunch until we get rid of these weeds. I don't see the point. They'll just be back tomorrow."

Ruby usually rode over on her bike to help with the lighthouse chores; in return, Lena sent her home with wild blackberries or some vegetables or herbs from the garden. Shiloh appreciated the company, though Ruby could be incredibly annoying, like now.

Ruby rolled her eyes. "Those bugs on the tomato plants are fruit worms, aphids, and flea beetles. We can dust the plants with plain talcum powder to repel them. Your aunt is growing basil, which works, too. We can make a homemade spray with a couple of drops of dish soap."

Shiloh stared at her like she'd grown a second head. "What are you even talking about? You're speaking a foreign language. All I hear is blah, blah, blah."

Ruby cracked a hint of a smile. "You think you're the only one who knows stuff around here? My mom was always working at the store with my dad, but when I was little my grandma took care of me. She's the one who taught me how to can applesauce, how to freeze-dry strawberries, and how to grow things. You know."

"No. I don't. My grandfather taught me how to kill things and how to stay out of his way when he was falling-down drunk."

A memory of Cody flared through her mind: they were six or seven, hunkered behind the wood pile, peeping through the logs as her grandfather stumbled, yelling drunkenly, violence in his clenched fists. Cody crouched beside her, one finger to his lips, his small hand gripping her shoulder to offer comfort, determined to protect her from the big bad wolf.

The jolt of sorrow struck her like an arrow to the chest. It took her breath away.

Ruby wrinkled her brow, concern in her blue eyes. "Are you okay—"

"Fine. Just dandy." Shiloh waved a hand at the garden to distract Ruby, as well as herself. "Okay, hotshot. I defer to your genius. Why the living hell did you let me make a fool of myself for so long? You could have told me what I was doing wrong."

The tiny smile grew broader. "It was a little bit funny."

"Whatever. Get back to work, smarty-pants."

Shiloh's stomach rumbled. She and Lena were far from starving, but they ate less than they were used to. Every meal took so much damn prep work—no more stops at Pizza Hut or Subway for fast food or runs to Dunkin Donuts for coffee.

She retrieved the stupid spade and got back to weeding. Her knees were covered in dirt, her back ached, and the sun was burning her alive. "I'm so freaking sick of salad and canned beans and fish. Fish, fish, fish. If I see another trout, I'm gonna cram it down someone's throat. I would kill for a double cheeseburger dripping with cheddar cheese and slathered with ketchup and mayo, topped with a whole pile of juicy pickles. Or a Snickers bar. All that melting chocolate, gooey caramel, and crunchy nuts..."

Ruby gave a wistful sigh. "I miss turkey paninis and broccoli cheddar soup from Falling Rock Café, our favorite restaurant. Every Friday night, Mom and I would get whatever we wanted, no calorie counting allowed, and watch a Hallmark movie together."

Shiloh made a face. "Barf city. No wonder you ran away."

"Don't knock it 'til you try it. It wasn't that bad."

"Yeah, well, I don't have a mom, so I'll never get to try it, will I?"

Ruby's eyes widened in horror as she realized what she'd said. "I—I didn't mean it like that, Shiloh. I'm so sorry—"

Shiloh forced a careless shrug. She didn't want anyone's pity, not even Ruby's. "It's fine, I'm fine. Don't worry about it."

Ruby looked concerned. "Are you sure?"

"Of course." Shiloh pulled a bunch of weeds choking the nascent snap peas and tossed them into the wheelbarrow. "Besides, I don't think Mom was the Hallmark type. If she was anything like me, we'd both be into barbeque chicken pizza, Snickers candy bars for dessert, and an *Avengers* movie, or *Star Wars*, but only the original trilogy."

Shiloh glanced down at the oversized green *The Last Jedi* T-shirt that had been one of Cody's favorites: it featured a picture of a fuzzy Ewok emblazoned with the words "Endor Forest Summer Camp."

"You remember your mom much?" Ruby asked quietly.

Shiloh stiffened. "Nope."

"Not at all?"

Shiloh closed her eyes. Saw the darkness. A shadow moving across the wall. Terror a coppery taste like pennies in her mouth. Long dark hair strewn across a pillowcase, blood spattered on satin sheets.

Her strongest memories of her mother were of that night. Faint recollections, like wisps of smoke dissipating through her fingers, ghosts vanishing when she chased them.

She opened her eyes and focused on the sunlight shining through the trees like a patchwork quilt of light and shadow, the green blades of grass tickling her bare legs, the dirt beneath her fingernails, the steady sound of the waves beating the shoreline.

Grief was a dagger. It cut anything it touched.

"I'm working on remembering, but mostly I see her in the way other people talk about her. Lena and Jackson tell me stories, about how bright and vivacious she was, how beautiful. Everyone is perfect after they die."

"I promise to only say nice things about you when you die."

"True friends keep their friends' secrets to the grave," Shiloh quipped.

Ruby stilled. She shot Shiloh a questioning look. "Is that what we are? Friends?"

"Things were going so well until you had to get all weepy and emotional."

Ruby's sober expression broke into a tentative smile. "We're friends."

"Keep talking sentimental nonsense like that and I'll abandon your lazy butt to finish the weeding yourself."

Ruby went back to work, but the contented smile stayed on her face.

Shiloh watched her for a second, blinking hard. Ruby had invaded her nightmares again, her plaintive cries mingled with Cody's, their sorrowful voices haunting Shiloh as she searched and searched and never found them.

In the real world, Shiloh had unearthed Ruby from beneath the floorboards of Walter Boone's cabin, yanked her from the pit, and faced Boone while Ruby fled, traumatized but alive.

Gradually, day by day, Ruby was coming back to life, blooming like a flower with its petals coaxed open in the sunlight. Shiloh would never admit it, but when Ruby smiled a real smile, it warmed a little spot in the center of her chest.

Ten minutes later, Shiloh had finished her section. Dirt crusted her hands, rimmed her fingernails, and stained her knees and shins. She sat back on her heels and rubbed her aching back with one hand.

Stillness eddied around them. The heat was stifling. She squinted against the harsh sun bouncing off the placid reflection of the lake. Bear had flopped onto his side, snoring loudly, his jowls vibrating with every grunted breath.

Perspiration dampened the back of her neck. She lifted her thick hair and tied it into a knot with the hair tie on her wrist, then took off her polyester neck gaiter, dunked it in the bucket of water, wrung it out, and repositioned it on the back of her neck, which helped cool her entire body for at least a good hour.

Ruby followed her lead. They drank from their water bottles, filled with rainwater from the water containment system, which was filtered and sanitized.

Lena had lectured her on the dangers of heatstroke, especially without air conditioning or a hospital when things went wrong.

"I think we're about done," Shiloh said. "I need a freaking break."

"I could whip up some raspberry juice. You want some?"

Lena had taught them how to make a fruity drink from the raspberries they'd gathered on the property, heating the berries on the wood stove to tenderize them, using a potato masher and cheese cloth to strain the seeds, and then mixing in cold, clean water.

"I'd sell you my soul for some raspberry juice right now."

"You're undervaluing your soul."

"I'm not. My soul is as black as my black thumb."

Ruby pushed the wheelbarrow across the yard to dump the weeds inside the tree line, grunting as she shoved the heavy load through the overgrown grass.

Shiloh finished adding the ripe cucumbers and zucchinis to her basket, wiped the dirt off the spade, and stuck it in the basket to wash later. Her mouth watered as she fantasized about a cold drink, the chilled glass tinkling with ice cubes—

Ruby gave a little yelp. "What the hell!"

Adrenaline kicked her chest. Shiloh dropped the basket. Tomatoes, zucchinis, and cucumbers spilled every which way. Instantly on her feet, crossbow in hand and a bolt drawn, she sprinted toward Ruby. Bear shook himself awake and trotted after her. "What's wrong?"

Ruby pointed at a bare patch of ground at the base of a tall spruce tree. At chest-height, deep claw marks scratched the soft bark. Several paw prints marred the dirt around the tree. Large paws, too large to be Bear's.

Shiloh sucked in her breath. "A black bear. A big one, too."

"Why would it come so close to the house?"

"I bet it's the same damn bear Lena saw a few weeks ago. Mrs. Grady said something got three of her chickens last week. Maybe it was the bear."

The animal was getting brazen. Shiloh loved God's creatures as much as the next person, probably more, but a black bear that didn't fear people was dangerous.

The Newfie sniffed the base of the tree in avid interest. A low growl emanated from deep in his barrel chest, the hackles rising along his ruff.

Shiloh's neck prickled as she scanned the woods, the crossbow stock snug against her shoulder, her muscles tensed. With a shudder, Ruby stepped closer to her. "You think it's out there right now? Watching us?"

Unbidden, another memory flashed behind her eyes—the unsettling feeling of being stalked in the woods, a calloused hand closing over her mouth, the terror of the attack. She blinked and forced the terrible images out of her head.

"I don't know," Shiloh said.

She told herself she was safe now, she was safe. She didn't feel safe. In the wilderness, animals weren't the only predators. She knew that too well.

12

JACKSON CROSS
DAY SEVENTY

Jackson sat at his new desk in the sheriff's office, his shoulders hunched, his elbows resting on the polished oak surface, his head in his hands. Case files were stacked perilously on both sides of the desk, the folders starved of evidence.

A Coleman lantern shone warm yellow light on the framed photos hung on the wall behind him—Underwood hamming for the camera, glad-handing with the superintendent, the governor, several senators, and a few judges.

The sheriff's office no longer had a working generator. During the heat of the day, the interior was nearly unbearable even with the windows open. Half the department had quit.

The remaining officers showed up with no pay, no thanks, and no reason to stay—other than an unerring sense of duty, a stubborn commitment to the cause, and a desire to protect their community.

Those who remained were true believers, people he trusted with his life.

Outside the sheriff's office, the large main room was cluttered with cramped workstations separated by shared partition walls. The air smelled of stale coffee and gun oil.

It was well after midnight, but sleep eluded him. Lily Easton's case binder sat unopened in the middle of the desk. She haunted him: her deep throaty laugh, her dark curls rippling in the wind, that mischievous glint in her brown eyes.

He could hear her whispering to him late at night. In the wind whistling through the eaves, it soughed and howled like a woman's mournful cry.

He would find her killer; he'd sworn it to Lily's ghost, to Lena, and Shiloh. With each day that passed, the world descended further into chaos; he felt further from solving her murder than ever before.

Darius Sykes and his escaped convicts presented a clear and present danger. Sawyer was a constant threat, as were thieves, raiders, and desperate citizens on the verge of rioting.

He was the sheriff now. It was his job to safeguard the living.

"Soon," he whispered. "Soon, Lily. I promise. But I've got to protect your sister and your daughter first."

He rose heavily to his feet and went to the whiteboard he'd brought in from the conference room. A detailed map of Alger County had been taped on one side. On the other end, he'd pinned up a larger map of the U.P.

A red pushpin marked the spot where the first corpse had been found. He didn't doubt there would be others. It was only a matter of time.

Tomorrow morning, he would create a task force to hunt for Sykes.

Before the world had crashed, he would've combed through video security footage from local businesses, ATMs, and nearby residences. He could have pulled up building plans and schematics, and run credit checks and public records searches.

There had been social media accounts to scan, license plates to run, photographs to run through facial recognition software, cell phone carriers to subpoena, and computers and phones to search for evidence—every clue a bread crumb he could follow.

That was all gone, burned to dust and ashes.

Jackson found himself once again on the hunt, searching in the dark for a killer.

13

ELI POPE
DAY SEVENTY-ONE

Eli bent over a stump next to the lean-to he'd built to store firewood, splitting wood in the darkness.

The steady *thwack, thwack, thwack* of the rising and falling axe drowned the voices in his head and kept the nightmares at bay, at least for a while.

He grunted with each blow, straining as if each rise of the axe physically hurt him. Sweat slicked his skin and rolled down his temples, plastering his damp hair to his forehead. Shirtless in cargo shorts, his biceps bulged as the axe rose and fell, rose and fell, his sinewy muscles rippling beneath battle-scarred skin.

The pile of fresh-cut firewood next to him stood chest-high. There had been none this morning. He had chopped wood for hours. Eli and Shiloh had collected deadfall. Eli had felled oak and maple trees along the perimeter of the meadow to season for next year.

Earlier, he'd run his ten miles as if he could outrun the demons hot on his heels. It was late, past 11:00 p.m. He should be in the assistant's cabin, restlessly tossing and turning, but instead, he was outside in the dark, weary and exhausted, his muscles burning with lactic acid, unable to stop.

Eli heard her footsteps before he saw her, his senses acutely attuned to his surroundings. Lena strode around the corner of the assistant's cabin and halted a few yards away. She wore striped pajama shorts and an oversized, white T-shirt hanging off one shoulder, a glass of water in one hand, her M&P held low at her side in the other.

Despite himself, his heart stuttered in his chest. Furiously, he wiped at his wet face with the back of his arm. He knew what she saw, her gaze scanning the puckered flesh of a bullet wound, the slashing white scars of multiple knife wounds. Fading yellowed bruises from his beating on the yacht still marred his ribs, his back, his chest.

"Hey," she said softly.

"Hey." His shoulders stiffened, then he continued chopping. *Thwack, thwack.* He placed a new log on the stump. The axe plunged again and again. *Thwack, thwack.*

She watched him in the dark. "You need a break."

"I'm fine."

"Talk to me," she said.

"I said I'm fine."

"You're not." She stepped closer. "Eli, stop."

Obediently, he lowered the axe, breathing heavily. "You ever take no for an answer?"

"No."

He grunted.

She thrust the glass of water at him. "Take it. You're already dehydrated."

His arms shook from fatigue as he sank the axe into the stump. He guzzled the water and then set the glass on the stump next to the axe.

They stared at each other in the dark. His face was veiled in shadows, his eyes dark pools that reflected the dwindling light. The lighthouse beacon passed back and forth, casting an eerie glow across the grass, the buildings throwing long shadows as night insects chirred.

"You're not fine."

An involuntary shudder went through him.

"What's wrong?"

"You have enough on your plate already. I don't want to burden you."

"I'll decide what I want to be burdened with."

He stared down at the axe jutting from the heart of the stump. "You don't want to know. No one does."

Anger flashed across her face. "You don't know that. You don't get to choose for someone else. That's not fair."

She took a step toward him until they were less than two feet apart. "I'm asking, Eli, because I want to know. I'm not leaving until you tell me."

He looked at her, stared her down with a ferocity that should have cowed her but didn't. She stared right back, unflinching. Lena was stubborn, always had been. "It's ugly."

She lifted her chin. "I can handle ugly."

Instinctively, he touched the Saint Michael's medal hanging from his neck next to his dog tags. His mouth wouldn't work properly. The silence stretched between them. He half expected her to leave, but she didn't. She waited him out.

After a long moment, his shoulders slumped in resignation. He said the thing he hadn't spoken aloud, the thing he hadn't been able to bear, to see who he truly was reflected in her eyes, the rejection when she feared and hated him.

The words were like barbed wire on his tongue. "I killed an innocent. A non-combatant."

Lena stared at him in shock. He waited for the revulsion, the horror, and judgment. It didn't come.

"Tell me," she said.

He did.

"On Sawyer's yacht," he said in a broken voice, "when I broke free in the safe room. One of the wait staff came in. He was still a kid, just a grunt Sawyer used to run errands for his crew. He brought me water against Sawyer's orders. And he died for it. I killed him for it."

He carried the burden with him, the guilt and the shame. He'd been carrying it since the night the yacht burned and Jackson rescued him from Sawyer's clutches. This bloody millstone blighted his soul and tortured his mind.

He looked at her like he was drowning. "I can't get his face out of my head. He's in my dreams, my nightmares. I see him everywhere. That kid and David Kepford—a man I never met who died for me. How am I supposed to live with that? What kind of person does that make me?"

"Eli—"

He shook his head, adamant. "I murdered an innocent, just a kid doing a good deed. I murdered him. He was no threat to me. I was in kill mode, survival mode, seeing red. If I had hesitated for even an instant, I could have prevented it. I didn't."

"You were fighting for your life."

"That's no excuse."

Lena folded her arms across her chest. "You have done everything in your power to protect me and Shiloh. You risked your life to stop a killer of women, Eli. You found it in yourself to forgive Jackson for what he did to you. You've done nothing but sacrifice yourself for others. How can you not see that?"

He heard her words, but she was speaking of someone else, someone without a soul deformed by death and killing, someone unsullied by innocent blood on his hands. It was the devil inside him, what he feared most in himself.

"I'm not—"

"I know who you are."

"No—"

"I know you."

He started to say something, to argue again.

"Listen to me," she said.

He listened.

"The things you did, the things you saw, what happened to you and what you did to others, for your country, for your survival—it all haunts you. I know that. I see that. You can't bury what happened to you. You pretend it's dead, forsaken, and left in the past, but it isn't. The past is in every breath you take, every memory, every emotion, every reaction you have. Soldiers and survivors—we all have something in common. It's trauma. We try to drown it, to numb it, to erase it. It doesn't work. It never works."

She touched her heart. "There are different kinds of battle-fields. Not everyone is in Syria or Afghanistan or Ukraine. Some are here." She touched her head. "Some are here. You have fought battles you never should've had to fight. You endured years in prison for a crime you didn't commit. You're still on that battle-field, but you don't have to fight alone. You don't have to suffer alone."

Eli's chest constricted. It was suddenly difficult to breathe properly. Lena had somehow peered deep inside him; she knew his history, his past, his demons, all the ugly things he hated about himself. He felt exposed and vulnerable.

And yet, she did not look away. She knew the worst of him and didn't run. Strange, unfamiliar warmth radiated through him, from his fingers to his toes. It was uncomfortable, disconcerting, unsettling—and yet not entirely unwelcome.

He wanted this. He yearned for it, but didn't know how to ask for it or deserve it.

"You have to let the darkness out to let the light in."

He went still.

She took a step toward him. "You have to talk about it. It's how we heal."

"I don't know how."

Lena came closer. Another step and she'd bridged the gap between them. She reached for him, wrapped her arms around his waist, and leaned her head against his bare chest.

His arms hung rigid at his sides; he was afraid to move lest he frighten her away. His heart thumped in his chest; his breath caught in his throat as he inhaled her vanilla scent, her sweetness, her warmth.

His blood buzzed beneath his skin. Everything came rushing

back: the way she felt in his arms, the passion that burned bright between them. That he remembered clearly, maybe too clearly.

Above their heads, the sickle of the half-moon hung in the immense bowl of the sky. Bats soared and dove as frogs croaked in the night.

He could have lived in this moment forever.

Lena pulled back and stared up into his face. "You care, Eli. Don't try to deny it. You've stepped up. You're trying with everything you are to be that person, to be better. You're good."

When he started to shake his head, she frowned up at him. "Don't mistake me. Goodness doesn't mean nice. And it sure doesn't mean harmless. It means you care, and you try. I see it every day. I see it in you."

He longed to pull her into his arms, to kiss her as she'd never been kissed, as no one had ever kissed anyone in the history of the world.

He held himself back. She was the good one. She was kind, compassionate, gentle, and tender-hearted—he did not deserve her. He never had deserved her.

But maybe he did deserve something more. To heal, to forgive himself, to allow himself moments of peace, contentment, and joy. Maybe in this world a thing like that was possible.

14

LENA EASTON
DAY SEVENTY-TWO

"I'll be right back," Lena said to Moreno, who was sitting on the sofa with his leg propped on the coffee table, surrounded by bandages and antiseptic creams. With the proper care and a dose of precious antibiotics, the infection was improving.

"Take your time." Moreno lay back with his arms splayed across the sofa cushions, closing his eyes with relish. "I'll just take a little cat nap while my pretty nurse nurses me back to health."

She snorted. "Flattery will get you nowhere."

He kept his eyes closed and flashed a mischievous grin. "Just speaking the plain truth, ma'am. I'm completely innocent. Zero ulterior motives, I promise. Besides, Eli would kick me into next Tuesday if my good looks and electric charisma turned your pretty head."

"Oh, Eli and I aren't—"

Moreno pretended to snore loudly.

It was a good thing his eyes were closed. Flustered, she shook her head and left him in the living room, heading into the kitchen to retrieve a few sprigs of lavender to reduce the inflammation around his cut.

She'd spent the morning and afternoon tending to minor

injuries and illnesses. Two days ago, she'd officially opened the lighthouse clinic to the public.

Word had spread fast. Trey Gleason, a retired local pediatrician, had agreed to help her three afternoons a week in exchange for a weekly basket of fresh vegetables, canned in winter.

Last week, she and Jackson had raided the aquarium store in downtown Munising. Fish antibiotics were similar to those prescribed for humans—amoxicillin, ciprofloxacin, and penicillin.

While she'd never advocated for the human use of animal antibiotics when the world was functioning, things were different now. Something was much better than nothing. But even fish antibiotics would disappear soon, and they needed alternatives. The antibiotics she would ration for the worst cases, like Moreno and his infected leg.

She'd gone to the library, still open with limited hours and run by the formidable Mrs. Grady, and checked out every book on natural and herbal remedies, then collected the recommended herbs from a vacant landscaping store outside of town.

No one had touched the packets of lavender, evening primrose flowers, ginger, goldenseal, or chamomile seeds. Most people were thinking of immediate caloric needs rather than long-term solutions.

So far, she'd offered chicory root to the child suffering from bouts of diarrhea to reduce inflammation, and chamomile to Sandra Miles for her arthritis and James Wood to relieve his constant toothaches. Aloe vera and raw honey had antiseptic properties and were excellent for soothing minor cuts and lacerations.

As Lena entered the kitchen, a bent figure closed the pantry door and tottered around to face her. An old woman hunched her narrow shoulders and patted at her wispy hair with a liver-spotted hand. With her other hand, she clutched an oversized canvas bag to her scrawny torso. Lena recognized the old neighbor lady from down the street, but she didn't know her name.

Startled, Lena halted. "What are you doing here?"

"You've got quite the set up here." The old woman's pinched gaze roamed the hydroponics wall garden system, the counters crammed with jarred tomato sauce, and the table set with a bowl of ripe zucchinis. Her watery eyes shone with greed.

Unease slithered through her gut. "The clinic is in the living room. This part of the cottage is not available to patients. You're trespassing."

"Is that so? You got something to hide, is that it? You a hoarder?"

Lena stiffened. "I have nothing to hide. We are entitled to our privacy. You're on private property."

The old woman gestured at the wall of hydroponic plants with a withered arm. "What's all that? Why do you have it and we don't?"

Hydroponics was a system of growing plants without soil which used less water and promoted faster growth, higher yields, and best of all, allowed for indoor growing year-round.

Currently, she used it for her medicinal herbs—rosemary, mint, sage, basil, and peppermint—but she had plans to build a DIY system in one of the spare bedrooms to grow vegetables suited to hydroponics, such as lettuce, spinach, peppers, and cucumbers.

Jackson had told her that David Kepford, the principal of Munising High School and a formidable Marine, had used it in his office. Before he'd died, he'd told Jackson to put it to good use. While Lena could never repay the gift Kepford had given her and others, she could give back unselfishly, the way he had.

She said none of this to the intruder, however. "They're medicinal plants I use in my clinic. Now, please leave and return to the living room if you'd like to be seen as a patient."

The old woman scratched at a red rash that started at her wrist and traveled up her arm, disappearing below the sleeve of her baggy, faded sundress. Dirt crusted her high heels, strange footwear for a grandma.

"Is that eczema? Both coconut oil and sunflower seed oil have soothing and antibacterial properties that can reduce itchiness and blisters and improve skin barrier function. I can help you, but you need to wait with everyone else."

The old woman ignored her generous overture. "Why do you have all this stuff that no one else has, huh? That's what I want to know. We have to bring you Band-Aids, beans, or bullets to pay you with what little we have left, while you have so much already?"

Lena gritted her teeth. "I take little payment. I'm helping people instead of doing other valuable things with my time."

The old woman pursed her wrinkled lips. "Like what?"

"Like cooking meals from scratch, growing and tending to my garden, scavenging for supplies, preserving food for winter, hunting and fishing for tonight's dinner, cutting firewood and hauling water from the lake and then purifying it for drinking and cooking, studying first aid and emergency medicine so I can heal patients without a hospital or doctors, identifying and using wild plants that can be used for food and medicinal purposes. The list is endless."

The woman sniffed in derision. "I haven't eaten in two days. The only thing I can make for my nephew is watery, lumpy pancakes and a few potatoes. All we got left. What are you going to do about that?"

A mixture of revulsion and pity flared through Lena. She hesitated, unsure what to do. On the one hand, the elderly woman was too old to do much for herself, and Lena felt compassion for her plight. On the other hand, the woman expected handouts, and when they weren't forthcoming, she felt entitled to demand them.

The thought of a greedy stranger rummaging through her belongings and invading the sanctity of her home made Lena's skin itch. "I see that you're in a tough situation. We all are—"

"You keep saying that, but I don't see the skin falling off your bones from starvation. You're plump as a bug in a rug, aren't you?"

Lena half expected the crone to reach out and pinch her cheek like the witch in Hansel and Gretel.

"And I don't see your girl going hungry, do I?" the woman continued with a nasty tone. "You got enough supplies here to share with the whole street, but I don't see you sharing nothing. I see you hiding what you got from everyone. You've got some secret stash you're hoarding like you're better than us. You think you're better than me? That you deserve to live all high and mighty, with heat from your wood stove and water from the lake right behind you, with all that food in your pantry and that fancy springhouse you got out back?" She hooked a gnarled finger at the kitchen window overlooking the backyard and the creek. "You don't deserve any of it."

Lena stiffened at the mention of the springhouse. "You don't know me."

The woman sneered, scratching incessantly at the rash on her shrunken arm. Beads of blood appeared. "Don't I? Everyone knows who you are and who you've got in your pocket. You're the sister of that dead girl that caused so much trouble. You ran away, but now you're back, causing more trouble."

Lena blinked but quickly regained her composure. She wasn't going to take verbal assault in her own home, even if it was from a grandma. "Leave my house."

"Not without my share," the crone snarled, spittle spraying from her mouth.

"You heard her." Shiloh entered the kitchen, one hand resting casually on the butt of the pistol at her hip. There was nothing casual about the fiery look in her eyes. "Leave now, or we'll toss you out on your bony backside."

Bear wandered in beside Shiloh, his ears pricked, his bushy tail wagging in a friendly greeting. He'd sooner lick the intruder to death than bite her, but the old woman didn't know that. His simple presence was intimidating.

The woman shot Shiloh a baleful look, then hobbled past them, her head down, mumbling something to herself that sounded a lot like a witch's curse.

Lena said firmly, "Next time, if you'd like something, you can come and ask instead of sneaking around."

Lena went to the bathroom window and watched the woman shuffle down the long driveway with a mix of relief and consternation. Her knobby shoulders were like coat hangers, the back of her spotted scalp gleaming through thin clumps of hair white as a spider's web.

Once the old woman was good and gone, Lena checked the pantry to see if anything had been stolen; luckily, everything was still in its place, including the canned goods they'd started storing for winter, though most of their supplies were kept in the root cellar.

Despite her misgivings, compassion swelled in her chest. The woman was too old to help herself. "I don't know if we should have sent her away. I could have fed her a meal, at least."

"If she needed help, she could have asked like a normal person. She didn't. She was spying on us, scoping the place out to rob us blind."

Lena sighed. "Perhaps."

"I'm telling you, that old witch is sketch."

"Maybe, but she's frail and elderly. She couldn't have hurt us."

"Maybe not, but her nephew who lives with her is a full-grown man. Kinda slow, but strong. He could do plenty of damage."

"Who is her nephew?"

Shiloh narrowed her eyes. "That ornery old lady is Mrs. Fitch. She lives half a mile down the street off that dirt road, in the saggy green house that matches her dress. I've seen her at the mailbox a few times. She keeps checking it like one day there'll be a letter or a bill for her to pay. Her nephew is Calvin Fitch, the creepy janitor at the school. He lived in a dilapidated trailer outside of town, but Mrs. Carpenter told me he moved back into his aunt's house after the whole thing with his cousin, Boone."

Sometimes she forgot how interconnected and insulated the small towns of the Upper Peninsula could be. Her years in Tampa made it easy to forget. "Mrs. Fitch isn't Boone's...?"

"His mother? No." Shiloh waved her hand like she couldn't be bothered with the tangled family trees of deranged adults. "A sister of his mother's brother, I think. Something like that. The brother, her husband, died of cancer ages ago. All I heard was that Mrs. Fitch took Calvin Fitch in after the owner of the trailer he was renting threw him out. Boone set him up, so they got lumped in together as creepy perverts. Mrs. Carpenter says he's a recluse, afraid to leave the house because adults call him names and kids throw rocks at him."

Lena watched the girl intently. Shiloh no longer flinched when she spoke Boone's name. That was a good thing. "You okay?"

"I'm dandy. I'm happier than a unicorn pooping rainbows." Shiloh shot her an exasperated look. "We're talking about that crazy old lady. She's gonna be trouble, I'm telling you. This is why Eli doesn't want strangers coming here."

Lena rubbed her temples. Her nerves were raw. She understood Eli's side and agreed with him. She also believed in doing something for the suffering in the community. She couldn't stand by and watch it happen; apathy wasn't part of her makeup and never had been.

"Did you see the people we helped today? Little Keeley with her bacterial infection? Nick Piper's foot because of that rusty nail he stepped on?"

"Yeah, yeah, I know. We need to give more than we take. It's how we balance things, karma, fate, and the universe. Whatever. It's nobody's business what we do or don't have."

"I don't disagree with that." Lena's limbs felt heavy. She needed a nap, but there were still two patients waiting in her living room. After she finished with Moreno, she had Ned Warden, a devoted single father in his fifties who needed something to alleviate his rheumatoid arthritis.

She moved across the kitchen to the counter where her diabetic paraphernalia was stored. Her supplies were neatly organized on the counter beside a bucket of sudsy dishwater and a Coleman lantern: glass syringes and needles, a sharps container, extra batteries, the glucometer, test strips, and a box of glucose tabs.

The pump was useless, as she was out of infusion sets and sensors, and she'd used her last emergency glucagon injection during the attack on the lighthouse. The insulin vials, both long and short-acting, were stored in her solar-powered mini fridge in her bedroom and the springhouse outside.

Without her pump, she could no longer simply check the pump readout; she had to inject herself multiple times a day and test herself often with the glucometer and test strips. Already, her fingertips were bruised, swollen, and tender to the touch.

Shiloh watched as she found one of the few remaining spots on her pinkie finger that wasn't bruised and poked her skin, wincing at the painful prick, then added a drop of blood to the test strip and checked her blood sugar numbers.

Her blood sugar was over 450. She was running high again, so she pulled a vial of short-acting insulin out of her Frio wallet and injected herself with the units she'd memorized to get her numbers back into a normal range.

"There has to be some middle ground between helping others and protecting ourselves," Lena said as she worked. "We'll tell Eli about Mrs. Fitch's visit, and we need to pay close attention and make sure nobody snoops around, but I want to help people and give when we can. I'm not going to stop."

"We won't be helping anyone if all our stuff gets taken."

Lena gritted her teeth. "I'm well aware of that. I'm stubborn, not stupid."

"You sure about that?" Shiloh offered her an evil grin. "Want me to go give that bag of bones a beatdown she won't soon forget? Bet you I can make sure she never breathes a word of our stash to anyone."

"Shiloh," Lena said in a reproachful tone.

"What? I'm just saying. It's an option."

"Scorched earth is not the only option we have available to us."

"You're no fun."

90

"We can't go off and beat the crap out of people preemptively."

"Maybe we should," Shiloh retorted.

Bear's ears pricked. His big head swung back and forth between them like he was trying to figure out what in tarnation his humans were arguing about. He must've given up, because he ambled over to his water dish and gulped big mouthfuls, spraying water everywhere.

Shiloh had a good point. The thought of intruders poking around made her flesh crawl. They couldn't be at the lighthouse twenty-four seven, and she needed a better way to protect the insulin stores. "You're right. Tonight, you can help me move the solar fridge up to the tower. Raiders probably won't look there first. We've already planted bushes around the spring house to hide it from prying eyes."

"Sure, whatever." Shiloh spun on her heels and headed for the back door, grabbing one of the five-gallon buckets they kept next to the shoe rack along with the loaded shotgun hanging on a hook.

Shiloh slung the long gun over her shoulder. Since finding the black bear tracks a few days ago, they didn't leave the house without it.

"Come on," she called to the Newfie.

Bear lifted his head, drool dribbling from his jowls, and bounded eagerly after Shiloh, almost shoving her aside with his burly torso when he reached the door ahead of her.

"Where are you going?" Lena asked.

"To lug a bucket of water to the bathroom so I can use the damn toilet!" Shiloh said over her shoulder as the screen door slammed behind her and Bear. "You want the gory details?"

Lena sighed wearily. Parenting a teenager in the apocalypse was harder than it looked.

15

SHILOH EASTON
DAY SEVENTY-FOUR

"I 'll catch more fish than you," Shiloh said, hands on her hips.

Eli grinned. "We'll see about that."

"I know how to fly fish," Shiloh scoffed.

"Course you do."

Eli picked up the fly-fishing rod leaning against a nearby boulder along with a net and a burlap sack, which he attached to his belt, before he walked down to the bank and started upstream.

They'd ridden their bikes to the Au Train River to catch dinner. The sixteen-mile river meandered through Alger County west of Munising, springing from the .Cleveland Cliffs reservoir and flowing north through Au Train Lake before spilling into Lake Superior.

Shiloh was sick of fish, but she didn't tell Eli. She enjoyed tramping through the woods with him, though she'd much rather be shooting things. Eli promised to continue her combat and weapons training; she was gonna hold him to it.

Shiloh left her crossbow resting on the rock and followed Eli. Sweet ferns tickled her bare shins. Birch trees, cedars, and pines grew tall along the banks. She scrambled over fallen logs worn smooth and gray by the water, slick to the touch.

Sunlight glittered off the tea-colored water. Removing her

socks and hiking boots, she rolled up her overall cut-offs and waded knee-deep, the icy water raising goosebumps on her skin. The rocks were sharp underfoot, but she was used to being barefoot.

Little rapids and eddies swirled through the shallows and around mossy boulders, creating deep pools where the river curved around the base of a tall outcropping. The pebbled bottom shone clear in the dappled sunlight.

Thirty minutes in, Eli reeled in a big trout. He raised the rod high and brought the fish in, then took the net at his belt and placed it beneath the fish. He wet his left hand as he cupped the trout and removed the barb from its lip.

The gold and brown trout writhed and wriggled in his hand. He opened the burlap sack and dumped the fish inside it, letting the sack sag in the water so the fish didn't drown in the air.

"Your turn," Eli said. "You sure you know what to do?"

She shot him a withering look. He shrugged and handed her the fishing rod and net. Shiloh waded deeper to her knees, then began to cast. Jackson had taught her when she was little, and her cast was smooth and practiced.

Time passed easily and comfortably. The river burbled over rocks, birds sang in the trees, and no-see-ums skated above the surface of the water. They moved from eddy to eddy and pool to pool. After an hour, she'd reeled in a smallmouth bass and a wriggling perch.

"Great job," Eli said.

Shiloh couldn't keep the grin off her face. "No biggie."

She loved the lighthouse, but she was at home in the woods, too. The forest had been her escape when her grandfather was in a foul mood, gripping a bottle of Jack Daniels, with violence in his eyes.

Shiloh handed Eli the rod and sat on a sun-drenched flat rock and watched him. Cody would have loved this. She watched the light glitter off the water until her eyes blurred. She blinked fiercely. Her hands started shaking.

A sudden swell of grief welled in her chest. Her grandfather was dead and buried. Cody should be here with her, laughing and drawing and running and living, but he wasn't. He was dead and gone, like her mother was dead and gone, forever and ever, amen.

Shiloh's throat went tight. The water sparkled brightly through the wetness clinging to her eyelashes. Sorrow like a pit opened up beneath her, grieving for a thing she couldn't remember.

Her mother. She was a wisp of a memory, a snippet of a song, a dream of a warm smile, soft hands, and long luxurious hair.

Every time Shiloh thought back, things fell apart. Fractured memories like rafts floated on the gray sea of her consciousness. Tiny lights flickered in the deep. She couldn't dredge them up, couldn't capture them in a bottle before they winked out.

Darker things she had pushed down deep...dormant and waiting for the right moment. She felt it like a scream locked in the back of her throat, a bone-deep terror woven into her marrow.

When her vision cleared, Eli stood in front of her, shin-deep in the river, fishing rod in one hand, gazing at her intently. "What is it?"

She shrugged, embarrassed, and looked away. "Nothing."

"Is it the attack? Are you okay?"

"He deserved what he got. He tried to kill me, so I defended myself. That's it."

"You sure?"

"Yeah."

"Because no one else will hurt you. I'll make sure of that."

She didn't answer. He couldn't promise her that and she knew it.

After a protracted silence, he said, "You can talk to me, you know."

She rubbed the back of her arm across her eyes, inwardly cursing herself for her weakness, her vulnerability. She looked down at the water, unable to meet his gaze. She was so tired of being afraid. She hated it. "Everyone leaves. Grandfather. Cody. My mom. Everyone."

"Not everyone. Not Lena or Jackson." Eli hesitated. "Not me."

Shiloh made a noncommittal noise in the back of her throat. She grabbed the crossbow resting on the rock at her side and wrapped her hands around the grip. Touching the weapon centered her somehow, made her feel less exposed.

"I'm serious."

She forced herself not to feel it, to show him that he couldn't hurt her. But that was a lie, a fat, blubbering lie. "You saved me at the cabin. You've put up with me for a while, but you don't owe me anything. Everybody leaves, one way or another."

"I don't."

"Why the hell should I believe you?"

Eli watched her with those penetrating eyes, dark as anthracite, like her own. "Shiloh," he said. "I have to tell you something."

16

ELI POPE
DAY SEVENTY-FOUR

E li couldn't breathe properly. His lungs constricted. He'd faced armed killers in battle and hadn't experienced trepidation like this.

He busied himself with the task at hand, eager to distract himself, to put off the thing that terrified him more than mortal combat.

He took out his knife, stuck it in a nearby moss-slicked log and picked up the sack attached to his belt, then reached in and brought out one of the trout, wriggling and slick, its scales shimmering in the sun.

Eli gripped it near the tail and whacked it hard against the log.

The fish quivered, its neck broken. Eli set it on the log and repeated the task with the second trout. After gutting the fish, he placed them in the cast iron pan and set it over the fire he'd instructed Shiloh how to build using a ferro rod. As a fire starter, they'd wrapped a strip of dryer lint in wax paper, both of which were highly flammable. Dryers everywhere were full of lint; it was an easy item to scavenge from the laundry rooms of abandoned houses.

Eli set the solar kettle on a sun-drenched ledge to boil water to make coffee. Once the fish were sizzling over the fire, he squatted on his heels and leaned back. He felt Shiloh's coal-black eyes on him, intent and piercing, asking the question he needed to answer.

He recalled the half-feral child who'd crept into his campsite, her crossbow pointed at his chest, wary and curious, shy and brave. There had been an instant connection between them, but he hadn't recognized its power.

He did now. He knew, now.

Minutes passed in silence. Mosquitos buzzed around them, and clouds of gnats swirled over the placid surface of the river. The air smelled fresh, of moss and wildflowers.

He cleared his throat.

She wrinkled her pert nose. "Whatever you're gonna say, spit it out already."

"Fair enough," he said. "I know you didn't know who your father was. I...I didn't know, either, not until I got out of prison. I would have done things differently if I'd known. I would have done everything differently."

Shiloh stared at him, a wrinkle between her brows, her expression frozen. Her eyes wide like a deer caught in headlights, crouching like a wild animal on the verge of fleeing.

"Say it," she whispered, so low he had to strain to hear. "Say it out loud."

Powerful emotion bubbled up from some deep space within him, a thing he hadn't known existed until Lena had spoken the words aloud and the thing was made real—fatherhood.

What if he failed her? Disappointed her? What if he couldn't be what she needed? What if she hated him? The only thing he knew how to do well was to kill people. What the hell did he know about being a father?

It didn't matter what he didn't know. The whole world was filled with things he didn't know. But this child here in front of him, with her sullen expression and fierce eyes—she was worth every fear, every failure, every sleepless night.

Lena believed love could conquer all obstacles. He didn't know what he believed in, if anything, but he knew he would try, with all his might.

This girl was the best thing he had ever done. Loving her would be the best thing he would ever do.

That was enough.

Eli said, "You are my daughter."

She didn't move or react, just remained there, utterly still. He saw himself in her eyes: her doubt and fear, her guardedness, expecting the worst, afraid to believe in something. He saw it in the way she gripped her weapon for comfort, as if it could protect her from loss.

"I'm not going anywhere. I won't leave you. Not ever."

She stared at him with flinty black eyes, unblinking. For an endless minute, she said nothing. Finally, she spoke. "You gonna order me around like Lena does?"

"Isn't that one of the few perks of parenthood?"

Shiloh let out a snort. The tension in her shoulders eased. She sank back on her haunches and released her death-grip on the crossbow.

For a moment, they watched a hawk circling in the blue cloudless sky, swooping low and skimming the tops of the trees before skating higher on the currents and vanishing in the sunlight.

Shiloh jutted her chin at the trout sizzling in the pan. A singed smell filled the air. "You gonna take those out before they turn black? So far, I'm super unimpressed with your cooking skills."

Eli grinned at her.

Shiloh grinned back.

He felt it, the pieces falling into place, a rightness of things, this moment of grace. The world could burn, and it wouldn't matter as long as he had her. His daughter.

17

LENA EASTON
DAY SEVENTY-FIVE

Lena stiffened and strained her ears. The sound she'd heard came again: a snorting, snuffling noise.

`Something was in the woods.

Adrenaline kicked her chest. She spun toward the woods as she reached for the M&P. Unsnapping the strap of her holster, she eased the pistol up enough to grip it with one hand, her finger on the trigger guard. The shotgun was slung over her shoulder.

"You smell anything?" she asked Bear.

At her side, Bear perked his ears, sniffed the air, and wagged his tail. He tilted his head from side to side and gave her a confused look. Whatever was out there was downwind; the Newfie couldn't scent it.

Dusk had descended, turning the sky deep purple as bats wheeled above the trees, darting and diving after insects. Bear loped at her side, sniffing the ground. She'd been so busy that they hadn't practiced the search-and-rescue games to keep them both sharp.

They'd continued their evening patrols of the perimeter, monitoring for strange footprints or anything out of place. Since it contained half of her insulin stores, Lena felt compelled to check and recheck the springhouse they'd constructed along the bank of the creek that fed into Lake Superior. She'd hidden the insulated cooler containing her insulin behind the glass milk jugs and goat cheese; relief filled her each time she verified her medication was safe.

Often, Eli and Shiloh joined them, but not tonight. Shiloh was up in the lighthouse tower, and Eli was training a group of citizen volunteers in operational security and hand-to-hand combat tactics.

Leaves rustled off to the left. The sound came from inside the tree line to the west.

The yard was empty, the cottage quiet and still. In the twilight, the colors of things leaked into gray. The branches of the trees reached for the sky like wraiths. To the north, soft waves ruffled the pebbled shoreline. She swiped a swarm of mosquitos away from her face and peered into the shadows.

All around her, the forest throbbed with sounds. Over the trill of insects came another loud swishing noise. Something heavy moved through the underbrush.

The hairs rose on the back of her neck. She kept her voice low. "Stay close to me, boy."

Cautiously, Lena stepped through wild columbine and milk-weed bushes, searching the thorny blackberry thickets and the snarls of rhododendron, the underbrush thick and impenetrable. In the gathering dusk, the trees looked the same—sugar and red maple, beech, yellow birch, and hemlock.

Perhaps Mrs. Fitch was spying on them again. They'd seen her lurking about their property twice since their altercation in the cottage three days ago. Once, she'd been caught peering through the living room window, her withered face pressed to the glass.

When Lena confronted her, she claimed she heard the dog barking and wished to "make sure you people are feeding it properly."

Lena said loudly, "If you're out there, step out of the trees. I'll give you half the loaf of sourdough bread I just baked, but you're going to have to show yourself."

The rustling grew louder. Lena set her jaw and stepped toward the trees, exchanging the pistol for the shotgun. Snicking the safety off, she held the gun low in both hands.

Not sixty feet away, a huge creature emerged from a thicket of blackberry bushes. The enormous black bear halted and stared at her in surprise. The densely furred animal was at least six feet tall if it stood on its hind legs and a good five hundred pounds.

Lena froze. At her side, Bear let out a throaty growl in warning.

The black bear shook its head and let out an angry growl that dwarfed the dog's growl. The sound reverberated in her chest. She couldn't tear her gaze from those powerful jaws.

"Easy now," Lena said in a calm voice, though she felt anything but. Fear clawed her throat, and her pulse roared in her ears.

Every warning she'd heard about bears barreled through her brain. Appear non-threatening. Don't panic. Be slow and calm. Whatever you do, do not run. Never play dead; that's an invitation to get eaten.

Its small, rounded ears twitched. It made a snuffing sound and shook its head back and forth, staring at her with beady eyes. It lumbered a few steps toward her, blowing loudly through its snout and swatting at the ground with one of its huge paws, a clear threat.

Black bears were typically shy, reclusive, non-aggressive animals, except for this one. Was this the same bear she'd seen a month ago? It was hard to tell. But this must be one of the black bears released from Oswald's Bear Ranch in Newberry, located fifty miles east. Black bears could travel incredible distances, especially to visit old hunting grounds.

To a once-captive black bear, humans represented food. In the wild, food was more difficult to come by. Perhaps this bear had forgotten how to hunt or had suffered an injury that prevented it from surviving as nature intended.

This black bear saw Lena not as a source of food, but as the food itself.

Bear gave another savage bark. His hackles raised as he darted forward, bravely defending her.

"Bear, stay back!" Her mouth had gone bone dry, her tongue thick and swollen against the roof of her mouth. Trembling, she raised the 12-gauge double-barrel shotgun. "Go away!"

She loathed the thought of killing a creature so regal, but she would if she had to. She had a weapon. She wasn't helpless. But how many slugs would it take to bring down a five-hundred-pound animal if it charged her? What if she missed?

It was so close she could see its nostrils flaring, the glint of claws as it raked the ground and huffed at her hungrily.

"Go!" she screamed. "Just go!"

It peeled back its jowls and gave an earth-shattering roar. It stood on its hind legs, impossibly tall. One swipe of those powerful paws, and the Newfoundland was dead. So was she.

Primal terror coursed through her veins. Thousands of years of instinct screamed at her to run. She did not run. Lena braced the butt against her shoulder and welded her cheek to the stock, her legs shoulder-width apart as she aligned her sights and squeezed the trigger.

The shotgun boomed, her shoulder absorbing the recoil.

Nothing happened. She'd missed.

The Newfoundland ran at the black bear, barking and snarling. The black bear roared at the dog. It swiped at him with a massive paw. Bear scampered just out of its reach.

It dropped to all fours with a tremendous crash. The ground shook beneath Lena's feet.

Time slowed. She desperately realigned the oncoming target, pulled the trigger again, and fired the second shell. The boom of the shot rang in her ears.

The bear faltered but kept coming. His hind leg dragged. She'd hit him, but it wasn't enough. A chest or a head shot would take him down. She had to fire again, and quickly.

She opened the breech and both shells ejected into the grass. Her numb fingers fumbled in her pocket for two more shells. With the shotgun hinged open, she inserted two shells into the barrel, then firmly snapped the gun closed to load it, but not quickly enough.

The bear lumbered toward her. Thirty yards away now. Much too fast—

A whooshing sound. Something punched past her face, so close her hair stirred.

The black bear bellowed in outrage. A bolt quivered from the matted fur of the animal's barrel chest. With an incredible roar, the black bear charged.

In the same instant, the Newfoundland attacked.

"NO!" Lena raised the shotgun, pressed the butt to her shoulder, and fired twice in quick succession. The black bear shuddered but kept barreling toward them.

Another twang and whoosh. The second bolt struck the bear's haunches. The bear roared, slowing but not stopping. It kept coming, closing the space between bear and dog. Ten yards, then five.

The dog lunged for the black bear's thick neck.

The black bear swung its great head, snapping for the Newfoundland's throat, attempting to crush his spine beneath its powerful jaws.

Shiloh ran to the side, the crossbow snug against her shoulder, and unleashed another bolt. It sang through the air and sank into the center of the black bear's throat directly below its jaws.

With a tremendous groan, the black bear shuddered, swaying heavily. Finally it toppled. The great beast slammed to the ground less than ten feet from Lena and Shiloh.

The Newfoundland toppled with it and somersaulted off its haunches, tumbling head over paws. Luckily, he was thrown free of the black bear's crushing weight.

For a horrible moment, the dog lay still.

Lena ran toward him. "Bear!"

The dog clambered up and shook himself, stunned but very much alive. He snorted at the indignity of it all.

"He's fine," Shiloh said. "He's okay. We're all okay."

Bear seemed not at all impressed by his namesake. He pranced in circles around the immense black carcass, his hackles bristled, jowls pulled back in an affronted snarl as he darted close, pawing at the bear's haunches and limp hind legs, as if daring it to rise so he could face it down again.

"It's dead, Bear. The danger is over." Shiloh grabbed his ruff and pulled him in close. He whined in delight and licked her face. Shiloh leaned down and whispered in his floppy ear, "You did so good. You protected Lena. Good boy."

Bear wagged his tail, preening beneath her praise.

Staring down at the dead animal, Lena felt no triumph, only a deep sadness. Unlike humans, wild animals could be dangerous, but they held no malice. They were not cruel, not conniving, had no concept of evil. Killing was necessary for food, but this creature's death seemed needless, senseless.

As if reading her thoughts, Shiloh said, "It was going to kill you or Bear or a little kid next time. It would have happened if we didn't do this."

Lena nodded numbly. You could know something was true, but that didn't mean it felt good. Sometimes the right thing felt downright awful.

Bear trotted to her side and pushed his snout against her hand, licking her fingers in concern, his ears pricked and head tilted as if asking if she was okay. She rubbed behind his ears.

"We won't waste this." Shiloh circled the carcass, studying it. Her oil-black eyes gleamed in the semi-darkness, a steely determination in her gaze that Lena recognized in Eli: pragmatic practicality, a willingness to do the hard things. "The Ojibwe carry a deep respect for the land and all its creatures. We thank you, black bear, for the gift of your life. We promise we will use every part of your gift to survive."

Shiloh glanced across the dead black bear and met Lena's gaze. "We need to field dress it before the meat goes bad. It's gonna be messy and hard work. If we preserve it correctly, we'll have enough meat to last us for months, maybe even the winter."

Pride surged in Lena's chest. A burst of fierce affection for this girl who had been a stranger to her. In only a couple of months, she'd grown to love Shiloh like her own heart. "I think it's time to build that smokehouse."

18

LENA EASTON
DAY SEVENTY-SIX

Eli handed Lena a large hammer. "Ready to learn basic construction?"

Lena rolled her eyes. "I guess I'm still lacking in my apocalyptic skillset."

"Not too lacking." He gave her a wry grin. "Bear hunter."

She snorted. "Shiloh was the one who took it down."

"You both did."

They had hundreds of pounds of freshly butchered meat they'd stored in the springhouse; they needed to preserve it so that it wouldn't go to waste. Last night, it had taken hours to field dress and butcher the black bear, but they'd gotten it done.

Shiloh wanted to tan the bear hide so she could wear the pelt in winter like a cape. She and Eli had fleshed and salted the hide before storing it in the springhouse until they had time to tan it.

This morning, she'd discovered an axe in the cottage root cellar and now wielded it like a sword, pretending to be a post-apocalyptic Viking queen who hacked people's heads off for fun.

Eli shook his head at her in chagrin. "Everyone thinks the apocalypse is about making weapons out of barbed-wire baseball bats and outfitting themselves in spike collars and leather armor. The reality is that death in the apocalypse is far more mundane."

Absently, Shiloh touched the arrowhead knotted in her hair. "I dunno, I think we've seen plenty of battles in the apocalypse so far. My crossbow has come in handy on a few occasions."

"That's not something to be proud of," Lena said.

Shiloh grinned. "Speak for yourself."

"We're just asking you to be careful. There are lots of ways to die." Lena ticked the list off on her fingers. "Tuberculous. Diphtheria. Diarrhea can kill you in a matter of days. Starvation in weeks. Accidents with no access to medical care will take you out like that." She snapped her fingers. "The little things will get us if we're not careful."

Shiloh rolled her eyes. "No way am I biting it from diarrhea. What a pathetic way to go. If I ever go down like that, tell people I perished saving a drowning baby from a school of hammerhead sharks."

Lena said, "That's why we work so hard on purifying water and preserving food for the winter."

"Boring," Shiloh said. "And I know, which is why I spend half my day purifying water that tastes like bleach and the other half weeding the garden from hell."

Lena wiped sweat from her brow and pointed at the pile of wood planks, nails, shingles, and concrete blocks they'd scavenged from hardware stores and the woodsheds of abandoned homes. "Enough talking. Time to work. You wanna help?"

Shiloh made a face. "I'd rather sit on a chair full of thumbtacks. Besides, Eli and I built the springhouse. The smokehouse is all you guys. I have better things to do. Have I mentioned how much I love weeding?"

Despite her best attempts at teenage angst, Shiloh was beaming. Lena didn't have to ask if Eli had told her the truth about her parentage. The knowledge radiated from her very being, bright as the sun.

Shiloh couldn't keep her eyes off Eli; she watched him wherever he went, like an adoring love-starved puppy. Eli, for his part, returned her adoration tenfold.

Lena's heart warmed at the sight of them. Despite the chaos and tragedy, this was a beautiful thing, a good thing. Together, they would rebuild something new from the ashes.

Lena pointed at Bear, who was frolicking near the creek, chasing butterflies. A distinctly fetid stench wafted from him. He'd rolled in something gross, his fur grimy with dirt, leaves, and burs. "Can you give Bear a bath, then? I dumped several buckets of water in the tub, and there's oatmeal soap on the counter."

At the word "bath," Bear's ears flattened. His tail lowered in abject misery as he gave her a woeful look at the indignity about to be forced upon him.

"Sorry, buddy," Lena said, "but you stink to the high heavens. Have you been chasing skunks again?"

Bear moaned in trepidation.

Shiloh dropped the axe and coaxed a wretched Bear into the cottage, murmuring sweet nothings into his floppy ears and tugging on his collar while the dog went stiff with futile resistance —he hated baths with a ferocity usually reserved for mailmen.

Once Shiloh was gone, Lena turned her attention to the task at hand. Using plans she'd found in a homesteading book, they constructed a base of concrete blocks to create space for the air to draft in from the bottom before exiting out the top.

The hours passed quickly as they built a frame the size of an outhouse, constructing four walls and a slanting roof covered in sheets of corrugated metal. They built wire rack shelves and lined the inner walls with aluminum foil, then added a hinged door scavenged from an old chicken coop. Eli installed a woodstove outside the smokehouse and vented it underneath.

As they worked, the late afternoon sun beat down relentlessly. Her shirt clung wetly to her hot skin, soaked with sweat. She took a swig of lukewarm water from her filtered bottle and wiped her mouth as Eli hammered the last board into place.

With a sigh, he removed his sweat-stained T-shirt, tossing it over a nearby log.

Against her will, her stomach flip-flopped. She averted her

eyes and focused on a bank of white clouds scrolling across the sky. "You're going to be just fine, you know."

He glanced at her, a confused line between his brows. "What?"

"At fatherhood, I mean."

Eli was adept at everything he put his mind to. He was a natural at survival, hunting, fighting, and tracking, his every movement capable and efficient, but parenting was a foreign frontier to him; he was anxious around Shiloh, worried about screwing things up.

Frankly, it was adorable.

"You don't know that."

"Some things I just know."

"My father wasn't around. My mother..." His voice trailed off.

He didn't need to explain his past—she already knew. She'd been there for all of it—his dead mother, his absent father. "Mothers and fathers are supposed to stay. They're supposed to protect us. Sometimes they don't. Sometimes they can't. And that scars us, the emptiness, loneliness, and isolation, that feeling of unworthiness. It makes a hole inside us that we spend the rest of our lives trying to fill."

Eli didn't speak. She sensed him beside her, still as a statue.

Her voice softened with compassion. "You and I know what that feels like, but she doesn't have to feel that way, not ever again. She has you."

He hesitated, still uncertain, then nodded as if steeling himself. "You're right."

The sun was setting by the time they stepped back to examine their handiwork. The shadows lengthened. Dusk descended over the tops of the trees as the breeze died, and the mosquitos returned in full force. Michigan mosquitos were savage and relentless, especially in the U.P.

Eli slapped at a bite on the back of his neck and cursed. "That one was big enough to put a saddle on and ride."

Lena reached for her pack sitting next to the smokehouse foundation and pulled out a small spray bottle. It smelled strongly of vinegar. "I've been reading about natural insect repellent. I mixed some crushed basil leaves in an oil base and added some apple cider vinegar. Sorry about the smell."

"If it keeps the critters away, then I'm all for it."

"Crushed lavender is good, too. I planted some around the cottage. Pick it, crush it in your hands, and spread it on your most bite-prone spots. Lavender is soothing and antibacterial for whatever insect bites you do get."

He tried to swipe at his back but couldn't reach it.

She cleared her throat, suddenly awkward. "Um, I can help you."

Eli went still. "Yeah, sure."

As she got close, she smelled the dense woodsy scent of him. She sprayed the oil on his back and rubbed it in, her hands running across his muscled shoulders, down his spine, over skin scarred from years of combat, fighting brutal enemies to survive.

Eli had returned from prison a stranger to her. He didn't feel like a stranger. He felt like the boy she'd loved since first grade. He was her first kiss, her first everything. There was nothing as familiar to her as the strength of his embrace.

Her face burning, she stepped back quickly and wiped her hands on her jeans. "That should work."

He peered intently at her as if he could read her thoughts. She hoped not, but he'd always had that preternatural ability to know what she was thinking, to anticipate her actions before she knew herself. "You okay?"

She fumbled for a glucose tab in her pocket and made a show of popping it in her mouth. At least diabetes came in handy as an excuse when she needed it. "A bit lightheaded. I'll be fine."

"You sure?"

They stood less than two feet apart, close enough to kiss. Her cheeks flushed, a flood of heat rushing through her insides.

A part of her would always love him. It didn't mean she was in love with him. The thought of opening her heart to Eli Pope again terrified her. And yet...

Her pulse quickened. "Eli, I—"

Bear burst from the back door of the cottage, barking with great enthusiasm, startling several robins pecking through the overgrown lawn for worms. The birds took flight, squawking in alarm as the giant dog dashed into their midst.

Bear's freshly dried fur stood up all over his body, so thick and fluffy that his eyes were invisible. He looked like an overstuffed teddy bear that had gone through the dryer.

Shiloh stood in the cottage doorway grinning like a maniac; her T-shirt and cut-off shorts were drenched and covered in tufts of cinnamon-brown fur. She pumped her fist. "Mission accomplished!"

Eli chuckled out loud. Lena found herself laughing with him.

They exchanged an amused glance, holding each other's eyes for a second longer than necessary. Her stomach fizzed. Suddenly embarrassed, she averted her gaze and focused on the sunset.

Behind the lighthouse tower, the sun touched the watery horizon, setting the sky ablaze and tinging the clouds in shades of scarlet and tangerine. The lake looked as if it had caught fire, the glass-smooth surface burnished a fiery red. It was beautiful.

At that moment, the world seemed almost normal, as if anything was possible—maybe even love.

19

JACKSON CROSS
DAY SEVENTY-SEVEN

"What's wrong?" Jackson asked.

Lena's face was pale and drawn, a line forming between her brows, her mouth flat. "Someone broke into the lighthouse."

Lena had met Jackson and Devon at the gate to the driveway, opened the padlock, and swung the gate open. They rolled their bikes through and leaned them against the fence post.

Bear greeted them anxiously, tail wagging low, sniffing at their hands, then returned to his mistress, sticking close beside her as if sensing her distress.

Lena buried her hands in the thick fur along his ruff as she explained that she'd returned from a house call to the Miller place in Christmas, where she'd reset their ten-year-old son's dislocated shoulder after he'd fallen from the twelve-foot-high sniper's nest the parents built to protect their homestead from thieves.

Lena pointed toward the cottage. "The front door is ajar, but I locked it before I left."

He didn't bother to ask if she was certain she'd locked the door; this was Lena, practical, pragmatic, responsible Lena. If she was worried, there was a reason to worry.

"Where's Eli?" Devon asked.

"I called Eli and Shiloh on the radio. They went to a clearing in the woods to target practice. Eli is training Shiloh in weapons and combat. They'll be back in ten minutes."

"I'll clear the cottage," Jackson said. "Devon, stay with Lena."

Devon frowned but nodded as she drew her service weapon. She disliked leaving her partner, but she understood protecting a civilian was paramount. "Got it, boss. She'll be safe with me."

"Stay back here in the tree line," Jackson ordered.

After checking Eli's caretaker's cabin, which had also been ransacked but was empty, Jackson approached the main cottage. The eight-story lighthouse tower loomed above him, casting a long shadow across the grass.

The front door was open, the door jamb splintered as if someone had kicked it in.

With growing trepidation, Jackson pressed his spine against the wall to the left of the front door. Taking a deep breath, he steeled himself. Weapon up and held out in front of him with both hands, he spun into the doorway, scanning left to right, high then low, taking in everything in an instant.

His heart punched into his throat. Inside, shadows gathered in the corners, the air thick and heavy with the heat of the day. The place had been ransacked, lamps knocked over, pillows ripped from the sofa and strewn about the living room, and antique knickknacks broken.

The kitchen table had been toppled onto its side, the cabinet drawers jerked open and their contents spilled across the wood floor. The rack of hydroponic plants had been ripped off the wall and tossed aside, the herbs trampled.

"This is the police! Come out with your hands up!"

Silence. The screen door squeaked behind him.

Dread iced his veins. Swiftly, he cleared the small cottage, checking each room, behind furniture, under the beds, and in the closets—nothing. The floor was swept clean except for a few pieces of reddish gravel, possibly dragged in by the perpetrator's shoes.

He was alone in the cottage. The sense of wrongness did not dissipate.

In Lena's bedroom, he halted in the doorway. He scanned the room, his gaze settling on the corner where Lena kept her solar-powered mini-fridge. The corner was empty.

Relieved, he remembered she'd started hiding the fridge up in the tower.

He hurried up the rickety tower steps and checked the lantern room. It, too, was empty. The solar panels were gone, as was the fridge.

The beacon in the center of the room had been shattered as if someone had taken a baseball bat to it. Glass, plastic, and metal littered the floor.

His heart punched into his throat. Whoever did this had destroyed the Fresnel lens for the hell of it. Who would do such a thing?

In the corner, something snagged his attention. Several pieces of crushed glass glinted in the sunlight streaming into the lantern room. The floor beneath the glass was wet.

Jackson squatted on his haunches, reached out, and touched one of the cylinder-shaped glass shards. He recognized the shape: the remnants of a few insulin vials. The thieves hadn't just ransacked the place, they'd taken the solar fridge and the insulin.

They'd either known it was here or they'd come up to destroy the beacon for fun and found it. But had they stolen all of the insulin? His pulse quickened in dread.

He closed his eyes for a moment, breathing deeply before he forced himself to stand and make his way back down the eight flights of the tower. Returning to the cottage, he checked the back door to the kitchen. It was closed but unlocked. A bloody smudge in the shape of a thumbprint marked the door above the handle.

Jackson turned and sprinted for the springhouse beside the

burbling creek, which was built into the bank and carefully camouflaged with artfully arranged tall bushes. Muddy footprints trampled the matted grass around the concrete structure.

Inside the springhouse, a couple of plywood crates obscured the cooler Lena used for her secondary insulin storage. He moved them aside to find an empty shelf. The cooler was outside, resting on its side a dozen yards down the pebbled bank. It too was empty.

Jackson stared blankly at the cooler, appalled. The thieves had stolen most of the insulin, destroying a few vials in their haste to collect the medication. Or maybe they relished the destruction of something precious for the sheer despicable thrill of it, just like the lighthouse beacon.

"It's clear," he said dully into the radio. "You can bring Lena to the backyard."

A moment later, Lena rushed across the grass with Bear at her side. Devon followed close behind them, her weapon drawn.

With a moan, Lena dropped to her knees and knelt over the broken vials scattered across the riverbank. Hunched, she picked through the grass, pebbles, sand, and twigs, clawing through the dirt in search of unbroken vials.

The liquid that gave her life soaked into the ground beneath her. There was no way to retrieve it, to claw it out of the earth.

Distraught, she lifted her head, tendrils of hair sticking to her sweat-dampened cheeks, her eyes wide with shock. "The fridge in the tower."

Jackson shook his head. "I'm sorry. They took that, too."

A strangled cry tore from her throat. "Who did this? Who would do this?"

Jackson squatted on the ground next to Lena. He wanted to comfort her but there was no comfort to give. "I don't know, but I'll find out."

"The diesel generator for the lighthouse is gone," Devon said quietly. "They took that, too."

Jackson pulled an evidence envelope from his pocket, slipped several shards inside, and pulled out his notebook. He focused on what he could do next, catching the culprit responsible for this disaster. "Who's been here recently? Give me names."

"Lots of people," Lena said woodenly as if this was a thing that was happening to someone else, a nightmare she would wake up from at any moment, except she wouldn't. "Neighbors, friends, regular town folk who need help. No one who would do a thing like this..."

"Tell me anyway, anything suspicious, anything out of the ordinary. Anything at all that comes to mind."

Her shoulders slumped in defeat. She rocked back on her heels and let the shards slip from her mud-crusted fingers. Blood dribbled from a cut on her index finger; she didn't seem to notice.

Bear sat next to her, whimpering with a worried look in his expressive brown eyes. He nosed at her face and licked her cheeks to try and comfort her. She leaned against his furry bulk for support. "Mrs. Fitch, the nosy neighbor who lives down the road. She's seventy-something, but I get this feeling that she's watching everything I do, cataloging everything I have. A few days ago, I caught her sneaking into the kitchen and going through our pantry."

He had the sensation of sliding on slick black ice. "Janet Fitch. As in Calvin Fitch's aunt?"

Lena nodded and stared at the creek, her eyes glassy. She was dazed, in shock. Jackson doubted she was seeing anything but the nightmare inside her mind.

"We'll check it out," Devon said as Jackson rose to his feet. "Soon as Eli gets here to stay with you, we'll go."

The sun shone bright and hot, not a cloud in the cobalt blue sky. Clear water burbled over moss-carpeted rocks. Behind them, Superior stretched smooth as glass to the distant horizon, Grand Island rising in the distance.

It was too beautiful for such a tragedy.

A minute later, Eli appeared around the corner of the cottage, Shiloh beside him. Eli headed straight for Lena. Sweat dotted his forehead. His face reddened from exertion—and rage. His hands balled into fists like he was prepared to fight the whole world if necessary.

But there was nothing to fight.

The insulin was gone. All of it.

20

JACKSON CROSS
DAY SEVENTY-SEVEN

Jackson and Devon approached the residence of Mrs. Janet Fitch and her nephew, Calvin Fitch. The peeling ranch house was set off the road a half-mile from the lighthouse.

They waded through shin-high grass. Grasshoppers buzzed and leaped from stalk to stalk. In the yard, weeds sprouted through the springs of a rusted bed frame. Two ancient push mowers leaned against a dilapidated shed.

A dirt-splattered Velocity Blue Ford F150 truck stood in the driveway, complete with special order Maxxis Trepador off-road tires. The truck belonged to Calvin Fitch, the same truck that had run down Shiloh Easton on her four-wheeler.

Jackson repressed a shudder and gestured to Devon, pointing at the reddish gravel of the driveway, the same color as the pebbles he'd found inside the cottage. The pebbles had probably caught between the treads of the perp's shoe and transferred to the crime scene.

A glint drew his attention—tiny glass shards with curved, cylindrical shapes mixed with the gravel at the edge of the driveway. It was reverse transfer from the suspect stomping on a couple of vials.

Calvin was likely the perpetrator, egged on by his jealous, entitled aunt.

His heart hammered his ribs as they reached the front door and mounted the porch steps. Dead leaves shorn off in the last storm rasped beneath his feet. Three rocking chairs filmed in dust sat on the porch, squeaking in the breeze.

A crow cawed from somewhere nearby. Sweat beaded his forehead, dripped down his spine, drenched his underarms.

No movement came from inside or outside the house. No swishing curtains or furtive shadows. The property was eerily silent.

Jackson took one side of the front door and Devon took the other, almost bumping into wind chimes hanging from the porch ceiling.

"This is the sheriff!" Jackson shouted. "Open the door!"

Before the grid went down, they wouldn't force their way inside. If the suspect refused to answer the door, law enforcement had to leave and return with a search warrant. If they entered a residence illegally, the evidence they uncovered in the house was inadmissible in court. The one exception was exigent circumstances.

As civilization frayed, it was hard to know which rules still applied and which had fallen by the wayside. Right and wrong didn't cease to exist because the system had crashed and burned along with half the planet.

The law was humanity's best attempt at justice. As far as possible, Jackson was determined to do things by the book.

"Mrs. Fitch?" Devon called. "We're concerned for your well-being. We want to check and ensure you're okay. Please respond if you're able."

Still nothing. There were no sounds but the squeak of the rocking chairs, the jangling wind chimes, and the insects whirring in the grass.

Devon nodded at a spot on the peeling front door, an inch shy of the brass door handle. The door was painted red; he'd missed it: a smudge of blood, like he'd found on the cottage's back door.

This was the exigent circumstance they needed to enter. Fresh blood meant someone inside was likely hurt or had hurt someone else. Concern for homeowners was the golden get-out-of-jail-free card.

Jackson drew his service weapon. Across the doorway, Devon did the same.

He jutted his chin at the door and mouthed, "On the count of three."

On three, he swung out, raised his leg, and slammed the flat of his foot against the weakest spot on the door, just below the lock. Once, twice, three times.

The wood splintered. The door burst inward.

Devon rushed in, weapon up and sweeping right. "Police! On your knees!"

Jackson came in low behind her and swept left, heart hammering, pulse roaring as he scanned for threats. Every sense on high alert.

Oppressive heat hit them like a wall, then the smell, rancid and fetid. Coughing, he glimpsed a shadowed living room, a low sofa, a flat-screen in the corner, and a TV tray set in front of a dingy La-Z-Boy.

His gaze was drawn to the La-Z-Boy. A deep gash cut a wide swath in the pleather fabric, the inner foam oozing from the jagged cut. It looked like someone had taken an axe to the chair.

Behind the La-Z-Boy, two thin stockinged feet stuck out.

"Cover me." Jackson moved to the oversized chair and peered behind it. The stench was overwhelming: the putrid stink of feces mixed with vomit, the ammonia smell of urine, and coppery blood.

Mrs. Finch stretched out behind the La-Z-Boy. The same fate that had befallen the armchair had befallen her. She lay on her back with her shriveled arms at her sides. There were defensive slashes across her palms. In death, her dour expression had slackened.

He nearly vomited but held it down. "We've got a body."

"What the hell is happening?" Devon said. "You think Calvin did this to his aunt?"

"It's possible."

While Devon covered him, Jackson squatted next to the victim. Her pupils were blown; rigor mortis was starting to set into her face and limbs. He checked her body for livor mortis: her heels, calves, and buttocks had darkened to purple as blood pooled.

The assault had occurred within the last couple of hours. If someone was still alive or hurt in the house, time was of the essence.

Devon called for backup, though it might take thirty minutes to an hour or more to get additional officers on the scene. She half-turned to keep her gaze on the hallway into the bedrooms and the archway that led to what Jackson presumed was the kitchen.

Jackson signaled to Devon. She nodded without speaking. Together, they cleared the rest of the house.

Piles of rotting trash in the kitchen gave off a gut-clenching stench. Unwashed dishes crusted with scraps of food were stacked on the counter. The bathrooms were worse.

The bedrooms were small, dark, and empty. A man's clothes filled the closet of the second bedroom, with size twelve boots set at the end of the unmade bed. There was no sign of Lena's mini-fridge.

At the stairs to the basement, Devon pointed out a bloody handprint on the wall at chest-height. She flicked on her tactical flashlight, held it beneath her pistol, and lit the perilous, narrow staircase.

Jackson did the same, descending first.

"Be careful," she said behind him.

Sinister darkness greeted him, so dense it felt like moving through pitch-black water, deep into the depths of the unknown.

Jackson's lungs constricted. The stairs creaked as he descended lower, weapon in front of him, his finger itching the trigger guard.

The narrow beam of the flashlight illuminated a typical Michigan basement with concrete walls, a dirt floor, a big rusted furnace in the corner, cardboard boxes everywhere, and an old washer and dryer set against the far wall.

The musty air cooled his skin. The fetid stink of death was down here, too.

With cautious steps, he ducked to avoid hitting his head on the exposed ceiling—a network of lead and copper pipes filmed with spider webs and crusted with mouse droppings.

Footsteps echoed behind him as Devon descended the stairs, her flashlight bobbing over the water-stained walls.

His light caught the deeper shadows of a second room. Jackson rounded the corner and swept his light across the room. Like the rest of the basement, it was narrow, the ceiling low.

A face loomed out of the dark. The body was strung from the low rafters with an extension cord. Jackson recognized the rotund body encased in dirty overalls, the dun-colored hair, the dull features. It was Calvin Fitch.

Stifling a gasp, he stepped closer and directed the flashlight at the swollen head, the protruding purple tongue, and the petechiae —the tiny red dots in the whites of the eyeball caused by a hemorrhage due to strangulation. Bloody rips in the victim's shirt across his chest indicated a flurry of stab wounds.

He thought of the corpse hung from the telephone poll on M-28, Sykes' calling card. This victim was hung and carved like the last one. It was eerily similar, too similar.

"Is this Sykes' handiwork?" she asked.

"It looks like it. Whether it was Sykes himself or his minions, they came here first, judging by the red gravel near the spring-house, the same gravel from the Fitch driveway. Maybe the old lady offered up Lena's supplies to save herself. The thugs went from here to the lighthouse, and then they came back and killed them, possibly for the hell of it. It doesn't look like the Fitch family had much worth stealing."

"How do you know they came back here again after the lighthouse?"

"Shards of the insulin vials on the Fitch porch—at least one suspect transferred trace evidence in the treads of his boots."

Devon nodded and remained quiet for a moment. "Sykes wanted us to find the bodies," she said, "and to find Calvin down here. If not for the break-in at Lena's, the victims might have been dead for weeks before anyone thought to check on them. You think he knew Calvin, that this was vengeance like that last case?"

"We need to find out."

Devon nodded without taking her gaze from the victim, then holstered her pistol and pulled out her phone to take notes and snap photos. They would do their best to work the crime scene by tagging evidence, gathering fingerprints, and collecting DNA, hair, and blood samples.

The process of working the case maintained some semblance of normalcy although nothing in the world was normal and never would be.

"What about Lena?" Devon asked. "What if these two told Sykes about Lena's connection to Eli?"

"If that was the case, I think Lena or Shiloh or both would already be dead or taken. If this was payback for something Fitch did, Sykes wouldn't think to ask about Eli. The lighthouse was randomly targeted—this time." A sense of menace plagued him, the dark fear that nothing he did would halt the impending storm of violence. "Until we hunt him down, none of us are safe."

21

ELI POPE
DAY SEVENTY-SEVEN

"How much insulin do you have left?" Eli asked.

"Only what's in the Frio wallet." Lena curled on the window seat. Bear splayed on the rug beneath her. She stared out the window at the rain spattering the glass, her fanny pack with the Frio wallet held tightly in her lap. As long as she dipped the Frio wallet in water every forty hours, it kept her remaining insulin refrigerated.

She'd barely said a word since they'd found the lighthouse ransacked hours ago. Her face was slack, her eyes glazed and distant. She was still in shock.

Devon had taken Shiloh for a walk around the property to allow Lena, Eli, and Jackson to speak frankly. Now, Jackson leaned against the wall in the cottage living room, his arms crossed over his chest, his expression strained.

"How much?" Eli repeated.

Lena didn't look at either of them but instead kept her gaze locked on something out the darkened window. Dense clouds blocked the moon and stars. "Three weeks."

The words struck Eli like a punch to the solar plexus. He couldn't lose her. Could. Not. Lose. Her. It wasn't an option. His mind refused to contemplate it.

His combat experience, survival skills, his talent for violence of action, and death—none of it mattered against this disease, this terrible thing he couldn't fight, conquer, or overcome.

He was helpless against it and his helplessness tore him to pieces.

Eli paced the small living room like a restless panther. He kept his fear bottled up tight. "We need to scour every pharmacy and every big box store from here to Wisconsin. We'll go below the bridge—"

"You know those meds have been gone for months," Jackson said. "We've already done that."

Eli knew it as well as he did. "Then we'll search every house, every clinic, every—"

"We have," Jackson said bitterly. "Everyone has! Every pharmacy is empty. Every clinic and every hospital in the UP has been scoured. I'm working on tracking down our list of informants with connections in the narcotics trade who we've turned to inform on our drug cases. I've been pulling them in and interrogating them on insulin sources through the black market. Last week, I went to the local pharmacies and got lists of local diabetics and cross-referenced that with our known meth and cocaine users. There were three. I visited them personally to see if they'd managed to source meds through their contacts. I figured if they had insulin, then they had a source I could track down."

"And?" Eli asked impatiently.

"And." Jackson swallowed. "They're dead."

Lena made a noise in the back of her throat like an animal caught in a trap.

"There is no more to get, not anywhere. Not even downstate. We've communicated via ham radio with as many counties as we could get into contact with. There's nothing. I'm so sorry."

"No." Eli's hands balled into fists, a vein pulsing in his neck. "What about the manufacturing plants?"

"The pharmaceutical company, Eli Lilly, is the largest insulin manufacturer in the U.S. They have a plant in Indianapolis, another one in North Carolina—"

"Then we're going there. I'll go."

"Alone?" Jackson scoffed. "Even if you could make it, that place would be armed like Fort Knox, if it were operational, which it is not."

Eli whirled on him. "How do you know?"

"I talked to the FEMA rep, Milton Sanders, before the riot. He said the entire country is in a pharmaceutical crisis."

"What a genius," Eli said.

Jackson ignored him. "Ninety percent of the U.S.'s crash cart meds are made in India and China. The same goes for our antibiotics. We don't make much of anything anymore. We do make insulin. Or, we did. Sanders said that the Indiana governor struggled to keep that plant open for the first month, but they couldn't keep the workers fed and couldn't get shipments of the secondary supplies critical to making synthetic insulin.

"The fuel ran out for the generators a few weeks ago, even the emergency supplies for government officials and first responders. They dispatched a National Guard unit to protect the plant, but desperate people overran it. A couple of scientists died in the altercation. It was a mess. Sanders said the feds have promised to ship in critical meds from the Southern Hemisphere—South Africa, Indonesia, and Australia—to increase production, and they're charging an arm and a leg for it. Once it arrives in port, the governors will disperse the goods to the diabetics in their states."

"When is that going to happen?" Eli spat. "What's the time frame? Exactly how long can a Type 1 diabetic wait for the useless feds to get their act together?"

Jackson shook his head, his mouth thinning as if struggling to rein in his frustration and grief. He loved Lena, too.

"That FEMA agent is lying. He doesn't know what he's talking about—"

"He does. I confirmed it with the governor."

Eli threw up his hands. "I'm not going to sit and wait while

Lena—while Lena—" He couldn't say the words, couldn't speak the horror into existence. "How long do they think diabetics can last without insulin? What do they think is happening right now?"

"They're dying," Lena said softly. "They're dying or they're dead."

Eli halted in his tracks and stared at her.

She turned her head from the window and looked at them with haunted eyes. "Most people weren't lucky enough to stock up like I did. Let's be real here. Type 2s have a chance. They can cut carbs severely and use an extremely strict diet to moderate their insulin needs. But Type 1s? There are 1.5 million Americans with Type 1 diabetes. Almost seven million with Type 2 diabetes need insulin to control their diabetes as well. Uncontrolled diabetes leads to blindness, kidney failure, gangrene and loss of limbs, coma, and death. The federal government has abandoned us all to die."

Her words permeated the room with an ominous dread that crouched in the corners and lurked in the shadows, waiting to take its pound of flesh.

"We'll make insulin, then," Eli said. "Find a chemist. Get the supplies, figure it out."

Lena shook her head bitterly. "It's impossible, or nearly so. In the old days, it took something like eight thousand pounds of pancreas glands from more than twenty-three thousand animals to make one pound of insulin. Put another way, two tons of pig parts are needed to extract just eight ounces of purified insulin. Even if we could get that many pigs, how could we purify the insulin, then measure it and make sure contaminates didn't kill me anyway? Before the solar flares, I researched it to see what would happen. What if, you know? There was an open-source group of college chemistry kids who tried for years to make insulin in their garage. They couldn't get it to work. I found a few old wives' tales on the internet about a diabetic woman surviving in the ghetto during World War Two, but when I tried to verify a legitimate source, it was all hearsay and rumor. This is not something we can DIY. It's not going to happen."

"There has to be an answer." Pain laced his voice and contorted his features. "Tell me what to do and I'll do it."

Lena's voice was barely a whisper: "I don't know."

"I won't give up," Eli insisted.

Jackson scrubbed his face with his hands. "No one is giving up."

"Someone, somewhere, has to know where to get insulin."

Lena turned to him, her face in profile. For once, the night outside was dark without the glow of the beacon. The dim lamp-light shimmered around her, so beautiful it made his chest ache. She looked ethereal, ghostly as if she was already half-gone.

"Shiloh can't lose you," he said, but what he meant was, *I can't lose you.* He couldn't say the words aloud.

Eli's chest felt too tight as if his heart was about to explode from the pressure. He needed to do something, to act, to beat the problem they faced into submission. After all the things the solar flares had taken from them, not this, too. Not her.

Three weeks. Lena had only three weeks.

The door opened and Shiloh entered. Devon offered to remain outside on the porch to keep a lookout. Shiloh's eyes went straight to Lena, dread and concern etched across her face. "Are you okay?"

Lena gave a sharp shake of her head. "I'm okay," she said, though everyone knew that she wasn't. Everything was far from okay.

The lack of insulin was only part of the threat looming over them. Eli forced himself to focus on the danger they could do something about. They had more than one enemy lurking out there, a fact they couldn't afford to forget for a second.

Eli said, "We need to talk about Sykes."

22

ELI POPE
DAY SEVENTY-SEVEN

Eli stood by the back door, half-turned so he could keep an eye on the exit points and the people in the room. His HK417 rifle rested on the kitchen counter next to a bowl of tomatoes, three loaded magazines beside it.

Lena and Shiloh sat at the kitchen table across from Jackson. Jackson had questioned whether Shiloh should be present for such a conversation, but Eli had insisted. It didn't matter that she was thirteen; she'd been forced to fight for her life more than once. His daughter might be the toughest one in the room.

He was glad he'd told Shiloh the truth. She hadn't run, she hadn't freaked out. They'd figure this thing out together, father and daughter. Whenever he looked at her, his chest filled with bright sparks of joy like fireworks. And fear.

He had to figure out a way to protect both of them.

Jackson stared intently across the table at Lena. "I suspect the lighthouse robbery was random, spurred by the old lady offering up Lena's supplies, possibly in exchange for her own life, though that didn't work out so well for her. But I don't know for certain."

Eli shook his head. "If Sykes knew what Lena and Shiloh meant to me, things would've turned out very differently. This was a random attack performed by his minions, intended to instill fear or gather intel, but he will find out. Eventually, someone will tell him. Everyone breaks under torture. Everyone."

Rain pattered the roof, steadily dripping down the window-panes, obscuring the view outside. It made Eli antsy. He peered through the glass, scanning the yard through the rain-swept darkness.

The goons had trashed Eli's cabin, but he'd hidden his weapons and ammo in a vent, and they hadn't found anything of value. Only the smokehouse had been left alone; maybe it was too much work to try and move the bear meat, which wasn't completely smoked yet.

His mind buzzed with plans and backup plans, measures and countermeasures. Every single one had flaws, leaving his loved ones exposed and vulnerable.

"It's not safe here," he said. "Darius Sykes is a dangerous man. Unlike Sawyer, who at least has a reason for what he does, Sykes is a psychopath. He relishes chaos, destruction, and cruelty for the sake of cruelty. He *wants* us to know he's here. More than that, he's known to go after his adversaries' families. He's slaughtered children with zero remorse. No one and no thing is off-limits to a man like Sykes. He has no moral code, no limits or boundaries. Above all, Sykes is vindictive. He retaliates against any slight, real or perceived, with tremendous brutality. If he finds out..." He couldn't finish the sentence. The thought was untenable.

"Not to mention the hired gun that attacked Shiloh," Jackson said. "Someone hired him to take out Shiloh. Just because that particular meth head is no longer a threat doesn't mean the killer won't try again."

They'd found no other leads to point them toward Lily's killer or whoever had hired the dead thug. Whoever had hired him could send someone else at any time.

The threats against them seemed to multiply by the day.

Shiloh stared at him, crossing her arms with defiance. "I'm not scared of Sykes or whoever sent that guy to hurt me. I took care of him. I can do it again. I'm not afraid."

"You should be!" The words burst out of him before he could stop himself. "I am."

Shiloh blinked, startled. "You're afraid?"

"I'm terrified. Fear is the primal warning signal in your brain that you are the prey, not the predator. Ignore it at your peril. Fear keeps you alive."

After a second, Shiloh nodded.

Eli had made up his mind. "You two need to leave the lighthouse."

Lena blanched. "What?"

He'd known this would be her response and had steeled himself for a fight. If he could sling her over his shoulder and drag her out of there kicking and screaming, God help him, but he'd do it. He'd drag Lena and Shiloh both if that's what it came to.

Gritting his teeth, he tried again, attempting politeness instead of making demands. "I would like you to consider moving to the Northwoods Inn for security reasons."

"The lighthouse—"

"Is a security nightmare."

"We can take care of ourselves," Shiloh insisted.

"Not against these threats, you can't. I can't, either."

Shiloh bit her lower lip, looking forlorn. "Forever?"

Eli's jaw flexed. If he had his way, yes. But he couldn't deny the way Lena and Shiloh had flourished at the lighthouse. They needed this place. He'd felt the same peace, the same solitude, and companionship. The lighthouse was a balm to his soul.

"Temporarily," he said.

"You think the Inn is safer?" Shiloh asked.

"I do. Tim and Lori will find a spot for you. There are at least a hundred people there. They have a secure perimeter and sentries, guards, and sniper hides. David Kepford was training a civilian security element, and I've agreed to take over. I can't be around every second. Sykes and his minions can't breach that property easily. Lena can still see patients at the Inn. It's the best solution."

Lena shot a questioning glance at Shiloh. Something

unspoken passed between them. After a minute, Shiloh nodded grimly. "Okay."

"Okay?" Eli's brows shot up in surprise. "Did I hear you correctly?"

Shiloh gave a long-suffering sigh. "We're stubborn, not stupid. Right, Lena?"

"Right," Lena said softly.

Eli scanned the yard again, checking for threats, and saw nothing. Bear lay on the floor at Lena's feet, his head down, snout resting on his paws, but his eyes were alert, his ears flicking as he listened to his humans talk.

"We can pack you up and transport your things in the morning," Jackson said.

"In the meantime, I need to talk to Sawyer," Eli said.

"That's a hard no," Jackson said. "We're not going to Sawyer."

"Sawyer has his ear to the ground when it comes to criminal activities. If someone invades his territory, he'll know about it. He may be able to provide information on Sykes. Hell, maybe he even has access to insulin through the black market, or knows who does."

"If you recall, the last time you saw Sawyer, he tortured you, then tried to kill you. He would like nothing more than to kill both of us. It's a very bad idea—unless you have a death wish."

"I can handle it."

Jackson grimaced. "That's exactly what I'm afraid of."

Eli almost smiled. In an instant, he was transported to their childhood, to inside jokes and crooked grins, to lazy afternoons fishing and swimming and rock jumping. The times he'd shown up at Jackson's house to escape the heavy silence at home, which had felt like a coffin after his mother's death.

He thought the bad blood between them had washed away the good memories, but they were still there, faint as fireflies flickering in the dark: two boys who had each other's backs, shared each other's secrets, who'd known the other's thoughts like their own.

Much as he'd tried, the past would not erase itself.

The semblance of an idea formed in the back of his brain. "I have a plan. I won't go directly to Sawyer. I have a backdoor option."

"Who?"

"One of Sawyer's men. I saved Antoine's life. He owes me. I'm going to call in that favor."

Jackson gave a disbelieving grunt. "The last time you saw Antoine, didn't he put a burlap bag over your head, knock you unconscious, and deliver you to the man who wanted to kill you?"

"I said it was a plan," Eli said. "Didn't say it was a good one."

23

JACKSON CROSS
DAY SEVENTY-NINE

Devon barged into Jackson's office, let the door slam behind her, and perched on the edge of his desk, her favorite seat. She glanced around the sheriff's office and whistled. "Nice digs. Much better than my squashed cubicle. Maybe you can get some real police work done for a change."

Jackson rolled his eyes. "You think you're so funny."

"I don't think I am, I *know* I am." Devon pulled two objects wrapped in aluminum foil from her backpack and placed them in the middle of the desk on top of Jackson's current case file. "I figured you'd forgotten to eat. Again."

His stomach growled loudly. She was right. He'd barely paused for more than a drink of water all day. "You brought me pasties. I forgive all your shortcomings."

"That should be easy since I have none."

It was after 10:00 p.m., and night had fallen outside the windows. They'd been putting in twelve- to fourteen-hour days with zero breaks. Jackson's eyes were gritty with fatigue. Dark smudges ringed Devon's brown eyes.

"You look exhausted," he said around a delicious bite of onions, diced beef, and rutabaga wrapped in a scrumptious pastry shell. Invented as portable meals for Cornish miners in the mid-nineteenth century, the famous pasty was pronounced with a soft "a" as in "pass."

"Looked in a mirror lately? Have you shaved in the last month?"

Jackson rubbed the thick bristles along his jaw with his free hand. "I'm going for the rugged mountain man look."

"And here I thought it was the homeless meth-head look you were going for."

Jackson laughed. No matter how dire the circumstances, Devon could always make him laugh. "You should be at home sleeping, not wasting your precious little downtime with me."

Devon took a bite and wiped a few crumbs from the side of her mouth. "We spent the day trying to keep the county from imploding on itself, and here you are, still working as if you're showing off or something. I couldn't let you hog all the glory for yourself, boss."

"That's the spirit." Devon was a breath of fresh air when he most needed it. He didn't know how she managed to keep her chipper mood, no matter the situation. She was no Pollyanna, but she was consistent, even-tempered, and optimistic in a way he admired.

They ate the pasties, savoring every bite. It was preternaturally quiet. Everything still. No sound but their breathing, no hum of the generator or buzz of fluorescent lights, no murmuring of coworkers.

He still wasn't used to it. It felt like they were completely alone in the universe, like being sucked into a black hole with no escape.

Devon wiped the crumbs from the aluminum foil, folded it neatly, and slipped it into her pocket. Gone were the wasteful days when people threw things away with such casual indifference. Now, everything was precious; anything that could be re-used or recycled was salvaged.

"What's new?" She jutted her chin at the whiteboard covered with maps, photos, and scribbled notes. Jackson had stuck a second red pushpin at the newest murder location—the Fitch crime scene.

They'd spent the last two days gathering evidence at the Fitch house as they investigated the murders. As with the first case, they were left with little to go on.

They'd gone door to door up and down the road. Three additional houses had been robbed. Luckily, they were empty at the time. As with the lighthouse, they'd been ransacked, with personal belongings destroyed. The perpetrators had stolen a propane generator, several solar chargers, and a diesel truck parked in a garage.

No evidence at the scenes had tied to Sykes' potential location, though they'd dusted for prints, taken photographs, and made castings of several tire tracks. If the tire castings matched past or future scenes, they could tie the crimes together.

Strangely, no one had heard anything. The houses were set back from the road, and each property boasted several acres, so it wasn't that surprising. However, engine sounds should've been notable in this new world with few running vehicles.

Tomorrow they would expand their door-to-door search to nearby neighborhoods. Jackson needed to deputize two dozen additional volunteers to start canvasing the county, searching for anyone who'd witnessed Sykes' coming and going.

Someone had to have seen something.

Jackson pointed to the row of names scribbled at the bottom right of the whiteboard. "We've got a list of the escaped convicts from the prison. Some are local. A few we arrested ourselves. Between the sheriff's office and the police department, we know some of their ties to the community. Moreno and I made a list of known girlfriends, ex-wives, kids, parents, et cetera. Tomorrow, I'm deputizing a dozen citizen volunteers who'll stake out the homes and businesses we know of. Their role is strictly observation, but we need their eyes and ears. If they see something, they'll alert us, and we'll interrogate the family or set a trap, depending on the situation."

"Did you find a connection between Fitch and Sykes?"

"Fitch's uncle on his mother's side served ten years for fraud. He'd cooked the books for criminal organizations and had connections with Hells Angels as well as other biker gangs. It was rumored that Sykes killed him in prison last year over a territorial dispute. It looks as if Sykes didn't feel that he'd suffered enough and decided to come after his remaining family. He's done it before."

"More vengeance. Sykes is settling scores."

Jackson nodded.

"But he doesn't know about Lena's connection to Eli?"

"Doesn't look like it. If he's out for vengeance, he'll eventually come for Eli. We've got to catch him before that happens."

Sykes had set his sights on Alger County, and he would not cease marauding and slaying its citizens until Jackson stopped him.

In the meantime, Lena and Shiloh had moved to the Northwoods Inn along with Eli. They would be safe there, as safe as possible in a world on the cusp of anarchy.

All day, he'd felt torn and conflicted, his thoughts returning to Lena's dwindling insulin. "I managed to hunt down three of my best informants: a low-level drug dealer for Sawyer who'd served a nickel in prison several years ago, an armed robber out on parole, and a middle-aged meth head who lost her kids to the system and still can't break her habit. I offered them cash and propane camping stoves to buy insulin off Sawyer or from any black-market source they can uncover. The second they get their hands on anything of value, they'll trade for crack or opioids, but I can't worry about that now. If there's one thing that motivates an addict, the promise of a high does the trick."

He didn't have high hopes, but he was desperate.

"It's something." Devon glanced at her watch, eased off the desk, and stretched, kneading the small of her back with her fists. "It's late. You can't keep burning the candle at both ends. You're not a vampire, even though you're starting to look like one. Obey your own orders for once and get some shut-eye. We can start fresh tomorrow."

"Aye, aye, boss lady."

"It's just boss to you." She grinned. "Boss."

Wearily, he nodded. Devon took his hand and pulled him to his feet. As they left the sheriff's office, he had the sinking sensation that they were going around in circles, like a lost man wandering feet from his own house in a blizzard, freezing to death within reach of safety.

24

SHILOH EASTON
DAY SEVENTY-NINE

Shiloh hated Northwoods Inn already, and she hadn't even made it out of the parking lot yet.

She wasn't stupid; she understood why she and Lena had to leave the sanctuary of the lighthouse. Sykes was a savage psychopath, and she had no desire to be attacked again. The fight for her life in the woods and the assault on the lighthouse were still fresh wounds in her mind.

Still, that didn't mean she had to like it, and it didn't mean she had to show an ounce of joy. Another killer was after them. At least one, maybe more. And Lena was nearly out of insulin.

The fear of losing Lena was like a noose tightening around her throat, dread like an anvil squeezing her chest. Lena would be okay; she had to believe that she'd be okay. There was no other option.

Shiloh hoisted her duffle bag over her shoulder and wiped a bead of sweat from her forehead with the back of her arm. Bear trotted at her side as Devon helped pull Lena's suitcase and backpack full of medical textbooks from the back of the patrol truck.

Devon had brought them from the lighthouse in one of the sheriff's vehicles since Lena's tan turd was out of fuel; luckily, law enforcement still had an emergency fuel supply.

Eli was gone doing investigative stuff with Jackson, so Ruby had offered to come and help move them in. Later tonight, Eli and Jackson would haul the hydroponics system, the remaining food stores in the root cellar, and whatever else they could transfer to the Inn in a trailer drawn by horses. The smoked bear meat would follow as soon as it was ready.

Despite her best intentions to the contrary, she had to admit that the Northwoods Inn made an impression. Built during the logging glory days of the nineteenth century, the Inn looked like a great mansion constructed of massive logs, large stones, and huge windows.

She still hated it.

A goat bleated at her.

Shiloh spun, startled. "What the heck is that?"

The big white goat stood on the cab roof of a black pickup truck, glaring down at her and Bear with an irritated, impertinent air as if they were invading her territory and she was affronted.

Beside her, Bear stiffened. His hackles went up.

"That's Faith," Devon said. "Resident mascot of Northwoods Inn."

"Does she always sleep on cars?"

"It seems to be her favorite pastime. I think she poops on them, too."

"That's Jackson's truck she's scratching with her hooves."

Lena smiled. "Indeed, it is."

Faith scrabbled from the truck's roof, her hooves scraping the windshield, and leaped from the hood to the asphalt. She strutted right up to them, hooves clopping, and her big white butt swaying.

Bear whined in alarm and backed his hind end into Shiloh's legs.

Faith glared at Bear with her strange rectangular pupils. The goat had a stout body, small horns that curled back from her skull, and a short, scruffy beard on her chin that gave her a perpetually obstinate look.

Though the Newfoundland outweighed the goat by close to a

hundred pounds, Bear was clearly frightened of the strange creature. His ears flattened.

Faith lowered her head, her little horns flashing in the sunlight, and made an irritating baaing sound.

Bear yelped in terror.

The goat charged him headfirst, attempting to headbutt the big dog.

Bear turned and fled, his bushy tail tucked between his legs. Faith bleated angrily as she charged after him, as if yelling at him to come back and face her like a man.

Shiloh nearly choked on her laughter. Lena held her stomach, she was laughing so hard.

"Well, that made my day," Devon said with a smile. "Let's get inside before we die of heatstroke."

"What about Bear?" Shiloh asked. He'd run off somewhere into the woods.

"Bear will come around after he recovers his dignity," Lena said.

Shiloh snorted. "After that display, I think his dignity is the last of his concerns."

"Should we rescue him?" Ruby asked.

Lena chuckled. "Maybe we should."

A moment later, the goat reappeared, her head straight and high, glaring furiously as if daring them to challenge her to a duel. She flounced past them and bleated demandingly at the front door.

"By all means, you first." Shiloh pushed open the giant cedar double doors. The goat sashayed in ahead of her, showing her a cheeky view of her white fluffy butt.

They followed Faith into the grand foyer. It was a ritzy but rustic lodge with wood paneling lining the walls and great cedar beams arching across the two-story cathedral ceiling. Sunlight spilled through the two-story stained-glass windows and stretched across the slate floors.

A floor-to-ceiling masonry fireplace stood in the center of the foyer surrounded by clusters of leather armchairs where guests were gathered. A huge stuffed black bear stood on its hind legs in one corner, its arms spread like it wanted to hug you—or squeeze you to death.

"Wow," Ruby breathed. "I've heard about this place, but I've never been here. It's awesome."

"It's not the worst place I've ever seen," Shiloh muttered darkly. She watched Faith wander off to torment a couple of the guests. The brash goat stole a sandwich right out of a man's hands.

"There you are!" gushed a warm female voice. A chubby woman in her sixties strode toward them. Laugh lines wrinkled the corners of her pale-blue eyes as she smiled warmly. She wore sneakers and a plaid shirt rolled up to her elbows; flour smudged her cheeks as if she'd just come from the bakery.

A slender white-haired man around the same age came around the bar and stood next to her, still polishing a cup with a hand towel. He had a kind, weathered face, and his eyes glinted with mischief like someone's favorite uncle.

With his free hand, he put an arm around the woman's shoulder and smiled. "Welcome."

Devon made the introductions. "Shiloh, Ruby, and Lena, meet Tim and Lori Brooks."

Before Shiloh could react, the woman pulled her into an embrace, squeezing her gently. The aroma of woodsmoke and baking flour filled Shiloh's nostrils.

Shiloh stood stiffly, her arms at her sides, until Lori pulled back, still smiling as if she'd just met the queen of England. If she noticed Shiloh's discomfort, she didn't show it.

"We're so glad to have you!" Lori gushed. "Please, make this your home for as long as you need."

"Thank you so much," Lena said. "We appreciate your hospitality. And we'll work for our keep."

"We have no doubt," Tim said. "It's wonderful to have you. We have a space for you to keep seeing patients, Lena. We're thrilled that you're willing to help like this."

Despite her best intentions, Shiloh liked them immediately. Warm and kindhearted, she could tell they were good people, people who would give the shirts off their backs to help others even if they didn't deserve it.

A loud bleat sounded as Faith made a sudden beeline for the restaurant kitchen, hooves clopping across the stone floor. People scattered as she pranced across the foyer, threatening to headbutt anyone who got in her way.

"Faith! Get out!" Lori clapped her hands at the offending creature. "Get out! Before we decide to make dinner of you!"

Faith scampered out of Lori's reach with a saucy bleat that sounded more than a little smug, too.

Lori rolled her eyes. "Ugh, that goat thinks she's human. She's always stealing people food. She refuses to eat her own darn hay. Either that, or she's climbing the guests' cars or nibbling on their clothes. I don't know what to do with her."

Tim shook his head, grinning good-naturedly. "Those goats. Lori treats them like children. They're a pain in the you-know-where, but boy are they coming in handy. They provide as much milk as we need. You ever had goat cheese? Lori has some great recipes. And they're great lawn mowers; they eat all the grass, so it doesn't get overgrown. They have their uses."

"I love them," Ruby said. "I'd love to learn how to make goat cheese."

"We'll teach you." Lori wiped flour from her hands onto her jeans and gestured at them to follow her. "Leave your bags here; Tim will take them to your rooms. I'll give you a tour."

They followed her through the foyer, past the bar and the main hallway leading to the guest rooms. Lori pointed at rows of Styrofoam cups filled with water lining the stained-glass windowsills. Romaine lettuce stuck out of each cup with toothpicks propping up each lettuce leaf.

"This is a small part of our DIY hydroponics system. We're growing food from kitchen scraps. Once the romaine stalks grow new roots, we transfer them to the garden outside or a pot inside.

We're also adding seedlings for our autumn and winter crops, focusing on higher-calorie foods to get us through the winter, like carrots, potatoes, sweet potatoes, and pumpkins. I'll show you our growing room filled with hydroponic plants we built with PVC pipe and a gravity-fed watering system."

Ruby nodded, eyes wide. "Cool."

They passed the large industrial kitchen where a dozen people were busy cooking something that smelled like heaven and exited the Inn. Set on twenty acres along the bluff, the property boasted spectacular views of Lake Superior.

Gardens sprouted everywhere with raspberry and blackberry bushes thick with berries, apple and walnut trees, and even some pear trees. Goats and chickens wandered the lawn beneath huge oaks and hemlocks. Several one-room cabins were scattered across the property. There were many people hammering and framing, busy constructing new cabins.

A dozen wind turbines built along the bluff spun in the breeze coming off the lake. Solar panels lined the roof of the main building and a few of the cabins. People walked or drove around in golf carts with solar arrays attached to the roofs.

Lori waved a hand. "When we bought the place twenty years ago, we envisioned a self-sustaining enclave for artists and writers to create while inspired by the stunning beauty of the Upper Peninsula. We built a gravity-fed well system for running water. The food we serve is harvested from our gardens and small working farm."

Several two-man security teams patrolled the perimeter of the property, shotguns slung over their shoulders. Sniper hides had been built into the trees. Slender trip wires with alarms strung along the tree line glinted in the sunlight.

Lori followed her gaze. "David Kepford set this up for us and started to train volunteers in operational security. We were devastated when we heard he'd passed. What a wonderful man."

A pang struck Shiloh's chest. She'd always liked the principal;

he'd taught science class and had always treated the kids with dignity and respect.

"Eli Pope has agreed to step in and continue weapons, security, and combat training. I wish it wasn't so, but everyone needs to know how to operate a gun and shoot safely. We would never intentionally harm others, but we are also prepared to defend the people who have sought shelter within our boundaries. I'm a firm believer in self-protection."

So was Shiloh. "Who can volunteer?"

"Everyone who stays here has duties based on their skill set and interests. We do rotate the chores no one wants, like latrine and trash duty."

"I want to be security."

Lori frowned. "I don't think it's a good idea—"

"I'm good with weapons, not lettuce."

"But you're so young, honey—"

Shiloh fisted her hands on her hips. "I can shoot the balls off a mosquito. You know, if a mosquito had balls."

Lori's eyes crinkled merrily. "You're a firecracker, aren't you?"

"You have no idea," Lena said.

"All right, then. If it's okay with your guardian, it's okay with me."

Lena gave a resigned shrug. "Not my decision."

"I'll ask—" Shiloh's tongue caught on the word *father*. It was still so new and strange. It would take some getting used to, though in a good way.

She had suspected somewhere deep down that Eli was more to her than a friend. She'd felt an instant connection to him from the very beginning, even when she'd still believed him to be a killer, a kinship with him that she hadn't been able to explain. She had known somehow that he was dangerous and yet not a danger to her, not ever—in fact, the complete opposite.

It was all still new and foreign, but she had a family. She was part of a real family; she was no longer an orphan. It was a feeling of warmth and comfort, like being wrapped securely in a fuzzy blanket and knowing nothing could get to you.

She'd never felt that in her life and now that she had it, she never wanted to let it go, not ever. Still, she wasn't ready to call him daddy or anything yet.

"I'll ask Eli," she said instead.

Lori kept walking. "We've set up classes to teach some of the old ways that we've forgotten. Classes include canning, smoking, dehydration, and salting. We're building brick rocket stoves, solar ovens, and spring and smoke houses. We've got a fire-building class that starts tomorrow. It includes making homemade fire starters, like cotton balls drenched in petroleum jelly."

"What are those for?" Ruby asked, pointing to a pile of solar landscaping lights stacked on a picnic table.

"These are great outside and inside. We let them charge in the sun during the day, and people bring them inside at night for lighting." Lori showed them the latrines which they'd dug far from water sources. "It's gross, but sanitation is high on our priority list. All the guns in the world won't protect you from a lethal case of dysentery."

"Do you have room for two more?" Ruby asked. "I know my mom would love this. We're excellent gardeners. And I'll do the sanitation stuff, no problem. I'm not afraid of gross."

"Of course, honey." Lori turned to Shiloh, hands on her plump hips. She looked every bit like a warm, loving grandma, the kind of grandma who'd bake you cookies every day after school. "This is a healing place, a good place if you give it a chance."

"I miss the lighthouse," she blurted. "That's home."

"We would never take your home from you, honey. Think of this as your second home, your home away from home. A place of safety, a shelter in the storm."

Lena shot Shiloh a nervous glance, weighted with everything they'd been through, everything they faced. The noose around her throat seemed to loosen, just a little.

Slowly, Shiloh nodded. She had intended to hate this place, but her hatred drained out of her, replaced by something she couldn't quite name or identify—something a lot like hope.

25

JACKSON CROSS
DAY EIGHTY-TWO

"I'd like to ask you a few questions," Jackson said.

Scott Smith glared at him from his front stoop. "Hurry it up, Sheriff," he drawled in a thick Yooper twang. "It's hot as blazes and we've got work to do, eh?"

Jackson wiped sweat from the back of his neck and felt himself wilting. It wasn't even 10:00 a.m. and the temperature had been rising exponentially, with the humidity nearly unbearable, the sun merciless in the cloudless sky. His uniform stuck to the small of his back, his underarms soaked.

It was the hottest July on record. Half of his volunteer force had spent several afternoons handing out battery-operated fans, advising people to sleep outside, block off the hottest rooms in their homes, and install heat-blocking curtains over the windows.

Still, he'd responded to five cases of heatstroke in the last week alone with two deaths: an older couple had perished in their home.

Now, he stood on a too-familiar street. The Easton place was just down the road, the battered sign for Amos Easton's salvage yard at his back.

A rail-thin young man in his twenties slumped on the front step beside Scott, gripping a crumpled unlit cigarette with a glazed expression, his hand trembling and shaky. It was likely his last one. Jackson recognized Mark Smith, a high school dropout who'd been arrested a few times for possession. His collarbones poked beneath his ratty T-shirt as he hunched forward, his eyes glassy and blood-red. An open sore oozed puss from the corner of his cracked lips.

Meth was his poison of choice. Disgust filled Jackson. Sawyer continued to distribute his merchandise of death, no matter the circumstances.

Scott squinted down at Jackson. "If you're here about that diesel, yeah I still got some, but no freebies. I gotta get it out by hand with a hand pump and it's a doozy. You'll pay for it just like everyone else."

In his fifties, Scott was dressed in grease-stained overalls over a short-sleeved button-up shirt with tan work boots. He'd owned the Shell gas station on Cedar Street for the last thirty years, and his father had owned it before that. He had probably expected one of his kids to inherit it from him.

"That's good to know, but I'm here about the murders down the street. Chad and Cindy Marlowe."

Two more bodies had been reported early this morning a mile down the road. Chad Marlowe, in his sixties, a former manager at the local Family Dollar, had been gutted and hung from an oak tree in his front yard. His wife Cindy had run the Episcopalian church's food bank. She'd suffered a slightly less gruesome fate.

Jackson had known them. They were good people, the salt of the earth. The senseless violence sickened him.

This time, the victims appeared to have zero ties to the Hells Angels or organized crime. The corpses showed signs of torture. The attack so close to the Easton place concerned him. Had Sykes discovered a link between Eli and Lena? Or had the convicts escalated to random acts of carnage?

Jackson and his team worked the entire road, hitting every house without netting a single actionable lead. Several houses had been abandoned. Those at home didn't recall anything.

Even without phones or internet, word was spreading like wildfire. People were scared and jumpy, not only because of Sykes, but because of everything and everyone. He didn't blame them.

Beneath his thick reddish beard, Scott's mouth thinned into a scowl. "Before you get comfortable, we didn't see a thing. Didn't hear a thing. Nothing."

Maybe he hadn't, or maybe he feared being targeted next.

Behind Scott and his son, the two-story bungalow was tidy. A vegetable garden grew along the west side of the house in long wooden planters built with screened canopies to keep the deer, rabbits, and coyotes out. Along the side of the house, portable solar panels were attached to a generator. A half-built fence would shield the generator from prying eyes.

"Never expected the government to take care of us, but the least ya'll could do is keep those murdering psychopaths you let escape from slaughtering us good law-abiding citizens."

"We didn't let them escape," Jackson said. His words fell on deaf ears. "Sir, I assure you that we are doing everything in our power to capture the escaped convicts."

Scott stiffened. "Well, we can't help you. Why don't you let us be?"

A young woman rounded the corner of the house carrying a jug of drinking water, dressed in a sweat-soaked tank top and cut-off jeans, a damp handkerchief tied around her neck.

Her red hair was no longer in pigtails, but her round cheeks and bright eyes were familiar. Back when she was a kid, she used to run a lemonade stand from the driveway. Jackson and Lena would stop by after school and purchase plastic cups for a quarter.

"Fiona, right?" he asked.

She shielded her eyes with her hand and offered him a half-smile, revealing two crooked front teeth. On her, it was charming. "That's right."

A tangle of tubing was coiled at her feet next to a pile of PVC piping. Two large barrels were situated beneath a gutter spout at each corner of the house.

Fiona saw him looking. "Our rain containment system. We've rigged up a gravity-fed system to water the garden. An outdoor shower is next on my list. It'll suck in winter, but it's better than a sponge bath."

There was a flash of despondency in her gaze. Then she blinked it away and forced a fragile smile like it might peel off her face like a sticker. "I'm a senior at the University of Michigan, studying architectural design. Or, I was. I should be there now taking summer classes. I wanted to create beautiful buildings. Skyscrapers, museums. Hard to imagine building anything like that now."

He saw it in her face—that grief, grief for lost futures, lost dreams, and lost possibilities. People could moan about coffee and Netflix, but the ability to pursue creativity and passion, to create nuclear fusion or send astronauts to the moon, was no small thing.

Humanity had built monuments that scraped the sky. Now they were reduced to scratching in the dirt for survival.

He had no energy for uttering empty platitudes. "I'm sorry."

She gave a slight jerk of her chin, acknowledging his words.

Jackson shifted his attention to the meth-head son. He hung his head while still staring at the unlit cigarette like it could solve all his problems. While meth could be manufactured, cigarettes were something of a hot commodity on the black market. Insulin might be as well.

"Can I ask you a question?"

The young man didn't respond, didn't act as if he'd heard him.

"He doesn't have to answer your questions. You don't have anything on him."

"I'm not here for him," Jackson said, quiet and even. "But if he could help me with a bit of information, I'd greatly appreciate it."

Scott started to say something else but Jackson ignored him. "I've got no interest in arresting you for anything, Daniel, or your supplier, but I am interested in medications on the black market. If your supplier might have access to insulin."

Daniel raised his head then. His hands twitched in his lap. His fingernails were bitten to the quick, his thumbnail bloody. "I don't know, man. I don't know anything."

"If you found out anything useful, I'd be willing to pay you, in cash, or Band-aids or bullets, which you could trade for anything."

Daniel's bloodshot eyes gleamed. "Yeah, yeah. Okay."

"That's quite enough." Bristling, Scott moved in front of him, attempting to shield him from Jackson's view. "Those auroras, the solar storms, they took everything. Their futures gone in a blink. He's got nothing else. What am I supposed to do? Kick him out? He'd die. I take him as he is." His jaw bulged as he clenched his teeth. "Now get the hell off my lawn."

Jackson was unperturbed. Scott wasn't a threat—he was stressed and afraid and worried about his son. "Are you sure you didn't see any vehicles last night? Or in the last few days? Anything out of the ordinary?"

"You deaf? We saw nothing." Scott spun on his heels and yanked open the screen door, gesturing at his son with his other hand. "Daniel, get on up and get back to fixing that solar array."

Sullenly, the boy obeyed, with his head down and his shoulders hunched, avoiding Jackson's gaze as he shoved the cigarette into his pocket.

"If you hear or remember anything at all—" Jackson called after him.

The front door slammed behind Scott and his son, leaving Jackson alone on the front stoop. Asking a meth head to source insulin was a long shot, but he was desperate enough to try anything at this point.

A throat cleared behind him. "I saw something."

Slowly, he turned around.

"My dad's scared," Fiona said. "When he's scared, he gets mean and defensive. Circle the wagons, you know?"

"He has good reason to be scared."

"My brother...he can't handle the hard stuff. And now everything, every damn minute of every damn day, is hard. He's using drugs to escape reality, and it's poisoning him, fast rather than slow. He knows it, and I don't think he cares. I think he'd rather die from an overdose than deal with this." She waved her hand as if to encompass the entirety of the world, its cruelty and suffering and terrible unfairness. "Are you going to arrest him?"

Jackson had no interest in arresting a pathetic nonviolent drug addict. Law enforcement didn't have the resources to keep detainees at the local jail, and the prison had closed its doors. He didn't know what to do with the real criminals.

"I'm just trying to stop the monsters who are killing people."

Cicadas and crickets buzzed in the long grasses. The air hung heavy and listless, waves of heat rippling from the asphalt road on their left. Fiona looked at him for a moment, her brow furrowed as if undecided.

"We can't catch the bad guys without intel. If you saw something, what you know could help us catch them before they hurt anyone else."

Fiona nodded. "Okay. I'll help if I can."

He pulled out his notebook and pen. "Tell me everything you remember. Don't leave anything out, even if it seems irrelevant. Any detail could be important."

"It was late last night. My battery-operated alarm clock still works. When I woke up, I remember looking at the time. It was after midnight. I got up to use the bathroom. We're on septic, so we can use the toilets but we've gotta dump a bucket of water into the tank each time. We use the water from the rain containment barrels. Usually, I get a fresh bucket before I go to bed, but I forgot last night, so I had to go outside with the bucket to get water. I was around the side of the house when suddenly, these SUVs drove past. I didn't even hear them approach. And I would have noticed. It was the middle of the night, dark and quiet. And engines aren't a noise you hear much anymore. I mean, I haven't seen a plane overhead in two months. They were so damn quiet it was like a mirage. I thought I was dreaming. There was a red film over their headlights so they let off a reddish glow, not bright at all."

His pulse accelerated. "Electric vehicles. That's why no witnesses have heard them."

"Yeah. That makes sense."

"How many vehicles?"

"Three. Maybe four. They weren't going very fast, otherwise, I would've heard the tires and wind. One right after the other."

"Could you tell the make or model? Color? Any distinguishing characteristics?"

"Some kind of big bulky SUV. All dark colored. Dark blue or black, maybe gray. The windows were tinted and I couldn't see anything inside."

"Which direction did they come from?"

She pointed east, in the direction of the crime scene. "They were headed west."

Despite the heat, a chill touched the back of his neck. They were on County Highway 589, northwest of Munising. To the west was the Gwinn State Forest Area; to the southeast lay the Hiawatha National Forest, covering miles and miles of dense wilderness.

"Did you notice if or where they turned?"

"The old logging road at the end of the road. They turned left off the paved road up there." She shrugged. "That's all I saw."

Sykes was using the hundreds of miles of old logging roads that crisscrossed the U.P., mostly used for off-roading and snow-mobiling in winter, traveling mostly by night in electric vehicles. If he'd deactivated the National Highway Traffic Safety Administration required safety sounds, their vehicles would be virtually silent below eighteen miles an hour. With dark-colored SUVs and dimmed headlights, they could travel in and out of rural towns nearly undetected.

It was the best break they'd gotten thus far.

"That's plenty," he said.

"Mrs. Marlowe was a nice lady. She would buy a cup of lemonade every single day in summer. Sometimes she paid me in fifty-cent pieces and told me to save up for college. It's not okay what happened to her, what could happen to anyone of us."

"No, it's not."

Fiona pursed her lips. "I heard that citizens could volunteer to help the police."

"That's true. We need every hand we can get to protect our community."

"I want to do something, you know? Otherwise, it feels like waiting to die, slowly or quickly but still just...waiting. Giving in. I *need* to do something, to fight back." She didn't say against what, but she didn't have to.

Jackson said, "Welcome to the team."

26

SHILOH EASTON
DAY EIGHTY-THREE

"Thank you for helping us," Lena said.

"It's my pleasure." Mrs. Grady smiled. "Please, call me Ana."

"Sure, Mrs. Grady," Shiloh said, grinning. Once Mrs. Grady, always Mrs. Grady.

Ana Grady was a trim, attractive woman in her late forties who wore flowing, colorful skirts and billowy peasant blouses; her long silver-streaked hair was in braids. Though she wasn't that old, she'd been the town librarian for as long as Shiloh could remember.

Mrs. Grady lived on a homestead and knew how to do a bunch of stuff the old-fashioned way, so Lori Brooks had asked her to come to the Northwoods Inn and teach a class about food preservation.

They'd spent the morning building several solar dehydrators out of plywood and window screens with a couple of hammers, some nails, and a handsaw. Dried foods were easier to store than canned and didn't require refrigeration. Using the power of the sun, it didn't need electricity to work, either.

They'd built a large, open-faced box about five feet tall with the front angled toward the sky, with six-inch blocks of wood for legs. The shelves were constructed of window screens with a swinging Plexiglas cover to protect the dehydrating food from the elements.

Now, Ana Grady and Lena sat at one of the many picnic tables on the sprawling Northwoods property and drank homemade thimbleberry tea. After checking to make sure no goats were around, Bear had fallen asleep at Lena's feet, his paws twitching like he was deep in a doggie dream, chasing rabbits or maybe black bears.

Shiloh and Ruby plopped down at the picnic table across from Mrs. Grady. Bear woke up and stood, stretched with a wide, black-jowled yawn, and nuzzled their hands, hoping for snacks.

"You're very kind to help us, Ana," Lena said.

"It's selfish. I help you now, you help me next time when I need something. Also, self-sufficient people don't need to steal and rob from each other, and we can trade with each other as well, including our skills. Then each member agrees to share the knowledge with their friends and family, and so on."

Tears glistened in Lena's eyes. She leaned forward across the picnic table and gripped Mrs. Grady's hands. "Just when I start questioning what this world is becoming, why we keep killing each other, someone like you shows up to remind me to keep the faith."

"You're welcome, dear."

Shiloh slurped her delicious tea and listened to them talk. Her eyelids drooped. She could take a nap next to Bear and fall asleep instantly.

"How do you like the Northwoods property, Shiloh?" Mrs. Grady asked.

Shiloh blinked away the tiredness. "It's okay, I guess."

Truthfully, this place was blowing Shiloh's mind. When she wasn't training with Eli, she had chores at the Inn, just like at the lighthouse. There were gardens to tend, firewood to gather, meal prep and clean-up shifts to sign up for, and laundry day, which was magnitudes worse than weeding.

Though the Northwoods Inn had some solar and wind power, it wasn't enough for full electricity, so a lot of laundry was done by hand using a washboard and bucket, or a hand-cranked agitator. Billowing sheets, pillowcases, and towels hung on dozens of clotheslines strung between trees to air-dry.

Chickens waddled around, squawking and pecking the dirt for worms. Surprisingly, she enjoyed gathering eggs almost as much as she liked Lori's goat cheese omelets.

She liked the goats, especially ornery Faith, who followed her around, bleating to be fed or petted, climbing on cars, the chicken coop, and the shed, and eating anything in sight, from scraps of aluminum foil to pillowcases; it was a miracle Faith hadn't choked to death.

Whenever Faith saw Bear, she lowered her horned head with a belligerent bleat and chased after him. Bear was still terrified of her and turned tail and ran whenever she showed him her horns. It was hilarious.

The property hummed with activity. Kids ran everywhere, and people worked on different tasks, laughing and talking, and listening to music on solar-charged phones. This wasn't some utopian nirvana—there was plenty of arguing and complaining, bugs and sweating, blisters and sore muscles.

People were still people, but Lori was right. This place brought a strange peace to Shiloh's soul, a respite from the chaos brewing beyond the property's boundaries.

"It's a safe place," Lena said. "That's what matters. What about you, Ana? Are you okay living by yourself? Things are getting more dangerous every day. Tim and Lori are taking people into their community. I'm sure they'd have room for you."

Mrs. Grady shook her head. "Thank you for your concern, but I birthed my daughter in my house. I lived with my husband for twenty-seven years on the homestead. It is my home. I'm not leaving."

"You have a daughter?" Ruby asked.

A shadow passed over Mrs. Grady's face. "Had. She died in a car accident fifteen years ago."

"I remember Allison," Lena said. "I was away at college when the accident happened."

"What accident?" Shiloh asked.

Mrs. Grady's words were slow and measured, her hands on the table trembling. "Sometimes I wake up and it feels like it just happened. A head-on collision on a winding road. It was pouring rain that night; the roads were slick. Gideon Crawford was dating my daughter at the time. They'd been together for two years. We thought they'd get married someday. They were attending Michigan Tech in Houghton on the Keweenaw Peninsula where Allison was studying wildlife management. She wanted to be a forest ranger stationed on Isle Royale. They'd come home for spring break and had gone out to party, headed for some popular dance club in Marquette. I asked them not to go, but Allison got stir-crazy whenever she was home. She didn't want to listen. They said she died instantly and felt no pain."

"Astrid Cross was driving the other car," Lena said. "I remember. Lily called and told me about it. She was really upset. They were friends."

Mrs. Grady rubbed her temples, a deep sadness in her eyes. She had never seemed old to Shiloh but now, suddenly she did. Up close, a network of wrinkles spanned her face, lines of grief bracketing her mouth.

"It was a tragedy. The whole town was in mourning. The grief eventually killed my husband. He died two years later of a broken heart."

"I'm so sorry, Ana," Lena said.

"Me too," Mrs. Grady said. "He was a good man and a good father. He never got over that he hadn't protected his baby girl."

Mrs. Grady tilted her chin as she studied Shiloh. "You always reminded me of her, you know. She was small but strong, with long dark hair, like you. She loved animals, trees, rivers, and lakes. She could be outside all day exploring and forget to come home until past suppertime. Whenever you'd come into the library, when you were little, seeing you was like a glimpse of my baby come back to me. For a moment, for the space of a breath, I'd feel her with me again."

Maybe that was why Mrs. Grady had looked out for her all those years. She was the only person other than Jackson who'd cared about the half-wild kids surviving on the edge of civilization.

Whenever Amos Easton had gotten particularly drunk and nasty, Shiloh and Cody would hide out in the library for hours at a time, Shiloh reading science fiction tomes like *Dune* or *The Hitchhiker's Guide to the Galaxy*; Cody was always hunched over a drawing pad in one of the carrels.

Mrs. Grady never turned them in for being unsupervised or for skipping school. Once, she'd even kicked their grandfather out of the library when he'd stormed in, drunk and shouting, searching for them, his big hands curled into fists.

Shiloh blinked away the memory, her heart twinging at the thought of Cody. Her memory of him was already fading, slowly dissolving even as she reached for it. Every day, he seemed further away from her, his smile, his laugh, the way he bit his lip in concentration.

Mrs. Grady watched her. "I know how much you've lost too, honey." She reached out and squeezed Shiloh's hand. Her fingers were dry, her skin papery thin. "They're always with us."

"It doesn't feel like it."

"Give it time. Grieving is a long process."

Shiloh was pretty sure it would never end. Grief was like the waves crashing against the Lake Superior shoreline, ruthlessly wearing away the shore's resistance, relentless in its undoing.

27

JACKSON CROSS
DAY EIGHTY-FIVE

Jackson stood in the Northwoods Inn parking lot. The husks of a couple of dozen vehicles surrounded him. Dead leaves, twigs, and pollen filmed hoods and trunks. Weeds sprouted from cracks in the asphalt and choked wheels and fenders.

A big white goat lay on the once-pristine candy-red BMW M760i parked next to Jackson's Chevy Silverado. Her hooves had left dents and scratches all over the sports car. Matted tufts of white hair clung to the windshield.

Faith glared at Jackson with her rectangular pupils and bleated in annoyance.

"Sorry for disturbing your nap, your highness," he said as he watched his informant approach on his bike, zigzagging through the parking lot, wobbling between vehicles.

Mikael Kotila didn't bother with the kickstand as he clambered off the bike and leaned it against the red BMW. Faith grumbled her disapproval.

A jittery, skinny skinhead in his twenties, Mikael grinned, revealing yellowed teeth with his too-large smile. He wore a dirty *Avengers* T-shirt with sagging shorts and unlaced red Nike shoes. "Nice goat."

"Nice bike." The bicycle was a gleaming expensive-looking

BMX, likely stolen. Jackson had bigger fish to fry. "Please tell me you have something good."

Mikael scratched at the red marks scarring the inside of his arms. "Sorry, dude. I did my thing, went to all the spots, talked to my usual dealers. Nobody's got anything like the insulin you're talking about. I heard it's worth more than an ounce of coke, man. That's hardcore. Sawyer's guys got candy up the wazoo, though. You need zanies, chill pills, or hydros? Brown sugar? Rocket fuel to keep you up all night? You look like you could use something, man. I can get you any of that for a good price, a good deal, just for you."

Jackson gritted his teeth. "I'll pass."

With great sincerity, Mikael assured him that he'd gone above and beyond for the law, breaking into seven different pharmacies; they'd all been ransacked weeks ago.

Mikael examined his dirty fingernails. "Remember I did you a favor, man. You got anything for me?"

"Not until you get something for me," Jackson said. "Keep looking. Oh, and go see Lena inside. She'll give you a glass syringe and teach you how to sanitize it. Be careful. You get infected with a dirty needle, and there's no 911 to call."

Mikael bobbed his head on his scrawny neck. "Yeah, yeah man. For sure."

"And eat something. Please."

His informant shot him another too-wide grin, then seized his bike, hopped on, and rode away, probably to feed his habit. Jackson watched him go, frustration souring his gut.

He'd found no solution to Lena's insulin problem and had zero leads. The situation became more dire with each passing day. If they couldn't find insulin, within weeks Lena and every diabetic like her would die.

At least he could do something when it came to Sykes. This week, he'd deputized twenty-five additional citizen volunteers, including Gideon Crawford and Fiona Smith, and assigned each of them posts at various checkpoints along the county roads.

He'd set up more checkpoints on M-28 west of the Au Train River, Highway 58 out by Bear Trap Inn, Interstate 94 at the intersection in Shingleton to the east and across from the Village Inn in Chatham to the west, and along Highway 13, which ran north-south between the Nahma Junction in Delta County and Munising.

Thanks to Fiona Smith's intel, at last, they had a lead to follow. The Upper Peninsula boasted more than six thousand miles of state forest roads maintained by DNR. Jackson had obtained several maps from the Down Wind Sports outdoor store in downtown Munising. The shop had been looted of tents, camping stoves, propane tanks, and survival gear, but the maps had survived intact.

With thousands of miles of logging roads to monitor, there was no way they could check them all. Jackson ordered a group to scavenge the local outdoor shops for deer trail cameras. Many local folks were hunters; they'd scavenged empty houses for hunting gear in basements and garages and scrounged up several more.

Using solar-charged battery systems, they'd spent the last three days planting the cameras at various locations along the logging roads throughout Alger County and into neighboring Delta, Schoolcraft, and Marquette Counties. They traveled deep into the Hiawatha National Forest, the Gwinn State Forest Area, and even further west into the Crystal Falls State Forest Area north of Iron Mountain.

Where they could, they used bikes, horses, or ATVs to travel, but for the areas farther away Jackson authorized the use of their emergency fuel supplies.

Once they'd caught Sykes on camera, they could start zeroing in on his location and follow him back to whatever hideouts he might be utilizing. He still had volunteers staking out the friends and family members of the escaped convicts.

It would take time. Time was the thing he was fast running out of.

"Look who it is."

Jackson spun at the familiar voice.

Bradley Underwood tottered toward him, a mason jar brimming with amber liquid sloshing over his hand as he made a show of a mocking bow. "If it isn't the false king of Alger County."

Jackson stiffened. He caught the sizzle of rage behind the drunken affect. Though he'd resigned, Underwood was furious at the world for losing his position, no less in such a humiliating manner. "What do you want, Underwood?"

Underwood swigged another drink, his Adam's apple bobbing as he gulped it down, then glowered into his mason jar. "Dana Lutz's grandfather used to make moonshine. He taught her; the equipment he used is still in his work garage. She's been making the stuff and selling it to Tim and Lori so they can keep the bar open. Tastes like warm piss."

Jackson didn't respond.

"Who do you think you are?" Underwood slurred.

Jackson's hand strayed to his service pistol. He didn't fear Underwood, but the man was angry, bitter, and desperate, and desperate men were unpredictable. "If you recall correctly, you were the one who resigned."

"No thanks to your father." Underwood reeled, swaying on his feet. "I had no choice. It was go along to get along or else, and I went along. You think just because you're his son that you're exempt? You better toe the line like the rest of us."

"My father is no longer the sheriff. He has no power anymore."

Underwood scoffed. "If you believe that, you've got another think coming. He has his grasping hand in many pots. Not all of them clean, if you catch my drift."

Jackson didn't want to, but he did. He thought of the generator still running at his parents' house, the meds for his mother and sister that miraculously appeared. However his father had gained access to critical medications, maybe he knew where Jackson could get insulin, too.

He kept his voice steady. "If you have something to say, come out and say it."

"Maybe mistakes were made. An oversight or two. But I am not corrupt."

He was still making excuses, deflecting the truth. The former sheriff was a bureaucrat, a chaser of power, fame, and influence. He'd coveted the limelight over catching bad guys. Due to being inept, bullheaded, belligerent, and petty, Underwood's failings had hampered investigations and hamstrung his deputies.

Jackson kept his opinions to himself, loath to kick a man while he was down. And Underwood was down.

Underwood stared morosely down at his mason jar without taking a sip. "I never made a deal with the devil."

"Are you saying that my father did?"

"You didn't hear it from me, eh?"

"I'm hearing it from you right now."

Bitterness crept into his tone. "You'll find out in your own sweet time, *Sheriff* Cross. The badge is nothing but a piece of plastic, and the role you play is the noose they hang around your neck. There's a cost to everything."

"My soul is not for sale."

Underwood gave a scornful laugh. "You tell yourself that. Everyone is for sale for the right price."

"No," Jackson insisted. "Not me."

"Mark my words—one day you'll look in the mirror and realize you've made the same deal with the same devil. Or maybe it'll be a worse devil."

"I won't," he said as guilt needled him. He'd acted the part of the devil; he knew that shame intimately. "Go somewhere safe and dry out."

"Ask your father," Underwood slurred. "Maybe he'll tell you the truth."

Jackson didn't have the time or the pity to waste on Bradley Underwood. He had a thousand things to do if he was going to catch a bigger monster than even Cyrus Lee. He left the former sheriff staggering in the parking lot, guzzling moonshine and muttering of devils.

A raft of clouds drifted across the sun, casting long shadows. For the first time in months, Jackson shivered, suddenly chilled, as if a ghost had walked across his grave.

28

LENA EASTON
DAY EIGHTY-FIVE

L ena stared at her empty plate. She'd eaten a few pieces of bear jerky and three leaves of romaine lettuce drizzled with lemon juice. Her gut was an empty knot, hunger constantly gnawing at her insides.

"You have to eat more," Shiloh admonished her.

Her stomach growled. "I can't."

"You can. You have to."

Bear stretched out on the rug at her feet, his fur tickling her bare toes. She and Shiloh sat at a table in the conference room formerly used for creative writing critique sessions and live poetry readings. Perched high on the bluff, the third-story room boasted floor-to-ceiling windows and fantastic views.

Bookshelves lined the remaining walls; they were filled with leather-bound, first edition books, poetry by Emily Dickinson and Dylan Thomas. Novels from Daphne du Maurier and Earnest Hemingway mingled with modern bestsellers by John Grisham, Karin Slaughter, and Lee Child.

A cheery fire flickered in the fireplace that was framed between two bookcases. Above the fire, Lena had hung a pot from a thin iron rod. The glass syringes boiling in the pot tinkled like wind chimes. Since she'd run out of disposable syringes, she'd resorted to glass ones that could be sterilized and reused.

Lena took her blood glucose meter from the table, pricked her finger, and squeezed a droplet of blood onto a test strip, then inserted the strip into the meter. Her fingertips were bruised and sore from the repeated pricks for the glucose monitor.

Holding her breath, she waited. The number appeared. Ice-cold dread shot through her veins.

"What's wrong?" Shiloh asked.

"The number is a little higher than I'd like." It wasn't a lie. It wasn't the truth either. In the upper 400s, it was much too high.

Her fingers shaking, she pulled a vial from her Frio wallet and produced a syringe, her mouth moving as she silently counted the carbohydrates, then withdrew six units of insulin and injected herself with the needle. She should be injecting more, but she needed to ration the little she had left.

"What happened to your fingers?" Shiloh asked, aghast.

"I ran out of the sensors and infusion sets for my pump. I could stockpile syringes and vials of insulin, but not the parts to the pump. They only came in ninety-day supplies through my insurance. I couldn't get more. So now, I'm forced to do things old-school which includes pricking my fingers multiple times a day. And I give myself shots of long-acting insulin every morning. Plus, every time I eat, I count the carbs and give myself an injection of the short-acting insulin for every meal."

Shiloh scrunched up her nose. "It looks painful."

"It's not that bad," she lied.

"That's why you're not eating as much. Fewer carbs, less insulin?"

"Something like that." Lena gestured at the stack of library books on the table. "I've been reading some books that I asked Mrs. Grady to get for me. They're about the history of medicine. I've been researching the discovery of insulin in the 1920s, and how they treated Type 1 diabetics before modern medicine. Diabetes has been around since ancient civilizations. Archeologists found ancient papyrus scrolls written by Egyptian physicians describing the disease to the best of their knowledge at the time."

"Well?"

"It's not good. I'd hoped to find some little nugget or old wives' tale that might be helpful, like how doctors used desiccated pig thyroid for hypothyroidism for decades before synthetic Synthroid was developed. Some people still use it even today. But insulin is different.

"Before the 1920s, doctors would put their newly diagnosed Type 1s on a strict, near-starvation diet. Zero carbs, or as close to zero as possible." Reading about the agonies of starvation and excruciating deaths—the same death she faced—was disconcerting, a terrible kind of torture. "It gave the patients a few more weeks, sometimes a few more months."

"And then what?"

"You know what," Lena said quietly. Never one to shy from the truth, she forced herself to say the words aloud. "It's a death sentence."

"Eli and Jackson will figure something out," Shiloh said with confidence. "They always do."

How Lena longed to believe her. She knew they were doing everything they could. It wasn't enough. The world was in dire straits, with death and suffering on a global scale. With every passing day, her impending demise stared her in the face.

It was awful. She hated it; the anxiety was a stone in the pit of her stomach, a constant awareness that never faded, not in sleep and not in her waking moments. She did her best to distract herself, but it did little to help.

Lena had spent the last several days seeing patients, and when she wasn't attending to patients, she poured over medical textbooks and herbal remedies. Several times, they'd gone foraging for medicinal plants.

Lori Brooks was a veritable fount of knowledge. Lena had learned to use elderberry leaves and flowers for pain relief, swelling, and inflammation, as well as utilizing the dried berries to ease respiratory ailments and headaches. They'd harvested the white-flowered common yarrow weed, whose astringent and antiseptic properties made it a potent wound healer.

Lena had used a yarrow poultice on Moreno's infected leg to reduce the inflammation. It seemed to be working. Chewing on the leaves had alleviated Ruby's toothache.

She was learning, bit by bit.

Shiloh shot her a reproachful look. "You're too damn skinny."

Her head pounded, her mouth too dry although she drank constantly. No amount of elderberry juice could fix this headache. It wasn't the lack of carbohydrates sapping her energy, but the relentless spike of her insulin levels as she rationed what she had left, her blood sugar climbing toward dangerous levels.

"It'll be fine—" She swallowed the words at Shiloh's alarmed expression.

"You promised you wouldn't lie."

"You're right. I'm sorry. Things aren't fine. I'm not fine." Her voice cracked. Lena longed to be brave, to stare death in the face with grace and dignity. The fear was there, nipping at her heels, a shadow with teeth.

"Why are you helping everyone else when you should be helping yourself?"

"I'm doing what I can. I'm rationing the insulin so I'm taking enough to keep me alive and not much more, and I'm eating a near-starvation diet to stave off the inevitable for a few more weeks. Jackson and Eli are searching far and wide for an answer. I'm researching everything I can—"

"It's not enough!"

Lena leaned forward and grasped her niece's hand across the table. Shiloh took one look at her bruised fingers, snatched her hand back, and shot to her feet, knocking her chair back. It clattered to the floor and landed on its side, the sound loud as a gunshot.

Startled, Bear lifted his head with a grunt.

Lena rose and started around the table, reaching for her niece, but Shiloh flinched from her grasp. They stood facing each other, the pain in Shiloh's eyes so stark that it stole Lena's breath from her chest. "Shiloh—"

"No!" Shiloh's chest heaved. Her eyes bulged, her fists clenched in grief and anger. "It's not enough."

"I'm helping people. It's my purpose. I'm doing what I'm supposed to be doing."

"What purpose? What meaning?"

Lena waved a hand helplessly, encompassing more than she could say. "To do some good. To make a difference while I still can."

"You think doing good stuff for other people is going to make up for you running away and leaving me and Cody behind? It won't and you can't."

Lena blanched. "That's not—"

"There's no reason for any of it, for anything. The stupid solar flares wrecked the whole world! There's no purpose to any of it. It doesn't mean anything. Not Cody running off a cliff. Not Eli going to prison. Not my mom getting killed in her bed while I hid in a corner. You can't tell me there's any purpose in that!"

"Shiloh, please understand—"

There was a knock on the door.

"Excuse me," a deep male voice said. "I'm here to see Lena Easton about my wife's lupus."

Shiloh's face hardened. "Better go see your patient. Can't keep them waiting, after all."

Lena opened her mouth to call after her, but Shiloh spun and stalked from the conference room. "You're her top priority," Shiloh snapped to whoever was waiting in line. The door slammed behind her.

The girl was running from the pain. Lena understood it but that didn't mean it hurt any less. It hurt. Everything hurt.

Bear clambered to his feet and padded over to Lena, thrusting his head beneath her palm to comfort her, his ears cocked and head tilted, his soft brown eyes searching Lena's with a mournful expression as if somehow, he could sense what was coming.

Lena's heart had broken into a thousand pieces, for Shiloh, for herself. Still, she forced a smile as her next patient shuffled through the door.

29

JACKSON CROSS
DAY EIGHTY-SIX

"Son?" Dolores's voice was weak and reedy.

"It's me, Mom." Jackson sat in the chair next to the bed, leaned forward, and hugged his mother, her spine beneath his fingers sharp and knobby. Her cheeks were hollow, her skin papery, almost translucent.

Dolores slumped against the satin pillows in the shadowy master bedroom and looked at him with rheumy eyes, a haze filming her pupils. Gone was the clarity, the sharpness in her gaze.

His mother had once been a gorgeous socialite, overseer of charities, country club outings, tennis tournaments, and lavish Christmas parties. Though her beauty had faded, Dolores was an arresting woman. Always slim as a whippet, she had shrunken seemingly overnight.

Not overnight. When was the last time he'd been home? Three weeks ago? A month? He was working almost every minute of every day, trying to keep everything from falling apart with his bare hands.

Even now, he'd come home not for his mother or sister but to interrogate his father and ask him about his source for medications, hoping to follow the trail to find insulin. But Horatio wasn't at home.

Guilt tasted bitter as rotten fruit in the back of his throat. "I'm sorry, Mom."

"I've missed you, Garrett."

Jackson stiffened. "Mom. It's me, Jackson."

She didn't blink, didn't show any sign that she realized her mistake. She gazed up at him with a dull smile. "Why did you leave us, Garrett? We need you. Everything is falling apart."

"I'm here, Mom. I'm your other son. Garrett left a long time ago."

Garrett Cross, the prodigal son. He was Jackson's older brother, the golden boy, the high school quarterback, and homecoming king—at least before he spiraled into drugs and addiction, lost his sports scholarship, and was expelled from MSU the spring before Astrid's car accident.

Weeks after the accident, Garrett had fled and never returned, sending occasional postcards from Mackinac Island and Saginaw Bay—then nothing, no birthday calls, no visits, not even a Christmas card.

It was as if he'd dropped off the face of the earth.

The double blow of Astrid's accident and Garrett's abandonment had shattered Dolores. In many ways, she'd never recovered.

"We can fix this," she said, her voice raspy as dead leaves scraping the pavement. "We'll take care of it, your father and I, like we always take care of everything."

A shiver went through him. "Fix what, Mother?"

Dolores clutched at him with shriveled fingers like claws. Everything about her felt insubstantial; at the next strong wind, she might disintegrate into dust.

Pity tugged at his heart, pity and a deep, abiding love. This was the woman who'd birthed him, sung to him when he was a toddler, and laughed as she danced with him in the kitchen while he stood on her toes.

He needed to find Horatio, but he could spare a few minutes of his time. "Mom, are you hungry? How about some soup? Chicken noodle is your favorite. I'll heat a can."

"Forgive us," she whispered in a tremulous voice that sent shivers down his spine.

"Forgive you for what?"

"Come back to me. Come home."

"Mother, why does Garrett need to forgive you? What happened?"

Dolores mumbled something unintelligible, her mind drifting within the fog of her memories.

He leaned forward, straining his ears, barely noticing the mahogany four-poster bed, the great stone fireplace, and the marble tile flooring. Thick shadows gathered in the corners of the well-appointed bedroom, bleak and uninviting.

Despite the heat of the day, a chill gripped him. She was incoherent, confused, and almost delirious. He'd never seen her like this. She took sedatives and had for years, but this was different.

"Don't leave me." Tears glimmered in her sparse eyelashes. "It's so dark."

He leaned down and kissed her forehead. "You'll be okay. I'll make you some food."

Much as he loved her, he couldn't escape the dark bedroom fast enough. In the kitchen, he scoured the cupboards. The supplies he'd purchased in Marquette three months ago crowded the shelves. They still had food.

Crumbs filmed the marble countertops, and dirty dishes were piled in the sink. Dust swirled in the panels of sunlight. His mother kept the house pristine; more than her mind was slipping. It worried him more than he wanted to admit.

He had too much to do, but he couldn't leave Dolores in this state. He felt obligated to care for her, too. She was his mother, for Pete's sake.

Jackson opened a can of Campbell's chicken noodle soup with the manual can opener and dumped it in a copper pan. He turned the knob on the gas stove; the little flame leaped to life. He stared at the flickering flames until his eyes blurred.

He hadn't been inside a building with full electricity in over a month. The Northwoods Inn had solar panels for partial power—hot showers once a week, and laundry twice a month. Washed clothes were hung to dry, and cooking was done by outdoor grill and woodstove to conserve energy.

The generator still worked, which meant his father was dealing with Sawyer to procure fuel. He swallowed down his irritation. Using electricity, especially at night, made the house a target. At least the house was camouflaged from the road, but it was only a matter of time.

"It's a stove. You gonna stare at it all day or cook something?" Astrid's voice rang out in the quiet house. She appeared from the living room and hobbled across the kitchen, leaning heavily on her cane, which thunked against the tile. "Thought you were too good for this place."

He placed the pan on the stovetop and turned to face her. "Where is Father?"

"I have no idea. Some meeting or another. I think he said he was getting more fuel for the generator."

Jackson grunted. "Did you know about this?"

"You're going to have to be more specific."

"Mother's memory, or lack of it."

Astrid's eyes glittered with a bright flash of anger—and something else, something that surprised him—sadness. "Father says it's Alzheimer's."

That surprised him. "Really?"

"Yeah. Or dementia. Pretty soon she's going to start wandering outside without telling anyone and stroll over the edge of the bluff." Her voice was hard and sardonic, but he caught the undercurrent, the catch at the end of her words. Much as she tried to hide it, this was upsetting Astrid, too.

"You didn't bother to tell me."

"You're the one who stormed out of here, remember? After accusing us of stealing and betraying your precious state secrets."

He'd accused Astrid, not the rest of his family, but before he could correct her, she spoke. "Father got pills to keep her sedated through all this, but she's just..." Astrid waved her hand as if searching for the right word to pull from the ether. "Wilting."

"Does she eat?"

"She says she's not hungry. I try to make her, but I'm not exactly up to the task."

"That's B.S. You're fully capable and you know it. Don't allow Mother to coddle you when you can take care of yourself. She's the one who's ill. She needs you to care for her."

Astrid's eyes narrowed. "I certainly am. No thanks to you. It's not like Father's any good at caretaking, and he's gone half the time, anyway."

"Where does he go?"

She gave a careless shrug. "Who knows? Who cares?"

"You have no idea?"

"Are you hearing impaired? He's got meetings with people. How should I know? I'm not his keeper. Or Mother's."

Frustrated, he stiffened as he turned back to the stove, stirring the soup with the wooden spoon clenched in his fist. "Mom was talking about Garrett."

Astrid hobbled to her wheelchair beside the breakfast table, sank into it with a pained sigh, and leaned her cane against the back of a chair. "Good riddance. What did she say?"

Jackson repeated everything his mother had said. He half-turned from the stove so he could watch Astrid's facial expressions. He expected his sister to lie through her teeth. Hell, Astrid lied for the fun of it, to get a rise out of people, poking the ant's nest to watch them boil over and scatter.

"Why would she ask Garrett for forgiveness?" he asked.

"I don't have the faintest idea." Her expression remained placid, and serene, but he detected the contraction of her pupils, a tiny twitch at the corner of her mouth.

"Surely, you have a guess."

"If anyone should be asking for anyone's forgiveness, it should be mine, don't you think?" She placed her hands on the tops of her thighs as if to emphasize her infirmity and stretched out her legs to reveal the misshapen flesh, the jagged scars crisscrossing her skin from her ankles to her thighs.

She'd never been one to hide her disfigurement; she seemed to take a perverse pleasure in the revulsion and pity of others, mocking their discomfort at her hideousness.

Jackson didn't look away. He hadn't forgotten how Astrid would scream in agony for hours each night, all night, for endless days, weeks, and months. No one and nothing could comfort her.

Sympathy pricked at him. For all her faults, Astrid had suffered immensely, maybe more than anyone. "It was an accident, Astrid. It was no one's fault."

Astrid quirked an eyebrow. "Wasn't it?"

"Certainly not Mother's," he said. "It doesn't make sense."

"She's losing her marbles; even you can see that. Her mind is turning to Swiss cheese. Why should it make sense?"

"She thinks it's the past. It doesn't mean it's a false past."

Anger flared in her eyes. "Maybe you should just let her be. All you do is poke and prod at people better left alone."

Jackson sighed. He felt old, old and tired. Conflicted emotions tore at him. He should still be out there hunting for Sykes and searching for Lena's insulin, but his mother needed him.

He took a ladle from the container of utensils on the counter along with a bowl from the cupboard and scooped steaming chicken noodle soup into the bowl. He set the bowl, a glass of water, a spoon, and a napkin on a wooden tray and carried it to Dolores's room.

"She's not going to eat it," Astrid called after him. "As usual, you're just flogging a dead horse!"

30

JACKSON CROSS
DAY EIGHTY-SIX

Nudging the bedroom door open with his shoulder, Jackson went to his mother's bedside and set the tray on the end table, raised Dolores to a sitting position, and fluffed the pillows behind her back.

Dolores blinked heavily. "We did the wrong thing."

Her words were soft and insubstantial as the brush of feathers against his cheek. He leaned forward to hear her. "What?"

"God will never forgive us," she whispered. "I told you it was wrong, Horatio. I told you there would be punishment."

"What do you mean, Mom?"

Something shifted behind her bleary eyes. Her mouth thinned to a pinched frown. "I need my pills. Give me my pills."

"I gave you your blood pressure meds an hour ago."

"No, the other ones."

"The sedatives—"

"The other ones!"

"What other ones?"

"I need them. Where are they? Did you take them? Bring them to me! I can't sleep, I can't sleep without them…"

"What pills? What do they look like? How many do you take?"

Dolores only raised her voice in agitation. "You promised me! I need to sleep! I can't sleep. I need my pills!"

"Okay, Mom. I'll find them."

Only with repeated promises did she settle down. He managed to get her to eat three or four bites before she clamped her wrinkled lips and refused more. Finally, he placed the uneaten soup back on the tray and held his mother's hand as she drifted into a restless sleep.

He couldn't get his mother's words out of his mind. What had made Dolores feel so ashamed that it had taken hold in her mind, rising through thousands of disjointed memories to emerge, of all moments, now?

How did Garrett factor into it? Was this relevant to the here and now or was it simply the guilt of a mother unable to protect her child from tremendous pain, as Astrid claimed? He didn't know, and that bothered him, the unknown niggling like an annoying gnat in the back of his mind.

Time passed. His eyelids felt heavy; he might have dozed a bit. The sky darkened outside the windows, shadows crept across the floor like wraiths reaching with crooked fingers, seeking the living to devour.

He rose heavily to his feet and stood over his sleeping mother. Her hair spread like gossamer across the satin pillow, thin and silvery. In sleep, her face slackened, her chest rising and falling in fluttery breaths.

"I'll visit more often, I promise." He hesitated, besieged with love and guilt in equal measure. "I'm sorry."

Jackson fled the bedroom. He had to get out of this house. Memories crouched in every corner: the criticism, the vitriol, the resentment. It was a childhood where no one raised a hand but the hits kept coming.

He exited through the French doors to the deck.

"Jackson." Astrid wheeled onto the deck, her strong biceps flexing as she adeptly maneuvered the wheelchair to face him. "Don't leave."

Jackson squinted at her, suspicious. "What do you want?"

"I want to know how you're doing."

"You don't usually care one way or the other."

"I do care." She smiled at him with startling affection. "You know I love you, right?"

He started. "What?"

"Can't a sister be nice to her brother?"

"Not when that niceness comes with a price."

Astrid pouted. "That's not fair."

"Call it cynicism." And when had he become so cynical? He was the idealist, the naïve one who believed in the best of people. Lately, he'd felt that idealism withering along with mankind's civility. Too many dead bodies would do that to a person.

She wheeled closer. The starlight softened her features. She looked younger, vulnerable and beautiful. "You were right, Jackson. Father had it wrong. You were right about buying and storing extra food and supplies. You knew what was happening, and you tried to warn us. I shouldn't have given your supplies away. I'm sorry."

Jackson stared at her, stunned. He couldn't recall a time he'd heard her apologize, especially not to him. She was arrogant, prideful, and spiteful, like their father.

"What do you want from me?" he asked warily.

She gave him a guileless look. "Nothing. I swear it."

He opened his mouth, then closed it, unsure how to respond. He wasn't sure he believed her.

"I don't want things to end like this between us. We're still family, you and I."

The hard lump in his chest softened. He reached out and touched her shoulder. She grasped his hand. Her fingers were cool and dry.

Things could change. People could change. Mistakes could be undone and wrongs righted. He still believed that. He had to believe that.

When he smiled at her, it was genuine.

31

LENA EASTON
DAY EIGHTY-SEVEN

S omeone pounded on the door to Lena's office.

Lena shoved her chair back and stood, a wave of dizziness washing over her as she swayed on her feet. Holding the desk for support, she blinked back the white spots floating in front of her eyes. "Come in."

She'd just seen her last patient for the day and was about to forage for more herbs and plants while Shiloh and Eli practiced at the firing range the Brooks had built at the rear of the property.

The door flung open. Traci Tilton and her husband Curtis burst into the room. Curtis carried a limp bundle in his arms. Beside him, Traci's face was ghost-white, her blonde curls in disarray, and her eyes wide with panic.

"How can I help—"

"It's Keagan!" Traci cried. "He passed out. I'm afraid he'll go into a diabetic coma. He'll die."

Curtis gently laid his son on the sofa across from the fireplace. He rose and faced Lena, his expression tormented. "Please help us."

When she had first offered insulin to the Tiltons, Lena had been careful to keep the location and the amount hidden. Though she'd acted like she'd procured the insulin from elsewhere, Traci had easily seen through the ruse.

"I know how much this is asking of you," Curtis said, "but you are the only person who has insulin."

"Had." Lena's mouth went bone dry. "Thieves broke in and stole it. They destroyed the rest."

Traci looked at her in desperation. "All of it?"

They saw the flicker of hesitation.

"Please, Lena," Traci begged. "Please."

Lena forced herself not to glance at the desk drawer where she stored her Frio wallet and the last of her insulin. Instead, her gaze was drawn to the boy lying barely conscious on the sofa. His labored breathing filled the room. His thin chest rose and fell, and his skin was a ghastly grayish-blue.

Kneeling beside the sofa, she felt his clammy skin and checked his pulse and vital signs, her years as a paramedic kicking in. Her movements were slowed, her thoughts muddled from hunger. "Get me the glucose meter and a test strip from the bookcase."

Without a word, Curtis obeyed.

Bear trotted up to Keagan, his tail low, his ears flattened. Pressing his furry bulk against her shoulder, he whoofed softly and nudged Keagan's cheek as if to wake him.

The boy hardly stirred. His shallow breath smelled sickly sweet; his urine would smell the same. "My stomach hurts," he mumbled. "My head hurts."

"I know, sweetheart. Hold on." With growing alarm, Lena checked his blood with a test strip and glucose monitor: over 600 and climbing. His numbers were dangerously high. If they didn't bring his blood sugar down quickly, he could slip into a diabetic coma and never wake up.

It was a choice for a fraction of a second. Then it wasn't a choice at all. The choice was not just to live, but how to live. Lena could not stand by and watch this child die. She could not.

Lena opened the Frio wallet and removed the remaining vial and a glass syringe. Tension crackled through the room. No one moved. Everyone stared at the vial of clear liquid, so small, innocuous, and ordinary, this miraculous product of modern medicine.

"This is the last of it," Lena said.

Curtis' fists opened and closed at his sides like he longed to lunge at her, seize it from her hands, and inject his son himself. Naked anguish etched his face. Greedy hope flashed in Traci's eyes.

"Traci," Curtis said, his voice cracking. "She'll die, too. We can't ask this—"

Tears streamed down Traci's face. "I know that! We have no right to ask you this, Lena. No right at all. As a woman, I'm appalled at myself. As a mother, I am asking you anyway. I hate myself for it and yet I'm still doing it. It's unpardonable, unforgivable. I'm asking for the sake of my son."

"Even if I share the last of what I have, he'll be in this same position again in a week, maybe less."

And so will I. The words remained unspoken but hung heavy in the air, the terrible elephant in the room. *And then we'll both die.*

"It gives him precious time," Traci croaked. "Time for the sheriff to find something."

Lena nodded. With trembling hands, she administered the units of insulin. Bear gave a forlorn whine, rested his head in the boy's lap, and thumped his bushy tail.

They didn't have to wait long. Within a few minutes, Keagan let out a gasp. His papery eyelids fluttered open. He looked around groggily, his gaze focusing on Lena's face. "W-what happened?"

Traci sobbed in relief.

"You went hyperglycemic and fainted," Lena said. "You're okay now. It'll take a few hours for your numbers to get to a healthy range. Your parents will monitor you, okay?"

Bear eagerly licked his face. The boy mustered a weak grin and petted Bear's head, who sighed in canine contentment.

Lena rechecked Keagan's vitals as his cheeks pinked, his heart rate and pulse steadied, and gradually, his BS numbers dropped. Before her eyes, he regained his vitality.

A few minutes later, Keagan tottered to his feet, albeit unsteadily, his mother's arms wrapped around him, his father hugging them both and affectionately tousling his hair.

It was a happy moment. It wouldn't last, couldn't last. Diabetes was an insidious, relentless killer. Without insulin, they had no weapons with which to fight.

Death would come for both of them.

Keagan half-turned, his cheek mashed against his mother's torso, and gave her a tremulous smile, revealing sweet dimples, a lock of blond curls slipping over one eye.

He was so young. Too young to die.

"You helped me." He scrunched up his boyish face. "Thank you."

Lena swallowed the lump in her throat. "You're welcome."

Traci released her son and touched Lena's arm, gratitude and relief on her face. "I will never forget this. Never."

"Come back tonight and tomorrow morning. I'll share the rest of what I have until it's gone."

"We couldn't—" Curtis started, but Traci shot him a pleading look.

Traci said, "We can never repay you—"

Abruptly, Lena's legs turned watery. She was tired, so tired. She barely had the strength to stand. "Please take your son and go."

Without another word, they did.

Lena sank into one of the leather armchairs and rubbed her gritty eyes with her fists as she fought back waves of despair. Had she done the right thing? The boy was alive. It was the right thing, it had to be. The right thing didn't feel noble, benevolent, or righteous. It felt horrible.

Lena was standing on the edge of a cliff as the ground crumbled beneath her feet, seconds before she plummeted. There wasn't a thing to do to stop it.

The only thing left was the fall.

32

JACKSON CROSS
DAY EIGHTY-SEVEN

The late afternoon slanted through the trees, gilding the vehicles sitting like inert humps in driveways, clotting the empty streets of downtown Munising.

Piled trash bags littered the sidewalk, many knocked over, the bags split and trash strewn across the road. Wood planks boarded the windows of several houses. The distinct stench of sewage permeated the air.

Here in town, folks were on public sewage and water, not septic or well systems like the rural areas. People dug latrine pits in their backyards and used trash cans as rain catchment systems. A few people continued using the toilets until sewage backed up into their houses; the smell contaminated the entire neighborhood.

Jackson made a mental note to return with deputies to clean up the street and instruct residents on the importance of hygiene and sanitation before their kids got sick.

Gideon Crawford's neighbors had reported an armed robbery to the sheriff's office that morning. Kevin and his wife, Rosa, had been robbed at gunpoint by a teenager claiming he needed food to feed his younger siblings. In their sixties, Kevin and Rosa weren't fit to fight back. The robber took everything they had, down to their last can of green beans.

Much as hunting down Sykes consumed him, he couldn't ignore the increasing crime besieging their community. He had a dozen officers checking the deer trail cameras. The listening posts weren't activated until nightfall.

A scream rent the air.

Adrenaline kicked Jackson's chest. He drew his sidearm and bounded up the steps to the dental building on Main Street and banged on the door with his elbow. "This is the sheriff! Open up!"

The door flung open. Gideon Crawford glared at him. Built like a linebacker, he'd lost weight, but his barrel chest, broad shoulders, and large meaty hands were still formidable. Years of alcohol abuse had aged him. He looked tired, bitter, and angry.

"I'm with a patient. What the hell do you want?"

Jackson attempted to peer behind him. "I heard a scream."

"You try pulling teeth without lidocaine or nitrous oxide."

Behind Gideon, Jackson glimpsed a messy reception area and a doorway leading to an exam room, a dental chair in the center next to a metal tray with stainless steel instruments laid across it—cotton, pliers, periosteal elevator, extraction forceps, and suture material.

A patient sat in the dental chair. Jackson recognized Fred Combs, a local mechanic, and owner of Combs Auto Body Shop on Adam's Trail. He moaned in pain, his mouth propped open with cotton rolls. He held blood-speckled gauze to his mouth; a few bloody teeth lay on the steel tray.

Gideon glowered at Jackson. His sleek black hair and dark eyes revealed his Native American heritage on his mother's side. "Do you know what pulling teeth feels like without anesthesia? Not pleasant. For me or the patient. That's what I'm reduced to. I'm out of lidocaine, filling materials, and fluoride. No power to run the dental drill or use the CBCT machine. I can still use a scaler to scrape plaque, but that's about it. That, and pull infected teeth."

Instinctively, Jackson touched his jaw and shuddered.

"Don't forget, a tooth infection can allow bacteria to enter the bloodstream, leading to sepsis, shock, and death. So don't wait if you've got a toothache. And make sure you're brushing and flossing. As long as we have toothpaste, anyway. You can use baking soda mixed with water as toothpaste or make a paste out of coconut oil and bentonite clay with peppermint drops for taste."

"Good to know," Jackson said.

Gideon regarded him like an aggravating cockroach he wished he could squish with his shoe. At least Gideon didn't look sloshed for once. He spent most of his days half-drunk.

"We need your help identifying a victim."

Gideon scoffed. "If I recall, last time we talked, you accused me of being a serial killer."

"I didn't accuse you of anything. We cleared you."

"Don't expect any thanks from me."

Gideon had helped them identify one of Cyrus Lee Jefferson's victims utilizing forensic dentistry. He'd also been a suspect in both Lily's death and Elice McNeely's. Though he'd been cleared, Jackson still had his suspicions. As Lily's jilted lover, he'd had the most obvious motive.

There was little love lost between them, of that Jackson was certain.

Gideon stared at him, bristling with resentment. "I'm incredibly busy."

"So am I." He had a list of things to do as long as his arm: several burglary cases to follow up on, another dead body, apparently heatstroke, and an altercation at the checkpoint on I-94 by Alger Falls where the sentry and a resident came to blows. The citizen volunteers needed better training.

The danger Darius Sykes posed to his community, and Lena and Shiloh, weighed heavily on him. So did Lena's insulin. He'd put out feelers with his old network of CI informants and sent deputies to Marquette and the Soo to see about medical supply shipments. They'd returned empty-handed.

Gideon sighed. "I heard you're deputizing citizen volunteers."

Jackson didn't trust Gideon as far as he could throw him, but beggars couldn't be choosers. They needed his expertise, but Jackson harbored an ulterior motive, a suspicion that had been niggling at the back of his mind, growing stronger with every passing day. "We sure could use your help to protect the county. You're strong and skilled with a gun, and your forensic dental expertise is invaluable for the identification of potential victims, especially now that we're out a medical examiner."

Before Gideon could answer, a moan came from behind him. "I'm hurting over here while my dentist is busy blowing smoke up the sheriff's rear end!" Fred yelled in a muffled, nasally voice. "I'm bleedin' through near every orifice I have! And it ain't pretty!"

"I'll be right there, Fred." Gideon narrowed his eyes. "Yeah fine, I'll help, but not because I owe you anything or even like you. Let's get that straight."

"It's straight."

"Perfect." Gideon Crawford slammed the door in his face.

33

ELI POPE
DAY EIGHTY-EIGHT

Eli moved light and fleet-footed through the dappled shadows of dense trees lining the Munising Tourist Park Campground west of the ferry service buildings in Munising.

Minutes before, the man he sought had beached his motorboat on the sand. He'd come from Grand Island—Sawyer's fortress.

Eli had been expecting him. His target had a weakness for the U.P. delicacy known as pasties. The only place still making them in Alger County was Falling Rock Café. Eli had known Antoine would eventually desert the fortress for his fix.

He'd needed to do a snatch and grab with zero satellite or drone footage, no technical overwatch, no recon team to conduct surveillance or HUMINT—human intelligence or assets on the ground, other than a gang of hungry, scrappy teenagers.

Since Eli couldn't recon Grand Island 24/7 himself, he'd paid several teenagers to keep an eye on things. He'd worked with what he had. In exchange, he'd had to give up his Biolite camping stove, which charged small electronic devices by burning kindling. The kids wanted to charge their phones and listen to their downloaded music.

It had taken well over a week, but he'd finally hit pay dirt.

He'd just completed his ten-mile run weighted with full gear when one of the kids reached him with the news—his target was on the move.

Eli stepped out of the shadows. "Don't move."

With a startled curse, Antoine Toussaint spun, reaching for the FAMAS 5.56 x 45mm NATO rifle slung across his back. Used in the French Legion Army, Antoine affectionately called his weapon "the bugle" for its distinctive shape.

"I wouldn't," Eli said, calm and measured, his VP9 aimed between Antoine's bushy eyebrows. He wouldn't miss; Antoine knew it.

The Frenchman glowered at him, glowered at the gun, then glowered at him again. "It's you," he hissed with a faint accent.

In his thirties, the former French Legionnaire was powerfully built with short light-brown hair, a thick bristly beard, and squinty eyes. He'd been working as a security contractor for Sawyer's criminal enterprises for a decade and had a reputation for boldness in battle, taking reckless risks and winning, and running into combat with a bloodthirsty grin plastered on his face.

"You going to kill me now, brother?" Antoine asked, guilt etched across his face.

Eli recalled the battle against the Côté cartel when Eli had saved Antoine's life. Antoine had repaid Eli's loyalty by shoving a burlap bag over his head and relinquishing him to Sawyer. "That depends on you, *brother*."

"You've been following me."

"I could've killed you a dozen different times."

"I seriously doubt that."

"I could've crept up and slit your throat while you were pissing against the birch tree five minutes ago. Snoopy boxers, huh?"

Antoine reddened like an overripe tomato. "Now you're just bragging."

"Weapon on the ground, on your knees, hands laced on your head."

"Come on, man—"

"Fine. Then take off your belt, drop your pants, and kneel in those cute boxers."

Antoine cursed.

"Your choice."

Glaring at him, Antoine obeyed.

Eli lowered the pistol a few degrees. He took a steadying breath to calm his nerves, to push out his constant, consuming worry for Lena and his daughter. "I need to talk to you."

"Sawyer wants your head on a platter."

"I'm aware." Eli pursed his lips. "I need some intel. You're the only one in Sawyer's crew that I trust enough to give it to me straight without running to Sawyer or shooting me in the back."

"Don't count your chickens before they're hatched," Antoine muttered with a dour expression.

Eli kept very still. He projected an easy calm, a man utterly confident, but his heart stuttered, his nerves raw. He needed Antoine far more than he could let on. "How are things on the island?"

"Fine," Antoine said. "Not enough women and too many sweaty, unwashed, horny men for my taste. It's kinda claustrophobic if the truth be told. I miss my old life, playing poker with the guys, fishing with my dad, and even my dead-end job at the bank. There's something to be said for ease and predictability. You hate it until you don't have it. Know what I mean?"

"Half the world knows what you mean."

"You're gonna tell me I owe you."

"I don't have to tell you jack squat. You already know."

Antoine made a face like he'd taken a bite of something sour. "You're putting me between a rock and a hard place. I got no personal hard feelings toward you. The opposite, actually. But the boss man who provides shelter over my head and food on my plate says otherwise."

"He doesn't have to know. Nobody has to know unless you open your big mouth and tell them. That's up to you."

Antoine sighed, resigned to his fate. "What do you want?"

"I need black market medication."

"Sawyer's got plenty. Prescription medication demand is sky-high. No one's manufacturing anything and FEMA quit delivering. People will pay any price, anything, for their heart meds."

"They want to stay alive."

"Guess so. What do you need specifically?"

"Insulin."

Antoine frowned. "Someone you love has diabetes."

Eli didn't bother to answer.

Antoine shook his head. "You've got it bad."

"Answer the question."

"It's better to be alone. When you've got something to love, you've got something to lose. This broken world will keep taking and taking. People starving, dying of diseases and accidents, no health care, no one to keep the monsters in check."

"There is."

"There is what?"

"Someone to keep the monsters in check," Eli said. "Me."

"We're all becoming monsters, man."

"I don't need a philosophical discussion, Antoine. I need information."

"Sawyer doesn't have insulin. Not a drop. Without his source, Cyrus Lee Jefferson, around anymore, his supplies have dried up like everyone else's."

Eli believed him. He had no reason to lie. Sawyer's black market drug trade had been Eli's last best hope.

A flicker passed over the man's features. His mouth tightened, his eyes darting sideways; it was a tell. Eli caught the micro-expression—Antoine knew something, something he wasn't keen on sharing.

"What is it?" Eli asked.

Antoine didn't answer.

"You do owe me. If you have an ounce of moral fiber, pay that debt now. The price is cheap. I only need information."

"It's more expensive than you think," Antoine muttered.

"Tell me."

He shrugged. "It's your funeral."

Eli surged forward and raised his gun. "Antoine, so help me—"

Antoine threw up his hands. "Hey! Easy!"

Eli had no patience left. He hummed with fear, dread, and anger, emotions he knew intimately. He aimed the pistol at Antoine's temple.

Antoine's eyes widened. Eli wouldn't hesitate to squeeze the trigger and Antoine knew it. Anyone who got in the way of protecting the ones he loved was fair game. "Don't make me."

"Okay, okay!"

Eli waited.

"There's a train."

"What train?"

"A train of supplies: medications, Penicillin, antibiotics, Chlorpromazine, Prozac, Morphine, Methadone, Oxy, and Vicodin. Every pill is worth more than gold, more than food."

Eli's mind whirred. A thousand thoughts spin-cycling through his brain in a microsecond. "Where is it coming from and where is it going?"

"They've got an old engine with steam or coal or something to run it. The route loops from the Soo across the U.P. down through Escanaba. There's a branch that heads up to Copper Harbor, while the main line runs west to Wisconsin, curves south, and hits Green Bay before terminating in Duluth, Minnesota."

"Where did the supplies come from?"

"A freighter loaded with FEMA medical supplies from the feds, apparently sourced from South America and Australia, where they still have power. It originated in the Atlantic through the St. Lawrence River, through Lake Ontario, Erie, and Huron before reaching the Soo. They can charge a mint for whatever they export. I suppose the fed's dollars still count for something, though up here, they're only good for toilet paper."

"WHEN, damn it!"

"August third."

Eli made a silent calculation in his head. His heart sank. "That's tomorrow."

"Hell, I didn't even know it was August yet."

Eli studied him and checked for signs of deception: profuse sweating, an eye twitch, the quiver of a hand, or the tightening of the mouth. There was nothing. "How'd you hear about this? Who told you? Is the source reliable?"

"One of Sawyer's assets in Sault Ste. Marie. My asset, really. My second cousin. He works at the Soo Locks on the docks, which are still functional since they're gravity fed. He saw the crates being unloaded. There's a large contingent of the National Guard protecting the Locks, though the Côté Cartel has staged small-scale attacks on the Locks, stealing shipments and sinking smaller ships. One of the soldiers told him where the train was headed. FEMA is skipping over us hillbilly hicks and dispersing supplies in Green Bay, Detroit, Duluth, and Chicago as if the city slickers deserve it more than we do."

Eli made the calculations. It didn't come out to a palatable equation, no matter how he looked at it. Attacking a train guarded by the U.S. military meant harming fellow Americans, the good guys, and his brothers in arms.

Could they ambush the train without taking innocent lives? Was it possible? Could they afford not to risk it?

"Why the hell didn't you lead with that?"

Antoine shot him a rueful look. "Didn't think you'd actually consider attacking an armed train."

"I'm not considering it."

Antoine sagged in relief.

"I'm going to do it."

Antoine let out a string of colorful curses in French. Several startled robins took flight from a nearby tree, their wings beating the air. "Hell, even Sawyer isn't that crazy. He knows a losing gambit when he sees one. But if you're desperate for insulin..."

Eli lowered his pistol. The weapon felt incredibly heavy in his hands. "She has less than two weeks."

"I'm sorry, man. I truly am."

"I have to do something."

"It's probably a suicide mission."

"I've survived suicide missions before."

"If anyone can hijack a federally protected train, it would be you, my friend. I've seen you fight."

Eli had no desire to harm soldiers or federal agents. He wasn't leaving Lena to die, either. There had to be a way; he needed to figure it out. He only had a day to do it.

"Keep this to yourself, or I'll hunt you down and skin you alive."

"Goes without saying, my friend." Antoine glanced at his mechanical watch. "I'm supposed to be back on the island in thirty minutes. I've still got to make it to Annelise Anders' to get one of her pasties before she closes the shop. It's the only thing in life I got left to look forward to. Don't deny a man his small pleasures."

Eli gestured with his pistol for Antoine to stand and retrieve his rifle. "Wouldn't dream of it."

Antoine grinned. "Let's do this again sometime."

"Let's not and say we did."

"Fair warning, though. Next time you sneak up on me like that, I will have to kill you. A man's got his pride."

Despite the circumstances, Eli's lips twitched. He'd always liked Antoine. His affection for the Frenchman had only grown with time. "You can try."

The odds were grim. But when had the odds ever been in his favor? He didn't think of the risk to his own life; it didn't matter to him. He thought only of Lena and Shiloh.

For them, he would do anything.

34

JACKSON CROSS
DAY EIGHTY-NINE

"What do you want, Jackson?" Horatio asked.

His father stood on the front steps of the porch, blocking Jackson's entrance into the house, his features hard and sharp as a knife's edge. Insects buzzed in the grass. The steady beat of waves crashed against the base of the bluff behind the house.

"I'm concerned about Mother."

"She's sleeping."

"She's hardly eating. She's wasting away."

"I'm taking care of my wife. It's a little late to start thinking of your family," Horatio said coldly.

"She's confused, dazed, and out of it. I'm worried."

Horatio did not move from the doorway. "She's fine."

Cool air from the air conditioner inside the house caressed Jackson's skin. Outside, heat shimmered from the brick walkway in waves. The sun beat down on him like a malignant force attempting to melt his flesh from his bones. The breeze off the lake offered little relief.

"Her memory is impaired. She said things that don't make sense. She talked about Garrett, and she mentioned Astrid's accident. What is she talking about?"

"I don't have the faintest idea. Patients suffering from dementia have an altered sense of reality."

"She doesn't have dementia."

"Stress-induced," Horatio said without missing a beat. "She's been declining for months. You've been too self-absorbed to notice."

The familiar sting of his father's words struck him like a slap. He stiffened, steeling himself against the blows that would keep coming. "She was incredibly upset."

Horatio narrowed his eyes. "Which is why I keep her calm and sedated. It's critical to her health and continued well-being. She gets worked up whenever you're around. Seems you have that effect on people."

As a child, it had been devastating, that wretched yearning for the thing he would never have. A slow-burning anger singed his skin. At his father. At himself.

Jackson mopped sweat from his forehead with a damp hand-kerchief. He wore a cooling neck bandana, along with a Wolverines baseball hat to shield his face. Temperatures had soared into the nineties with full humidity, breaking records for the Upper Peninsula left and right.

In the last two days, he'd responded to three calls of heatstroke. A man in his eighties had succumbed. A ten-year-old girl had wandered around her backyard, naked and hallucinating, yanking up handfuls of dry cracked grass and eating it to fill her empty belly.

The horrible sight was seared into his brain. More would come.

Chief McCallister had written up heatstroke prevention guidelines, made photocopies with Jackson's portable solar generator, and sent out volunteers to knock on doors and spread the word.

Lori and Tim had organized the kids and taught them to make cooling neck bandanas, which the volunteers passed out to the young and elderly. The cotton fabric was sewn with water beads or crystals they'd scavenged from craft and hobby stores. When dunked in water, the beads expanded; the water evaporated over several hours and cooled the blood flowing through the carotid artery in the neck, which helped cool the whole body.

Jackson returned his attention to his father. "Lena is almost out of insulin. We've been looking everywhere and can't find any. Do you know where I could source some? It's important."

His father stared at him impassively. "No, I do not."

"You've procured antidepressants for Astrid and sedatives for Mother."

Horatio said nothing.

Jackson had zero desire to be indebted to his father for anything, but for Lena, he was desperate enough to do almost anything. "I would owe you."

Horatio gave a harsh bark of laughter. "You already do."

"Your years as a sheriff have given you access to some unsavory resources—"

"I'm going to ignore your unseemly insinuations, son. No one I know has insulin, Jackson. No one."

Jackson nodded heavily; he'd expected as much. Still, he'd had to cover his bases. Against his better judgment, a question formed in his mind, the question he hadn't dared to ask but he could no longer hold back.

As a law officer, he knew better. He would never confront a suspect without evidence in hand to trap the suspect with his own words. He had no evidence, only an accusation from Underwood and a dark suspicion he despised himself for entertaining.

But as a son, he couldn't help himself. He had to know. He had to ask, had to see the answer in his father's eyes.

"Were you dirty?" Jackson asked. "Are you dirty?"

Horatio froze. "How dare you ask me that?"

"Underwood said you were corrupt."

"Bradley Underwood is a simpering coward who can't bear to face that he's barely a man, let alone a competent officer of the law. He was no cop. He was a bureaucrat with no talent for the hunt, only an inane ability to brownnose the right asses in power."

Horatio could have been speaking of himself, but Jackson chose not to point out the similarities. "You're saying he's lying."

"Of course I am."

Jackson didn't detect deception in his father's words or demeanor, but then, he seldom did. His father was impenetrable as a brick wall. He knew he should stop, that this path led nowhere good. He wanted to believe his father, this man who had stood for honor and justice his entire childhood.

"As sheriff, were you crooked? Did you make deals under the table, maybe turn a blind eye to criminals who paid the right price?"

"No. I'm frankly insulted that you would even ask me such a thing." Horatio sneered. "And besides, you're one to talk, aren't you?"

Jackson flinched as the arrow landed. He could not afford to show weakness. To his father, weakness was a sign of blood in the water. "I've made peace with what I've done. I'm making restitution."

"Restitution? Is that what you call it? Or cowardice?"

Jackson said nothing, but he did not drop his eyes beneath his father's scathing gaze.

"Don't forget I own you!" Horatio jabbed at Jackson's chest with his finger, his voice rising, a crack in his iron control revealing itself. "I'm the one who owns you, body and soul. I am the one who promoted you from bungling deputy to undersheriff of Alger County. I am the kingmaker who placed you in your current role, *Sheriff Cross*."

"I am good at my job," Jackson said quietly. "Is that what you're afraid of?"

"Watch your step, son. You need to be very careful what you say and do next." A flicker of rage shimmered behind those icy eyes. His mouth thinned into a bloodless line as he shook his head in disgust. "Sometimes I wonder how things would have turned out if you were the one who disappeared, if your brother were here instead."

Jackson recoiled. A low thrumming dread started at the back of his neck and spread through his limbs, his arms and legs, his fingers. That familiar wriggling shame filled him, a gnawing unworthiness. His father had always made him feel diminished.

"You are no longer welcome here." His spine straight, Horatio shut the screen door, withdrew into his palatial estate, and turned his back on Jackson.

Jackson forced his watery legs to move as he turned and walked down the driveway. He hadn't gotten the answers he wanted, only more questions. He'd known his father would never tell him the truth, not without evidence, and he'd confronted him anyway.

Maybe he *was* speaking the truth. Maybe Jackson had made a terrible mistake, alienating his own family in the process.

The radio crackled. "Boss!" Devon said. "I'm at the Inn with Eli. He has an informant who claims there's a shipment of meds headed west on the Canadian National Railway. On a train."

Jackson stilled. "Did you say a train?"

"Eli's source says there's insulin."

His breath snagged in his throat. "Are you certain?"

"We got our miracle, boss, but there's a catch."

"What is it?"

"The freight train is under federal jurisdiction. The feds are prioritizing large population centers versus rural areas. The train isn't stopping here or anywhere in the U.P. The train will go right past us, and we won't get any of it."

Jackson cursed.

"Eli wants us to go after it."

Jackson didn't hesitate. "So do I."

"Problem is, the shipment is FEMA's, so the train is protected by National Guardsmen."

"Oh, hell."

"My sentiment exactly. The train will head through Escanaba tomorrow night. We've got a narrow window of time to act. So—"

"I'm coming to you right now."

Jackson ended the radio call and glanced back up at the house. To his surprise, his father stood ten feet away, staring at him with an inscrutable expression. He had surreptitiously followed Jackson down the driveway while his back was turned.

Jackson steeled himself. His hands clenched into fists at his sides. "If you're hiding something, I will find it."

For a second, astonishment flared in Horatio's eyes. And a flash of something behind the anger and derision—was it fear, or something else?

Before his father could respond, Jackson spun on his heel and hurried toward his bike. The dark hum of dread in the back of his mind grew louder. Cyrus Lee's ugly words echoed in his mind: *you're blind. You've always been blind.*

He couldn't think of any of that now. They'd found insulin.

It was time to save Lena.

35

ELI POPE
DAY EIGHTY-NINE

E li sensed the threat before he heard it. Something crept through the underbrush to his rear, lurking in the darkness, stalking him.

His heart rate accelerated, adrenaline spiking through his veins. He spun, drew his pistol, and aimed at shadows.

It was 10:30 p.m. He had left the Northwoods Inn on foot and headed to the spot where he'd hidden his 4x4 in a hide along the southeastern perimeter of the Northwoods property. After dinner with Lena and Shiloh, he'd checked the Inn's security before conducting weapons training with a dozen recent recruits.

Afterward, he'd jogged ten miles with his forty-pound pack to keep himself in peak physical condition. Shiloh had gone with him. She'd made it six miles. Last time, it had been five.

Now, he was headed to the Sheriff's Office in Munising to meet with Jackson and his team to plan an operation to ambush the train.

Though the sun had set, the heat hadn't broken. Sweat beaded his forehead and collected beneath his armpits, humidity clung stickily to his skin, and mosquitos the size of swallows swarmed around him.

Moonlight gilded the street and empty houses, the massive oak trees standing tall and silent. Everything was still. Nothing moved but those damn mosquitos.

Eli squinted, his finger itching the trigger guard. The hairs on the back of his neck rose. There, at his nine o'clock, was the slightest flutter of a leaf.

"If you don't want to be turned into Swiss cheese in the next three seconds, I suggest you come out now."

"We're friendlies," said a familiar voice in a French accent. "Don't shoot."

Two figures emerged from the darkness twenty yards to the northeast.

Eli aimed his pistol at them. "Not another step."

Antoine offered a wide grin visible through his beard. He wore camo pants and a hunter green T-shirt, "the bugle" hanging on a sling across his chest. "Long time no see, brother."

A woman in her late twenties stood beside him. Her name was Natalia Reyes, but everyone called her Nyx, the Greek goddess of the night, and for good reason.

She had a combat knife strapped to her left thigh over black leggings, a revolver strapped to her right thigh, and a bandolier outfitted with shotgun shells slung across her chest. A Mossberg 500 shotgun hung from a sling on her shoulder.

He motioned with his chin. "Weapons out and on the ground."

Antoine groaned. "Come on, man—"

"Now."

"Hold your damn horses. We're doing it." Nyx raised both hands, palms out in surrender, and lowered to her knees. She unslung her shotgun and set it on the ground in front of her.

Antoine followed her lead, groaning as his knees popped in complaint. "I'm too old for this."

"You're not even thirty. How about that revolver, Nyx?"

With great reluctance and several muttered curses, the revolver was placed next to the rifle. The long sleek barrel glinted in the faint moonlight, the wood butt polished and worn smooth as silk.

A Smith & Wesson Model 29, famously used by Clint Eastwood in the *Dirty Harry* movies, the .44 magnum six-shooter was accurate, firing fast in double action or more precisely in single action, not to mention it looked beautifully lethal and intimidating.

Nyx saw his admiring glance. "Try stealing it and see what happens. I've carved out men's eyeballs for less. My granddaddy gave me this, may he rest in peace. It's mine."

"Wouldn't dream of it." He gestured with the VP9. "Knives out, too. I know you keep a Smith and Wesson three-inch carbon blade in your boot, Nyx."

"Damn it all to hell." She shot him a crooked scowl but complied. Her white-blonde hair was buzzed close to her scalp, which emphasized her feline cheekbones and symmetrical features. She managed to be muscular and feminine, her strength accentuating her beauty.

Satisfied that his captives were weapons-free, Eli lowered his pistol a fraction. "Why are you following me?"

"We're not following you," Antoine said. "Can I stand up now?"

"No. And that's a stinking load of B.S. if I ever heard it. Lie again and I put a bullet through your teeth. Try telling tall tales with enamel splintering your tongue."

Antoine rolled his eyes. "I came back to talk to you earlier, but you were ensconced in that Northwoods enclave. They've got a decent security team going over there."

"I know. I'm training them."

"It's not like we can walk up to the front gate and ask for you, can we? We'll be arrested for crimes against the state, or maybe Jackson won't bother—he'll just execute us. We're not exactly buddies with local law enforcement."

"It's true. Jackson has your faces on wanted posters all over town."

Nyx perked up. "What's the reward?"

"A roll of toilet paper," Eli quipped.

"I'll take it," Antoine said.

Nyx made a face. "How disappointing. I bet we can do better."

Eli relaxed slightly and loosened his shoulders, acting as though he'd let his guard down when he'd done anything but.

He liked Antoine, even respected him. They'd survived a wildly dangerous Hail Mary mission together and come out on top. That didn't mean he trusted him as far as he could throw him.

Nyx was cunning and tough. Unlike Antoine, who was bold, brash, and good-humored even in a foxhole, Nyx was a hunter. Stealthy and observant, she could sneak up on anyone and put a dagger in a man's heart before he heard a furtive footstep. She was also an ace shot.

He couldn't read her and that worried him. In Sawyer's camp, she was a chameleon, altering herself to suit her environment as easily as opting for a new hat.

Antoine said, "We've been waiting hours for you."

"Why?"

Nyx looked up at him, half her face obscured in heavy shadow as a raft of clouds slid across the moon. "Antoine told me what you're doing. You need help."

"I don't need a damn thing from Sawyer."

"You do from us."

"Not the way I see it."

"I already gave you help, brother," Antoine reminded him. "You wouldn't know about the train if not for me."

"What train?" Eli deadpanned.

"Come on, the train you're planning to ambush tomorrow night. The one chock-full of party supplies."

Eli stared at them blankly. "I have no clue what you're gibbering on about."

"Cut the act, Eli. We're serious. Why do you think we're submitting to your gun in our faces? For funsies? 'Cause I can tell you, this part is far from fun."

"You want to help," Eli said, incredulous.

"He's got major wax in his ears," Nyx muttered.

"What's the catch?"

"No catch."

"Sawyer always has strings."

"Sawyer didn't send us," Nyx said. "We came on our own."

"Does he know you're here?"

"No," Antoine said. "We got someone to cover for us at the fortress. We'll handle Sawyer if it comes to that."

"He'll kill you if he finds out."

"He won't find out," Nyx said.

"You sure about that?" Eli asked.

Antoine and Nyx exchanged a weighted look. Eli was terrible at relational cues, but he sensed something between them, an intimacy he hadn't noticed back on Grand Island. Were they colluding, plotting to backstab him? Or was it something else, something less menacing?

"He's our problem," Antoine said. "Not yours."

"Why would you abandon a sweet gig with all the food and supplies you need? You've got water, food, security, and a brotherhood."

Nyx raised her chin. "Grand Island isn't all rainbows and sunshine. Sawyer's getting paranoid, suspicious, and controlling. Ever since we stole those weapons from the Côté cartel, he's looking over his shoulder every second, expecting a bomb to drop from the sky or a sub to launch a missile from the middle of Superior and obliterate his little fortress."

"It wasn't the brotherhood we thought it'd be," Antoine said quietly. "I won't pretend to be something I'm not. I'm a mercenary for hire. I knew Sawyer was a drug kingpin when he brought me in, and I was okay with that, but the world going to hell in a handbasket has changed things. The end of life as we know it alters a man's priorities."

Eli was torn. Doubt wormed inside him. He needed to trust his team one hundred percent. On the other hand, the weapons and combat expertise these two brought to the table added huge value to this mission and any future battles. In addition, their intel about the goings on at Sawyer's compound could prove invaluable.

Nyx bit her lower lip. A hint of vulnerability flashed across her features, softening her hard expression. "Those meds can help us. My grandmother lives up in Grand Marias. She has heart disease. She ran out of her beta blockers a week ago. She raised me, her and Grandpops, but Pops is dead. I owe her. If Sawyer got those meds first, he'd charge a bounty no regular person could afford. If you're willing to share, I'll fight with you."

"We would share," Eli said.

"You want Nyx on your side. Even if you don't want me for what I did on the island..." He cleared his throat with a guilty expression. "Nyx has military experience. She has training in intelligence and weapons. Graduated both Army and Marine sniper schools."

Nyx straightened her spine and grinned. "I'm damn good, too."

"Then what happened?"

"Come again?"

"How the hell did you fall so far? From a skilled soldier to a glorified bodyguard for a drug kingpin."

Her jaw clenched, anger in her eyes, but she kept her gaze steady. "Four years ago, I was an Army SF sergeant working in Afghanistan. An officer blatantly caused a friendly fire incident that could have—should have—been avoided. He was trigger-happy, careless, and lacking discipline. A civilian mother and her six-year-old son were casualties. I got pissed and headbutted my superior officer. Dropped him, too. The Army didn't look kindly on that."

"You were dishonorably discharged."

She nodded.

"And now here you are, part of a criminal organization that peddles drugs to children."

Her eyes flashed again. "It's not the same. Mercenary work pays the bills. I do what I need to do to survive."

"And when survival requires you to turn on your teammates?"

"I have a code I choose to live by. That's part of why I'm coming to you. My morals may be grayer than most, but I do have a line."

The Hope We Keep

Eli considered her words. At least she was honest. That meant something.

He had his misgivings. He could despise Antoine for throwing him to the wolves and Nyx for standing by—or he could move on.

He thought unbidden of the boy he'd killed in the bowels of the *Risky Business*. Guilt ate at him. He pushed it down somewhere deep and dark.

Antoine and Nyx had survived. So had Eli.

The truth was that they desperately needed the fighters. Two skilled soldiers increased their odds of commandeering the meds exponentially, the meds that would save the life of the woman he loved.

In the end, was it even a choice?

The pistol still aimed at his prisoners, with his free hand, he swiped his phone from his back pocket and snapped a few pictures with the camera app. Phones were mostly paperweights these days, but they had their uses, which is why he kept his charged with a solar charger.

"What was that for?" Nyx demanded.

"You turn on us, and I'm handing these photos to Sawyer. I'll tell him you're joining deputies on raids. I'm sure he'll understand."

Nyx's mouth puckered like she was sucking on a lemon. She looked about to say something rude, but Antoine spoke first. "We're risking a lot, doing this."

"And we're risking a lot if we take you in. I'm sure you understand *our* risk. You could betray us. You're exposing us to Sawyer's wrath. He's not going to take two of his best soldiers defecting lying down."

Nyx said, "Yeah, we get it."

He slipped the phone into his pocket. "This isn't a one-time thing, and you go back to Sawyer afterward with your spoils. If you switch sides, you stay switched."

Nyx and Antoine exchanged another wary glance. Whole

conversations passed between them that Eli couldn't read. Nyx gave an almost imperceptible nod.

"We know," Antoine said.

"My team of deputies and cops are good, but they aren't operators. They don't understand operational security and have never held a security clearance. No matter what I say, someone is going to spill the beans that you defected. They'll tell their mom, their wife, or their best friend's brother. It makes for great gossip, and it will get out. If you go back to the island, the chance of being caught and tortured is high. We'll give you as little intel as possible about our organization and resources, but simply joining this operation will give you intel on us that would be incredibly valuable to Sawyer."

"We're in," Nyx said. "For good."

There was a beat of tense silence.

"Okay," Eli said.

Antoine brightened. "Okay? We're good?"

"As long as you keep your word."

Nyx holstered her revolver, retrieved her knife, and ankle pistol, and stood. "What about the others? The cops. Will they accept us?"

"You'll have to convince them."

"Piece of cake." Antoine jumped to his feet and pumped his fist with great enthusiasm. "It's good to be back! Pope and Toussaint strike again!"

Eli couldn't help himself; warmth sprouted in his chest and spread through his torso, a strange but not unwanted feeling. A faint twitch tugged at his lips. "Don't start thinking we're friends."

A broad grin spread across the former Legionnaire's face. "Wouldn't dream of it, brother."

36

ELI POPE
DAY NINETY

The team gathered before midnight. Eli cleaned his HK417 with the twelve-inch barrel and nightscope. A stack of 7.62x51mm NATO ammunition and empty magazines waited to be filled on the folding table beside him.

Next to the stack of ammo was a nest of radio equipment and headsets, a stack of armored vests and plates, and an array of pistols, revolvers, and long guns. He'd already disassembled, cleaned, and reassembled his other weapons.

The door to the conference room opened, and two people sauntered in, grim and armed to the teeth.

A shocked silence descended over the sheriff's office conference room. Officers exchanged wary looks and stared at the newcomers in alarm.

Nyx and Antoine glared back in open hostility.

"Hello to you, too," Nyx drawled.

"What the hell is this?" Hart cried.

"They're traitors," Moreno spat.

"Watch who you're insulting," Nyx snapped back. "You might just find yourself with a broken nose or worse."

Jackson raised a hand and stepped between the law officers and the newcomers. "Everybody take a breath."

"Took you long enough," Eli said.

"You *invited* them here?" Alexis sputtered.

Hart went to draw his weapon. "Oh, hell no."

Eli had briefly considered inventing covers for Antoine and Nyx to deceive the deputies and police officers but swiftly dismissed the idea. A French Legionnaire and a beautiful Black-water-type mercenary weren't exactly gray men. They both had notorious reputations.

"They're with us now," he said simply.

Nash crossed his arms with a scowl. "They work for Sawyer."

"Not anymore," Nyx said.

"They'll put a bullet in our spines the second one of us turns around," Alexis said.

"They won't," Eli said. "They're solid."

Jackson moved to the front of the room. His voice was steely with no give in his posture or his expression. "If Eli says they're solid, then they're solid. We need the manpower, and these two are ex-military. They add a level of skill and tactical experience that we sorely need."

"You're going to pardon their crimes? Is that what we're doing now, Cross?" Chief McCallister looked at Jackson in disbelief. "Joining up with killers and drug dealers?"

"No one's crimes are being absolved."

Hart scoffed. "There's no way I'm fighting side by side with criminals. With killers! Sawyer's people killed Charlie. They shot me in the leg! Have you lost your freaking minds?"

McCallister's posture stiffened, with one hand resting on the butt of her service pistol, the other curled into a fist at her side. Charlie Payne had been her officer. The loss was personal—Eli could see the resentment written across her face.

"We defected," Antoine drawled. He alone remained calm. Nyx was scowling like she was about to headbutt somebody. Eli tightened his grip on his VP9; this was not how he wanted things to go down, but he'd expected the distrust and animosity.

McCallister shook her head, appalled. "How do we know

they'll follow orders and won't turn on us halfway through the mission?"

"Because if they disobey a single letter of an order, I'll drag them to Sawyer myself," Jackson said. "Sawyer will behead them for their betrayal. They understand the risks—and the consequences."

McCallister returned Nyx's stare, not in the least bit cowed. "People like you are the reason we're in this mess in the first place."

Nyx took a step toward her. "What's that supposed to mean?"

Antoine laid a steadying hand on Nyx's forearm. She flinched but didn't draw back. She clenched her jaw, nostrils flaring in anger. "We said we're good. And we are. You don't trust us? Fine. We'll leave. We're not here to be insulted. You don't think you need what we bring to the table? It's your funeral."

"Chief," Jackson said. "We've got to work together on this."

McCallister frowned. "I don't like this at all."

"No one cares if you like it," Eli said. "This is what's happening."

"Chief," Moreno said tightly. "Eli and Jackson are right. Much as I hate the idea, we need them to pull this off."

"Please stand down, McCallister," Jackson said.

The tension was palpable. Finally, McCallister's shoulders slumped. She raised a hand in surrender. "This is on you."

"Fine." Jackson was the first to move. He strode across the conference room and thrust out his hand to Antoine. "Glad to have you on board."

After a moment's hesitation, Antoine shook his hand. Nyx stared at McCallister, still disgruntled but no longer oozing hostility. When Jackson offered his hand, she was slow to take it, but she did.

"Good," Jackson said. "Now that's settled, let's get to work then, shall we?"

To Devon's credit, she offered the newcomers the two empty seats next to her, though her expression remained dubious. Reluctantly, Nyx and Antoine sat, with their spines stiff and weapons close, uncomfortable as hell.

Eli didn't need them comfortable, only compliant. "Read them in, Sheriff Cross."

The team consisted of fourteen people: Eli and Jackson, along with Moreno, Devon, Alexis Chilton, the former Marine Jim Hart, the rookie Phil Nash, Police Chief McCallister, and four of her police officers, including Baker and Flores, who had participated in the yacht attack last month, and finally, Nyx and Antoine.

The citizen volunteers Jackson had deputized included Gideon Crawford and Fiona Smith as well as several retired police officers, correctional officers, and former soldiers. They would remain at the checkpoint and patrol locations to protect the county.

Eli touched the St. Michael's medallion next to his dog tags beneath his shirt and thought of David Kepford, the man he'd never met, with a physical ache in his chest.

Jackson turned to an old man standing silently in the back. "Johannes, it's your turn."

In his seventies, Johannes Heikkinen had served as a train engineer before his second career chartering fishing boats for rich downstaters. Tough and grizzled, he wore a hunter-green shirt and cargo pants that hung from his slight frame, a camo bandana tied around his forehead.

Johannes leaned over the wrinkled map spread across the table, wisps of white hair clinging to his liver-spotted pate. "Since the collapse of the mining and timber industries, many of these railways have been abandoned or outright dismantled. The current Canadian National Railway route through the U.P. starts at the Soo where the freighters unload shipping containers onto the railcars. The route heads southwest, following the southern coast of the U.P. along Lake Michigan to Escanaba."

Johannes continued, "From Escanaba, at the mid-south point of the U.P, a branch heads north to Marquette, where the Escanaba and Lake Superior railroad branches off into the small towns near old sawmills or mines, like the Iron Ore Mountain mine. This track heads south into Green Bay, Wisconsin, while this line continues southwest to Duluth, Minnesota."

Jackson said, "Whoever controls the rails controls a means of dispersing goods throughout the Midwest."

Antoine leaned over the map next to Johannes. "According to our intel, the train departs the Soo late afternoon tomorrow. It'll reach Escanaba approximately between nine and ten p.m., tonight. From there, it's headed northwest into Wisconsin to Green Bay. We need to hit it before then."

Eli traced his finger along the Escanaba River, winding northward to the spot where the train crossed the bridge. Henry Wadsworth Longfellow described how the Native American Hiawatha had "crossed the rushing Escanaba" in the famous poem.

An old timber and mining port, the town had a population of around twelve thousand and was located about sixty miles south of Munising on U.S. 41, nestled on the coast of Little Bay de Noc, which opened into Green Bay on Lake Michigan.

Eli did several calculations in his head. He moved his finger slightly south to a railroad spur, asked Johannes a few questions, and got the answers he needed.

He didn't want to conduct an operation within spitting distance of civilians. The freight train also needed to be far enough from the Soo that a QRT, or Quick Reaction Team, couldn't hit them in the middle of the mission.

"North of Escanaba will work," Eli said. "What about security on the freight train? How many Guardsmen?"

"There should be four National Guardsmen and two railroad personnel," Antoine said.

"What are the rules of engagement?" Nyx asked.

Eli said, "We're going to stop the train, overwhelm everyone on board with non-lethal force, then handcuff and blindfold them under guard while we do what we need to do." He shot a warning glance at Nyx and Antoine. "Absolutely no collateral damage. We are not harming American soldiers."

"Got it," they said in unison.

Devon bit her lower lip. "Even if we do this without hurting anyone, if we get these meds, then we're taking it from others who need it. I'm not saying we're not going to do it, but it feels like something we need to acknowledge."

Eli set his jaw. "I'll live with that guilt if it saves the people I care about."

"The government abandoned us," Jackson said. "I understand your hesitancy, but our people deserve to live as much as those in the cities. FEMA can send another shipment. It's not right to simply ignore entire swaths of the country. We'll do everything we can to spread the wealth, I promise."

Grudgingly, Devon nodded.

Johannes cleared his throat. "I don't know what your plan is, but it's practically impossible to stop a train without getting caught. Both the Federal Railroad Administration and the PTC, the Positive Train Control System, have tracking and alarm systems in place for such a thing. Soon as this train stops when it ain't supposed to, government agencies will be alerted, and all hell will be on its way within minutes."

"Not this time," Eli said. "The tracking and safety systems are connected to GPS. For once, the downed satellite and communication systems will help us."

Johannes scratched at his whiskery jowls. "Guess you've got a chance, then."

"We'll take that chance," Nyx said brightly.

"What about fuel?" McCallister asked. "We're critically low on gas. Traveling to Escanaba in several vehicles will completely deplete our stores."

"We can help there," Antoine said. "Sawyer has fuel. We know where he keeps it on the mainland. We can walk right in and take what we want."

McCallister looked dubious, but she nodded.

"How the hell are we going to stop a train?" Moreno asked.

Eli studied the topography, considering the options, playing out the potential scenarios, the pros and cons. An idea began to form in his mind. It was risky, but it could work.

If Antoine's inside man was reliable. *If* there were no surprises. Too many ifs. The uncertainty and unknowns tied Eli's stomach in knots. It felt like going in blind.

As a Ranger on a sanctioned mission, his team would've reenacted the mission dozens of times until they had every move and countermove memorized.

Eli said, "Leave that to me."

37

ELI POPE
DAY NINETY

E li slowed his breathing and his heart rate, entering battle mode. Everything else fell away, even Lena, even Sykes—everything but the operation at hand.

Dressed in his battle gear—dark camo, plated vest, and helmet with headset—he studied the scene through binoculars. Nestled in an overwatch position on a hill, he looked down upon a collection of dilapidated buildings, rusted railcars, and a cluster of train tracks several miles north of the town of Escanaba.

Known as a siding or spur, the area was used to store cars or provide transit—in this case, for an ore mine a half-mile away. The ore mine had ceased production decades before, but the railroad still occasionally used the site to park railcars.

The spur was deserted save for some tank cars and a dozen open hopper cars, now empty, which had been used to carry coal or ore.

An LPG tank car full of liquid propane gas sat on a sidetrack. They'd uncoupled the LPG tank and moved it thirty yards with a switcher, a small engine left in the yard that acted as a tug.

Antoine and Nyx were already proving their value. Not only had they secured additional gasoline for the trip and shaped explosives, but they'd also procured the propane tank from one of Sawyer's depots in Chatham.

As members of Sawyer's inner circle, they'd walked right past security. Sawyer would be pissed as hell when he discovered the theft, but that was a problem for another day.

Two hours earlier, Eli, Antoine, Nyx, and Devon had planted several shaped charges while Eli instructed them on where and how to place the charges for the diversion he'd planned.

Along with other tier-one units, the Seventy-Fifth Rangers Reconnaissance Company had learned this particular procedure. It was part of an intensive training course on neutralizing WMDs and railway response for hazardous materials, in preparation for some clandestine missions in Eastern Europe inspecting old Soviet military storage depots.

It was a simple vent and burn technique to cause a large fire on the tracks which would force the oncoming train to halt. They'd dug a trench to direct the propane to flow away from the other railcars and buildings.

A single mistake and the tank could detonate and explode all at once, destroying not only the trucks, but also incinerating the nearby buildings, potentially leaping to the tree line on either side of the tracks. If that happened, the ensuing forest fire would be devastating.

They would conduct the operation very, very carefully.

A fire wasn't the only way to stop a train without derailing it, but it was the safest method. Using trucks or laying down huge trees to block the tracks might destroy the train and cause major injuries to the Guardsmen onboard.

Eli was adamant—no harm could come to the good guys, even if they were on opposite sides on this mission.

He didn't want to damage the train, either, as it was one of the few methods of transporting goods to people who desperately needed them.

Five miles northeast along the tracks, Johannes and Nash were nested in an overwatch position over a flat stretch of terrain. Nash manned their tactical drone while Johannes was needed to identify the refrigerated intermodal from the drone's images. Out of the forty railcars, only one was refrigerated.

Eli went over the plan for the hundredth time in his mind. Once the train stopped, three teams of three people would breach the train cars, then disarm, cuff, and detain the guardsmen without harming them.

Simultaneously, Eli's team would beeline for the refrigerated intermodal, breach it, and offload the insulin and whatever medications they could take within a seven-to-ten-minute window.

Stacked front to back, the shipping containers' doors couldn't open until they'd been offloaded with a crane, but Eli knew a way around that. In his pack, he carried a blow torch, a battery-operated circular saw, several pry tools, a sledgehammer, and a breaching shotgun along with his H&K rifle.

Nyx and Devon carried backpacks with containers of dry ice in case they needed to exfil on foot without the vehicles and had to keep the meds refrigerated, while the trucks contained Styrofoam containers filled with cold packs.

"This is Echo Five," Nash's voice came through Eli's headset. "Our eyes in the sky have sighted the train."

"Alpha One to Echo Five. Have you sighted the target?"

"Not yet. Still looking. Damn, but this is a long train."

Eli waited for a beat, his pulse thudding in his ears. Mosquitos buzzed around his face. One landed on his forehead. He didn't bother to swat it away. He couldn't see the drone, couldn't see the train. "SITREP?"

"Echo Three to Alpha One," McCallister said into the headset. "I see it. Two miles out."

His heart rate accelerated. He willed himself to stay calm, taking deep slow breaths.

Nothing moved below him. The rows of tracks glinted in the glow of the sunset, the sky ribboned with orange, crimson, and lavender-tinged clouds. The shabby buildings sagged, the shadows lengthening as the sun dipped below the horizon.

"Echo Five, do you have eyes on the target?" he repeated.

Silence for a moment. He didn't dare breathe. If they couldn't locate the refrigerated container quickly, all hell might break loose. Speed was a key component of the entire plan. Every second counted.

His mind raced with all the ways the mission could tip sideways, go pear-shaped—

"Got it!" Nash said. "Johannes ID'd the target. Second to the last car at the end."

Eli exhaled sharply. "Roger that."

"One point five miles," McCallister said.

Eli swung his binoculars, peering up the track, and waited expectantly for the telltale glint of oncoming lights. So far, nothing. The train remained out of sight.

"This is Echo Two. I hear the train," Hart said.

A moment later, so did Eli. A low rumble grew louder and louder. The ditch lights appeared, two powerful lights affixed above the top rail of the train. As it drew closer, the piercing beam painted the tracks with a widening halo of light.

"One mile!" Devon said.

"Game time!" Jackson said. "I repeat, game time!"

"Echo Two, let's blow something up!" Moreno yelled gleefully.

Two clicks came through static: Hart's signal to blow the top charges. Sixty seconds later it came: a loud *bang, bang, bang.* The top-shaped charges blew small holes in the top of the tank car to vent pressure. A second later, there was another chorus of bangs as the lower charges blew holes in the bottom of the tanker.

Liquid propane gas poured out onto the ground and burst into flames. The flames expanded rapidly, exploding in a massive fireball over the main tracks.

With a roar like a rocket engine clawing for altitude, the fireball leaped to three stories tall. Fed by the gushing fuel, the fire burned with the intensity of a blazing sun.

The inferno across the tracks was a hundred yards from the rail yard and the woods. The air seemed to bend and warp from the searing waves of heat.

No train would be able to pass through the fireball for the next thirty minutes at least.

Even a mile away, the conductor and assistant conductor would see the massive explosion and billowing smoke. They might panic, but they would know there was no way they could drive through the flames. They had no choice but to engage the emergency brakes.

They would stop. They had to stop.

A deafening screech split the air.

"Emergency brakes are engaged!" Jackson said.

The engineer put the train in full emergency stop mode. The train slowed as rapidly as possible for a forty-car freight train. The locomotive shook as if a great fist had slammed into it, the railcars behind it trembling so violently it seemed a few might jump the tracks. None did.

Eli squinted through the binos. It was difficult to see through the leaping flames and swirling smoke. The roaring of the fire and screech of metal on metal rent the air. The stink of ash and burning plastic stung his nostrils and gagged him. He coughed and spat.

The train ground to a shuddering halt not two hundred yards from the blistering fireball.

"Go, go, go!" Eli shouted.

Engines roared to life as three vehicles burst from the tree line. The teams had been waiting in Wildland fast-attack fire trucks they'd borrowed from the Marquette County fire station. The heavy-duty trucks were designed with off-roading capabilities to fight wildfires in dense wilderness.

Each team raced for its assigned section of the train. Their overhead lights streaked across the trees, lighting up the train, the tracks, and the dilapidated buildings. The fierce bloom of the fireball burned against the blackening sky.

Eli leaped from his position and sprinted down the hillside, his pack banging against his spine, the rifle slick in his hands. He jumped over roots and rocks, branches slashing at his face as he reached level ground.

A pickup truck sped toward him, raced behind the rail spur buildings, and slammed to a halt not ten feet away. At the wheel, Antoine whooped and punched the steering wheel with his fist. "Let's go, slowpoke! We don't got all day!"

Eli hopped into the truck bed beside Nyx, who knelt with her AK-47 up against her shoulder, aiming for the rear section of the forty railcars. Firelight glinted off her weapon and lit up the side of her face. Her eyes glowed like a demon out of hell. "Welcome aboard!"

A duffel bag of extra ammo and magazines sat next to the Styrofoam containers. Eli took up a position on the opposite side of the truck and brought his HK417 to bear.

The first team approached the locomotive in the lead Wildland truck. Sudden gunfire rang out. The Wildland truck's windshield blew out. The truck swerved violently to the right, its tires bumping over uneven ground as it spun to avoid more fire.

Panicked cursing filled Eli's headpiece.

"They're already firing at us!" Jackson shouted.

Eli's breath froze in his lungs. "That was AK fire."

Another barrage of gunfire blasted the night. Again, it was from AKs, definitely not the smaller rounds of a military-issued M4. Half a dozen shadowy figures leaped from the rear of the train and raced along the tracks parallel to the train. A second group of six to eight men poured from the front of the train.

Eli shouted into his radio. "Contact! Contact! Team One is taking fire north of the train and toward the rear. A group of hostiles has dismounted and is moving toward us using covering fire. They appear heavily armed and dangerous. Make that two. Two groups of six hostiles each!"

A figure near the front of the train crouched, a long thin object resting on his shoulders. Before Eli could react, an RPG arced across the sky. It was headed straight for Team Two's Wildland truck.

"Echo Two, incoming!" Antoine shouted.

Team Two's truck careened wildly, rising on two oversized tires and nearly rolling as it skidded to avoid the rocket-propelled grenade.

The RPG impacted thirty feet to the right of the racing truck. Instead, it punched through the nearest building like tin foil. The metal storage facility burst into a thousand chunks of twisted steel. Smoke and flames erupted as the blast lit up the sky.

"What the hell!" Nyx ducked to avoid flying shrapnel. "That was a freaking RPG!"

Eli shook his head, bewildered. This made no sense. Unless—

They weren't being fired upon by American soldiers. These clowns didn't move or fight like soldiers. Their weapons were different. There were more fighters than the four Guardsmen their intel had reported.

These guys were prepared for battle, not taken by surprise, almost as if the hostiles had known they were coming.

Fear settled in his gut like a stone. "This is NOT the Army National Guard. I repeat, they are NOT Guardsmen. Weapons free! Weapons free!"

Gunfire exploded from multiple locations along the woods on both sides of the tracks. Muzzle flashes burst like fireworks. Rounds punched the side of the pickup with *thuds* and *pings*.

Antoine swerved, performing counter moves to avoid the oncoming firepower. Eli seized Nyx's arm and dragged her down. "Get down! Head down!"

Lying prone, his belly pressed against the ridged floor of the truck bed with Nyx cursing beside him, Eli pressed his mic. "This is Alpha One! Pull back! Everyone retreat to the front of the train as fast as you can drive. When you get there, find cover. Only engage the hostiles from cover. I repeat, retreat to cover!"

If he had his spec ops team with him, they'd aggressively

attack the hostiles. A Special Forces team would move into the attack, shooting and moving, hunting down the enemy.

But Eli's ragtag team consisted of law enforcement officers, not a Marine Recon platoon. Above all else, he had to protect them.

"Keep them pinned," Eli said. "Give us five minutes!"

"Roger that," Jackson said. "We'll give you the cover you need."

"No dilly-dallying around!" Moreno shouted. "These psychos have crazy firepower!"

"Echo Four, stay on course," Eli instructed Antoine. "How copy?"

"Good copy," Antoine shouted back.

Nyx popped her head up, fired a controlled burst, and then ducked. "What's the play? We running or fighting? Please tell me we're gonna waste some bad guys."

An image of Lena flashed through his mind, her kind smile and her bright eyes. The way she'd looked at him once and might someday again. No way in hell was he running.

"We're gonna waste some bad guys," Eli said. "And I'm getting that damn insulin."

38

ELI POPE
DAY NINETY

The massive fireball cast the world in an eerie orange glow. Smoke snaked low to the ground, spreading like a thick fog across the train yard. The shapes of buildings and shipping containers turned blurry and indistinct.

Eli crouched in the bed of the pickup, his back to the rear cabin window, covering their six. Nyx rose and aimed her AK-47 in wide sweeps, firing at the shadows darting between trees, abandoned railcars, and empty buildings.

Antoine cranked the steering wheel and jerked the pickup into a sharp spin, rumbling over uneven ground as they raced parallel to the train, speeding past rows of shipping containers stacked on flat railcars, one after the other, forty cars long.

Eli kept one eye on their six, the other frantically scanning for the refrigerated intermodal container, the second to last car. "Come on, come on!"

"Echo Four to Echo all, we're taking heavy fire by the rear western building!" Jackson shouted.

Eli poked his head above the side of the pickup bed to fire two quick bursts at four hostiles sprinting toward them from the front of the train.

One figure stuttered and fell. The remaining three darted between two railcars before he could get off another shot. Further down, more shadows disembarked the train and scattered, muzzle fire flashing.

"I've got eyes on the target!" Antoine said through the headset. "Dead ahead!"

There it was, the second to last railcar, a white forty-foot-long intermodal container with "Cold Train INTERMODAL" scrawled in huge blue letters across the side.

Lead struck the shipping container directly to their left, three feet above Eli and Nyx, stitching a line of holes through the metal panel.

"Go! Go! Go!" Eli shouted. "Swing around to the back side!"

The pickup's tires squealed in protest as Antoine swung the wheel hard. They made a U-turn at the rear of the train. Gravel sprayed beneath their tires. The truck bumped across the tracks, then lurched around the SBU—the sense and braking unit, mounted on the end of the freight train.

Eli kept his HK scanning the shadows, searching for movement, the glint of a barrel or flash of muzzle fire. There was nothing. The stink of fumes and melted plastic singed his nostrils. The railcars cast long flickering shadows.

The ongoing firefight was concentrated on the opposite side of the tracks; the train itself provided cover and concealment. Antoine pulled the pickup within a foot of the refrigerated container and slammed the brakes.

Eli slung his rifle over his shoulder, leaped to his feet, and clambered up the side of the container while Nyx covered him. Antoine remained in the truck, ready to peel away at a moment's notice.

Once on top, Eli crouched and brought his weapon to bear, the stock braced against his shoulder, his eye squinting through the optic, finger itching the trigger guard. He spun on his heel in a circle, weapon up and searching for enemy combatants.

He covered Nyx while she climbed up. Two blocky rows of

solar panels lined the refrigerated intermodal's roof. The smoke made it difficult to breathe, even more difficult to see.

Further north, a gun battle raged between the buildings, railcars, and shipping containers littering the rail yard spur. Figures hunkered behind cover. Others darted between trees and buildings. Muzzle flashes sputtered through orange-tinged smoke.

A figure dropped. Then another. From here, it was impossible to distinguish the good guys from the bad. He could only pray his people were okay.

Distant rounds punched into the shipping containers with *pings* and *thunks*. Instinctively, Eli ducked, but not before noticing a small figure sprinting into the open from the tree line, headed for one of the storage buildings two hundred yards north.

He peered through his sights and recognized Devon's long braids flying behind her. Thirty yards to her rear, two figures rose from cover behind a shipping container and crept toward her. To her right, another hostile peeled out, trapping her in a pincer move.

Eli aimed, exhaled, and squeezed the trigger. The hostile about to fire on Devon dropped to the ground. Eli spun and swept the shipping container with a barrage of firepower. The move exposed his position, but it didn't matter. Two more hostiles went down as Devon made it to cover behind one of the buildings.

Return fire raked the shipping container in front of him.

"Head down!" Nyx shouted.

Eli dropped to his belly as she released several short bursts. The rounds zinged above his head. The return fire ceased for a moment.

With Nyx covering him, Eli unzipped his pack and yanked out the circular saw. He'd made sure it was freshly charged with a solar charger that morning. He found a section clear of the solar panels and started cutting through the roof of the shipping container.

Eli wished he could decouple the last two railcars to ensure the train wouldn't start back up and leave with the meds they needed, but he couldn't. The train's control wires were fed from the rear of the train, and the brake release had continuity through every railcar from front to back.

If brake continuity was lost at any point, the brakes would apply full emergency pressure, and everything would remain at a standstill.

He had to get the insulin out now.

Moreno's tense voice came through his headset. "There's too many of them!"

Fear knifed through him. They didn't have the manpower or ammunition for a battle like this. The ambush had turned into a FUBAR of epic proportions. He clenched his jaw so hard he thought his teeth might crack. There was only one viable option left.

He turned to Nyx. "Leave one of the backpacks with the dry ice. You and Antoine get to Jackson and drive back those hostiles. All teams fall back and exfil. Get the hell out of here."

Nyx scowled. "No way. We don't have the meds yet."

"Our teams are about to get pinned. I've got this."

"What about the beta blockers?"

"I don't know if I'll have time—"

"The meds for my grandma are non-negotiable! I'm not leaving without them. Or you."

"Yes, you are. That's an order."

Nyx snorted. "I'm not a soldier anymore. I'm a merc. And I don't answer to you."

"On the field, you do!"

"Jackson won't leave you behind."

"Then tell Jackson I'm with you."

"Eli—"

"Whatever it takes to get them out of here alive. That's the priority. You understand?"

"I don't want to—"

"But you will. That's why I'm telling you, not them. You're a mercenary, and you'll do what you need to do to save your skin.

Look around you. This is a losing battle. It was a well-organized ambush. They have three times the fighting force we do and better weapons. They aren't the National Guard, and they sure as hell aren't a Jr. ROTC Unit out of Detroit. This is a death trap unless we get our people out. That's what I need you and Antoine to do."

Firelight flickered across her hardened features and her fierce eyes. "If I have to, I will, but we're not there yet. Keep working."

A burst of gunfire tore through the shipping container to their right. Nyx returned fire while Eli continued to work the circular saw. Within a minute, he had a three-by-three square cut through. The section of the roof dropped and clattered against something inside the darkened container.

Without hesitation, Eli dropped inside. He landed hard in the dark. His knee knocked the edge of a crate. Ignoring the stab of pain, he started moving.

Rows of refrigerated cartons, cardboard boxes, and Styrofoam crates filled the long narrow container. Frigid air raised goose-bumps on his flesh as he flicked on his tactical flashlight and scanned the rows looming above him and to either side. He squeezed through a narrow passageway. There must be a hundred containers or more.

The seconds ticked like a bomb in his blood. Every second he spent in here was a second one of his people might get shot or killed.

Every nerve on high alert, he moved quickly, scanning crates labeled Roche, Pfizer, Novartis, Vertex Pharmaceuticals, and Merck. Each crate was filled with critical life-saving medications, but not the ones he sought.

Lead punched through the top of the shipping container and slammed through the opposite wall, ripping holes in the panels. Narrow beams of reddish light shot through the darkness.

"Echo Two, we're running out of ammo!" Moreno yelled through his headset. "The bad guys are closing in!"

Above him, Nyx cursed. "What's taking you so long? You napping down there or what?"

Eli put his tactical flashlight between his teeth and pushed at a crate, moving it aside to reveal a refrigerated container the size of a cooler, with Ethitech stamped on the side. Ethitech was the main African distributor for some of the world's leading diabetes companies like BioCorp, Diasend Glooko, and Dexcom.

There were a dozen similar containers labeled Ethitech. He ripped off the packaging and lifted the lid of the first container to verify the contents: vials of insulin nestled in Styrofoam.

He sucked in a sharp breath. Relief flooded his veins. This was it: liquid gold. Lena's life in his hands.

Eli seized the first container, squeezed his way to the opening above him, and thrust it toward Nyx. She leaned down, grasped it, and hauled it to the roof.

A flurry of gunfire split the air. *Boom, boom, boom!* Two rounds ripped through the shipping container a foot from his face. Thin lines of fiery light pierced the shadows like laser beams. His ears rang.

Nyx yelped. Above him, her form vanished.

Dread scrabbled up his spine. Using the stacked crates as a ladder, he climbed from the intermodal container. Leading with the muzzle of the VP9, his head eased above the lip of the hole as he scanned in every direction. "Nyx!"

To his right, Nyx was on her stomach, one hand gripping her shoulder, blood pulsing between her fingers while she fired her pistol one-handed.

A group of four hostiles had managed to sneak up on them, scurrying between railcars, leapfrogging each other to provide cover. They were only two railcars away.

Eli unslung his HK417 and burned through a magazine driving them back, then slapped in a fresh magazine while Nyx fired several shots before she ran dry. "I'm out!"

He handed her his rifle and drew the VP9, firing a half-dozen shots before they managed to drive the closest hostiles back behind a railcar and keep their heads down behind cover.

Eli risked a glance at Nyx. "You're bleeding!"

"I'm fine!" she said between gritted teeth.

"That's the adrenaline talking."

"Don't worry about me. We're running out of time. Look!"

It was incredibly difficult to see through the black smoke billowing thick and heavy in the air. Eli's throat was parched, his nostrils singed, his eyes stinging as he turned to look ahead of him.

The massive fireball in front of the train had gradually diminished. It was only ten or fifteen feet high now, not nearly as dangerous to an oncoming freight train. In a minute or two, the conductor might find the bravery to forge ahead despite the flames.

"I've got company!" Antoine shouted. "Four more on my side, coming in hot! We've got to go, stat!"

Eli fired several covering rounds one-handed as he pushed Nyx off the top of the shipping container. She dropped light-footed to the truck bed and looked up at him, gesturing wildly with his HK417. "Come on!"

He handed her the insulin container and was about to follow her. A sudden shiver of apprehension rippled across his skin. The back of his neck prickled. A primal instinct, a warning in his reptilian brain.

He sensed an approaching predator like a shark senses a drop of blood in the ocean.

Dropping low, Eli spun to face the length of the train. A figure approached them. Not from below but from above, striding across the tops of the railcars, ten cars away. Two men behind him carried automatic weapons.

Jackson's panicked voice filled his headset. "We're boxed in! The enemy flanked us on two sides. We're trapped and running out of ammo!"

"Eli, come on!" Nyx shouted.

Eli risked a glance down at Nyx and waved her away. "Save them, damn it!"

Reluctantly, Nyx obeyed. She banged on the roof with her injured arm. "Go! Go! Go!"

Below him, Antoine spun the truck, gravel flying as the wheels squealed. The truck raced back along the tracks in retreat. Nyx fired the HK417 as the truck shot toward the cluster of buildings.

The men atop the railcars ducked for cover. Gunshots blasted from several directions. Rounds zipped over his head, one so close it kissed his ear. He felt no pain.

The concussive sounds thrummed in his ears, his teeth, his chest. Eli dropped to his belly and fired the last three rounds from his VP9. The slide locked back.

Quickly, he reached for a magazine from the pouch on his vest.

He heard the menacing click of a safety sliding to "off."

"I wouldn't do that," said a familiar voice.

Eli turned to face his adversary.

Darius Sykes stood before him.

39

ELI POPE
DAY NINETY

E li faced Sykes.

Fear sprouted in his chest. His pistol had run dry. Nyx had his rifle. His only weapon was the fixed-blade knife at his hip.

Darius Sykes was a large man, thick and beefy with paradoxically delicate facial features and full lips, his voice silky-smooth. It was disconcerting as hell. He wore black cargo pants with a plated chest rig over a camo T-shirt, with both a knife and a pistol at his hip.

Sykes' minions stood behind him, grinning and armed to the teeth. Eli recognized the Hispanic gangbanger, Angel Flud, and a ham-fisted goon Eli recognized from prison.

Memories crashed through his head: the years buried alive in Alger Correctional Facility trapped with killers, the stench of desperation and terror, resignation and rage, always on high alert, waiting for the shiv to the ribs, the silent attack in the night.

The last time he'd faced Sykes in hand-to-hand combat, he'd fought with the reckless boldness of someone with little to lose.

That was before. Now he had everything to lose.

"Imagine my pleasant surprise when I discovered you were leading the attack on us," Sykes said. "Here I was, minding my own business, and you fell right into my lap."

"How the hell did you get the weapons? So many men?"

"A mutually beneficial partnership."

"Sawyer?"

Sykes shook his head. "Guess again."

The realization struck him like a bucket of ice water in the face. "You're working for the Côté cartel."

"The cartel took over the Soo Locks this morning. We own Sault Ste. Marie. All those freighters, all those containers brimming with supplies—they're ours now."

"You mean the cartel's."

Sykes' lips slithered back from his teeth in a lecherous smile. "I AM the cartel. The king of the Côté family personally invited me and my followers to join forces with him. Luis Gault has been assimilating criminal organizations for months, solidifying more territory and strengthening our numbers. We're taking over the U.P., then the Midwest, then the whole country."

"You murdered National Guardsmen."

Sykes shrugged with calculated indifference, but he was boasting. He wanted Eli to know his power. "Gault himself gave us the order to ambush it. The train was loaded before the cartel attacked the Locks, so we went after it and hijacked it within an hour after it left the Locks. They put up a fight, but they're kids playing with toy guns. No match for us."

Outrage burned in his chest. American soldiers had been murdered by hardened criminals with no souls, and no consciences.

Sykes needed to die.

Eli wanted to kill him, to make him suffer.

"Let me take him." Angel aimed his rifle one-handed at Eli, his other hand massaging the collar bone Eli had fractured in prison. The teardrop tattoos on his cheeks stretched and distorted in the firelight as he grimaced, hatred in his eyes.

On Sykes' other side stood a bald white guy the size of a rhino, with meaty ham-sized fists, huge pecs, and bulging biceps writhing with tattoos.

Eli smirked. "Where's Fat Tommy?"

"You killed him, you scumbag," Angel snarled. "You broke his neck like an animal." He surged forward, weapon up. "I'll murder you for that!"

"He's mine," Sykes said. "Pope, take your pistol out and toss it over the side."

"I ran it dry five minutes ago."

"Then you won't mind tossing it. Do it now."

With reluctance, Eli pitched his VP9 over the side of the train. It thudded to the ground twelve feet below. It was a solid pistol, and he would miss it.

If he lived long enough to miss anything.

Angel's finger slid to the trigger. Sykes thrust out his hand to stop him. "I told you he was mine. Go back and finish the fight. Kill all his friends."

"But—"

Sykes' eyes flashed. "You have a job to do. Now do it."

Obediently, his attack dogs retreated. They climbed down the rear of the nearest shipping container. Seconds later, they'd disappeared into smoke and shadow. The boom of gunfire grew distant as the battle continued among the sagging buildings.

Sykes and Eli stood alone on top of the train.

"I was hoping you would come," Sykes said in his soft voice. "That it would be you."

Ten feet apart, they squared off. The container they stood atop was eight feet wide by forty feet long. Two containers were squeezed together on each railcar with a space of approximately four feet between each coupled set of containers.

Sykes drew a karambit knife from the sheath at his belt. The sharp curved edge glinted in the dark firelight. Designed to impart the maximum damage to the human body in the shortest time, the curved blade resembled the claw of a raptor, the better with which to disembowel someone.

Knife fighting was brutal, messy, and lethal. On any given day, even an amateur could get lucky. It was not the choice of someone with something to lose.

Except for a sadistic sociopath like Darius Sykes.

He believed he was above physics, above consequences, and above all, a god of his own making. Eli knew better than to think the odds had been evened in his favor. Still, he was determined to prove Sykes wrong.

"I loved Fat Tommy like a brother. He was my family, and you stole him from me. Now I'm going to return the favor, tenfold. I don't let things go, Pope. I follow through."

"Go to hell."

"I told you I'd get you on your knees. That you'd beg before you died. Before I slit your throat, carve up your belly, pull out your entrails, and tie them in a pretty bow before I string you up from a telephone pole for everyone to see. That day is here, Pope. That time is now."

"I'll kill you first," Eli said.

Hatred mingled with the dead calm of his training, the thirst for violence building inside him. There it was, the thing Eli could never admit to Lena or anyone—he enjoyed fighting for his life, the incredible rush from facing death, the high afterward from surviving.

If his adversary was truly evil, Eli *wanted* to murder, to cause pain. He relished the act of killing. This was the darkness he hid within himself at all costs. The devil inside.

"Get down on your knees!" Sykes screamed.

Eli wasted no more energy on words. His muscles coiled. He tensed, lowering himself into a fighting stance, legs planted wide and knees loose to keep his balance.

He drew his combat knife. It slid from its holster, sharp and deadly.

Eli held the knife in a forward grip, the blade angled forward and facing down, his left hand in a fist close to his chest, the faster with which to slash and strike. It gave him a critical six additional inches of reach to take a hand or thrust into enemy flesh.

Sykes smiled the slippery, malevolent smile of an eel. "You should know, I've trained with Filipino grandmasters in Kali, Eskrima, and Jeet Kune Do." Kali and Eskrima were martial arts known for lightning-fast, hand-to-hand combat techniques— particularly utilizing a choice of weapons like sticks, knives, double knives, and even swords.

"Whatever the army taught you, it's nothing compared to what I will do to you. I will peel your skin from your bones. And after I kill you, I will come for the ones you love. I made that promise to you before, and it is a promise I have never broken. Not once. They will scream for you in dark places, and you will not hear them. They will cry out your name, and you will not be able to save them."

Eli's vision went red. Terror flayed his heart and stopped his breath in his lungs. Stronger than the fear was his fury. He would kill this man to protect those he loved.

Eli slowed his breathing and readied himself. Time slowed. The action seemed to unfold frame by frame, a jerky, slow-motion movie.

Sykes sneered. "I am going to enjoy this greatly."

"No, I am." Eli charged. His knife whipped through the air. No windup or telegraph. No preamble. Just a fast strike. His knife slashed down at a diagonal and smacked Sykes' blade.

Sykes pulled back in time to save his hand. Swiftly, he parried. The karambit thrust once, twice, half a dozen times in rapid succession.

Their movements were swift and furious. A blur of motion. A terrible dance.

Eli managed to slip past Sykes' hand outside the arc of his slashing blade. Whirling, he smashed the butt of the knife against Sykes' skull.

Sykes threw up an arm and made a partial block. Steel thudded against bone. Blood gushed down the side of Sykes' face.

With a roar of rage, Sykes spun and slashed downward, aiming for Eli's temples. Eli managed to jerk his head back, but the blade was already singing toward him again.

Sharp steel sliced Eli's lower right side beneath his chest plates. The blade opened a ragged tear in his shirt and carved the skin over his hip. The cut stung, but adrenaline masked the pain.

Eli sidestepped fast to keep from squaring up with Sykes, where his opponent's skilled thrusts and downward strikes would connect. Sykes stayed close, lunging and feinting. For so large a man, Sykes was incredibly nimble, his footwork quick, and his knife thrusts lightning fast.

Sykes gave him no openings, no give, no vulnerability. The knife flicked like a snake's tongue in the fiery dark. The firelight gleamed in his eyes like the eyes of a demon.

Blade clanged against blade. Gasps and thuds rang in the night. Another slash and the back of Eli's thigh opened up. Sykes had aimed to sever the tendons behind his knee, but Eli had darted to the side at the last moment.

As Sykes spun right, Eli feinted left as he swiftly reversed his wrist and thrust into Sykes' chest. The blade bounced harmlessly. It had struck Sykes' ceramic plates beneath his chest rig.

Sykes leaped back with a fiendish grin. His body armor had saved him.

Before Eli could strike again, the shipping container shuddered beneath their feet. The rumble of the locomotive's engine sliced through the roar of the flames and the *rat-a-tat* of gunfire.

The train began to move.

Alarmed shouts echoed in his headset. The fireball had receded far sooner than expected; the conductor was making a run for it, likely with a gun to his head, held by one of the convicts who'd hijacked his train.

The shipping container jolted. Eli nearly lost his balance. Shifting his feet, he adjusted to the rhythm of the train as it accelerated. The wind rushed in his face. The smoke and firelight receded as the train barreled into the darkening night.

Sykes attacked. Again, they clashed in a ferocious blur of

bodies, thrashing and slashing, grappling chest to chest. Sykes' hot sticky breath hot on his face, gasping from exertion.

Sykes broke apart to get enough space for another attack. He lunged low, slashing for the artery in Eli's groin. Eli could hardly see the glint of the blade in the darkness.

Eli hurled himself backward. He narrowly escaped falling as Sykes pounced. Blindingly fast, the knife sang through the air. A sharp sting bit into Eli's left forearm. Blood poured down his arm and dripped off his fingers. His hip and leg were bleeding heavily, too.

Across the shipping container, Sykes crouched, grinning at him in triumph. This was the end game. All Sykes had to do was keep out of Eli's arc of thrusts and slashes. Eli would slow, growing cold and dizzy as shock took hold. Then Sykes would move in for the kill.

Eli needed to stop the bleeding and get a tourniquet on his arm, probably his thigh as well or he'd go into hypovolemic shock. He had one in his IFAK first aid kit, but Sykes was hardly going to pause while he tended to his injuries.

Eli stumbled, his legs going watery. His heart pounded to make up for the loss of blood, the shortage of red blood cells carrying precious oxygen to his brain, heart, and muscles. He was battered and bleeding out.

As the train chugged around a bend, Eli swayed, his heels sliding over the edge of the container. Gravity pulled him toward the edge, toward oblivion.

Sykes advanced toward him.

He had to escape, had to live to fight another day. He was the thing standing between this monster and Shiloh and Lena.

The wind roared, threatening to seize him and pitch him over the side. The train whistled, a haunting, mournful sound, a funeral dirge.

Out of the corner of his eye, he glimpsed a ribbon of midnight blue far below. The tracks rattled as the train chugged onto the bridge over the Escanaba River.

Then Sykes rushed him, coming in for the kill shot. With a deadly gleam in his eyes, he raised the knife.

Eli jumped backward. Backward and down, down, down. As the train roared across the bridge, he hit the water and sank like a stone.

40

ELI POPE
DAY NINETY

The black water swallowed Eli whole. The frigid cold struck him like a punch. A rush of silence filled his ears. Opening his eyes, he saw nothing but watery darkness.

Water gushed into his nose and mouth, filling his lungs, and drowning him. His chest tightened. His lungs ached for oxygen. Panic screamed inside his skull.

He hurled himself upward, arms windmilling, and broke the surface. Chest heaving, he spewed brackish water from his mouth. Before he could suck in any air, he was dragged down again.

Water poured into his nose and mouth. He gagged, choking, kicking with all his strength, but his armored plates were an anchor dragging him straight to the bottom.

Several feet underwater and sinking fast, he ripped at the straps and Velcro holding his chest rig and chromatic plates on. His movements were slowed by the rushing water and darkness, the pain, and the loss of blood. Unable to see or breathe, his pulse roared inside his head.

Seconds ticked past. It felt like drowning. He *was* drowning.

Finally, he freed himself from the body armor, his lungs exploding, and kicked upward. His head broke the surface.

Choking and spitting, his lungs convulsed. Then he was breathing precious air.

Pain seared his left arm with every stroke and stabbed his right leg with each kick as the cut in his side pulsed with blood in tandem with his heartbeat. The gashes steadily leaked blood.

His training took over. Twisting onto his back, he attempted to float. He expended tremendous energy kicking to stay above water as he pulled the tourniquet from his IFAK that had been under his body armor and wrestled to get it around his arm just above his elbow.

As he struggled to twist it tight, his body sank, his head dropping below the surface. He was still too heavy. His waterlogged clothes and boots still dragged him down, threatening to pull him under again.

Rolling over in the water, he kicked hard, brought his foot in close to his chest. Working first one boot and then the other from his feet, he tied a knot with both sets of laces so he could hang them around his neck. Already, he felt lighter.

Exhaustion pulled at his limbs. His lungs ached, his heart pounding out of his chest. He was freezing cold and shivering. With a punch of dread, he recognized the first stage of shock.

Moonlight glinted off the rushing brown water of the Escanaba River as the strong current whisked him along. Above him, the bridge rapidly retreated. The train was long out of sight, and Darius Sykes with it.

He refused to die like this, drowning in a river, his corpse washed ashore, left for scavengers to pick his bones clean. He had to protect Lena and Shiloh. He had to live.

Wrenching himself toward the western shore, he kicked out, fighting the current, plunging his good arm in strong arcs through the water, turning his head to gasp for breath. His legs and arms turned to lead, but he kept pushing.

Swimming hard, he crossed the current. His socked feet struck the bottom, silt shifting beneath his toes. The current was stronger here, pulling at him, tugging his legs, his hips, pulling him back out into the deep water, but he managed to wade through the shallows and slither up the bank.

Weary to his core, he tossed aside the boots wrapped around his neck and lay on the pebble-strewn bank for a long minute. Mud oozed against his cheek, and rocks poked his belly and thighs. Crickets and cicadas serenaded the moon. Frogs croaked in unison as black flies and mosquitos buzzed around him.

He took stock of himself—miserable, wounded, half-dead. Raising his head, he studied the shadowy line of ash and maple trees a dozen yards from the riverbank, half-expecting a threat to emerge at any moment. None did. Everything was still and cloaked in darkness: the woods, the river, the hunched dark shapes of distant buildings.

Worry consumed him. Darius Sykes had beaten him. The psychopath knew he was alive and would not rest until he came for those Eli loved most. Back at the train spur, Jackson and Devon had been trapped by Sykes' hooligans.

He needed to get to his team, then home.

And he needed weapons. His VP9 had been pitched over the side of the freight train. It was too dangerous to attempt to return and retrieve it. He still had his knife.

And he had a buried cache a half-mile from his father's old house—a five-gallon bucket sealed with an air-and-water-tight Gamma lid, then wrapped in an industrial trash bag for extra protection.

Inside it, he'd stored a Glock 19 handgun, along with boxes of 9mm ammo, a change of clothes, water purification tablets, a Leatherman multi-tool, an emergency blanket, a first aid kit, and protein bars.

His father's house was miles away. First, he had to get to the rally point.

With a grunt, Eli pushed himself to his hands and knees, then lumbered painfully to his feet. He put his waterlogged boots back on, grimacing as agony shot through his forearm, side, and leg.

Using his IFAK, he managed to wrap a bandage around his

thigh and pressed some QuikClot gauze against his side. He'd stopped most of the bleeding, but the wounds needed to be debrided, disinfected, and stitched.

By some miracle, he still had his headset though he was well out of radio range. Using the stars to orient himself, he headed west.

He wasn't certain how far the river had taken him, but he was at least five to seven miles from the rally point, an abandoned warehouse three miles west of Escanaba, located off a rural gravel road.

If they had survived, the team would be waiting for him. If they hadn't—he couldn't think about that. He focused on the here and now, the next breath, the next step.

Steeling himself, Eli began the long grueling walk, pain and worry his only companions.

41

ELI POPE
DAY NINETY-ONE

By the time Eli reached the warehouse, it was two a.m. Ragged ribbons of clouds drifted across the moon like burial shrouds. There was no movement, no sound but for the bugs, the swish of weeds against his thighs, the sigh of a soft breeze through the pine needles.

On high alert, he limped toward the building but remained within the tree line.

The warehouse had been abandoned for a couple of decades. Graffiti scrawled across the concrete exterior, vines crawled up the walls and snaked over the metal roof, and trash and debris were scattered everywhere. The upper windows were shattered, the lower windows boarded up.

He hesitated behind a pine tree, keeping the trunk between him and twenty yards of open pavement. His gaze swept the milky shadows, pulse quickening as he caught a glint on top of the warehouse roof: a sniper.

His hand slid to his combat knife. Little good that would do in a firefight.

"This is Alpha One," he whispered into his headset. He wasn't sure if it would still work. "Anybody alive in there?"

A crackle of static, and then Moreno's voice said, "Guess you're not dead, Alpha One. That's a pity. We had a bet going for the last five gallons of gasoline."

"Too bad you lost. That our guy on overwatch on the roof?"

"Yours truly," Hart said. "I don't see you anywhere."

"That's the point." They'd set up a defensive perimeter as he'd instructed. They were learning. "You gonna let me in or what?"

"Hart's got you covered," Moreno said. "Come on into the Hilton and make yourself at home. Hope you brought your best suit. The dining room is black tie only."

"Damn. My tux drowned in the river."

Eli waded through waist-high weeds; brambles snagged his clothes and scratched at his exposed skin. Ahead of him, the parking lot zigzagged with cracks as he made his way around to the rear entrance.

The rusted steel door hung on squeaky hinges, a cement block holding it closed, the padlock long busted. A shuffling sound came from behind the door, and then Jackson shoved the door open enough for Eli to slide through.

Jackson moved aside and gestured for Eli to enter, closed the door behind him, and shoved the cement block back into place. He carried a red-filmed flashlight low in his hand, so as not to draw undue attention.

Relief welled through him. He hadn't realized how strongly he'd feared Jackson hadn't survived until he laid eyes on his old friend's grim, sooty face. He resisted the bizarre urge to hug him.

Instead, he cleared his throat awkwardly. "Guess your ugly mug made it, too."

Alexis stood behind the door, guarding the entrance. She saluted Eli. "Good to see you, sir. We were starting to get worried."

"So was I. And I'm no sir."

Jackson scanned his injuries with concern. "You're hurt."

"A couple of scratches."

Alexis frowned. "Is that Ranger-speak for on your deathbed?"

"Something like that."

"We've been waiting for three hours. We thought—" Jackson

didn't finish what he'd thought, but his dread and worry were written across his face.

"Sorry to disappoint you."

Jackson's mouth thinned. "I'm glad you made it, you big idiot."

Eli only grunted. It had been three hours of hell. His whole body ached. He longed for a soft mattress, a bowl of soup, and maybe a painkiller or two. Hell, what he wanted was a morphine drip, to surrender to oblivion.

"What about our people?" he asked. "Who's hurt? How is Devon?"

"Devon is fine. Everyone made it." Still, there was something in Jackson's voice, a thread of sorrow, of defeat, that gave Eli pause.

He examined Jackson's face, searching for clues. "What is it?"

Jackson's expression hardened. He started down the hall and waved him forward. "I'll explain in a minute."

Alexis stayed behind to keep watch. Jackson led Eli deeper into the warren of rooms and hallways, his flashlight beam low and sweeping ahead of them. The warehouse smelled faintly of burnt plastic and something dead—the rancid carcass of a raccoon or possum, perhaps.

They entered the cavernous main room, which was three stories tall, the perimeter ringed with a one-story metal-grate catwalk. Smashed pop cans, shriveled condom wrappers, and shredded cardboard were piled in the corners. Deep wavering shadows lurched along the walls.

His boots crunched shattered glass. With every step, his anxiety grew.

In the center of the room, the team sat in a circle on stacked crates and pallets, slumped forward, elbows on thighs, their heads down. Fighters who'd escaped death but were drained, exhausted, and weary to the bone.

There was no elation, no exhilaration at surviving, at beating the enemy. They hadn't won; they had barely escaped with their lives.

At the sight of him, Nyx rose, picked up the HK417 she'd rested across her thighs, and handed it to him. "Thought you were a goner."

"I got lucky." He winced as he slung the rifle over his chest. He didn't feel lucky. He scanned Nyx and automatically checked her over for injuries. Her shirt sleeve had been cut away and her shoulder bandaged. Her right arm hung limp at her side.

She saw him looking and grimaced. "I can move it, but it hurts like hell. It was a through and through, a flesh wound. It didn't hit tendons, ligaments, or bones. At least, I don't think so. You, however, look like you got run over by a dump truck."

"I'm fine." In truth, his arm and thigh felt like someone had jabbed him with hot pokers. He needed to remove the tourniquet and get his forearm stitched up, asap. "On second thought, I'll take some Ranger candy."

Beside them, Devon raised her head. She was dirty and soot-streaked. Blood smeared her cheek from a nasty cut above her eyebrow. Other than that, she was unhurt. "What's Ranger candy?"

Nyx rolled her eyes as she pulled a packet from her IFAK, tore it with her teeth, and dumped the pills into Eli's outstretched hand. "Army-speak for ibuprofen. Between you and Antoine, those are my last two, you jerk."

"Thanks." Eli swallowed the pills without water. "What the hell's wrong with Antoine?"

Nyx offered a sharp smile. "He misses his mommy."

Antoine cursed in French. "Damn straight I do."

He sat beside Devon, nursing a second-degree burn to the left side of his face. His shirt hung in tatters from his left shoulder, the ends singed from his neck to his ribs. Blood oozed from a few lacerations along his ribs where shrapnel had struck him.

"What happened to you?" Eli asked.

Antoine winced. "Got kissed by a grenade."

"You look like death warmed over."

"Takes more than a damn grenade to kill me, brother. I'm a cockroach like that."

"In more ways than one," Nyx said.

Antoine winked. "Still here to fight another day. That's what matters."

"Yeah, well, you should have seen him two hours ago, crying like a big fat baby."

"Tears of joy at our reunion," Antoine quipped.

Nyx rolled her eyes. "He clearly needs to have his head examined."

"We were lucky as hell we didn't lose a man," Jackson said quietly. "In addition to injuries, we lost a truck to an RPG. We have barely enough fuel to return home."

Devon shot a grateful look at Nyx and Antoine. "We were trapped before these two came barreling in like kamikazes. They pushed back the shooters so we could escape. The bad guys retreated when the train left. Luckily, they didn't pursue us."

He could see it in their eyes: Nyx and Antoine had earned their grudging respect. No one could deny it—the mercenaries had saved their bacon.

Eli shifted his attention and scanned the shadowy warehouse. At the far end, two of the Wildland trucks were parked in empty bays, the rolling doors pulled down to shield them. He searched the dirty concrete floor around the group.

He didn't see what he was looking for. "The insulin. Where is it?"

Nyx's face darkened. "In the middle of the gunfight, as we were driving back the hostiles, one of them threw a damn grenade into the bed of the truck. Antoine and I managed to jump out in time. We dove behind a concrete building, which got most of the blast. The insulin was in the back of the truck. I'm sorry Eli, but it got blown to smithereens."

The blood drained from his face. He couldn't breathe properly. Everything they'd risked, only to fail, and to fail utterly. They had suffered far too many losses for such little gain.

All he'd done was expose himself to Sykes and paint a target the size of Montana on his back, and those he loved. Plus, he was now injured, weakening him for the next time he would face his enemy.

Then he remembered. With his good arm, he reached into his pocket, searching for something. He pulled out a handful of broken glass shards slippery with clear liquid.

Dread scrabbled up the notches of his spine. When he'd removed the lid of the refrigerated crate to verify the insulin, he'd grabbed a handful of vials and shoved them into his pocket. The vials had shattered, either during his battle with Sykes or his dive from the bridge into the river.

No. Not all of them.

He cradled two unbroken vials in his palm, a few weeks of life for the woman he loved. He closed his fingers over the vials and gently slipped them into a pouch on his chest rig, next to his heart.

"The beta blockers?" Nyx asked softly. "Did you find them?"

Chagrined, Eli shook his head. "I'm sorry."

Nyx didn't respond. Her mouth tightened. She stared dismally at a spot of fresh graffiti scrawled across the warehouse wall: *The end of the world is the beginning of hell.*

At that moment, he couldn't agree more.

Moreno grimaced. "How the hell did things go sideways so fast? And who the hell was that who attacked us? They weren't soldiers, but they sure as hell were vicious and armed to the teeth."

"The Côté cartel," Eli said wearily. "And Darius Sykes."

Jackson blanched. "What?"

"According to Sykes, the Côté cartel slaughtered the National Guard stationed at the Soo and took over the Locks. They're extending their reach into the Upper Peninsula. They hired Sykes and his convicts, gave them weapons and more men to ambush the National Guardsmen and steal the train."

Across the circle, Eli met Jackson's gaze. Jackson looked stricken. He knew what this meant. It was no longer a matter of time. Sykes was coming for them now, coming for everything they held dear.

A shocked silence settled over the room.

Chief McCallister shook her head, horrified. "Here on American soil?"

Devon let out a soft groan. "Holy hell."

"What do we know about the Côté cartel?" Nash asked.

"They're a Quebec-based organized crime network," Jackson said. "They've consolidated power from Montreal to Toronto to Vancouver. For years, they dealt mostly in narcotics trafficking, until seven years ago, when Luis Gault assassinated his cousin and several of his high-ranking Côté family members at a birthday party in Cancun. It was an organized coup. Under Gault's leadership, they've built underground networks with the worst of the Mexican cartels, the Sinaloa cartel and Los Zetas and sunk their claws into black market weapons smuggling and human trafficking. Gault has a particularly vicious enforcer known as the Jackal. Not much is known about him, other than his affinity for brutality.

"The cartel is organized, effective, and merciless. Cross them and they go scorched earth—they wipe you out and your entire lineage. Over the last few years, they've stepped up recruitment efforts and built themselves an army of foot soldiers. They have an arsenal of weaponry including RPGs, grenades, and automatic weapons. Hell, they have helicopters and rockets."

"We've seen what they can do," Antoine said with terrible awe. "They attacked us on the open highway, nearly slaughtered us. We barely got away. The National Guard and local cops showed up and were massacred."

"Sawyer stole from them," Eli said. "They don't know who or where he is, or they would have come already. If Sykes sniffs around enough, he might figure it out and relay that intel back to Gault. That wouldn't be bad news for Sawyer, but it would be bad news for us. The cartel wouldn't just destroy Sawyer, they'd kill whoever got in their way."

"Then we better figure out how to catch the SOB, and quick," Moreno said.

The somber silence grew thick and heavy. No one spoke for

several minutes. They listened to the wind soughing through the broken windows, the rustle of trash, a rat skittering in the corners.

Jackson glared down at his hands as if he could figure out a way to solve this mess if he thought hard enough or as if he could conjure up a solution through sheer force of will. When he looked up, his eyes were haunted. "They knew we were coming."

"What?" Nash said.

"We didn't surprise them. They were ready for us. This was an organized counterattack."

I was hoping you would come. Sykes' words echoed in Eli's mind. *I was hoping it would be you.*

Eli nodded. "He's right."

The group gazed at each other, aghast.

"Who?" Moreno's voice rose in anger. "The only people who knew about the mission are here right now. Hell, we've only been planning the op for a freaking day! What the hell happened?"

Suspicious gazes turned on Antoine and Nyx.

Nyx bristled. "We told no one. Our butts were on the line, too." She jerked a thumb at Antoine. "Look at his face. Why the hell would we ambush our operation? We didn't leak intel."

"Someone sure did," Nash muttered. "Someone ratted us out to Sykes, to the cartel, or both."

Jackson said, "I will not rest until I find out who did this. And they will pay dearly for it. Believe me."

"This is just the beginning," Moreno said what they were all thinking. "Sykes and his merry band of murderers will keep coming. Now that they're backed by the cartel, they're stronger and even more dangerous. They have more men and better weapons. They'll keep coming."

No one answered him.

Eli gazed at his disheartened team members, at the despondency in their expressions, their slumped postures. He felt it, too. Despair lurked at the edge of his consciousness, the darkness creeping in. His failure sharp as a razor blade.

Devon stood unsteadily and cleared her throat. "This is bad, but it's not over. It's not the end. We'll keep fighting."

Jackson reached over and squeezed her hand. She offered him a grim smile.

Eli had no energy left for smiles or comforting platitudes. The darkness did not recede.

42

LENA EASTON
DAY NINETY-ONE

"Hold still," Lena demanded.

She bent over Eli's wounded forearm, skillfully stitching the gash with a sterilized needle and sutures from her med kit. She had no access to topical anesthesia, but she'd iced the area using ice cubes from the solar-powered fridge in the Inn's kitchen.

It helped. A little.

Sykes' knife had opened a nasty four-inch gash in his forearm, biting deep into flesh and muscle and barely missing an artery. He was lucky a tendon hadn't been cut, or he might have lost the use of his hand.

The cuts on his side and the back of his leg were shallow although they'd bled profusely. Lena had debrided the wounds with sterilized water, then applied antibiotics and antiseptic cream before stitching the lacerations.

She winced with every puncture of the needle through his flesh. For his part, Eli was stoic, merely gritting his teeth against the pain. He held completely still, hissing an occasional curse.

The fire flickered cheerily in the fireplace, the flames casting the room in a warm comforting glow. The constant tinkling of her glass syringes boiling in the pot over the fire was the only sound.

They sat at the table in the conference room, Lena's favorite spot. She loved the oversized leather armchairs, the papery smell of hundreds of books, and the huge windows with beautiful views during the day, though night pressed against the panes now.

It was four o'clock in the morning, but Lena hadn't slept, hadn't thought of anything else until Eli and the others returned to Munising. Neither had Shiloh, though as soon as she knew Eli was safe, she'd passed out in her bed with Bear splayed half on top of her, both snoring soundly.

"Last stitch." Lena snipped the thread and leaned back in her seat. "The lacerations will be tender for a while. You need to take it easy, or the wounds will open up again. A deep wound like this one on your arm can easily get infected."

"I can't take it easy."

She placed her hand over his on the table. "I'm telling you to try. I'd be abdicating my responsibilities as a medical professional if I didn't."

He shook his head, his mouth flat, his black eyes burned with anger. "I failed. I failed you. I failed the mission. Sykes is still out there. Worse, now he knows I'm here. He will hunt for us. He'll find out about you. About Shiloh."

She heard the fear in his voice which scared her more than she wanted to admit. "We'll deal with it the same way we've dealt with every threat we've faced so far."

Eli shoved his chair back and rose abruptly as if he couldn't bear her touch. He paced the room, his body rigid, expression taut. "I didn't get the insulin, Lena. They were ready for us. I should have gotten more intel before we attacked. I should have seen it coming."

"This isn't your fault."

"I promised you insulin." He halted next to the desk, reached into his pocket, and pulled out two vials. He placed them almost reverently next to her glass syringes, test strips, and blood sugar meter. "This is all I could get. I'm sorry."

Lena released the breath she'd been holding. At least it was something. She tried not to show her fear, her exhaustion, the sickness she felt in her cells, her bones, her marrow. "Those vials buy me a few more weeks. It's good. It helps."

"That's nothing! That's not enough!" He started up his pacing, roaming in tight circles, the tendons standing out in his throat, hands balled into fists.

"It's something, Eli. Thank you."

He grunted as if he'd barely heard her.

She watched him helplessly. He was silent, tortured, and stewing in his pain. It hurt her to see him like this, like a pulsing wound in her own heart.

She rose from her chair and went to the desk, wincing as she pricked a tender bruise on her pinkie finger to check her blood sugar, then she injected eight units of insulin and placed the used syringe in the pan to sterilize later.

"Eli," she said.

He looked at her with glazed eyes like he wasn't even seeing her, as if he hadn't heard her. "I'm going to kill him. I *want* to kill him. I long to kill him with every fiber of my being."

He paused in front of the fire, his form silhouetted against the flames. "I kill people. Sometimes, I—I enjoy it. I like killing. I want to make it hurt, to make men suffer."

He looked down at his hands with revulsion as if he were seeing them drenched in someone else's blood. Shame shadowed his face and etched his voice. "I'm a monster. I kill worse monsters. That doesn't absolve what I am."

"I know what you are. You are no monster."

He started to shake his head.

Without thinking, she crossed the room, unable to help herself, drawn to him with every cell in her body. She placed her hand on his uninjured arm and forced him to look at her, to meet her gaze. "You're good, Eli. That is who you are. A good man."

This close, she inhaled the dusky, woodsy scent of him, took in the lean lines of his face, his slanting cheekbones, those hard black eyes that pierced her heart.

He watched her, desperately, almost hungrily. Heat swelled in her belly, quickening her pulse. They stood close, less than two feet apart.

"I know you," she said. "I know you better than anyone else."

"Lena." His eyes darkened with want, with need. The same need was reflected in her eyes, the desire she couldn't hide, couldn't bear to hide, not any longer.

Never had she been more aware of the time she'd been given. Nothing had felt more right in the world than this, here in this room with him.

"You don't have to hide," she said. "Not from me. I want the dark parts, the ugly parts, the broken pieces. The parts you don't want anyone else to see." She swallowed hard. "I want it all."

He stared at her for a long moment as if he couldn't believe her words, that it couldn't be real. His gaze questioning, hesitant, full of yearning. "Are you sure—I don't want to hurt you—"

"Shut up," she said. "And kiss me."

The years of pent-up longing burst like a dam breaking. One powerful stride and he reached her, seized her waist, and pulled her to him. Drawing her against his chest, he cradled her face in his calloused hands and tilted her chin toward him.

Eli bent his head and kissed her deeply. His lips on hers set her skin on fire. Her lips tingled and her fingertips sparked. Lena kissed him back. At first tentatively, then as hungrily as he kissed her.

Her pulse thudded wildly against her throat. She felt his heart beating in tandem with hers. Their bodies pressed together, Eli held her close as though he couldn't bear to let her go.

The years of want, of trials, of suffering, of loneliness, and heartache—it all fell away, burned to ashes and swept to dust.

Lena pulled away, her heart surging in her chest, breathless and giddy. She reached up and touched his cheek, looking into those dark eyes she adored.

"I've loved you my entire life." Eli's voice grew husky with emotion. "I would do anything to protect you. Anything. Even if it takes my soul."

She gazed up at him. "I know."

43

JACKSON CROSS
DAY NINETY-ONE

"Where is he?" Jackson asked. "Where is Horatio?"

Astrid blinked up at him from her seat in the living room, a novel in her lap. Her wheelchair sat next to the sofa, the cane leaning against the cushions beside her. "Where is who?"

"Father."

"He's out."

"Out where?"

Astrid gave a nonchalant shrug. "Out with whomever. Who knows? I'm not his keeper. He's a grown man in case you haven't noticed."

"Did he say when he would return?"

"Nope. Why do you care?"

Jackson forced himself to breathe, to be calm, to steel himself so he could think clearly. Since the train ambush, suspicion had been growing in the back of his mind, festering like cancer.

He needed to know for certain. He needed to confront Horatio in person, face to face.

Jackson strode through the expansive kitchen and vaulted living room, down the long hallway to his parents' master bedroom, looking for his father's things, searching for a hint as to where he might have gone.

Astrid hoisted herself from the sofa, grasped her cane, and thumped down the hallway after him. "Whatever you want, you won't find it here."

"Shut up for once."

"You only visit when you want something," Astrid spat at his back. "How do you think that makes Mom feel? Or how about me?"

Jackson was too stressed to worry about hurt feelings. Still, guilt pricked him. He did worry about his mother; he did care.

Wearing gloves like he was working a crime scene, he checked Horatio's master closet and dresser: several items of clothing were missing, his shoes were lined up neatly on the floor but a few were gone, though his suits still hung, immaculate and untouched.

His suitcase was not in the closet. On the dresser, Horatio's wallet and truck keys were gone, a clean spot in the dust where they were usually kept.

His father was gone. Where had he gone, and why?

"Horatio," his mother croaked.

Jackson turned from the closet, padded across the carpet, and sat on the edge of the bed. Dolores leaned against a pillow, her pencil-thin legs draped in a rose-pink comforter.

"Where have you been?" Her voice was thin and raspy. "I want my pills. I need my pills."

He winced at the sight of her. Leaning down, he kissed her cheek and took her hand in his, her wrist bones bird-thin beneath his fingers. "I love you, Mom."

She didn't seem to hear him or even register his presence.

There was nothing in the house, so he went out to the garage. At the back of the six-bay garage was a workshop filled with shiny tools his father enjoyed owning but seldom used. The workshop featured a marble half bath, a window for natural light, and a mahogany desk and leather chair. A new-looking ham radio system sat on the desk.

Strange. As far as he knew, his father had never owned a ham radio. Jackson picked up the mic with gloved hands and turned it over in his fingers. Next to the mic was a laminated book of call signs.

Why had his father procured a ham radio? Who was he in communication with? Why hadn't he said anything to Jackson? Was this how he communicated with Sawyer? Or someone else?

His concern deepened. That suspicion niggled in his mind, whispering terrible things. As he turned to go, something caught his eye. On the second shelf, a half-dozen prescription pill bottles lined up neatly next to a pair of speakers.

Jackson examined them. The medications were prescribed to strangers—Jason Myers, Callie Pine-Alton, and Taylor Ferguson. He didn't recognize the medications, so he wrote them down on his notepad.

These were not Astrid's antidepressants or his mother's sedatives. His father was in robust health and took nothing but a multivitamin.

Why was his father keeping meds in the workshop and not in the medicine cabinet in the house? He picked up another bottle and shook it, studying the tiny blue oblong pills.

A shiver of unease rippled through him. His father must have procured these meds from Sawyer as he did the fuel for the generator and gasoline for his vehicles. In exchange for what? For the years Horatio had looked the other way and allowed a parasite like Sawyer to gain a foothold and flourish unopposed?

Or was his father in bed with something even worse?

His anger didn't abate but burned bright, turned incandescent.

They were surrounded by wolves. Escaped convicts on the hunt, killing and thieving with impunity. A murderer living amongst them, hiding in plain sight. And the Côté cartel, a threat looming ever closer.

With a growl, he pounded the desk, feeling stymied at every turn due to the lack of communication, lack of transportation, lack of resources. Lack, lack, lack.

He kicked the office chair in frustration. The wheels squeaked.

Next to the office chair, parallel scuff marks marred the shiny wood floor.

Sawyer. He needed to confront Sawyer. Sawyer could tell him the truth about his father. He'd enjoy every second in the telling, but Sawyer had no reason to lie now.

Jackson took a last look at the mysterious pill bottles and headed for the door.

44

JACKSON CROSS
DAY NINETY-TWO

Jackson stood on the dock of William's Landing on Grand Island, arms in the air, palms out in a show of surrender, a dozen rifles pointed at his chest.

More armed men descended from the trail and exited the visitor station, weapons up and trained on Jackson. Two burly men stepped forward and frisked him roughly, then checked him for listening devices. Jackson recognized them from past arrests and surveillance.

He spoke calmly. "I'm unarmed. I'm alone. I'm here to talk to Sawyer."

One of the men took a step back and spoke into his radio. Jackson waited, outwardly calm, but his heart juddered against his ribs, his palms damp.

It was reckless to come alone without weapons or backup. Eli would have his hide for it. So would Lena. Jackson needed answers, and he was determined to get them—despite the danger.

He'd contacted Lena that morning about the prescription meds he'd found in the garage. She'd said, "Tolterodine is an acetylcholine blocker. Acetylcholine blockers are prescribed for IBS, depression, heart disease, Parkinson's, and insomnia. Treatments with anticholinergic effects in the brain can cause memory disturbances, agitation, confusion, and delirium. And lorazepam is a benzodiazepine, a medication meant to treat anxiety and insomnia, but it has sedative qualities and can cause cognitive problems, especially if he was giving her very high dosages. They could cause symptoms of dementia."

Her words had confirmed his worst suspicions.

He'd thanked her, then promptly borrowed a fishing boat from the marina and rowed to Grand Island. A mere half-mile from the Munising marina, the island was buttressed and fortified; it was a citadel set atop a three-hundred-foot sandstone cliff guarded by two hundred hardened mercenaries, skilled ex-soldiers, and violent criminals.

It was the middle of August. The heat wave had finally broken, and the day was a warm seventy-five degrees, the sun shining brilliant in the cobalt blue sky. Half a dozen yachts bobbed along the dock within the placid waters of Murray Bay.

Something glinted high above him along the cliffs of Wick Point. The gleam of sniper rifles. Sawyer had overwatch teams providing security 24/7. As if the plethora of weapons aimed at his head and chest wasn't enough.

A minute later, James Sawyer emerged from a trail leading to the bluff and strode down the dock toward Jackson, his movements languid and unhurried. Dressed in cargo shorts and a crisp button-down shirt, he was tall and muscular, his wavy hair sun-bleached, his tan skin weathered from years on the water.

He halted on the dock, his hands hanging loosely at his sides, his posture straight but relaxed, a hard alertness in his blue-gray eyes. There was no depth in that gaze, no emotion, just a wary watchfulness like a wild animal hunting its prey.

Sawyer didn't smile. "Well, if it isn't the Sheriff of Nottingham."

Jackson met his icy gaze. "Sawyer."

"Last time we met, it was under very different circumstances."

"Last time we met, you had snatched one of my men with the intent to torture and kill him."

"To be fair, you sent a rat into my organization. I deal with rats accordingly."

Jackson thought of David Kepford, how Sawyer's men had slaughtered him, shot him in the back, and dumped his body somewhere they'd never find him. His hands fisted at his sides as he struggled to push down his anger, to hide the revulsion burning his insides.

He longed to arrest Sawyer where he stood, slap handcuffs on him, and drag him to prison. He'd let him rot in a cell for the rest of his miserable life.

Those times were over. He had to deal with the reality they faced now. Justice was elusive when society supposedly functioned; now it threatened to slip forever out of his grasp.

"I took care of our little problem for you." Sawyer was referring to Cyrus Lee. "He's probably at the bottom of the lake wrapped in chains right now. I wouldn't know."

Jackson clenched his jaw, tension radiating from his teeth to his temples. "He was my suspect to arrest."

"You say po-tah-to, I say po-ta-to. "

He felt a dozen pairs of hard eyes on him, the gun barrels zeroed in on his torso from men and women who'd love to put a bullet between his eyes and call it a day.

"I'd feel more comfortable if your people would kindly lower their weapons. I'm no threat to them." Jackson knew better than to make demands. Sawyer was more amenable to requests that stroked his considerable ego. "Please."

"No threat at the moment."

"At the moment," Jackson readily agreed.

"Whatever makes you comfortable." Sawyer smiled without mirth and raised a hand. Two dozen rifles dropped into the low ready position. Itchy fingers moved from triggers, but barely.

"What do you want, Jackson?" Sawyer said in a low voice that wouldn't carry to his men. "I'm a very busy man."

"I've seen your handiwork. Overdoses are at a record high.

Drug-induced suicides. Meth heads robbing innocent families for supplies to trade for more drugs."

Sawyer offered his most innocent look. "I've no idea what you mean."

"Yes, you do."

Sawyer shrugged. "Life is hell. Hypothetically, if people want to escape that hell, what's it to you or me? People have a right to choose how to live. Frankly, for every person that chooses not to pass Go and collect two hundred dollars, there are more resources to spare for you and me. For Lena, and for that kid you care so much about."

"You're destroying people's lives."

"Hypothetically. And I'm not doing anything."

"It'll kill them."

"They're dead men walking anyway. The dregs of society. No one wants them. Let them go in a drug-induced haze. Everyone's better off. You're not stupid, Cross. You're stubborn and arrogant and infuriating, but you're not stupid. I know you see that."

Jackson thought of Daniel, Scott Smith's son. They weren't better off. He was physically present, but they'd already lost him, and they knew it.

Sawyer's countenance brightened. "Do you need something to take the edge off? Pick your poison. I'd be happy to make a deal with the new sheriff. Off the record, of course, for old friends."

Sawyer had grown up with Jackson and the others, but he'd never been part of the in-crowd, although he'd brought the goods to all the parties, and he'd always wanted to be an insider. His father had been a narcotics trafficker, serving as the distribution link between Detroit and organized crime in Quebec. When his father went to prison, Sawyer had taken over the business and transformed himself into a kingpin of the Upper Peninsula's criminal underworld.

Anything Sawyer did for him would have a price tag; it always did. "I'm not here to make a deal."

Sawyer looked disappointed. "Then why, pray tell, are you here?"

Seagulls soared and squawked above their heads. Clear jade-green water lapped at the dock. Behind Sawyer, the island rose, verdant with dense forests of pine, spruce, beech, maple, and alder, impressive sandstone bluffs jutting into the lake.

"I'm here for my father."

"Hate to disappoint you, but he's not here."

"I have some questions. Answer them, and I'll leave."

Sawyer's expression didn't change. "You're not wearing a wire. This isn't a trap conjured up by the FBI. Does the FBI even still exist? Wait, don't tell me. I don't care."

"I just want the truth about my family."

Sawyer's lip curled. "Be careful what you wish for."

Jackson decided to lead with the truth. "My father drugged Dolores and possibly Astrid, keeping them docile. He's using prescription drugs to artificially induce dementia in my mother. I believe she knows things he doesn't want getting out."

"I can say this with absolute certainty—those meds didn't come from me."

"My father is dirty."

Sawyer's eyes narrowed. "I don't know a thing about that."

Jackson put his suspicions into words. "I already know, Sawyer. My father has been working with you for years, alerting you to surveillance, tipping you off to raids, and exerting his power to keep the heat off you. Even after he retired, he still held political sway over Underwood, the mayor, the DA, and the governor. He still held value for you. In exchange, you've kept him cozy with fuel for his generator, food, and whatever black-market meds he needed."

Sawyer didn't react other than to flash a cunning smile. And in that smile, he confirmed everything Jackson needed to know. It wasn't evidence in a court of law, but it was enough.

Jackson exhaled slowly. Acid stung the back of his throat. He wanted to puke. Clammy sweat broke out on his skin. He felt sick.

Horatio had been corrupt from the beginning, selling himself and his office to the highest bidder, all along pretending to be the champion of the moral high ground. How far did his father's corruption go? He tried not to show how rattled he felt—horrified and ashamed.

Sawyer tilted his head, studying him for a moment like he was a bug beneath a magnifying glass. He took a step closer. "Who your father is and what he does is no concern of mine. As you know, I'm innocent of any wrongdoing. However, I do have something I'm sure you'd be interested in."

Jackson went still. "What is it?"

"You'll owe me a favor," Sawyer said slyly.

"I don't owe you anything."

"We'll see."

Jackson sighed. "Tell me."

"I'm only throwing you this bone because we have a mutual enemy, you and I, whom I happen to despise more than you."

"Spit it out, Sawyer."

Sawyer's eyes sparked with anger, but that anger wasn't directed at Jackson. "Your good old papa switched sides. He found a bigger fish and went and suckled that teat. My network has informed me that he's snitching, providing information to our enemy."

Jackson felt like he'd been sucked under water. He couldn't breathe. "The cartel."

Sawyer snapped his fingers. "Bingo."

He didn't want to believe it, but there it was, the evidence staring him in the face. The ham radio was the method Horatio used to communicate with the Côté cartel in the Soo and beyond into Canada, how Horatio had warned them of the train ambush.

Horatio had overheard Jackson and Devon speaking on the radio that day at the house. It was the only thing that made sense. There was no other leak. It was his father, in bed with brutal criminals, his father who had ratted them out to the cartel.

Anger burned through him. Outrage threatened to burst from

his skin and incinerate his bones. He struggled to rein in his emotions, to stay in control of himself.

Sawyer saw his fury and smiled. "Ah. The truth stings, doesn't it?"

Jackson took a hard look at his nemesis. Sawyer could be deceiving him, but he didn't think so. Sawyer was also incensed that Horatio had betrayed him and was out for blood.

Every answer he uncovered filled him with more questions. Why would his father jump ship on Sawyer when he had a good thing going, just to climb into bed with a worse criminal? Was that the reason? Horatio saw a chance to align himself with the most powerful entity in the region, and so he did.

To betray Sawyer was no small thing. Sawyer had an army and extensive reach; he had eyes and ears everywhere, almost everywhere. But the Côté cartel represented a criminal enterprise the likes of which they had not yet seen, rapidly consolidating power, growing exponentially, and spreading like cancer.

There was something he was still missing, a piece to the puzzle not yet in place.

"I'm going to have to find your father, Jackson," Sawyer said.

"He knows I'm onto him. He's in the wind. I don't know where he is."

"I believe you, though I have my ideas about it."

"You think he's already with the cartel."

Sawyer gave an insolent shrug. "You know what I have to do."

Jackson knew what Sawyer was insinuating, how he liked to wrap his enemies in chains and throw them to the fish in the deepest depths of Superior, the water so cold that bodies remained preserved for decades down in the frigid depths. "I'll find him first."

Something shrewd and calculating flitted across Sawyer's face. "May the best man win."

Jackson spun on his heels and headed down the dock toward his little boat bobbing against the pilings. "Don't shoot me in the back. That is not a war you want to start."

"Wouldn't dream of it." Sawyer paused. "Oh, and Jackson."

A foot from his boat, Jackson halted. His stomach in knots, he turned back toward Sawyer. He kept his posture relaxed, his voice nonchalant. "Is there something else? I'm busy."

"Speaking of wars, you wouldn't happen to know the whereabouts of two of my loyal soldiers, would you?"

Jackson stilled. His heart pounding, he kept his expression neutral. Two could play this game. "What are you talking about?"

"I'm missing a couple of men. To be exact: one male, one female. They're fairly attached to each other. It's odd that they would both fail to show up for their duties two days running. Also, I'm coming up short on fuel and propane gas. Very odd, don't you think?"

"I have no idea how you run things or what your people do or don't do, Sawyer."

"Because if you did know their whereabouts and you failed to tell me, it would be grounds for a war, a war that you and your boy scouts would certainly lose, even with Eli Pope batting for your team."

"Duly noted," Jackson said.

Neither man moved. Tension thrummed between them. Sawyer's men raised their weapons a fraction. Jackson didn't look at the guns surrounding him; he kept his gaze steady on Sawyer and didn't blink.

Sawyer broke the stare first. He waved a hand, dismissing Jackson. "Don't ever say I didn't do favors for old friends."

Jackson bit his tongue, stopping short of a snarky response. Sawyer still thought there was some connection between them, even after everything, and Jackson chose not to disabuse him of that notion. The Côté cartel was a common enemy, and there might come a time when Alger County needed something from Sawyer. A placated Sawyer was something Jackson could work with if necessary. He kept his true feelings to himself and forced a smile. "We'll see about that."

Sawyer grinned but it failed to reach his eyes, which were flat and empty as a shark's. "Like I said, be careful what you wish for."

As Jackson departed, he half expected a bullet to the spine, but it never came. He was on the fishing boat rowing for the mainland when his radio crackled to life. It was Moreno. "We've got something on Sykes."

45

ELI POPE
DAY NINETY-TWO

E li cursed. "We just missed him!"

He stood in the center of the cavernous room, Jackson at his side. Moreno and Hart worked one side of the factory while Devon and Chief McCallister took the opposite side. Nash was outside taking castings of the tire tracks.

They stood in a paper mill factory off River Rock Road, fifteen miles west of Munising and north of the hamlet of Chatham. A maze of machinery loomed above their heads, huge pallets of paper were stacked higher than his head. He inhaled the scents of dust, ink, and paper.

A couple of sleeping bags had been left in one corner behind one of the printing presses. Discarded trash wrappers from protein bars, bags of chips, and MREs were scattered everywhere. He inhaled the cheesy scent of Doritos, and his stomach growled.

Toward the rear of the factory floor stood five truck bays. Scuffs and scrapes in the dust revealed where large objects had been moved recently, likely loaded through the bay into trucks or SUVs.

"One of the volunteer observation posts called it in," Jackson said. "I put eyes-on surveillance on as many associates of the convicts as I could track down and cover. This warehouse is owned by Jared Huffman, the uncle of Jacob Huffman, convicted of strangling his ex-girlfriend when she attempted to leave him. We didn't know about it until two days ago. I put two guys across the street, and last night we hit pay dirt. They saw a bunch of SUVs entering through the back. They entered from the alley and cut the gate padlock. The factory is miles from town and out of radio range, even with the repeaters we've installed. It took hours for the volunteers to get back to town and alert us. By the time we arrived, the suspects had left."

"How many vehicles did they count?"

"Four."

Devon kicked at several candy wrappers strewn about with the toe of her boot. "Looks like they've got plenty of food."

Jackson walked around between the pallets, studying the scene and taking photographs with his phone. "The cartel supplied Sykes with meds and weapons. No reason to think they wouldn't provide food as well."

He bent behind a stack of pallets, retrieved something, and returned to Eli and Devon, holding it almost reverently on his palm: a Snickers bar, unopened and unsullied.

"Sweet!" Devon breathed. "I haven't had a candy bar in...two months, maybe more? My mouth is already watering. Finders keepers, damn it. I'd give you my left pinkie finger for two bites."

"That's Shiloh's favorite," Eli said.

"I know." Jackson tucked the candy bar into his pants pocket. "I'll save it for her."

"Lucky dog," Devon grumbled.

Moreno approached them from the factory side door. "The tire tracks we found outside match the casts we took from the Fitch, Marlowe, and M-28 crime scenes. No doubt this is Sykes."

"*Was* Sykes," Eli said in frustration. "He's long gone."

"We'll set up more deer trail cameras and checkpoints on all roads leading to and from the paper mill," Jackson said.

"Too late," Eli said. "They took everything but trash. They're not coming back. If I were Sykes, I'd move around, too. Never stay too long in one place. Especially not a safe house connected to my old life that someone could track, as we did."

"Any hits on the cameras?" Jackson asked Devon.

"Not yet. We're sending teams to check them every day. It's only a matter of time."

"Time we don't have," Eli said.

Jackson spread out the map of forest roads on top of a crate of shipping packages. He traced red Xs with his finger. "The last three crime scenes were located west of Munising, including the paper mill. We'll concentrate our resources to the west."

"That's hundreds of thousands of acres of wilderness and thousands of miles of logging and forest roads," Devon said. "What's even out there?"

Eli said, "Lots of old mines, campgrounds, caves, abandoned logging camps, and a few small townships. As good a place as any to get lost in."

"Once we sniff out his trail, we'll have him," Jackson said.

Eli nodded, barely listening. The stitches itched incessantly. He resisted the urge to scratch through his bandages, which he changed twice a day after applying topical antibiotics.

So far, he'd avoided infection, but the wounds hurt like hell and hampered his movements.

He kept thinking of Lena. He could still taste her on his lips, smelled her vanilla-scented hair in his dreams, felt her arms around his waist, her heartbeat against his chest, the sound of her laugh ringing in his ears.

She was more than he could've imagined. She was real, she was flawed, and she was everything he wanted. This woman, strong and sweet, tough and gentle, who believed in goodness, by some miracle believed in *him*.

Lena's encouragement had given him the strength and confidence to be a father to Shiloh. She and Shiloh had transformed his entire world in monumental, earth-shattering ways; he could never return to the small shrunken life he'd lived, trapped within a prison of his own making.

The thought of Sykes hurting Lena or Shiloh set his insides humming with rage. If anyone touched his daughter again, he would disembowel them with his bare hands. He would destroy the whole world before he allowed any harm to come to her.

"We need to set up listening posts," he said. "We'll do things the old-fashioned way, how the FBI and DEA used to do before GPS-tracking. Show me where the deer cameras are. If they didn't catch anything last night, then we focus on the forest roads without cameras, as one of those logging roads was the most likely path they took out of here. Where's the nearest one from this location that's heading west? That's where we start."

Jackson examined the map and then pointed. "This one goes north to Au Train before heading west, hugging the coast through Marquette. And this one here stays west through the center of the U.P., through Chatham into Marquette County, before branching off in several directions near Gwinn, less than fifty miles southwest of Munising."

"You think he's holed up that far from Munising?" Devon asked.

"With electric vehicles and a way to charge them, which he obviously has, then it's an hour's drive. Add some time for the rugged logging roads, but it's doable. I'll reconvene the task force, and we'll get the listening posts going tonight." Jackson turned to Devon and Moreno. "Keep working the scene."

They nodded and went back to work. Jackson hesitated, rubbing at his jaw. Dark circles ringed his eyes, a tightness around his mouth. He hadn't shaved in days if not weeks.

Eli's mind raced ahead to the task at hand, but he could tell when something was bothering Jackson. He always could. "What is it?"

Jackson lowered his voice. "It's my father. He's the one who ratted us out to the cartel. That's how they knew we were coming for the train. He overheard me on the radio and went straight to them."

Anger roiled through Eli. Horatio Cross was an arrogant dirtbag, always had been. His son had nearly lost his life in the ambush. So had Eli, for that matter. An image of Sykes' sickening smile seared his mind. He felt himself drowning again.

"I'm sorry," Jackson said, stricken.

Eli forced his rage down somewhere deep, inhaled a steadying breath and steeled himself. "Did you know?"

"Of course not, but—"

"Then you have nothing to be guilty for. Do you know how to reach him?"

"He's gone, probably fled to the protection of the cartel."

"What's done is done."

Jackson shook his head in misery. "I don't understand. How he could do this—"

"Put him out of your head, Jackson. He's been playing mind games with you since we were kids. He's getting to you, messing with your psyche, and he's not even here. Don't let him win."

Jackson nodded. "Yeah, you're right."

"I need to know that your head's on straight. Your people need you on top of your game. First, we get Sykes and those meds. Then we'll worry about your damn father."

A hint of a smile crossed Jackson's face. "You said 'we' just now."

Eli could tell he was thinking about the old times, when it was just them, two lonely boys against the whole world.

Eli scowled. "Don't get sappy on me. We've got a whole bunch of bad guys to kill."

46

SHILOH EASTON
DAY NINETY-THREE

S hiloh scrunched up her nose. "You want me to eat cattails? Gross."

"Marshland hot dogs," Lori corrected her. "Most parts are edible. The root, called the rhizome, is crunchy and fresh, like celery. I slice up the tops when they're still green and use them in stir-fries. The seed fuzz can be used as a fire starter. We can also dry the roots and grind them into flour or soak them to extract the starch."

"Sounds disgusting. I'll pass."

"If you're starving, you won't think so," Ruby said.

Shiloh gave her the middle finger.

Ruby only smiled.

Lori led a small group along a trail through the property, pointing out edible plants and mushrooms, teaching them the best times to harvest each plant, what parts to eat, and how to cook them.

Ruby and her mother, Michelle Carpenter, were visiting for the day. Michelle was considering moving to the Northwoods Inn. Two nights ago, their neighbors had been robbed at gunpoint. Lena had talked to Tim and Lori, who'd invited Michelle to check the place out.

Lena took up the rear, taking photos with her phone, scribbling notes, and collecting specimens. Bear wandered after them, enthusiastically snuffling every plant, twig, blade of grass, and tree root, his tail wagging as he took in the spectacular scents of his new home.

Bear looked relieved to have escaped the attentions of Faith the goat, who was busy tormenting the chefs in the kitchen, determined to steal as much human food as she possibly could.

Lori pointed to a carpet of wild violets growing in the shade of a huge oak. "Use the whole plant, stem and flowers, in salads. Or you can crush them and make a honey-violet cough syrup. They're high in vitamins A and C, and are antioxidant, anti-inflammatory, and good for colds."

She showed them nettle leaves and fiddlehead ferns, a swirly plant that tasted like asparagus, and mushrooms, cautiously distinguishing the edible from the poisonous ones.

"How do you know so much?" Michelle asked.

"When we bought this place twenty years ago, we envisioned it as a thriving artists' colony, a retreat for writers and artists. One of our early writers was a prepper of sorts. He's the one who showed me how to forage in my backyard and showed us all the amazing things we could be doing with the property. We were inspired. We've tried to grow everything we needed from our land as much as possible which is why we invested in goats and chickens, planted so many edible trees and bushes, and started hydroponics gardening. Things grew from there."

I bought every book I could get my hands on that had to do with edible plants, foraging, homesteading, prepping, and homeopathic remedies. The books have proven to be invaluable. No one person can know or remember everything."

Lena said, "I think you're pretty close."

Michelle stretched and rubbed her back. "I like what you're doing here, Lori. I never imagined I'd want to join a commune, but here we are."

"Desperate times call for desperate measures," Shiloh quipped.

Lori smiled, her eyes crinkling. "I admit it, I never imagined this place as a post-apocalyptic stronghold."

Shiloh liked the sound of that. Let a madman like Sykes try to infiltrate this fortress. They'd slaughter him. Eli would take him apart piece by piece, and leave chunks of him for the crows and vultures to devour.

Lori said, "I think as time goes by that more and more folks will return to living in groups, like clans, for protection and division of labor. It was how humanity survived for thousands of years. Many hands make our tasks not so burdensome. And while companionship won't end suffering, friendship lightens the load."

Lena knelt next to a bunch of morel mushrooms, plucking several and adding them to the canvas satchel slung across her chest. She was too skinny, her jean shorts hanging from her hips, her face pale, circles smudging the skin beneath her eyes.

Without enough insulin, Lena was fading more every day. Whenever Shiloh glimpsed her bruised fingertips, her guts knotted in apprehension. It worried her more than she could articulate. Eli had brought back enough for a few more weeks, but it wouldn't last. And then what? No one could answer that question.

"How many people can stay here?" Lena asked.

"We've got about one hundred and fifty residents, give or take," Lori said. "I think we'll max out around two hundred if we can scavenge enough supplies to build more cabins and dig another latrine. Any more and you start getting clans within the larger clan, and divisions. Us versus them, more politics, plus the hygiene, sanitation, trash, and septic problems—too many people and it gets overwhelming. The only thing we know for certain is that change is inevitable. We pray, do our best, and leave the rest in God's hands."

"Wish we could leave the laundry in God's hands," Shiloh grumbled.

Lori laughed. She had a kind laugh; it rang pure and sweet

through the trees. Fine wrinkles crinkled at her eyes and mouth, her cheeks were pink and plump like the grandmothers in fairy tales. Everything about the Brooks seemed too good to be true.

Shiloh fisted her hands on her hips. "Why are you so nice? You could keep this all for yourself. Most people would. If you weren't sharing electricity with so many people, you'd have enough to power everything—hot water, the washing machine, and lights."

"Two reasons," Lori said. "We could try to keep this place a secret, but someday, someone would find out. And then they would try to take what we have. If they had more people than we did, they would win. It's not ours if we can't keep it. We brought in others to help us protect ourselves and keep this place safe. We're stronger together, and that's the truth."

It made sense to Shiloh. "And the second reason?"

"It's the right thing to do. I believe in God. I have faith, and faith means living out your beliefs. You have to live your faith, or else, what is it good for? Faith without good works is dead."

Shiloh made a face. "There's got to be a catch."

"No catch."

"I don't believe in that stuff."

Lori's smile only broadened. "You don't have to believe in anything, sweetie. No one here is going to push anything on you. I do believe there is meaning and purpose to life. Otherwise, why don't we just give up right now and end it? Life is too painful if it's all meaningless. I choose to believe I have a purpose. As humans on this earth, we're responsible for each other. Commitment and responsibility are a part of life, a good life, a purposeful life worth living. That goes whether we have laws, electricity, and a functional society, or we don't."

Shiloh didn't know what she believed, but she knew the importance of family right down to her soul. She'd lost too much to take anything for granted. And she'd fight to the death to protect the people she cared about and the places worth keeping —like this one.

Lori walked further along the trail and paused at a thicket with large green, maple-shaped leaves and bright red berries. "The thimbleberry is a delicacy of the U.P. It's incredibly nutritious, a good source of vitamins A and C, plus potassium, calcium, and iron, and boosts the immune system."

Lena raised her brows at Shiloh. "And for those of you with a sweet tooth, thimbleberries make delicious jams and pies."

Shiloh's mouth watered as she plucked a berry and popped it in her mouth, the sour-sweet juice bursting on her tongue. She tried to banish her anxiety and forced a smile she didn't feel, for Lena's sake. "Now you're speaking my language."

47

JACKSON CROSS
DAY NINETY-THREE

Jackson stood in the doorway to his mother's room. Rain rattled the roof and poured down the glass. Lightning lit up the darkened windows in pulses. "Mom? Are you awake?"

Dolores blinked blearily up at him from the bed. "Jackson? Is that you?"

Relief flared through him. "It's me."

"You left me! I've been all alone, so alone..."

"I'm here now. I'm right here."

He helped his mother out of her nightgown, averting his gaze from her emaciated figure, and gave her a sponge bath. He brought in a bowl of warm water and rinsed out her hair, combing the brittle strands with his fingers. He talked to her, told her things would be okay, reminding her of memories and people and events she could no longer recall.

His chest ached. How quickly her mind had retreated into a fathomless nothingness. It broke his heart. "I won't leave again, Mom. I promise."

If only he could carry her in his arms, deposit her in his truck, and whisk her to a hospital where nurses would dote on her and the doctors would order a battery of tests and hook her up to machines to monitor her vital signs.

The loss of modern medicine was devastating. Humanity had taken the miracle for granted. Now it was abruptly, ruthlessly, gone.

"I need my pills," she mumbled. "I can't sleep, I can't sleep without them..."

"I know. I'll get them." He got her settled back in bed, fluffed the pillows, and lay her gently down. "I love you, Mom."

But his mother wasn't listening anymore. It was like she couldn't even hear him. Her shoulder blades were hunched inward like wings. Her silver hair was frazzled, her crepe skin loose around her jowls. She looked so incredibly frail.

Jackson stayed with her long into the night, listening to the rattle in her chest deepen along with his fear.

48

SHILOH EASTON
DAY NINETY-FOUR

Shiloh picked up her pace. "I wanna do security."

Eli jogged beside her. "That's a hard nope."

"Why not?"

"You're a kid."

"That's not fair."

"Seems perfectly reasonable to me."

Shiloh and Eli ran through the forest along the jogging trail that circled the perimeter of the Northwoods Inn property, the trail Eli ran daily, checking the perimeter's security measures, the sniper hides, and the patrols.

"I'm no little kid." She pumped her legs harder, dodging rocks and sidestepping roots snaking across the dirt path. "I'm nearly fourteen."

He halted, stopped right in the center of the trail and stared down at her with a stunned expression. The realization dawned on his face—he didn't know her birthday. He looked guilty as hell.

Shiloh harbored zero resentment toward him, but she wasn't beyond manipulating that guilt to get her way. Widening her eyes, she twisted her features to appear hurt.

"When—" He swallowed. "When is your birthday?"

"September sixteenth." Her nose scrunched up as she worked

out the days of the month in her head. "That's only a few weeks away."

He nodded soberly. "I'll remember that. I'm—I'm sorry I didn't know."

Shiloh took the moment of respite from their punishing run to grab her filtered bottle from her pack and guzzle several mouthfuls of lukewarm water. She wiped her mouth with the back of her arm.

"It hurts, Eli, down deep in my soul. A gaping wound I'm not sure I'll ever recover from. I'm gonna need years of therapy for this. Unfortunately, last I checked, the shrinks are all in hand-to-mouth survival mode like the rest of us."

"I'll look into it."

"You do that."

She still called him Eli. Late at night, lying in bed with Bear snoring in her ear, she considered the options. Dad? Father? Daddy? Too babyish. What if he didn't like being called dad? He'd lived his whole life without knowing he had a daughter. This was probably as weird for him as it was for her.

Everything between them had gone awkward as if they were feeling each other out all over again, learning how this strange new relationship would take shape. He'd never been a father. She'd never had one. Neither knew how this was supposed to work.

"Keep running," Eli said gruffly. "We've got to finish the circuit."

Ten freaking miles, with a backpack. Eli was a cruel taskmaster. She took one last slurp from her water bottle and stuck it into a side pouch. Her stomach rumbled; she'd donate a kidney for a Snickers bar right now.

His dark eyes glinted. "Unless you're too tired."

"Eat my dust!"

She took off ahead of him, but there was no outrunning Eli. They jogged together side by side. Eli slowed his steady stride, his breaths even. Shiloh was small but quick, her legs pistoning to keep up, gasping for breath like a dying fish. To be fair, they'd already pounded out seven miles today.

Everyone was so busy, with Jackson and Eli constantly on the hunt to track down Sykes, that she seldom saw Eli unless she joined him on his runs. She despised running. It nearly killed her, but she was getting stronger, faster and fitter.

Either that, or she was about to give herself a hernia.

Truth be told, it wasn't just the running. She was Eli Pope's daughter. She belonged to someone in a way she never had before. It was changing everything in ways she didn't quite understand yet. She'd never admit it out loud, but it was good. Everything about this father-daughter thing they were building together was good. Well, almost everything.

"How are things going at the Inn?" Eli asked awkwardly. "Making friends?"

"I managed to make it through the day without beating anyone with a chair, so I'd say my people skills are improving."

Eli guffawed.

She liked it when she could make him laugh. It was a rare event. "When are we gonna tan that black bear hide? I think I'll get more respect once I'm wearing it as my new apocalypse coat. It's gonna jazz up my vibe, you know? Then I'll just need some leather chaps to complete the outfit. Shock and awe, baby."

"I get the shock part; I don't know about the awe, though." Eli increased his pace. "When we have time. In case you haven't noticed, we've been busy trying to keep everybody from killing us."

Shiloh worked harder to match him, the stitch in her side burning. "Yeah, I've noticed, which brings me right back to my security proposal."

"Too dangerous."

"You've been training me! I'm even better than you at the crossbow."

"Doesn't matter."

"Sure, it does!"

"You're not ready."

"That's a big load of B.S. It's not like you've got elite tier-one warriors manning your checkpoints and perimeter security, by the way. I caught Jason Anders falling asleep at the northwest post two days ago. And last night, I was out using the latrine, so I thought I'd check on the southern patrol team. Amanda Martz was smoking a cigarette which blinds your night vision, right? Someone could've snuck up on her, easy peasy."

Shiloh looked up from the path ahead of her to sneak a glance at Eli. His profile was stern as if etched from stone. His jaw clenched, mouth flat. He wasn't happy.

Their sneakers thudded the packed dirt in rhythmic beats. Shiloh's pulse roared in her ears, her chest tight, her lungs bursting. "You're letting Drew Stewart on the security team, and he's sixteen! He doesn't know his butt from his tail end when it comes to weapons."

"He's not that bad."

"Dude. He can't hit the broad side of a barn ten feet away. I was better than him when I was seven. Hell, I was better than him when I was in diapers!"

Eli grunted and ran faster, his long legs outpacing her.

Shiloh's side ached, lactic acid building up in her muscles. It felt like she was dying. "I have the skills. I'm just as good as them, and I'll get better—"

"I said no!"

"That's not fair! Why should you have any say? Just because you're...because you're my..." Her voice trailed off. She halted in the middle of the trail, one hand pressed to her side, gasping. Hot tears stung her eyelids, and she blinked them back fiercely. "You can't treat me any different!"

Eli stopped and turned around to face her. They stood three yards apart. He was barely winded. A sheen of sweat dotted his forehead. "Like hell, I can't."

Birds twittered around them. Sunlight shifted through maple, beech, and elm trees, and violets sprouted in the shade on either side of the trail. Insects hummed. Two squirrels chased each other up the bark of a massive oak tree; its branches arched across the trail above them in a thick green canopy.

"I've more than proven myself! I survived Boone. I survived the lighthouse attack. I killed the black bear. That jerkwad attacked me in the woods, and I fought him off. Me! All by myself!" She pounded her chest fiercely with her fist. "I did that!"

"You did," Eli admitted like it was the hardest thing in the world.

"I'm sitting here stuck and helpless while people are dying! While Lena is sick and I can't do anything..." Whenever she thought of Lena dying, the ground seemed to drop out from beneath her. A sob clawed up her throat, but she forced it back and pushed out the words. "What was the point of everything I've done if I can't do something that *matters*?"

Eli stared at her for a long minute in silence. "I just found you," he said in a halting voice. "I can't—I don't want to lose you."

"What about me? Don't I get a say? You and Jackson are out there risking everything! Maybe I can't bear to lose you, either. Did you think about that? Did anyone think about that? The thing is that I already know how it works. I know it better than anyone. Death takes whoever it wants, whenever it wants. You can lose everything and think you can't possibly lose more, but you can." Her voice was a hoarse whisper. "You can always lose more."

Eli wiped sweat from his brow. His expression contorted. "Shiloh—"

"Don't you dare patronize me. Not me. Not after everything." She squared her shoulders, straightened her spine, and stood tall in the middle of the trail. Trees towered above their heads, blocking out the sun. She breathed in the scent of pine needles, peat, and rich soil. "Not me."

He stared at her like she was a feral creature he'd discovered inside his house; he didn't know how to get close without getting scratched or bitten.

She fisted her hands on her hips. "I have the right to defend my home and my people. You can't take that away from me. You don't have the right to take that from me. I get to choose!"

A long moment passed. Finally, Eli's shoulders slumped in resignation. He didn't look happy, but he blew out a breath and gave her a reluctant nod. "Okay."

She stared at him. "Okay, what?"

"This is the deal," Eli said. "I will give you security posts with the least chance of hostile contact. You will serve as a sentry, that's it. You will neither argue with me nor will you complain. You will accept my orders without question. You will train with the security team every evening for two hours minimum, in addition to your other chores."

Shiloh breathed deeply, her lungs expanding. She felt a lightness in her chest, spreading through her whole body. She stuck out her sweaty hand and offered her cheesiest grin. "Deal."

49

JACKSON CROSS
DAY ONE HUNDRED

J ackson squatted beside Gideon Crawford on a bed of pine needles beneath a tall jack pine two yards into the trees lining the forest road. He breathed evenly, inhaling the scents of pine needles, damp earth, and moss.

The night crouched low and dark over the trees. The sickle moon hung bright in the cloudless sky, the stars scattered in dense sparkling layers, the Milky Way arcing overhead.

A branch creaked above them.

Alarmed, Gideon whipped around, reaching for his weapon. On his knees, he gripped the rifle with both hands, brought the stock to his shoulder, and peered wildly through the optical sites.

Above their heads, a large shape burst into motion.

Jackson's heart kicked in his chest.

The large shape spread enormous wings and took flight—a great horned owl. The details blurred against the hazy green background of their NVGs. Large speckled wings beat the air as its head swiveled, glowing yellow eyes peering down at them for a moment before it lifted its mantle of wings and flew up and away, a black silhouette against the bright stars.

Gideon raised his rifle.

Jackson reached out and shoved the barrel down toward the ground. "What are you doing?"

"What the hell was that?" Gideon cried.

"Just an owl."

Gideon lowered the rifle, chagrined. "Sorry," he muttered. "I'm on edge."

"Calm your nerves."

"Yeah, okay. Guess I'm more nervous than I thought."

"This is an observation post only," Jackson assured him. "We use the gun only as a last resort since the sound might alert anyone nearby to our presence. We won't be fighting. They won't even know we're here."

Gideon nodded as he shifted his position, dropping the rifle to his side. They wore dark clothing, their faces smeared with Eli's grease paint, and their exposed skin slathered in natural bug repellent to fend off mosquitoes. Their helmets with night vision goggles attached allowed them to see clearly at night; the forest shone an eerie, alien green.

Jackson peered between the trunks of two powdery-white birch trees at the road. Weeds sprouted in the center of the two-track dirt lane with overgrown underbrush spreading into the trail. Overhead, leafy branches formed a dense canopy. Without the DNR, the wilderness was swiftly reclaiming the formerly groomed forest roads.

Jackson and Gideon were positioned in a hide a couple of hundred yards from the next intersection where the forest road headed straight to the west, turned east, or curved in an S-pattern to the north toward Marquette.

They would remain at this listening post for the night, taking turns on watch.

Four days ago, the motion-activated deer camera had captured several dark-colored SUVs driving this road headed west. Each night, they'd moved their listening post bit by bit, gradually zeroing in on Sykes' location.

Once the SUVs passed a listening post, after they'd gone a safe distance ahead, the observers would walk or ride via bike a few miles until the next fork in the road, and then stop. The next night, the observers picked up at the new location, again following the SUVs at a safe distance until the next fork in the road, then stopped again.

In this way, they were covertly trailing the convicts back to their hideout, cautious mile by cautious mile, night by night.

They couldn't follow the SUVs by car, since any vehicle on the road would automatically arouse suspicion. The process was infuriatingly slow and painstaking, but if Sykes caught on, he would move again, and they would lose him.

Gideon was antsy. He kept fidgeting, nervously clearing his throat and guzzling noisily from his water bottle. For a moment, Jackson wished he'd brought Devon instead. She was far better company, but she was manning another listening post on a logging road ten miles south of their position.

Besides, Jackson had chosen Gideon as his partner for a reason.

The desire to capture Sykes consumed him, matching the compelling need to track down life-saving meds for Lena, but he hadn't forgotten about Lily's case, not for a single second.

Jackson wasn't naïve; cold cases were extremely difficult to solve on a good day, and untangling a near decade-old murder amid a worldwide disaster felt overwhelmingly futile, searching for that impossible needle in a haystack.

The needle was out there. He knew it. He *felt* it.

And he was certain the citizen volunteer crouched beside him was a liar.

Jackson flipped up his goggles. The glowing green world vanished. In its place, the light of the full moon gilded the edges of things in pale glimmers. He blinked to adjust his eyes to the darkness. "We need to talk."

Gideon grunted. "I'd rather not."

"I have a few questions to ask you about Lily Easton's case."

"Oh, hell no."

"It won't take long."

"You already caught the killer."

He said the same thing he'd said to Astrid. "We're closing out the case, tying up the last few loose strings." Jackson didn't mention Cyrus Lee Jefferson or that he'd had an alibi for the murder. He didn't say that he suspected Gideon but couldn't prove it.

"What does it matter if there's no court system?"

"Everything matters. The law still matters. Someday, the world will get glued back together, and then we'll have to answer for what we did in these hard times. I want to be able to testify that I did everything I could. Don't you?"

"Everything's breaking down, including the law. Nothing is getting put back together."

Jackson feared Gideon was right. Even if the next decade or two brought power and order back to the Northern Hemisphere, everything would be a chaotic mess and remain so for years. No one would remember who did what to survive, let alone collecting evidence and holding trials. But there was more to justice than courts and prisons.

"We don't have to lose our humanity," Jackson said quietly. "That's up to us."

Gideon's mouth thinned in anger. "You brought me out here for this? I volunteered to protect my community, not subject myself to a pointless interrogation. I don't have to answer your questions."

"No, you don't. No one can make you." Frustration bubbled up inside him. He was sick and tired of being stymied at every turn. He paused, letting his words hang in the air. "Seems like you'd want to help me find out what happened to the woman you professed to love."

Gideon tensed, his hands balling into fists like he expected a fight and wouldn't back down. Emotion contorted his features. Was it guilt or something else? He didn't speak for a minute, as if struggling with his conscience, self-protection vying against the desire to do the right thing.

He looked away and shrugged his broad shoulders. "Whatever. Ask your questions."

"Where were you that night, during midnight and two a.m., the time of the murder?"

"My statement is in the file."

"It says you left the bar at ten p.m. and went to Ana Grady's house, the mother of your dead fiancé. And you stayed until eleven p.m. You don't have an alibi for the time of the murder."

Gideon deflated. "I went to Ana Grady's that night because I was drunk, all right? I drove to her place drunk, and I drove home drunk. She'd agreed to be my sponsor at AA, but I couldn't stay sober for more than a month."

Shame flared in his voice, his face. "She'd tried to help me for her daughter's sake, but it was too hard for her. I've spent the last eight years half-sauced, even at work. Is that what you want to hear? That I'm a louse, a self-flagellating loser who can't keep a relationship, who barely maintains my practice? That the only thing I look forward to in life is getting off work, coming home to an empty house, and drinking myself into a stupor? Now even that's been taken from me."

Bitterness and regret flashed in the man's eyes. The tragedies in his life had carved wounds that never healed. It made him pitiable; it didn't make him innocent.

Gideon scratched at a wormy scar that writhed across his collarbone and worked up the side of his neck—a scar from the accident that crippled Astrid. Jackson had seen him do it before, a nervous, instinctive gesture.

The details of the accident were vague in Jackson's mind. He'd been in college when it happened, though he'd read the incident report. His father had been first on the scene at 3:00 a.m. in the slashing rain, the roads slick, gleaming with broken glass and twisted metal.

"What happened that night? The accident."

Gideon rubbed the scars harder. "I lost control in the rain on M-28, went around a curve too fast, and hit an oncoming vehicle. That's what people told me when I woke up in the hospital. I have no memory of it. Zilch. It's in your father's report."

"I've read it. The report is slim. It says hardly anything at all."

"Not my problem."

"The report says no one was at fault."

Gideon's jaw stiffened in the moonlight. His right eye twitched. "That's what it says."

"If there's something else, I'm listening."

Gideon lowered his voice. "It was a long time ago. I've moved on. Everyone has moved on."

Part of him wanted to let well enough alone, but that wasn't the job. Things were niggling at him. Strings and snags that led nowhere and unraveled the more he tugged. Sometimes the tapestry made no sense until you viewed it from a different angle.

There was something here. He just didn't know what.

He took a chance. "Cyrus Lee Jefferson didn't kill Lily. He had an alibi. Someone else did. Someone we haven't found yet."

Gideon flinched. His head jerked up and he stared at Jackson like a deer caught in the headlights. "What?"

"You heard me."

Gideon's expression flattened. "You think I did it. That's why you brought me out here."

Jackson didn't deny it. He used the common tactic of identifying with the suspect, making them think you were on their side, that you were the same at heart. "She was cheating on you. If it was me, I would've been furious. Outraged and heartbroken. So upset I couldn't see straight."

Gideon stared at him, bristling with resentment. "Screw you."

"You went over there to confront her, and things got out of hand. It happens."

"No, no way. After I lost Allison in the car accident, I thought I'd never love anybody again. I loved Lily. I loved her with my whole heart. I would never have hurt her."

Jackson said nothing. He let the silence stretch between them, let the tension build. Most suspects couldn't handle that silence; they needed to fill it with something, with nervous chatter, an unspooling rope of words that Jackson used to hang them.

Gideon's eyes darkened. "As I said before, I didn't know about her and Eli, and even if I had, I never would have laid a hand on her. I would have forgiven her. I loved her that much. We could have worked it out."

Jackson didn't believe him. Gideon was lying, but about what, and why? And what did it have to do with Lily's death, if anything? Horatio was most certainly covering something up, but what was Gideon Crawford hiding, and for whom?

"It's in the past," Gideon said wearily. "What does it matter?"

"The past is never dead," Jackson said. "The past is right here, right now. Just a few weeks ago, someone tried to kill Lily's daughter to shut her up. If I don't stop them, they might try again, and soon. If you didn't kill Lily, help me find who did."

He saw when it happened, the dam breaking, the lies and deceptions crumbling. The man's whole body deflated. He exhaled like he'd been holding his breath for years.

"It's time, Gideon," Jackson said.

In a defeated voice, Gideon said, "It's time."

50

JACKSON CROSS
DAY ONE HUNDRED

G ideon met his gaze with dull eyes. "Lily was there. I don't mean the night she was murdered. I mean before."

The realization struck Jackson like a punch to the solar plexus. "She was in the car the night of the accident."

Gideon nodded. "We went out that night, me, Lily, and Allison. Lily and Allison were good friends. It was raining so hard. The official accident report said it was a head-on collision between two cars. But Astrid's car was stopped dead on the road. The car just appeared out of nowhere. In our lane. She was in our lane." His voice choked. "I didn't see the body until after."

Jackson got that feeling, that little shiver at the back of his neck when the hunter catches the scent of his prey. He didn't move, didn't alter his facial expression or tone of voice. "Tell me about the body."

"Astrid, she—she'd hit something. Someone. She hit a pedestrian. Who knew what he was doing on the side of the road at night in the rain? He had hiking gear, boots, a big pack with a tent, and a sleeping bag, like one of those guys who take eight months to hike the entire North Country Trail from North Dakota to New York.

"He was all torn up. Broken bones poked out of his skin. His head was...it was bad. It had just happened. Astrid was still in her car, trying to figure out what to do, I guess. Not believing it was real. Hell, steam was still boiling from the hood. And then we came barreling around the curve and slammed right into her.

"When I stumbled out of the car, it was like a scene out of a nightmare. The headlights highlighted everything. Blood and glass were everywhere. Allison...she was...she was already dead. In the other car, Astrid was screaming and screaming. I had blood running down my temples. I could feel the blood, but I didn't feel the pain, not yet. I was going into shock. Lily was in the backseat; she had some bruises, but she was okay.

"At first, when I saw the body lying crumpled on the ground on the shoulder of the road, I thought it was us. I thought we hit him and his body went flying across the road into the ditch. At that moment, I panicked. I knew how bad it was—this was going to ruin our lives. I told Lily to go, to run. She was five miles from home."

"You told her to flee a crime scene?"

"I thought I was saving her."

"Okay," Jackson said. "Okay."

"Once she was gone, I called 911, which goes through the sheriff's office. The car was mine, and it was wrecked. It wasn't like I could run. I'm sitting on the side of the road, sobbing, I know Allison is dead. I'm staring at the dead body of the hiker on the side of the road. I can't tear my eyes away and that's when it dawns on me: Astrid hit him, not us. That's why her car was in our lane. There was blood on her bumper and grille, but the rain was washing it off, washing the evidence right off the road.

"Sheriff Cross pulls up and walks around for a minute. He calls an ambulance for his daughter, but he doesn't call for backup, not yet. He sees the beer cans in my car. He shines the flashlight in my face and makes me take a breathalyzer, then he says I have a choice. I'm drunk, he says. I didn't think I was drunk, just buzzed, but I'm in shock, I'm terrified, I've got a concussion—what do I know? He says he can charge me with vehicular manslaughter and prosecute me to the fullest extent of the law and put me away for years, decades maybe, my future gone."

Gideon chewed his lower lip, staring at Jackson, wariness on his face, apprehension and maybe fear. "This is your father we're talking about. I don't—I mean—"

"I know about my father," Jackson said. "Keep talking."

"The sheriff says I can go to prison, or I can make the smart choice. He'll report that he found me concussed and unconscious. The concussion is real. I'm feeling like my head's gonna explode. He's gonna take care of the beer in the car and make it all go away for me. I don't have to think about it ever again. I get my future back in a blink. Not Allison's future but hey, we were drinking and driving, what the hell did we think would happen? Take the win, kid, he says. Take it and run. I did."

"Horatio covered it up."

Gideon nodded miserably. "And I let him."

"What happened then?"

"I did what he said. The ambulance came. That's it."

"Had other deputies or officers arrived by the time you left?"

He shook his head. "Just the sheriff. Another car was pulling up. It was unmarked. I remember seeing the headlights pass the ambulance."

Someone had helped get rid of the hiker. Perhaps someone known for weighting bodies with chains and dumping them in Lake Superior, the lake so cold and deep, she never gave up her dead.

Jackson recalled the missing hiker report around that time. A college kid from Wisconsin was taking a gap year to hike the 4600-mile North Country Trail that spanned eight states, five in the Midwest, crossing nearly the entire width of the Upper Peninsula through five hundred and fifty miles of old-growth forest, rugged hills, spectacular waterfalls, lakes, and rivers. There were lots of places to fall, to go missing permanently.

He was seen at a Munising gas station. Authorities suspected he'd slipped and plunged from a steep bluff where the trail hugged the jagged Superior coastline. The case was still considered open.

The pieces fell into place, the picture gradually revealing itself, everything making a horrible sort of sense. Horatio had called in a huge favor. He'd been in debt to Sawyer ever since.

"And Lily?" Jackson asked.

Gideon rubbed his eyes and made a wounded sound in the back of his throat. "She had seen the hiker, too. The sheriff didn't know she was in the car. I told her to keep her mouth shut and it would be fine, everything would be fine. She got pregnant with Cody soon after that. I asked her what good it would do to go to prison for telling the truth when she had a kid to take care of. We'd been drinking. We'd hit Astrid's car and crippled her. To out the sheriff was to out ourselves. The sheriff knew it. He knew I wouldn't talk.

"It ate me up inside, but I coped. Lily, though, it ate her up in a different way. It bonded us: the accident, losing Allison like that, and keeping that terrible secret. We grew close and then we fell in love. I loved her, though she was haunted by her ghosts. Hell, we both were."

Gideon shook his head, grief on his face, his eyes glassy with the pain of remembering. "Years go by. Every once in a while, she'd talk about telling the truth and coming clean. I told her she was crazy. She couldn't start telling people that Sheriff Cross had covered up a vehicular homicide to protect his daughter. I would lose my license and go to jail, too. But she became more and more obsessed with it. Justice for Allison, she kept saying. We never would've gotten in the accident if Astrid hadn't hit that hiker."

Gideon rubbed his eyes with his fists. "Lily told me the night before she died that she was going to come clean, no matter the consequences. She couldn't live with it anymore. She was going to tell you, Jackson. Did she ever come to you?"

Jackson swallowed a fresh wave of grief. "No, she didn't."

"She never got the chance, did she?" Gideon shook his head, angrily, in despair. "I knew she was messing with bad stuff.

Someone had gotten rid of that body that night, someone powerful and dangerous. Your dad was the sheriff. He'd lose his job, go to prison, and be humiliated, his house of cards tumbling down. A man like that doesn't go down quietly, does he?"

"No, he does not." It was silent for a few beats. Jackson said, "You had almost as much to lose, Gideon."

He lifted his head and met Jackson's gaze. His eyes were bloodshot, devastated but clear. "I did not kill her. I loved her. I would have married her in a heartbeat. If I'd stood by her instead of drowning myself in vodka, if I'd agreed to come clean with her... everything would be different. Harder to kill two people rather than just one, isn't it? I was a coward. I was a coward, and she's dead because of it. Believe me or don't, that's the brutal truth."

Jackson did. He believed him. No one could blame Gideon Crawford more than he blamed himself. The man had revealed his worst sins. He had nothing left to hide.

"And after Lily was murdered?"

"I thought...I thought it was Horatio at first. I was scared spitless. I thought the sheriff would frame me and kill two birds with one stone. The boyfriend is always the easy mark. Then Eli was arrested. It came out that Lily was cheating on me. They said he got jealous when he found out about me and flew into a murderous rage—you know the rest."

Jackson stiffened. He knew far too well. "You let the secret stay buried."

Gideon swiped at his tired face and hunched his shoulders as if to ward off a blow. "Yes. Yes, I did. I was afraid and I was a coward. I thought I had suffered enough but I had no idea. I had no idea."

Jackson had no answer to that.

"Are you happy now?" Gideon spat.

"No," Jackson said quietly. "Not at all."

Gideon scrubbed wetness from his eyes and cleared his throat. "Do you think...your father could have killed Lily?"

A shudder ran through him. If Lily had gone to confront

Horatio at his home...his father would've lost everything: his illustrious career, his reputation, his family, and his freedom. Horatio had motive, means, and opportunity.

"I'm going to find out."

"W-what's going to happen to me?"

Jackson looked at him, a man he'd known his entire life and barely recognized. "Absolutely nothing."

Gideon's features seemed to cave inward; he was hollowed out by pain, secrets, and guilt. All the years he'd spent in this town, helplessly watching Sheriff Cross shake hands with the governor, eat with the superintendent, win awards and accolades, while Gideon swallowed his dirty secret, the one his fiancé died for, the one he despised himself for, the sordid truth he'd buried to save his skin.

But it was half the truth, a piece of the truth—because something was still buried, rancid and rotting, and Horatio was somehow in the fetid center of it.

Whatever it was, Jackson was going to dig it up.

"I never thought—" Gideon started.

Jackson heard something. He held a finger to his lips. Gideon nodded tightly.

He strained his ears, listening hard. A sound reached them. It was different than the rustling and chirring of the night creatures. It was a soft and sibilant purr, the rush of wind on a windless night, the whirr of tires over dirt and grass.

Jackson whispered, "They're here."

51

JACKSON CROSS
DAY ONE HUNDRED

Jackson dropped to the ground and yanked Gideon down beside him.

Through the trees, the first SUV flashed past, dark green through the NVGs, and almost silent. A second SUV drove by, then a third, and a fourth.

Staying low on his belly, Jackson flipped his NVGs over his eyes and crept through the underbrush toward the road to get a clear view of the caravan.

Gideon scrabbled up beside him, making too much noise. He was a gorilla, big and unwieldy. He scraped branches out of the way, shaking bushes, dragging the rifle in one hand.

"Stay quiet," Jackson hissed.

Up ahead, the caravan of SUVs had reached the intersection. Instead of turning left or right or keeping straight, the lead vehicle halted. Brake lights gleamed like predatory eyes.

Adrenaline shot through his veins. Less than a hundred yards separated them. A dozen armed thugs in four SUVs against two men with rifles.

"What are they doing?" Gideon asked.

"I don't know."

"Why aren't they moving?"

"I don't know!"

And then he did. The brake lights grew larger. The SUVs had reversed, heading backward, straight toward them. The occupants must have seen something somehow, glimpsed the metallic gleam of Gideon's rifle barrel, or caught the unnatural rustle of bushes in the rearview mirror.

Either way, they were screwed.

"Get behind cover!" Jackson retreated, scrabbled low on his belly, and crawled rapidly behind the thick two-foot diameter trunk of the jack pine. Staying low, he peeked around the trunk. Ten yards to his left, Gideon lurched behind a log and flattened himself into the depression beneath the fallen tree.

On the forest road, the SUVs stopped directly in front of Jackson's hiding place. The windows of the SUV rolled down. Several wicked-looking gun barrels poked out.

Alarmed, Jackson withdrew behind the pine, shrinking himself, rifle gripped in his hands and held vertically between his thighs. He was immensely grateful for the black clothes and grease paint.

There were too many of them. Their only chance was to hide. Stay small, stay silent, and wait them out. If they didn't see anything, they would leave in a minute or two. No point in firing at them, which would only reveal his position. Fighting was a last resort.

He stifled his breathing. Fear soured his stomach, his pulse a roar in his ears, too loud. He was certain they would hear it, would find him—

Gunfire exploded. A cacophony of automatic gunfire split the night. Rounds smashed into the underbrush, shredding leaves and branches, and slammed into tree trunks. Several rounds pummeled the jack pine with powerful impacts. Bark splintered a foot from his skull.

Jackson winced as slivers of bark struck his cheek. He held the rifle to his chest with clammy palms. Cold sweat popped out on his forehead. His ears rang, sound going fuzzy.

A second wave of automatic fire stitched the trees. Pine needles and small twigs rained down upon Jackson's head. More rounds blasted the ground less than two feet to his right. Clods of dirt sprayed his legs.

Gunfire cracked all around him. The jarring barrage vibrated in his teeth and his chest. As abruptly as it had started, the thunderous *rat-a-tat* of gunfire ceased.

The night fell absolutely silent.

One of the SUV's doors creaked open. A thud as a pair of boots hit the ground. Footsteps drew closer. Jackson sensed a figure standing at the shoulder of the dirt track, peering into the dense forest.

He stopped breathing and pressed his spine against the base of the pine. Bark bit into his back and shoulders. The incessant buzzing of insects hushed. The woods had gone eerily still.His mouth was dry as a desert, his heart pounding, his sight narrowing with tunnel vision as panic bit at him. No matter how well he'd concealed himself, they only needed to traipse a few yards into the woods to discover him and Gideon.

A deep voice broke the silence. "You see anything?"

"Nah. Whatever it was is good and dead," said a second voice.

"Told you it was a deer," said a muffled voice, likely from inside the SUV.

"It wasn't a damn deer," the second voice snarled. "I saw someone. I know I did."

"Like you said, it's dead now. You punched a dozen holes in anything living within a fifty-yard radius."

There was a moment of silence as the thugs considered their next move. Jackson heard the stifled anxiety in their voices. They didn't like the darkness or the woods. They were far from thrilled at the thought of trolling through the forest in the middle of the night looking for threats.

No matter how skilled they were at moving with cover and concealment, there was the chance someone could get off a lucky round and put a bullet in your face. Even trained soldiers would hesitate to enter such hostile territory. These scumbags were brutal and violent but far from trained.

"I'm getting eaten alive by mosquitoes, man," a third voice whined. "We're already late."

"Come on, let's roll."

Another door slammed. Seconds later, the whirr of tires followed. In near silence, the SUVs departed.

Jackson closed his eyes for a moment in abject relief. His whole body was shaking, his jaw clenched so tight he thought his teeth might crack. He forced himself to crawl through the underbrush to the edge of the road in time to watch the caravan of electric vehicles drive past the fork in the forest road and head straight.

Moments later, the taillights vanished.

"Gideon!" he called.

There was no answer.

He could barely hear his voice over the buzzing in his ears. His head rang like a struck bell. They were damn fortunate the thugs hadn't bothered to hunt their quarry down.

He called Gideon's name again.

Still nothing.

Slinging his rifle over his shoulder, he pushed aside thorny thickets, branches clawing at him as he headed for the fallen log. The trees were clumped close together, blocking his view.

"Gideon!" he whispered. "Where are you?"

Still no answer.

Jackson rounded the log. Gideon lay on the ground. He was on his right side, half-curled in a fetal position, clutching his left leg with both hands. His rifle lay on the ground beneath a thicket of rhododendrons. Due to the wavelength of the night vision goggle's aperture, the blood gushing through Gideon's clenched fingers looked almost translucent.

Jackson sank to his knees beside him, aghast. He pushed the goggles up on his helmet. Blood spattered across the leaf litter and matted pine needles. The wet liquid glistened in the moonlight, black as tar.

Gideon hissed out a breath. "It hurts."

Jackson called for help on the radio but got only static. They didn't have repeaters out here in the boonies. Any backup was too far away.

Jackson reached for the first aid kit. He had first-aid training, but his skills were rusty, nowhere near Eli's or Lena's. Gideon needed a skilled surgeon. He needed a hospital and a surgical team on call ready and waiting.

Gideon was panting, his breathing shallow, his pulse thready. His femoral artery was pierced. He could bleed out within minutes.

"Hold on, just hold on." Frantic, Jackson fumbled for a tourniquet, ripped the packaging with his teeth, and pulled it around Gideon's thigh a few inches above the gunshot wound, then buckled it and yanked the end strap to tighten it. He twisted the windlass rod to further tighten the tourniquet, increasing pressure to stop the bleeding, then secured the rod with the strip of Velcro.

"You're gonna be okay," he said. "Just breathe, keep breathing, and hold on."

"Don't let me die. I don't wanna die..."

Jackson needed to get him out of there, but Gideon was too injured to ride his bike. Jackson would have to ride within radio range of Devon, who would bring the diesel truck. They could put him in the back seat and drive him back to town like a bat out of hell—

"My—my stomach hurts."

Jackson felt Gideon's torso and stomach and lifted his blood-soaked shirt. The darkness and Gideon's black clothing had obscured the wounds. Oil-black liquid leaked from several holes that punctured Gideon's stomach below his belly button.

Sour panic clawed at his throat. The bullets had most certainly shredded Gideon's internal organs. There was too much blood.

Gideon's skin had gone cold and clammy. His breath came in

shallow gasps, his pulse fast and weak. Even in the dark, Gideon's lips were tinged grayish-blue.

He was going into shock.

"Is—is it bad?"

Jackson swallowed his dismay. He tore bandages from the first aid kit and held them to the wounds. It was too late, already too late.

"We're going to get you back to the Inn and Lena will stitch you right up. You've got a few flesh wounds. You're going to be fine. Just —hold on."

Gideon grasped Jackson's arm with feeble fingers. "I—I loved her...I should have...done things different..."

Jackson checked his thready pulse. He could barely feel it. "I believe you."

"Forgive me," Gideon begged, his voice hoarse. "Please ... forgive me."

Jackson had no power to forgive Gideon of his demons or anyone else, including himself. He'd brought Gideon here to grill him for answers, to pursue his own goals. Gideon had bravely faced his ghosts and spoken the truth, only to be shot for his courage.

The terrible unfairness of it was incomprehensible.

"Please..." Gideon mumbled.

Jackson fought back bitter tears. If Lily were here, he knew what she would say. He hoped he did, for he had sins of his own to account for. "Lily would forgive you, Gideon. She forgives you."

Cicadas whirred in the underbrush. An owl hooted from somewhere nearby. Moonlight limned the leaves of the oak tree spreading above them. Gideon's eyelids fluttered closed. He gasped, blood bubbling from his lips.

"Stay awake!" Jackson leaned over him, desperately pressing the wadded bandage against the wounds gushing blood. It was no use. He squeezed Gideon's ice-cold hand. "Stay with me! Come on!"

Gideon gurgled something Jackson couldn't make out. His eyes rolled into the back of his head. His chest went still.

Distraught, Jackson sank back on his heels, his hands limp and useless in his lap. Gideon's blood was hot and slick on his palms.

He wanted to scream at the heavens, to demand that God rewind time, take it back. This wasn't supposed to happen. This was his fault. Gideon's death was his fault.

They were so close to catching Sykes. He was closer than ever to solving Lily's murder. Yet he'd never felt more lost and alone in his life.

52

LENA EASTON
DAY ONE HUNDRED AND TWO

"I'm out of insulin," Lena said.

"No," Shiloh said, stricken. "No, that's impossible."

Jackson and Eli stood in the conference room next to the fireplace. She'd asked them to come, to tell them together so they'd know, so they could prepare. The wind whistled outside the windows, the glass syringes tinkling, the flames in the fireplace popping and crackling.

Bear leaned against her leg and gave her a plaintive look, whining mournfully. Maybe he scented the sweetness of her breath and could somehow sense the dangerously rising sugar in her blood.

Squaring her shoulders, one hand on the desk so the others wouldn't see her weakness, she faced the three people she loved most in the world and told them the truth.

"I don't understand," Shiloh said thickly. "How can you be out so soon? You were supposed to have another month. Eli bought you another month."

"I've been sharing the insulin with Traci and Curt's little boy."

They stared at her in shock as her words slowly sank in. Grief and anguish crossed their faces. Their pain made Lena's chest ache.

"How could you?" Shiloh said in a wretched voice. "How could you!"

"It was my choice. Not yours." Lena tried and failed to keep her voice even. She wanted to keep a brave front for Shiloh. "I couldn't in good conscience keep it for myself. It wasn't fair."

"Fair? Who cares about fair? You'll die!"

Lena took a step toward her, her heart breaking with Shiloh's grief. "I help people. It's what I do, who I am. Shiloh, I need to tell you—"

"I don't accept it!" Shiloh said. "I don't!"

"I love you with all my heart. Death won't change that."

"You promised!" Her voice broke. "You promised you wouldn't leave!"

"I'm not choosing to leave. I would never—"

But Shiloh was disconsolate. She fled the room and slammed the door behind her.

Bear lowered his head and whimpered, nosing Lena's palm. Lena petted his head to soothe him with trembling fingers. "I'm sorry," she whispered. "I'm so sorry."

"I'll go after her," Jackson said.

Lena nodded, fighting back tears. "Thank you."

Instead of leaving, Jackson went to her first and touched her shoulder. "We're doing everything we can. We're closing in on Sykes and those meds. We're so close, Lena. Don't give up."

"I'm not. I won't."

She looked at him, really looked at him, affection squeezing her chest and tightening her throat. His face was haggard, his eyes haunted, a man pursued by ghosts. She knew Gideon Crawford had died with Jackson two nights ago. She knew how much he cared, how hard he fought for justice, the price he'd paid, and was still paying.

"I love you, you know," she said. "You're the brother I never had."

Jackson hugged her. "You're the family I chose."

She hugged him back. "We chose each other."

"I'll be here for her," Jackson said.

"She needs you, you and Eli. Now more than ever." Lena pulled back to look into his face. "I need you to find Lily's killer."

"You'll be there to see it—"

"I probably won't, and you know that," Lena said softly. "But I know you'll keep hunting. I know you'll find him. For Lily. But more importantly, for Shiloh. To keep her safe."

Jackson swallowed hard. "I will, Lena. I promise." He released her and headed after Shiloh, closing the door quietly behind him.

Alone, Eli and Lena stood facing each other.

Eli did not yell or lecture or rage. He stood like a man stunned into terrible stillness.

"I'm sorry—" she started.

"Don't apologize." His voice was gruff, raw with pain. "You don't ever have to apologize to me."

Her face crumpled. Her eyes filled with tears. She blinked rapidly. Fear strangled her lungs. No matter how strong she acted, the truth was, she was afraid, so afraid. "I'm trying to be brave. I'm trying so hard. I don't think I'm doing a good job."

"You don't have to be brave for everyone else. You don't have to be brave at all. It's okay. Whatever you feel, it's okay."

Words failed her completely. She didn't have to say anything out loud. He already knew. Eli opened his arms and every fiber of her being longed to go to him. He kissed her through her tears, fiercely, desperately. He wrapped his arms around her, drawing her into his warmth and his strength. So long as she was in his arms, she felt utterly safe.

She sank into his embrace, pressed her cheek against his chest, and listened to his steady heartbeat. She loved this man, was in love with him, truly and madly, with every beat of her heart. It had taken the end of the world to find true love. How ironic.

Tears coursed down her cheeks. Once they started, she couldn't stop them. He stroked her hair with tenderness. Her heart felt ripped out of her chest. "I'm so scared."

"Me too," he said into her hair.

They stood like that for a long time, holding each other, offering solace, a reprieve from the pain, from what they feared was coming.

She murmured into his chest, her words muffled. "I don't want to die."

"You won't." He spoke with conviction, but he was lying. No matter how hard he tried, no one could promise the impossible. He held her tight. "Whatever happens, I'm right here. I'm here until the very end."

53

SHILOH EASTON
DAY ONE HUNDRED AND TWO

Shiloh sat with Jackson on a mossy log along the riverbank on the Northwoods property. Beside them, a waterfall spilled into the river. Crystal-clear water rushed over mossy rocks and boulders. Birds twittered as small creatures rustled through the underbrush.

Nature went on like nothing had happened, like the world hadn't cracked in half, as if Shiloh's heart wasn't shattering into pieces as she sat there, trembling and devastated.

"I'm here if you want to talk," Jackson said.

She didn't want to talk; she wanted to open her mouth and scream and scream and never stop. She wanted to kick, to punch, to hurt someone as badly as she hurt. "You have to save her."

"We're doing everything we can," he said quietly. "But you need to know, it might not be enough."

She made a stricken sound in the back of her throat. She already knew. Of course, she did. Lena would leave her like everyone else; she was going to die and there was nothing Shiloh could do to stop it. The tidal waves of fury and sorrow nearly bowled her over and stole her breath from her lungs.

Jackson leaned toward her, compassion in his expression but his movements hesitant and unsure, like he wanted to hug her, but she glared at him with such animosity that he pulled back and held his palms up in surrender as if she were a rabid dog. "It's okay."

"Nothing's okay! Nothing's ever going to be okay."

"I know. I love her, too. She's my best friend."

She saw the suffering on his face and knew it was true. Jackson wasn't the bad guy; he'd gone above and beyond for her and Cody, more than anyone else. She tried to apologize, but the words sat on her tongue like a lump of clay.

"I know you're angry heartbroken, and scared. So am I."

"What am I supposed to do?" she whispered.

"Don't waste what time you have with her. Treasure every second. That's what I'm going to do."

Shiloh swallowed the lump in her throat and nodded.

"I won't lie to you. The conversations you have with Lena over the next week or two might be the very last you'll have together. After she's gone, you won't be able to take it back. You won't be able to tell her 'I'm sorry, or I love you.' Please, don't let your last words with your aunt be like this."

Her vision had gone blurry. She gazed up at the sunlight sifting through the leaves of the great oak spreading its canopy above them. Insects whirred, mosquitos and gnats and black flies. The tsunami of emotion threatening to drown her was almost too much to bear.

"Okay," she said and meant it. "I promise I'll make it up to her."

"Don't wait."

"I won't."

She listened to the breeze stirring the leaves, the rustle of grass and buzzing grasshoppers, the burble of the waterfall spilling over moss-covered rocks and steeled herself.

"I want to talk about my mom. About what happened."

Jackson looked at her, startled. "Now?"

Her nails dug into her palms. "Yes. Now. I...I was standing outside the door for a minute, trying to work up the courage to go back in. I heard what Lena said to you. She asked you to keep looking for my mother's killer. What if Lena—" She swallowed the hitch in her throat. "What if she dies without ever knowing the truth about her sister? That would be...it would be terrible."

"Yes," Jackson said. "It would."

"And that guy who attacked me...I know everybody's worried that someone else might try to hurt me again, that whoever killed my mom was behind it. I can't do anything about insulin, but maybe I can do this. If there's something in my head that could help."

He hesitated. "Listen, Shiloh. It would be better if a child psychologist did this with you. That's what I've been waiting on. I went through the directory I had saved on the hard drive of my laptop and did a search for child therapists the sheriff's office has worked with in the past. I wanted to find someone with experience in childhood trauma and associated memory loss to help you relive your memories safely. I rode out to Manistique, Grand Marais, and Marquette, but I couldn't find anyone. So many people have left, headed downstate ahead of winter, or they never made it home during the solar flares. Plane crashes, car accidents, and people stranded with no way to get home...I'm sorry, I tried. I can't ask you to do this—"

"I need to do this."

"Are you certain?"

Her fear tasted like battery acid in the back of her throat. "Yes."

Jackson looked unsure. "I had a couple of assault cases where I watched a therapist using techniques to help bring back repressed memories. She explained it to the district attorney while I was there. I am far from qualified to do this with you, but if you're willing, so am I."

She slumped forward on the log and rested her elbows on her knees, her head in her hands. She closed her eyes and thought of Cody, of her mother, of distant laughter, and of spinning in sunlight in strong arms.

After that came the darkness, the screaming, the blood.

Remembering felt like suffocating.

Jackson leaned forward and grasped her arm. "Shiloh. Hey."

She stared at him, wild-eyed. The ghosts were in her head, the darkness seeking her out.

"We don't have to do this."

"I'm—I'm okay."

Concern wrinkled his brow. "Shiloh, nothing is worth your well-being, not even this. If you think I'm going to risk your psychological health for the sake of this case, you've got another think coming. I care about you. I always have, from the moment you were born."

She blinked back a sudden rush of tears. "I know," she said thickly. "I do know."

And she did. The years he'd dropped by to check on her, brought her books and Snickers bars. After Boone had kidnapped her, Jackson hadn't given up. He'd cracked the case and brought Eli to save her. They'd both saved her.

"Why can't I remember everything?"

"Because the trauma was overwhelming, annihilating even. Sometimes, the only way to survive is for victims to leave their bodies, essentially. Complete dissociation. A total shutdown. It was too much for your mind to handle, so to protect itself, to protect you, your mind hid those memories from you. When something is unbearable, our brain finds a way to hide it from our conscious selves as self-protection. It's completely normal, Shiloh. You had a perfectly normal response to trauma, and you were a young child."

That explained the blackouts, how she would fade in moments of extreme terror.

"The memories are still there somewhere," Jackson said. "The body doesn't forget."

"If I have a clue inside my head, if I can finally know who took my mom away from me and Cody, if Lena can know before—" Her voice cracked. She hated her emotions for betraying her, but she couldn't help it. Grief threatened to pull her under.

Jackson nodded. "We can stop at any time, understand?"

"Let's just do it."

Jackson took her back in time slowly, gently, asking questions about her house, her bedroom, and her favorite stuffed animals, asking her to describe items in detail: her Paw Patrol sheets, the bedroom walls painted navy blue, not pink like her mom wanted, the Simba stuffed lion that slept with her every night.

With a jolt, she remembered that Eli had gotten her Simba for her fifth birthday. It had smelled like him—woodsy, like pine needles and wood smoke—and she'd loved it. Even then, Eli had been a part of her life.

Jackson took her through that night, the Paw Patrol episode she'd watched, the spaghetti they had for dinner. "What woke you up that night?"

"A strange sound. I don't know what it is." *Thump, thump, thump.* The horrible sound invaded her dreams, night after night. "Then someone is screaming. It's Mom; I know it's Mom. I'm holding the covers so tight, I'm so scared. There's someone in the house. Mom's here but somehow, I know it's not her. The footsteps are heavy and halting. They don't sound like her. They're furtive, secretive. I sit up fast, scared, my heart like a bird flapping out of my chest. I call out for my mom. The scream comes again. That's when I know it's not a dream. It's real. It's in the house."

Her fingers dug into the log, nails clawing soft bark. Her breathing was shallow and ragged. She couldn't get enough oxygen, her muscles rigid.

Everything rode close to the surface, memories sparking beneath her skin, the past touching the present. She closed her eyes and let the memories come as her surroundings faded.

"Then what? What is happening now?"

"The thumping sound is getting louder. Someone's coming."

Shiloh was breathing fast, almost hyperventilating. She trembled all over, her eyes stinging as the tears welled unbidden.

"Where are you? What's happening?"

"I'm trying to hide. I'm so scared. I'm cold. I may throw up. I'm trying not to cry. I want to scream for my mom, but I know something's wrong. A monster is in the house, a windigo. He's come here to devour me and my mom. I know it. I can feel it."

"Where are you?"

"I scramble out of bed and slide down between the wall and the side of the bed. It's only a foot wide. I'm tiny and I can squeeze in. It's where I go when grandfather starts yelling and Mom's not there. When Mom is there, she stands between me and Cody and him. But he's not here tonight. It's me and Mom and whatever is making her scream. Whatever is making those horrible noises—"

More sounds. Bumps and scrapes and a terrible, pained groaning. A muffled scream cut off in the middle, severed. And after, silence. Deafening silence.

"Someone's there. Someone's on the other side of the wall where I'm hiding. They're knocking on the wall like they know I'm there. Like they're saying, 'Come out, come out, wherever you are.' I don't move. I can't move. My body is locked up. I'm frozen. The darkness is coming for me, I'm so afraid but the dark will take me, it promises to make the fear go away. But it doesn't. It doesn't."

"Where are you? What's happening?"

"I'm crouched in my bedroom, huddled between the wall and the bed, trying to make myself small."

"Can you see over the bed? What do you see?"

"He's looking in the doorway to my bedroom. I think he can see me. The night light is on."

"What do you hear?"

"The thumping sound as he's walking into the room."

"Can you see his face?"

"He's got a hoodie on, he's holding the hood around his face so I can't see any details—"

Shiloh stopped speaking, stopped breathing and stared into space as back in her bedroom eight years earlier, she looked into the face of a monster.

It felt like she was occupying two places at once, here with Jackson and there with the monster in the same terrible moment.

The fear like a hook lodged in her throat, her heart thundered in her ears, vibrating through her chest.

"He's looking right back at me. In my dreams, it's a demon with holes for eyes and a mouth. The face turns toward me, but it's a blur. No distinction, no details, a smear of shadows beneath the hoodie. Then everything goes dark. I think I blacked out like I did at the salvage yard when Boone took Cody."

"What did you do next?" Jackson asked gently.

"It's still dark in the house. I don't know how much time has passed, minutes or hours. I'm standing beside my mother's bed, shaking her arm, trying to get her to wake up, but she won't. Her limbs are strange...they're floppy, like a doll's. Her eyes are open, but they're staring up at the ceiling like they're not seeing anything. She can't hear me. The blankets are pushed off the bed, like when you have a nightmare and kick the covers off. She's not wearing any clothes. There's a glint of a necklace, but I've never seen it before. It's not hers. She's so beautiful, like a porcelain doll, her dark hair splayed across the white satin pillow. But there's something very wrong. I can feel it.

"I put my hands on her face and call her name. There's slippery stuff on her skin. I can't see what it is; it's like black paint on my fingers but I know it's not. I'm little but I know. I knew it was the shadow, the windigo, the *thing* that invaded our house."

Shiloh started to cry. Her body was shaking, shivering, and she was cold, so cold. Her bones frigid, her flesh made of ice that might crack at any moment. The tears came slowly at first and then the dam broke and she broke into deep, wrenching sobs. "She's dead. She won't move. That...that monster killed her!"

She wrapped her arms around her ribcage and wept. She could see the blood so clearly, her mom's lifeless stare, the glint of the necklace around her bruised throat.

Jackson put his hand on Shiloh's shoulder. He scooted closer and drew her into him. "I'm here, Shiloh, I'm here. We're here. You're sitting here with me. Open your eyes. You're right here, you're safe now."

Shiloh opened her eyes, blinking blearily, and looked at Jackson as if from very far away, as if she had plunged a hundred leagues beneath the ocean and couldn't find her way back to the surface. She couldn't stop shuddering, her breath hitching in her chest.

"It's now, not back then. You're safe. You're safe now. Look at the grass, look at the trees, and pay attention to your breathing. Start slowing your breathing, Shiloh. Listen to the waterfall. You're not in that house anymore, you're right here. Come back now."

"Anchorage, Madagascar, Brussels, Dubai, Istanbul, Hong Kong, Auckland..." Shiloh mumbled the names of the places she desperately wanted to visit but probably never would. The familiar litany gradually calmed her.

The river returned, as did the burbling waterfall, the blue sky, the trees, and the crumbly bark of the log beneath her. Then the dappled sunshine, the singing birds, the rustling meadow grass tickling her shins, and Jackson sitting beside her.

Sniffling, she bit back the sobs, swallowed hard, and scrubbed the tears and snot from her face as the shuddering in her chest slowly subsided. She took deep, hitching breaths to steady herself.

"When he stopped in my room, he was deciding whether to kill me, too."

"I think so, yes."

"The killer didn't see me as a threat. He left me to spend the night in an empty house with my dead mother. He left me to find her like that, to see her after what he'd done. I should've done more. I should have recognized whoever it was and told the police, told you."

"You survived. Your mind protected your fragile psyche the only way it could. There's no shame in that, absolutely none."

They were the same things she'd told Ruby, over and over. Somehow it was easier to say it to someone else than to believe it yourself. It was strange the way people were hardest on themselves.

"You're stronger because of it."

"No," Shiloh said. "It's not the trauma that makes you stronger. It's every day you get up after you've been knocked down, every time you choose to keep fighting for one more hour, one more day. That's what makes you stronger."

"You're right." Jackson squeezed her shoulder again and kept his hand there, offering what comfort he could.

This time, she didn't pull away.

54

LENA EASTON
DAY ONE HUNDRED AND THREE

"Lena!"

Lena spun, holding her foraging bag across her chest with one hand and reaching instinctively for her pistol with the other. Her heart leaped into her chest.

Traci Tilton dashed toward her, breathless. "I hoped you might be here, at the lighthouse. The Inn is so much further, and there's no time. We're out of time." Her words came fast and jittery. The woman was hyperventilating, her face red with exertion and her blonde curls in disarray.

Lena eased her hand off her pistol. "What's wrong?"

Traci's frantic gaze dropped to Bear, who was sniffing a butterfly perched on a mossy log with great interest. "Shiloh said you do search and rescue, that your dog can find anyone."

The long shadow of the lighthouse tower stretched toward the beach, where waves pounded the shoreline in lacy white plumes. The wind had picked up, shaking branches and rustling the leaves.

Lena had slipped away for an hour to forage for wild cranberries which she'd only found in the peaty soil in the bog near the lighthouse. The sour berries budding from low-lying, trailing vines had begun to ripen in late August. Wild cranberries were high in antioxidants and lowered blood pressure, improved heart health, and prevented UTIs, among other things.

"Bear can find almost anyone," Lena said. "Traci, what is it?"

Traci looked stricken. "It's Keagan. We were hunting the ducks out by the Enchanted Cascades. There are so many of them, and they're used to being fed, so they come right up to you...We got turned around for a minute, and he was gone. He just vanished. We have to find him."

Alarm flared through her. Lena glanced at the overcast sky. It was late afternoon, heavy shadows slanted through the trees. They were losing precious daylight by the second.

Clucking her tongue at Bear, she headed for the driveway, calculating the distance in her head. It was ten miles or so and four hours to sundown. Instinctively, she reached for her pump with her bruised fingers before remembering that she had no pump and no remaining insulin.

She hadn't checked her blood sugar numbers since this morning, another painful prick to tell her what she already knew—her number was too high and climbing.

Traci hurried after her. Lena stumbled, nearly losing her balance, but the woman didn't notice; her focus was on her missing son. She ignored her pounding headache, her knotted stomach, and the constant ache of hunger. Thirst plagued her no matter how often she drank.

"When was the last time he had an injection?"

"This morning around ten a.m. His numbers were running high. He needs another dose. We have two left of the supply you gave us. A night in the forest alone will stress his system—"

Lena knew the dwindling odds. She knew how easy it was to disappear in a thousand miles of wilderness, to lose your way, trip over a root and sprain an ankle, slip and fall down a ravine, or wander in circles until one perished of exposure, or in Keagan's case, slip into a coma and never wake up.

A little boy was lost in the woods with the dark of night approaching. He had no food, no insulin, glucose tabs, or pump, no tent, fire starter, or water filter—nothing he needed to survive a night in the wild.

She reached the spot where she'd stashed her mountain bike behind a birch tree, her emergency medical first-in bag stored on the back.

Next to her bike, a horse stood in the driveway, saddled and sweating. In her desperation to locate Lena, Traci had run him hard. Traci mounted the horse and clutched the reins. The horse shook its mane and snorted impatiently.

Lena looked up at her. "Do you have an item of his clothing that he's worn recently, yesterday, or today?"

"His handkerchief he always carries in his pocket. We found it on the trail. I put it in a paper bag. Please, Lena. I'm begging you."

While she had strength left, she had no choice. She had risked herself to save Keagan's life once. If she failed him now, what was the point of her sacrifice?

There was meaning in this, a purpose for their collective suffering. There had to be.

"If not us, then who?" she asked Bear.

Bear nudged her side, his entire rump wriggling with enthusiasm, his ears cocked in anticipation. He'd sensed the tension, recognizing an adventure when he saw one. He loved SAR work. He was ready to go. He was always ready to go.

"Lena," Traci said. "Please."

Lena nodded tightly. White spots shimmered behind her eyes. She blinked them away and reached for her radio to call Jackson. She needed his help to organize a search party and find Keagan.

The radio was dead. She pushed the buttons, powered it off then switched it back on, removed the batteries, and replaced them, but still nothing. She checked her fanny pack where she kept a set of spare batteries and tried them—it still didn't work.

Her heart sank into her stomach. She had no idea why it wasn't working or how to fix it. "Traci, do you have a radio?"

Traci shook her head. "That's why I was out searching for you."

Lena hesitated, conflicted. She should not do this alone, not in the best of times, and certainly not ill, and not with a psychopath out there somewhere. She needed help. Eli would not want her to do this alone.

But the radio was dead, and the Inn was several miles in the opposite direction of Keagan's PLS, his Point Last Seen. They had a few hours of daylight remaining.

Once the sun sank, the odds of finding him alive plummeted.

Lena made the split-second decision. Time was of the essence, and they needed to start the search as soon as possible. Once they reached the gift shop, she could send Traci or Curt after Jackson and Eli. That little boy was her priority now.

She headed for the bike. "I know a shortcut between here and the Enchanted Cascades. There's a groomed trail through the woods. It'll save us time."

Traci said, "Hurry."

Bear gave an excited *woof* and gazed up at her expectantly, his tail wagging his entire body.

"That's right, boy," Lena said. "It's time to work."

55

LENA EASTON
DAY ONE HUNDRED AND THREE

S omething was wrong. The singular thought blazed through
Lena's brain as she approached the sign welcoming visitors to
the Enchanted Cascades.

The trail had cut through dense terrain and come out on
Prospect Road a short distance from the Enchanted Cascades.
They followed the dirt road half a mile, passing a storage yard, a
trailer park, and a big rusty building with a sign out front adver-
tising Ronald's Body Shop. Everything was still and quiet.

Once they'd hit the dirt road, Traci rode ahead of her to meet
Curt. Lena biked as fast as she could, but her weakness slowed her
down. Bear was a strong dog, but running long distances was hard
on his joints. Endurance was more his thing, as was Lena's.

Up ahead, a couple of horses were tied to a nearby tree. The
Enchanted Cascades gift shop stood in the center of the clearing
beyond. There was no sign of Traci or her husband.

It had rained last night; hoof prints and tire tracks were
evident on the muddy road leading to the gift shop. The tire tracks
were fresh. That was odd: she'd barely seen a handful of working
vehicles in weeks.

A dozen yards from the gift shop parking lot, Lena halted in
the middle of the drive, feet on the ground to balance the moun-

tain bike. The hairs rose on the back of her neck. She was tempted to call out for the Tiltons but something held her back. Eli's warning on situational awareness rang through her head. Something was off.

The manicured gardens surrounding the Enchanted Cascades Gift Shop had gone wild, the grass overgrown, the gift shop windows broken. She took in everything: the parking lot in front of her, a large pond filled with quacking ducks to her right, the thick woods to her left, and the dirt road behind her.

The wind blew through the needles of the jack pines. Sugar maples and hemlocks scraped against each other, their leaves fluttering. The overcast sky was heavy with swollen clouds that blotted out the evening sun. It would rain again soon.

Lena pulled the bike off the road and leaned it against a tree. Bear bounded up to her, panting hard. Uneasiness crawled beneath her skin. She reached for the pistol holstered on her hip and took an instinctive step backward. Then another.

Drawing her gun, she held it low, scanning everywhere for threats. Her instincts warned her to flee, to take the bike and run while she still could.

It wasn't something she saw or smelled or heard. The air itself seemed wrong somehow. It felt wrong against her skin. Heavier. Denser.

Why were there fresh vehicle tracks but no cars or trucks in the parking lot? Why weren't the Tiltons outside waiting for her? What if the Tiltons were in trouble?

Lena took a step backward. She should go get backup, get Jackson and Eli, and come back—

The gift shop screen door slapped open. A man stepped out. He was barrel-chested, tall and broad. Prison-made tattoos writhed across his huge biceps. He grinned at her with flat deadfish eyes.

"You know who I am," he said without preamble. His voice was soft and lilting, a trick to disarm you, to lure you in. "Of course, you do."

Lena's mouth went bone dry. Her guts turned watery with terror. She raised the pistol. "Stay back."

"I wouldn't if I were you," Darius Sykes said.

"Fire that gun and I'll put a bullet through your skull," said a gravelly voice behind her. Footsteps crunched as two men emerged from the trees and advanced on her from either side.

To her right stood a skinny Hispanic gangbanger with tattooed tears that dripped down his angular cheeks. The man on her left was bald and muscular, and covered in tattoos.

They wore camo and gear like soldiers, with pistols and knives at their hips and long guns slung over their shoulders. They didn't move or act like soldiers but henchmen. They trained AK-47s on her chest.

Lena resisted the urge to recoil, to turn and flee. If she ran, a bullet to the spine would follow or Sykes' thugs would chase her down and do even worse.

"Put the gun on the ground," Sykes ordered. "Or I'll cut off your head."

Obediently, Lena dropped the gun. With numb fingers, she grasped Bear by the scruff and pulled him close to her side. She didn't doubt Sykes' threat. This man slayed women and children without conscience, a demon dressed in flesh and bone.

She struggled to keep her voice steady. "Where are Traci and Curt Tilton? I'm here for them."

"But I am here for you." He jutted his chin at the two men closing in on her. "Meet Angel Flud and Jacob Huffman. They'll be your escorts."

Angel moved in closer, within ten feet.

Bear growled a warning low in his throat.

"Stay!" Lena whispered frantically. The Newfoundland was a sweetheart, but he'd defended her from the black bear. He would defend her again, she had no doubt. This time, there were too many predators for one brave dog. "Stay, boy!"

"That thing's the size of a horse." The gangbanger lowered his AK-47 and pointed the muzzle at Bear. "And dangerous."

Terror shot through her veins. "NO! Don't hurt him!"

Bear growled louder, a deep menacing bass vibrating from his barrel chest. His black jowls pulled back over his teeth in a snarl.

"He's certified search and rescue. He's a teddy bear. He won't hurt anyone!" Lena's words tumbled over each other in her desperation.

"Lady, that's no teddy bear," Huffman drawled.

Growling, Bear swung his big head between the approaching thugs. His muscles bunched and strained beneath his fur as he barked furiously, the booming sound ricocheted through the trees.

"I hate dogs," Sykes said. "Kill it."

"Bear, run!" Lena shouted.

Bear didn't run. He charged at Angel.

Angel aimed at Bear and fired.

The dog's hind legs collapsed. He let out a horrible yelp and tumbled to the ground. He lay on his side as blood dribbled from a gash along his haunches.

"No!" Lena screamed and ran for Bear. "Stop!"

Angel seized her from behind and jerked her backward. He shoved her to her knees on the ground. With his other hand, he aimed the gun at the dog.

Lena didn't think, only reacted. She flung herself sideways at Angel. Shoulder first, she plowed into his side.

The gun went off. The loud crack rang in her ears, dulling all sounds.

"You stupid slut!" Something hard struck her in the back of her head. She fell onto her stomach, the breath knocked from her chest. Disoriented, she sucked in air, her lungs screaming for oxygen that wouldn't come.

Gasping and dizzy, she scrambled to her hands and knees. Bear. Where was Bear? If they'd hurt him, or worse—her mind stopped there. They'd shot Bear. They shot her dog.

The round had gone wide; Bear was on his feet. Limping, he turned toward Lena, despite the men with guns trying to kill him.

"Run!" she screamed. "Run, Bear!"

Somehow, some way, the Newfoundland seemed to understand. Bear turned tail and fled, trailing blood but on his feet. Angel fired again, but he was too late. Bear disappeared between the trees, a fleeting shadow among deeper shadows in the lengthening twilight.

Angel started after him. "I'll finish it."

"No, you idiot!" Sykes said. "Who cares about a stupid animal? We have actual work to do. Bring her inside. Let's get this done."

56

LENA EASTON
DAY ONE HUNDRED AND THREE

The thugs shoved Lena into the gift shop. The screen door squeaked shut behind them. Lena stumbled. Panic tasted like copper pennies in her mouth.

Concern for Bear consumed her, but he was alive, he'd escaped. It was time to worry about herself now. Blinking back tears, she forced herself to focus, to think, to survive.

The ransacked gift shop smelled of sandalwood and candle wax. Racks of T-shirts and hats had been knocked over, shot glasses cracked, touristy mugs shattered, and ceramic figurines of bears, moose, and wolverines smashed. A few broken candles were on the floor, but most had likely been stolen to use for light.

In the center of the gift shop, between racks of sunglasses, key chains, and mugs, three people knelt, their hands tied behind their backs. Traci knelt beside Curt and Keagan, who were both gagged. Huffman and Angel trained their rifles on the parents.

Despite her fear, rage seared her chest. "You!" she choked out. "I trusted you!"

Head bowed, Traci made a despairing noise in the back of her throat.

"I sacrificed myself to save your son, and this is how you repay me? You led me straight into a trap!"

"You catch on fast," Sykes said. "Smart girl. You for their son; that was the trade. They made the right choice, in my humble opinion. They get to live their merry lives, and I get to use you to annihilate Pope. Everyone wins, except you, sorry to say."

"They shot my dog," Lena spat. "Because of you."

"They would have killed my son!" Traci blubbered. She was sobbing, her chest heaving. "I'm sorry, I'm so very sorry. Please forgive me."

Lena opened her mouth, but nothing came out. Terror clotted her throat. Time seemed to slow, her thoughts sluggish, as if she was trapped in a vat of molasses.

Panicked tears streamed down the woman's cheeks. She hadn't been touched. No bruising marred her face or arms. She didn't sport a busted lip or a black eye. Otherwise, Lena would've been alerted to the trap.

Curt Tilton hadn't been so lucky. His left eye was swollen shut, the blackish-purple color of eggplant; his lip was split and his shirt torn and bloodied. He was in deep shock, his face blank with fear, his eyes glazed, expressionless, empty.

Keagan sagged between his parents, his face slackened, low whimpers escaping his lips. A large knot swelled in the center of his forehead. Bruises marred his thin arms and his throat.

They'd hurt him in front of his parents.

The people they once were had ceased to be. Now they were paralyzed by shock, fear, and panic, rendered almost inhuman by terror. These people had betrayed her, lured her into a lethal trap, but they were caught within its savage jaws; she could not hate them.

"Let the boy go," she said. "Let them all go."

Sykes let out a displeased *tssk*. "I thought you'd know better."

"The boy is a Type I diabetic, and he needs immediate medical attention. He looks concussed."

Sykes leaned in, his demeanor affecting the intimate tone of a close friend. It repulsed her. His smile was beatific, death itself

343

grinning back at her. "Stop worrying about everyone else and start worrying about yourself."

"What do you want?" Although she knew. She already knew.

"They say revenge is a dish best served cold. I disagree. However, prison made certain objectives...unattainable. The world being what it is, everything has changed. I will maim and slaughter my way to the top as I always have. Not everything has changed. The powerful will still rule the weak. It's the way of things."

"This family has nothing to do with that. They're innocent."

"I needed them as bait. It worked. And I need *you* as bait for Eli Pope."

Lena met his gaze and didn't blink, keeping her terror locked inside. "I don't know who you're talking about."

Sykes laughed. It was a high, sweet sound. It made her flesh crawl. "I have little ears everywhere, little birds I reward for their intel and loyalty. I know all about you and your romance with that traitorous scumbag. Unfortunate taste, my dear."

"We're old friends. I'm not in any—"

"I'm not interested in debating facts," Sykes said coldly. "I made a promise to Pope. I reiterated that promise on the train he tried to steal from me. He killed my men. That is...unacceptable. He hurt the people I care about, so I hurt the people he cares about. It is simple arithmetic, a beautiful equation."

The terrible realization sank in slowly, then all at once. There was no escaping this, no way out but through. "Let them go and I'll go with you without a fight. I won't kick or bite."

Sykes smiled again. "Who says we don't like biting?"

A few of the convicts chuckled and leered at her.

Lena felt sick. Her head was spinning.

"I like your spirit, girl," Sykes said. "So, I'll humor you. One of the three must die. I need a corpse to string up."

Traci moaned deep in her throat. Her eyes were wild and bloodshot, the tendons in her neck standing out like cords. She knelt, trembling and terrified, though she'd managed to move in front of her son, partially shielding him.

"Which one do you pick?" Sykes asked.

Lena blanched. "What?"

"You pick. Who dies? Who lives? The mother is the one who lured you here. Should I put a bullet through her cranium? Or her husband? Do you think he stood up for you or capitulated as soon as Angel put his hands on his precious little spawn?"

His words struck her like a sledgehammer to the gut. Nausea clawed at her stomach, her intestines twisted into knots. Cold sweat broke out on her brow. Her tongue felt like a dead slug in her mouth. "I—I can't do that."

Sykes gave a nonchalant shrug. "Guess we'll shoot all three, then."

"No!"

"No? You're going to pick? Do it now." Sykes glanced at his watch as if bored. "I'm a busy man. You have thirty seconds."

Lena looked at the three of them in horror. The boy she'd saved who would die without insulin. The mother who'd betrayed her. The father she barely knew.

She smelled her own sour, panicked sweat. Her vision narrowed, her pulse loud in her ears. How could she make this impossible choice? How could anyone?

"I—I can't."

"Fine. Shoot them all in the head."

Angel raised his weapon.

"No!" Lena gasped. "Stop! I'll do it."

"Then do it."

Everything in her resisted but she knew the stakes, knew she must make a choice or three lives would be lost rather than one. Sykes might kill them all anyway. Or he might not.

Sykes liked games, but he did not bluff. She knew that much.

Curt squared his shoulders and lifted his head. Snot and tears smeared his face. He looked at her with the terror of a cornered animal, knowing it was about to die. Then his gaze cleared. He couldn't speak with the gag in his mouth, but he didn't need to. His eyes begged her—resigned, resolute—and she understood his request.

"You have five seconds or everyone dies!" Sykes sang with glee.

Lena met Curt's tortured gaze and nodded. Her head weighed a thousand pounds. "Save the mother. Save the boy."

Sykes jerked his chin at Angel. "You heard her."

Lena longed to look away but did not. She kept her eyes on Curt as Angel stepped forward, placed the muzzle of his pistol against the back of the man's head, and pulled the trigger.

A sharp crack split the air. Curt toppled forward face first. He lay motionless on the floor. Traci moaned in despair. Keagan's dazed expression went slack. He didn't make a sound.

It didn't seem real. But it was. It was real, all of it—the horror, the terror, and the blood.

Two of Sykes' thugs yanked Curtis Tilton's limp body up by the arms and legs and lugged him from the gift shop like nothing more than a sack of trash. Blood streaked the floor. Blood and other things. The air smelled like gunpowder and death.

Sykes pulled his knife. "Hang him from the flagpole out front. I want everyone to know this is my handiwork. Take the horses, they'll be useful. Everyone else, load up."

"And these two?" Huffman pointed at Traci and Keagan, cowering on the floor.

"Leave 'em. I'm a man of my word when I want to be."

"What about this one?" Angel asked.

"Get her to the storage depot and watch her. We need to make preparations before we let Pope know where she is. Don't say boo until I say so."

Angel seized her by the arm. Lena struggled, attempting to wrench free, to kick him in the balls, scratch his eyes, or elbow his Adam's apple.

Huffman stepped forward. He punched her hard in the face. There was a horrid crunching sound as her nose shattered. The explosion of pain was blinding.

Her muscles turned to jelly, her legs went limp, her vision going hazy. Rough hands lifted her into the air. As unconsciousness dropped over her like a black mantle, the last thing she heard was Sykes' silken voice as he leaned in close: "Don't worry, darlin'. I'm gonna take special care of you."

57

SHILOH EASTON
DAY ONE HUNDRED AND THREE

Shiloh stood on the catwalk ringing the lantern room at the top of the lighthouse tower. She had missed the lighthouse with a physical ache in her chest.

The walls were constructed of floor-to-ceiling glass and offered spectacular 360-degree views. Her rock collection lined the sills: pudding stones, quartz, red jasper, black chert, red and yellow agate, rare greenstones, and Yooper stones, which glowed under UV lights. Next to the rocks sat the lockpick set Cody had given her.

That morning, she and Eli had gone running together. He'd run ten miles without stopping; she'd made it eight miles this time. Afterward, they headed for the woods to check their snares, two rabbits and a raccoon, and then stopped at the lighthouse to weed the garden, collect the ripe vegetables, and check on things.

Eli had patrolled the perimeter of the property while she climbed the lighthouse tower to sweep up the shattered remains of the beacon. The generator was gone, the Fresnel lens was destroyed.

She didn't know what to do about that. If they could get another beacon, they could convert it and maybe use an oil-fueled lantern like in the old days.

Fishermen and other small boats still operated along the jagged shores of Superior, so it was still important to keep the lighthouse functioning to guide boats to shore, to save them from wrecking against the shoals and rocks. The great lake was beautiful, yet cunning; she hid danger beneath her placid surface.

Shiloh raised her face to the iron-gray sky. The wind tugged tendrils of hair free of her bun, whipping it around her face. Gulls squawked as they spiraled high, riding the currents. Her crossbow rested against the railing at her side.

Lake Superior stretched as far as the eye could see, with endless emerald-green water meeting the horizon in the distance. Along the shoreline, great sandstone bluffs jutted like long ragged fingers, layers of rock molded by centuries of glaciers.

It felt like a different world up here, a world without brutality and death. But of course, that was an illusion.

Her gaze was drawn to the canvas bag that held the harness and rope for an emergency descent. A month ago, she'd been stalked by a monster on this catwalk and had nearly died.

Closing her eyes, she thought of Cody, of her mother and grandfather, of everything she'd lost and everything she might still lose.

Grief left no physical mark. Losing Cody was like having her ribs cracked open and her heart carved from her chest, blood-red and raw, still beating. Grief was trying to hold yourself together, cradling your internal organs in your hands, your lungs, your guts, and your pulsing heart.

And Lena...if she lost Lena...she cringed at the thought of how she'd stormed out on her aunt like a petulant child. She needed to go to her, to apologize, it was pointless to be angry at someone who was dying.

It wasn't fair to Lena. Shiloh had to grow the hell up, and she would, right now. If this was the end...Shiloh could hardly bear to think about it. But she had to. She had to face this, and Lena needed her.

Something far below snagged her attention, some movement

in the shadows beneath the trees. She squinted. It was Bear. But that was odd because he was supposed to be with Lena back at the Inn.

Shiloh slung the crossbow over her shoulder and returned to the lantern room, closing the door to the catwalk, then opened the hatch and descended the rickety spiral stairs quickly.

Exiting the tower, she locked the door, pocketed the key, and whistled for Bear.

The Newfie moved with a clumsy, awkward gait as he loped across the meadow. Dark crimson matted his thick fur along his shoulder and front foreleg. It was spattered across his chest like paint. Not paint. It wasn't paint.

With her heart in her throat, Shiloh looked beyond the dog, expecting to see Lena burst through the trees behind the Newfoundland. She didn't come.

Eternal seconds passed and still, Lena didn't come.

A shot of liquid fear made Shiloh's scalp tingle. Her throat constricted. There was no Bear without Lena and no Lena without Bear, not unless Bear was with Shiloh, which he wasn't.

"Eli!" she shouted in alarm as she sprinted across the meadow, the crossbow thudding against her spine. Overgrown weeds and nettles scratched at her shins, but she didn't care.

The dog limped toward her, whining, his head down and his tail low. She knelt at his side. "What happened? Who did this to you? Who hurt you? Where's Lena?"

Bear whimpered and pressed his immense weight against her, almost knocking her over. Nettles and thorns stuck to his coat. Blood was everywhere. Aghast, she wrapped her arms around him, not too tightly, since she wasn't sure where he was hurt or how badly.

"It's okay now, it's going to be okay," she whispered into his floppy ear. "You'll be okay." However, she knew no such thing.

Rapid footsteps approached from the tree line. Eli dropped the snares and fell to one knee beside the girl and the dog, his body half-turned to face the woods, rifle braced against his shoulder as he scanned the shadows between the trees, the barren beach, the woodshed, and the springhouse.

"He's hurt," she said.

"Keep watch in case whoever did this is following him."

Shiloh leaped to her feet, crossbow in hand, a bolt strung and pulled taut. The buttstock nestled snugly against her shoulder, her cheek pressed to the stock with her dominant eye in line with the sight. With her trigger hand, she held the grip, her index finger balanced on the trigger, ready to fire at any threat that presented itself.

Eli set the rifle within easy reach and examined Bear. With efficient fingers, he ran his hands across the dog's haunches, hind legs, spine, front legs, shoulders, neck, and head, parting the thick blood-spattered fur to check for wounds.

Shiloh forced herself to keep her attention on the woods, scanning for threats without daring to breathe. She didn't speak, afraid to interrupt Eli's concentration. Fury burned beneath her skin. Someone was going to pay for this. Whoever did this to Bear was going to die. She'd do it with her bare hands.

Eli climbed to his feet and scooped the big dog into his arms. Bear was one hundred and fifty pounds, but Eli held him easily and with tenderness. He started toward the cottage with sure purposeful strides. "Follow me but cover our six."

Shiloh obeyed, scanning left to right, then right to left, cutting up ten degrees and scanning again as she moved gingerly backward. "Tell me how to help."

"Call Jackson and Devon on the radio. Tell them it's an emergency. Tell them to find Lena and that Bear has been shot."

Shiloh made the call one-handed, contacting Devon who promised to alert Jackson immediately, then raced ahead of Eli, checked the woods once more, shoved open the front door with her shoulder, and darted inside. Slinging the crossbow to the coffee table, she spread a blanket on the sofa and lit a Coleman lantern as Eli laid the dog on the cushions.

Kneeling beside him, Shiloh held the Newfie still and whispered sweet nothings while Eli retrieved a razor from his cabin, then shaved the fur across Bear's right shoulder so they could see the wound. As if sensing the urgency of the task, Bear submitted to the humiliation with his head low, whining, his ears drooping.

Shiloh's chest was too tight. She wanted to scream and cry and beat something with her fists, but she did none of those things.

Eli mopped up the blood and irrigated the wound with a syringe of purified water. He pulled his IFAK from his vest and removed QuikClot bandages, antiseptic, and antibiotic ointment. Shiloh watched as he tended to Bear's injuries, applied ointment, placed gauze over the jagged cut, and wrapped an Ace bandage around the dog's chest and shoulder.

He worked with intent focus, efficiency, and gentleness. His hands were skilled at violence, but they were much more. They were her father's hands.

A lump rose in her throat. "How bad is it?"

"Fortunately, the bullet skimmed his shoulder blade. The wound is about a half-inch deep and four inches long. I don't see any bone fragments or shredded tendons. The bullet nicked him and kept going. Another inch in either direction and we'd be having a different conversation. The round partially tore the muscle, but it can heal. He's in pain, but nothing crucial was damaged. He'll need to take it easy to recover. He should see a veterinarian. I'm no doctor."

Her concern for Bear abated as another fear grew deep and wide as a pit beneath her. She stroked the Newfie's furry side, his chest rising and falling steadily, and met Eli's worried gaze.

They were both thinking the same thing. "What happened? Where the hell is Lena?"

At the sound of his mistress's name, Bear's tail thumped the cushions as he tilted his head and whined. He rose onto his belly and attempted to leap off the sofa.

Eli restrained him. "Whoa, boy. You need to stay right here and recover."

Bear gazed up at them with forlorn brown eyes. He was trying to tell them the awful truth they already knew deep in their bones.

Shaking, Shiloh climbed to her feet. "Bear would never leave her. Never. If he was shot..."

She left the terrible words unspoken. They knew. They both knew.

Eli paced the narrow living room as he called Jackson on the radio.

"She's not at the Inn," Jackson's voice crackled. "We searched the place. Devon went to the Carpenters and Ana Grady's place. She's not anywhere."

"Someone could have come to her for help," Shiloh said. "She does that sometimes, goes to their house."

"She was supposed to report in if she did that," Eli said. "She didn't."

"It could be Sykes," Jackson said.

"We have to find her," Eli choked out.

Jackson said, "I'll be right there."

Eli clipped the radio to his belt and moved to the window, blading his body to peer through the glass, checking for threats. He radiated tension, ready to explode into violence.

He glanced back at Shiloh. His coal-black eyes mirrored her fear.

Shiloh brought Bear a bowl and poured purified water from the jug she'd placed on the counter before they'd left. While he drank, Shiloh hurried into Lena's bedroom and returned a moment later carrying a brown paper bag into which she'd placed one of Lena's shirts tossed in the dirty clothes pile. They'd brought few clothes to the Inn, optimistic they'd soon return home.

Bear perked up, his ears pricked. He clambered from the sofa to the floor, favoring the injured leg but on his feet, his tail wagging as he looked expectantly from Shiloh to Eli, and back to Shiloh.

Eli watched her. "What are you doing?"

"I have an idea."

"Bear can't—"

"He can! We need the PLS, the Point Last Seen. Bear can take us back there. Maybe he can track her scent. At least we can find where she was last. There will be clues, evidence."

"He could damage his shoulder further, possibly irreparably."

"I know," she said in a strangled voice, but she didn't back down. "We have to."

They stared at each other for a tense moment. Urgency crackled through the room.

Eli nodded in reluctance. "But how—"

"Lena taught me. I've watched her do it. I can do it, too. Bear will help me."

Shiloh sank onto her knees in front of the Newfoundland. Bear licked her cheeks and chuffed into her ear, blowing hot doggy breath in her face. Love burned like a bright hard spark in her chest.

"This is for Lena. For our Lena, okay?" Her voice broke. "I know you can find her. Take us to where she was last, and we can take it from there. You're so strong and so brave. I would never ask if it wasn't important."

Bear chuffed, his tail wagging low in agreement. His head cocked, his chocolate-brown eyes so expressive, so human, as if he could read her emotions and knew what she needed, and why. And he would do it. For her, for Lena, he would gladly walk into the fire.

"Shiloh, this is dangerous. We don't know what we're facing. I can't let you—"

"Do you know how to do this?" She didn't take her gaze off Bear. "How to handle a search and rescue dog? Do you know how to read him? What hand signals to give him? Because I do. I'm coming with you."

"Absolutely not—"

"You said the lone wolf dies," Shiloh said.

He stared at her.

"You told me once that the lone wolf dies. You made me

promise not to run into a lion's den alone." She glared at him. "You promised. You promised me back!"

She could see it in his eyes; he was conflicted, torn by doubt, worry, and fear. "I can't lose you, Shiloh."

"And we can't lose Lena!"

Eli needed her. He could argue all he wanted but he was wasting time. Besides, if he went off to play the hero, he'd be leaving her at the lighthouse alone. That wasn't an option, either. And he knew it.

He sighed. "You do everything I say, no questions."

"Got it." Shiloh opened the bag and pulled out the unwashed shirt with two fingers, holding it to Bear's snout. "This is Lena. You know her. You know this scent. We have to find Lena. Please take us to where she is."

Bear sniffed the shirt, his entire body quivering with excitement. The dog chuffed, shaking his head back and forth, searching for the scent.

Shiloh was his handler now. She gave the signal she'd seen Lena give him a dozen times—*time to work*.

Bear barked and loped for the door. Shiloh slung the crossbow over her shoulder and fell into step right behind him.

With reluctance, Eli grabbed his HK417 with one hand and followed them out as he radioed Jackson and Devon for backup.

The Newfoundland wore no bright orange Search and Rescue vest. He shuffled with a painful limp, bedraggled and bloodied, but he was tenacious, unshakable, resolute.

Bear had a job to do. To find the lost. To bring Lena home.

58

SHILOH EASTON
DAY ONE HUNDRED AND THREE

They moved deeper into the Hiawatha National Forest. Bear took the lead with Shiloh and Eli trailing him. Eli was a near-silent shadow beside her, his weapon up, scanning left and right, ahead of and behind them.

Shiloh watched Bear's tail, his hackles, his ears, and his mannerisms. Every reaction meant something, a clue to the unseen world he sensed but humans couldn't, invisible currents of meaning leading them onward.

Lena had explained how easily a scent could be lost: the constantly shifting air currents, how the scent could loop in on itself or pool into streams or ditches, funneling in the wrong direction, and how wind and humidity altered current patterns. On a hot day with no wind, the scent pooled without dispersing, limiting its range.

Every few minutes, Bear paused and glanced over his bandaged shoulder with a pained expression. Even injured, he worked with tireless, unflagging dedication, oblivious to his discomfort. His limp worsened.

Her heart felt split in two, with her fierce devotion to Bear pitted against her unrelenting love for Lena.

For the first time in her life, the forest felt hostile. Though they mainly followed a trail, writhing roots tripped her feet. Lurking shadows played tricks on her weary eyes. Her boots skidded on damp leaves; she almost fell on her butt but managed to keep upright by slamming into a pine tree. Thorny underbrush raked her right arm, drawing blood.

Abruptly, Bear stiffened, his hackles raised, his tail sticking straight out. That was his alert signal. The woods hushed. The trees crouched and listening, waiting with bated breath.

Adrenaline kicked her heart into overdrive. Fifty yards ahead, there was a wide break through the trees, an open circle of slate-gray sky: a clearing.

She glimpsed the roof of a building. In the distance, she heard a waterfall, the burble of water rushing over rock.

"Bear, come to me." She lifted a hand, palm out, to stop the dog from going farther. "Bear alerted. She's here. Or she was here. This must be where he was shot."

Eli moved ahead of her, weapon up and swiveling. He stalked closer, half-bent as he darted soundlessly from trunk to trunk, ducking beneath branches. As she watched, he seemed to fade into the background, almost invisible, melding as one with the forest, the dappled shadows.

He didn't need to tell her what to do. Grasping Bear's collar, she scooted behind the massive nine-foot root ball of a fallen oak tree and quietly radioed Jackson their position, one hand on the dog to keep him still.

Trepidation slithered up her spine. Who might be lurking inside the building, waiting for them to expose themselves? They had no clue what they might be walking into.

A minute later, Eli returned and squatted next to her. He handed her his binoculars while he examined the scene through the optical scope of his rifle, then he pointed to a spot past the root ball which gave them a better vantage point but still offered cover and concealment.

"Stay low, and keep your head down."

Belly flat on the soggy ground, she crawled alongside the huge log frilled with some kind of white fungus, scraping over twigs, leaves, and pine needles until she reached a shallow depression in the ground. When she lowered her head, she could peer between the ground and the log without revealing her position.

She raised the binoculars. A single-story building stood in the center of the clearing. It was a cabin, half log and half stone, with a red metal roof. They'd broached the rear of the property. She glimpsed overgrown weeds, a stone wishing well, a pond where ducks swam, quacking at each other, and a trail marked by a wooden sign.

"I recognize this place. The Enchanted Cascades. It's private land. There's a waterfall and gardens with a gift shop. It's mostly tourists who visit. Visited, I mean. Without tourists, I bet it's been empty since the solar flares."

Unlike most of the waterfalls on state land near Munising, the Enchanted Cascades was privately owned. One had to pay a fee to walk the gardens and visit the waterfall.

There was no movement. Everything was still, quiet, and peaceful. Butterflies flitted above clumps of zinnias, marigolds, lilacs, and petunias in the gardens behind the gift shop. The scent of fennel and parsley filled her nostrils.

A low moan echoed through the stillness.

The sound was unmistakable. It was human, a human in tremendous pain. Bear's ears pricked; he raised his head, his tail thumping, but Shiloh pulled him back down. He obeyed with a miserable whimper.

Shiloh went rigid. "Someone is hurt in there."

"Could be bait to lure us in."

"Or they're dying while we wait!" Panic seared her chest. Backup was still at least ten minutes out. "It could be Lena. You have to do something!"

With one hand, Eli pulled a radio headset from his tactical pack and placed it on her head. "Stay here. Keep Bear quiet, and keep your head on a swivel. If you see anything, tell me immediately, like we've been training."

Shiloh nodded soberly. She knew the risks, the stakes.

He looked at her with a hesitant expression, as if he dreaded leaving her, as if this might be a very bad idea. She stared back at him, scared spitless but rock steady. "I've got this."

Eli said, "I'm going in."

59

ELI POPE
DAY ONE HUNDRED AND THREE

E li raised his HK417, the stock braced against his shoulder, and peered through the scope. The cut on his forearm burned, but he hardly noticed. The compact Glock 19 he'd retrieved from his buried cache sat snug against his kidney in an inside-the-waistband holster.

He hated leaving Shiloh in the woods; he hated breaching the gift shop sans a team or backup, hated rushing into danger without intel, hated that Lena might be hurt, or worse.

There were no resources at his disposal, no overwatch other than a thirteen-year-old girl. No thermal imaging cameras or listening devices, not even a damn drone.

He couldn't wait for Jackson and Devon, not if Lena was hurt, maybe dying.

Choking down his fear, he forced himself to steady his breathing and slow his heart rate. The familiar dead calm of battle settled over him.

On high alert, Eli moved in.

Half-crouched, staying low and concealed within the tree line, he circled the perimeter, swiftly checking the gardens, the narrow stone paths, the pond and wishing well, and the little bridge that crossed the creek leading to the waterfall, scanning continuously for threats.

His head on a swivel, he darted across fifty yards of open ground. The meadow droned with insects—grasshoppers whirring, hopping from stalks of drooping grass, and clouds of no-see-ums swarming in the late afternoon sunlight.

He reached the rear of the gift shop, ducked beneath the window, then rose and peered inside: an office and a bathroom, both empty. The store must be in the front.

Blading his body, he moved along the right side of the building toward the front. The parking lot came into view ahead of him. A large crimson puddle stained the asphalt. Spatters of blood marred the pitted surface.

Another moan split the air, so distorted by pain that he couldn't tell if it was Lena.

Cautious, Eli cut the front corner of the building, leading with his pistol. He stared up in horror at the flagpole. An American flag snapped in the wind. Not just a flag.

Curtis Tilton sagged from the flagpole with his chin lolling against his chest, his gray face slack. His flaccid corpse slowly twirled from the noose around his throat.

Urgency crackled through him. Eli edged around the corner, sprinted to the front door, and kicked it in. Unlocked, the door burst inward at the first blow. Breaching the entry, he dropped to one knee to avoid head-on fire as he swept the room, slicing the pie with the HK417.

He took in the scene in a heartbeat: graffiti scrawled across the log walls, racks of trinkets toppled over, folded T-shirts and mugs on shelves, plastic displays of key chains, penknives, shot glasses, magnets, and piles of hats emblazoned with "Pure Michigan."

In the center of the gift shop, two people lay on the wood plank floor. One larger form was curled around a second smaller figure. The moans came from the small body curled into a fetal position, his mother's arms wrapped protectively around him.

Swiftly, Eli cleared the building. He transmitted a message to

Shiloh and told her to keep watch. Returning to the mother and child, he dropped to one knee, placed the rifle on its sling, and drew his Glock 19, setting it beside him within easy reach before examining the victims for injuries.

"I'm a friendly. You're okay, you're safe now."

The woman's pulse was strong but frantic. He checked their breathing, skimming their bodies with his hands. They appeared to be uninjured but for bruises and lacerations.

The boy's pulse was strong, but his pallor was sickly, his lips purple, and his breathing labored. He'd managed to loosen the duct tape at his mouth enough to make those eerie, keening moans. He was in a near catatonic state, nonresponsive.

The woman rolled onto her back and stared at Eli in abject terror. Snot and tears slicked her face. Duct tape covered her mouth and bound her wrists behind her back, her legs taped at the ankles.

Eli cut them both free. The woman turned her head and vomited. The sour-sick stench turned his stomach, but he ignored it. He'd smelled and seen much worse. Worse was outside, hanging from a flagpole.

The woman bent over her son, murmuring his name, stroking his hair and his cheeks. He groaned, his eyelids fluttering, and curled into a tighter ball. She pulled him into her lap and held him, clutching his small body to her chest like she could ward off all enemies.

"What is your name?" Eli asked.

Tears gathered at her chin and dropped onto his pale face. "T-Traci Tilton."

"Where is Lena?"

"They—they took her—"

Eli couldn't breathe, couldn't get enough oxygen. "Who are they?"

Her breaths came in hiccupping gasps, her words garbled with panic. "That terrible monster—he took my son and—my husband and tied them up. He—he held a gun to my son's head, said he'd torture him to death if I didn't do exactly what he said. I'm sorry, I'm so—"

"Breathe. You're okay, you're safe," he said with a calmness he did not feel. He wanted to shake her like a rag doll until she gave him answers. It took every ounce of self-control to hold back. "Tell me what happened."

She couldn't stop trembling. "I went to get Lena and told her that my son was missing. I—I had to do it. I had no choice. He was waiting for her."

"Darius Sykes."

She nodded miserably.

"He took her."

"Him and the awful men with him."

"Did they hurt her?"

"They hit her a few times, but she was alive when they left with her. They put a hood over her head and tied her up. That man— he shot my husband in the head. I did everything they asked and they still k-killed him. He's dead. I can't believe he's dead."

Eli wasn't any good at comforting victims. All he could think of was Lena. "Where did he take her?"

"I—I don't know."

"What did he say? Tell me everything."

"He—he said it was a trap for you. That Lena was bait. He said things weren't ready yet, that you would know when it was time."

"How long ago did they leave?"

"I don't know—"

"How long?"

"I'm not certain. My phone doesn't work anymore. The clock on the wall is broken—"

"Guess."

"A couple of hours, maybe." Traci hesitated. "My son is diabetic. He's been without insulin for hours. There's a vial in my backpack behind the cashier's counter."

Eli reared back on his heels. "Your son is Keagan."

She nodded wordlessly, frazzled curls falling into her face as she hunched over the boy. He curled into a tighter ball. His little chest rose and fell in shallow hitching breaths. She stroked her son's slack cheek as if he could save her, could redeem her for the terrible things she'd done.

His voice was an accusation. "Lena shared the last of her insulin to keep him alive."

Her swollen face flushed in shame. "She did. And I—I repaid her by betraying her to save my son. And he...he..." Her features contorted in despair, unable to say the words aloud. Her actions had doomed Lena but hadn't saved her husband or her child, who would perish within days.

Eli gritted his teeth, reining in his frustration, his fury, trying to be mindful of the trauma this woman had endured. The grief and guilt would haunt her for the rest of her life.

He tried not to hate her for betraying Lena, but he did. He despised her for it.

Jackson's voice came through the radio. "We're outside."

Eli didn't say a word. He rose to his feet, holstered his Glock 19, and stalked for the door.

"I'm sorry!" the woman shouted at his back. "Please—please understand, I'm sorry—"

He couldn't give her what she begged for; he couldn't even give it to himself. He had no pity left in him. His only thought was for Lena, for the seemingly impossible task ahead.

Outside, dusk had fallen. Heavy iron-gray clouds gathered as a menacing wall of darkness on the horizon. A half-dozen deputies and cops had arrived on bicycles, horses, and ATVs.

Nash set up a crime scene perimeter while Moreno and Hart worked on the corpse strung on the flagpole a dozen yards from Devon and Jackson, who was bent over a set of tire tracks in the dirt driveway. Nyx and Antoine were out searching for Sykes, following potential escape routes.

Bear circled Devon, limping but intently searching for Lena's scent, sniffing at the ground with anxious barks.

Shiloh ran up the drive toward him. "Where is she?"

He steeled himself. "She's not here."

Fear etched her face. "They took her, the men who did that." She pointed a shaking finger at the body hanging from the flagpole. "It's him. It's Sykes."

He couldn't lie to her. "Yes."

Her pupils dilated. She screamed a high keening wail of fury and grief. She came at him in a distraught frenzy, pummeling her fists against his chest.

He seized her wrists, gently, with one hand. She tried to rip away, but he pulled her close and hugged her against his chest, her heart thudding wildly against his ribs.

"I'm sorry," he said into her hair. "I'm so sorry."

"You have to save her! She can't die! You have to find her!"

A terrible powerlessness swept over him. Sykes had Lena and he would do terrible things to her until Eli came and did as Sykes wanted, which was to die slowly and in agony, while Lena was tortured to death in front of him. His thoughts spun in a frantic blur, his heart racing, his palms clammy with dread. How could he save her and keep everyone else safe? He did not know.

Eli held his daughter as his heart shattered into a thousand pieces.

60

ELI POPE
DAY ONE HUNDRED AND THREE

Eli stood with Jackson and Devon half a mile from the Enchanted Cascades Gift Shop. Bear had tracked his mistress to the paved road before losing the scent for good. The SUVs had headed west.

Eli fought the urge to shoot something, or someone, in frustration. Luckily, Sykes didn't know about Shiloh, or he would've taken her, too. His chest seized at the thought of losing Shiloh, of losing Lena, who was already halfway gone, slipping through his grasp.

He knew the madman who held Lena captive, what that madman would do to her, might already be doing to her. The mere thought of Sykes set his blood on fire.

He *wanted* Sykes, longed to hunt him down like an animal, to put a bullet in his temple or worse, much worse. God help him, he wouldn't be able to hold back. He didn't want to.

Nash had taken Traci and her son to the Inn, along with Shiloh, who'd gone kicking and screaming—but she'd gone.

Moreno and Hart had dealt with the corpse. They would bury him in the cemetery next to Gideon Crawford. McCallister and several others continued to work the scene. They'd taken casts of the tire tracks and matched them to the other crime scenes.

Jackson seemed deflated, shrunken somehow by stress, fear, and worry. "We lost a third of our citizen volunteers after they heard Gideon was killed on watch. We don't have enough manpower. I reached out to the state police with the ham radio for backup, but they've left the U.P. under the governor's orders. They've lost more than half their workforce, the remaining officers are trying desperately to bring order to the chaos in Detroit, Grand Rapids, Kalamazoo, and all the other major population centers."

Devon took the map of the DNR forest roads from her pack and spread it out on a boulder set along the shoulder of the road. "There are still dozens of potential storage depot locations within a hundred-mile radius of our last listening post location, mines, logging camps, et cetera. If you add campsites..." Devon waved her hand across the map. "There are still too many sites to check, at least quickly. With the lack of boots on the ground and limited fuel for vehicles, it'll take days."

Eli studied the map. "Once it's daylight, we can get the drone up and start searching the closest campsites for signs of recent movement. Include the abandoned nickel and copper mines west of Gwinn. It'll be more efficient than checking them in person and will use less fuel."

He pointed at the spot on the map where the last listening post had tracked Sykes' SUVs. "The forest road splits into several off-road tracks throughout the wilderness northwest of Princeton and spreads into Tilden and Richmond Townships, west of Highway 35 and heading northwest. I don't think he'll have holed up much farther than this range here, maybe a twenty-mile radius."

"It's almost dark," Devon said. "The SUV is likely headed straight back to their hidey hole, which means they probably won't pass a listening post tonight."

"We'll do it anyway, just in case," Eli said, though she was likely correct. So far, Sykes hadn't attacked multiple locations in a single day.

Jackson's mouth thinned into a bloodless line. "I bet my father knows where they're storing the meds before they offload them. Sykes could be there."

Eli shot him a questioning look. "Where is your father?"

"He knew I was onto him. He took off. He's in the wind." Jackson stared down the empty road fringed with trees where shapes gradually merged outlines in the gathering dark. In the twilight, his face was a pale, ghostly oval. "I will find him. Somehow, all roads seem to lead back to the same place—"

Jackson swayed on his feet. He flailed his arms, then grasped Devon's arm to keep from falling.

"Hey, you okay?" Devon asked.

"Fine." The blood had drained from his face. He swiped blearily at his glassy eyes. "I'm fine."

Eli studied him. Deep circles ringed his eyes, his skin gray with fatigue. Losing Gideon Crawford, and in such a brutal manner, had shaken him. He looked like he had one foot in the grave. "When was the last time you slept?"

Jackson shrugged, chagrined. "I...I don't know."

As a Ranger, Eli had trained to go days with little to no sleep. Back then, he'd had pills to help him. He had nothing now, but he could push himself beyond a normal man's endurance. Jackson couldn't. "You need rest. Go back to the Inn, get some sleep, and we'll start fresh in the morning."

"No. No way. Not with Lena out there—"

"You're a liability right now," Eli said firmly. "It'll be pitch black in ten minutes. We can't use the drone in the dark. Moreno and Hart will man the listening post tonight, not that it will do any good. Go home, Jackson."

"What are you going to do?"

Eli studied the map again, a line between his brows. "I have an idea."

"I'll help you," Jackson insisted.

Eli shook his head. "For this, I work alone."

61

ELI POPE
DAY ONE HUNDRED AND FOUR

E li was closing in on Sykes. One more bearing on his map and he'd be close to an approximate location.

He had traveled to the last known position on his ATV. Hiding the four-wheeler within some scrub brush, he'd covered it with his ghillie blanket and pine branches.

Now, he moved forward on foot to practice noise discipline. Outfitted in tactical gear, he wore his chest rig and battle belt, his rifle slung across his chest. The night vision goggles were pulled down over his eyes, casting the world in green.

In one hand he carried the map; in the other, he held a strange contraption—a homemade directional antenna he'd built using salvaged supplies he and Shiloh had scavenged from the local hardware store, abandoned garages and sheds, and Amos Easton's salvage yard.

The antenna consisted of several lengths of PVC pipe. It had four measuring tape "arms" cut at specific lengths that were attached to the PVC pipe body, with stainless steel hose clamps, a coaxial cable, and a receiver with an S-meter.

The antenna he'd built was rudimentary, but it worked. In this way, he could pinpoint directional signals. An hour ago, he'd picked up a transmission.

Attempting to get compass readings, which gave him bearings from different places in the woods in the middle of the night was proving to be a difficult task. He'd been forced to keep to the logging roads since it was impossible to wade through the dense forest carrying a six-foot-tall antenna.

Homing in on the source of the transmission, Eli had already taken a good compass bearing on an intercepted radio call, so he could plot the bearing accurately on his map. Where the lines crossed would triangulate the origin of the transmission—hopefully, Sykes's hideout, or at least a location nearby.

He needed a good second bearing from a new position, some distance from the first, so that the lines would cross on his map and give him a reasonably accurate location.

Unless he got a good third bearing, his result wouldn't be very accurate. He also didn't know whether the radio transmissions he was intercepting were from people traveling toward the hideout, away from it, or from there.

He was quite certain about his position when he took his first bearing; he was less certain about his exact position since then. Of course, all that assumed he'd plotted each bearing accurately on his map.

He'd just managed to mark the second bearing when the signal died. As if Sykes could sense his pursuer, the radio traffic went abruptly silent. For a long time, he waited, but he couldn't hear any more.

Was Sykes smart enough to practice EMCON—radio silence— or was something else at play? It was late at night, well after midnight. Whoever was communicating via radio may have gone to sleep, though he assumed patrols would remain in contact throughout the night.

Thick cloud cover obscured the moon and stars. Insects whirred, the night creatures stirring deep in the trees. He stopped at the side of an off-road track, ready to dart into the trees if he sensed any vehicles nearby. Weeds and thorns snagging his shins, he studied the map again.

Within five to seven miles, he counted too many potential locations: three campsites, a Christian youth camp, a regional airport, Kal's Rustic Log Cabins, the abandoned Eagle Falls copper mine, and half a dozen caves known for their large brown bat populations.

Exhaustion pulled at his limbs. Though his other wounds had mostly healed over the last two weeks, the laceration on his arm burned like someone had poured acid on his skin. Holding the antenna for hours had overworked the torn muscles.

Pocketing the map, he rested the PVC pipe contraption on the ground and leaned against the rough bark of a pine tree, inhaling the sweetness of the sap in the cracks, breathing through his fear, pain, and frustration.

As much as he wanted to, it was too difficult to continue. As soon as the sun rose, Eli would be back at it. He needed that third triangulation point to narrow down the target area.

One more day at the most and Eli would have him.

He prayed that Lena could hold out for that long. She might go into a diabetic coma without Sykes laying a hand on her. Time was running out.

He touched the St. Michael's medallion beneath his shirt and prayed like never before. He prayed to whatever supernatural power existed: to God, to the Great Spirit of his Native American ancestors, to whatever benevolent force up there might still care what happened down here on this cursed planet. *Help me save her.*

62

JACKSON CROSS
DAY ONE HUNDRED AND FOUR

Jackson sat in his chair, defeat curving his spine, his shoulders slumped. The Coleman lantern cast long shadows across the desk in his room at the Northwoods Inn. The air was still and stifling.

It was midnight. He was utterly drained and bone-tired. His eyes were gritty, his mind fuzzy with fatigue, but sleep eluded him.

Earlier, Lori Brooks had brought over a plastic container of chili soup that now sat on his dresser, untouched. "I'm so sorry, honey," she'd said, tears in her eyes. "We love Lena. Bring her back to us."

"I'll try," he'd said.

He was too sick to eat. Worry and fear chased him like beasts from nightmares. Despair coiled in his belly and crawled up his throat.

Sykes had kidnapped Lena. Everything he had done, everything he had given of himself, and it hadn't been enough. Gideon Crawford was dead. Curtis Tilton was dead, and his wife and child were traumatized.

Eli was still out there, looking. They'd narrowed down the vicinity of Sykes' location, but it might take days to find him—days that Lena didn't have.

Jackson was supposed to rest, but he couldn't. How could he? What good was he if he couldn't do his damn job when it mattered most?

The room was quiet. The silence pressed against his eardrums. His blood rushed in his ears. He rested his head in his hands. His jumbled thoughts blurred, spinning in manic circles.

Lena's final request kept coming back to him. She'd asked him to catch her sister's killer. If he could do nothing to save Lena tonight, then he could at least do this.

That feeling haunted him, that his family was somehow tangled up in everything, in ways he couldn't yet pinpoint. If his father had willingly jumped into bed with the cartel, and the cartel was working with Sykes, then he might know something about Lena's disappearance.

Even more damning, Horatio certainly knew something about Lily's death. Jackson thought of Gideon's words before he died regarding the suspicion that Horatio might have committed violence to keep the truth hidden.

Certain facts didn't make sense. Even if his father had covered up his and Astrid's crimes, there was more to Lily's case: the broken heart locket, the lock of hair, the strangulation, and the beating around the face.

Jackson raised his head. He pulled the half-melted Snickers bar from his pocket and set it on the desk. He stared at it, thinking of Shiloh.

He thought about all she'd been through and the things she'd remembered: the shadowy monster in the hoodie, the thumping sound she'd heard—the killer knocking on the wall to taunt her, her mother's last weak plea for help, or something else altogether, a vital clue he was missing.

He fumbled for Lily's case file and thumbed yet again through the witness statements, the crime scene photos, the notes from Underwood's press conference. He thought of Shiloh's testimony and his mother's disjointed memories.

His gaze snagged on something. A sentence, a few words. The fishing tackle box.

Jackson went still. The oxygen fled from his lungs and he felt like he was drowning.

The pieces fell into place with a terrible clarity.

And he knew, at long last, what he must do.

63

JACKSON CROSS
DAY ONE HUNDRED AND FOUR

Jackson opened the front door. "I brought you a late dinner."

Astrid beamed at him from her seat on the sofa. She'd been reading a paperback romance novel with a half-naked hunk on the cover. She put the book on the coffee table.

Jackson shut the door softly behind him. "I thought you might enjoy some hot black bean chili with chunks of seared bear meat. Lori made it."

"You know that it's past midnight, right?"

"You're a night owl, like me. I figured you'd be up."

"Lucky guess." Astrid's cane thumped against the floor as she limped from the living room into the kitchen. She sank into her wheelchair at the breakfast table and leaned the cane against an empty chair.

Jackson got out two bowls and spoons, opening and closing drawers noisily. He tucked an object into his pocket and then brought the bowls to the table. He served her the still-hot chili he'd warmed up on the woodstove in the Northwoods kitchen before he'd left.

Astrid sat back and watched him. The lights were off for once. A handful of candles cast a flickering glow through the room, her bright eyes glinting, her silken blonde hair shimmering around her head like a halo. "To what do I owe this pleasure?"

He pushed her bowl across the table. She took a bite and moaned with pleasure. The delicious smell wafted around them.

Jackson dipped his spoon in his bowl, took a few bites he didn't taste, then set the spoon in the bowl and left it there. He'd lost his appetite.

He'd considered how to tackle this conversation, how to get the answers he needed. He decided to go on the offensive.

"I know," he said. "There is no use hiding."

"You know what?"

"About the accident."

"I have no idea what you mean."

"I know what you did that night—you hit and killed a hiker. Then another vehicle came barreling around the corner and crashed into you. Gideon, Allison, and Lily were in the car. They were drinking. Their recklessness crippled you for life."

Her eyes darkened as he spoke. Her expression didn't change, not even a tic of a muscle at her jaw. She was good, very good.

"Nothing happened to them. You were the sacrificial lamb. That's how you saw yourself. You'd killed a man, hit him with your car. You were drunk, but you blamed Lily. Gideon was driving and Allison was dead, but Lily was the one who got away. She ran that night. She escaped all consequences, all blame. Everyone was drunk in the car that hit you. You wanted them to pay for what happened to you, but that couldn't happen. To cover up your crime, theirs had to go away, too. There was no one to blame, not publicly. But you knew. You remained conscious at the accident scene and never lost your memories. And you hated it. You hated her."

Astrid said, "You think you're so smart."

"I'm not that smart," Jackson said.

"You've got it all wrong."

"I know this," Jackson said. "Your future aspirations were ruined. Your dreams of college, of modeling, of a full life burned to ash, and no one paid for it. Your hatred for Lily festered through every minute, hour, and day that you suffered in agony, in horrific, unutterable pain for months. You lived, but you were left crippled for all intents and purposes, scarred and ugly. You had to live with that secret, that seething hatred, for years. And you wanted someone to pay for your misery. You wanted to make someone pay for it."

Astrid said nothing. The room was dead silent. She sat still as a statue.

"You can speak the truth now. There's no reason to hide it."

For a moment, she didn't move, then Astrid leaned forward intently, her eyes burning. "She walked away from the crash without a scratch. She deserved shattered bones, snapped tendons, and crushed limbs, to wake up in the hospital with ruined legs. That slut escaped unscathed, with no consequences. That wasn't right. It wasn't justice. You of all people should get that, Jackson."

Jackson kept his voice even. "So, you made her pay."

Astrid didn't blink. "Cyrus Lee Jefferson killed Lily."

"He didn't."

"Sheriff Underwood said so."

"He was wrong."

She stared him down and took a bite of chili, not breaking eye contact.

"There's more."

She cocked a delicate eyebrow.

"Back when Devon and I interviewed you, you mentioned Cyrus Lee's 'tackle box,' but when Underwood gave the press conference, he didn't call Lee's trophy box a tackle box, he called it a toolbox. I made a note to correct him. There's no way you could've known it was a tackle box unless you already knew, because you'd seen it before."

Astrid shot him an incredulous look. "You or Devon called it a tackle box when you interviewed me on horseback."

"We didn't. Neither of us mentioned it. Only you did. I checked my notes."

"Your notes are wrong."

"I recorded the conversation with my phone. I'm very thorough."

"I called a stupid box the wrong name. That's all you've got? An issue of semantics? That means nothing."

"Maybe it does, maybe it doesn't."

"Whatever you're implying, you're wrong."

"Not this time."

"A man killed her." Astrid smiled, not taking her eyes off him. "Alas, I do not have the hardware."

"Everyone made assumptions. You're almost six feet tall and broad-shouldered. You can easily pass for a man in the dark. You're strong, even now. Working the wheelchair strengthens your back and your biceps. You wore a black hoodie to obscure your features in case anyone saw you."

"Sounds like speculation to me. And a vivid imagination."

He spoke slowly, deliberately. "Then there's Shiloh."

"What about her?"

"Shiloh told me about a thumping sound in her nightmares, a sound she heard that night. She thought it was someone knocking on the other side of the wall, the monster who murdered her mother taunting her. I realized she'd heard it wrong. It wasn't someone knocking on the wall, it was you. You and your cane. The sound it made on the floor: *thump, thump, thump.*"

Astrid's pupils contracted ever so slightly. "That's nothing."

"Oh, it's not nothing. It's something. It's the something that led me straight to you."

Astrid took a large bite of chili. She chewed slowly, mechanically. She swallowed and daintily patted her lips with her napkin, then folded it beside her bowl.

The silence stretched taut. He waited her out. If she was going to break, it would be now, or never. There was a part of her that longed to boast of her exploit. He was counting on it.

She was proud of herself. All sociopaths suffered from enormous egos. Their biggest disappointment lay in the realization that the more cunning they were, the fewer, if any, people would ever get to appreciate their genius. So, he used that.

"It was late that night, but Lily opened the door because she knew you, which is why there were no signs of forced entry. She underestimated your strength—and your brutality. You used your cane to beat Lily in the face and render her unconscious so she couldn't fight you. Then you strangled her.

"And all these years, no one knew it was you. You were the poor crippled girl who could barely walk. No one suspected you. You weren't even on our radar. Thanks to the sheriff, no one knew you had a motive for murder. Even if a few cops got suspicious, our father had covered up a crime once for you; you knew he'd do it again. You got away with it, scot-free."

A twitch of her lips. A flash of something—arrogance. A glint of disdain. He knew then, without a shadow of a doubt, that he had the right monster.

Every discombobulated trail, every twisted clue, every lie and deceit and misdirection led back to his own corrupt family. First, to his father, and then, to his sister.

"You think you've got it all figured out," she spat. "What do you need me for?"

"The confession you're going to give me."

Astrid snorted and took another bite of chili. The only sounds were her steady chewing and the rattle of her spoon as she cleaned out the bowl.

Finally, she looked at him. And smiled. "Shiloh. That little rat."

64

JACKSON CROSS
DAY ONE HUNDRED AND FOUR

Astrid's eyes glinted in the candlelight, her skin dewy and glowing like an angel. It was disconcerting as hell.

"Killing is a rush," she said, "just like they say it is. It's all true. It's better than drugs, better than sex, better than winning the lottery. There's nothing like it. There is so much power in your hands, absolute power over another person."

Jackson felt gutted. He'd expected this, but still, it stunned him. He felt nauseous and repulsed, but he matched her step for step, as controlled and calculating as the predator sitting across the table.

"You tried to kill Shiloh. You hired that meth head to murder her in the woods, just like you hired the two druggies who tried to steal Lena's insulin."

"I should've killed her myself," she said absently, as if she were discussing the weather. "Lesson learned."

Jackson had thought he couldn't be more incredulous, but once again, he was wrong. He was horrified and dumbfounded by her callousness, her flippant cruelty.

Astrid frowned prettily. "I knew you were getting too close, that Shiloh might be remembering things. I made sure she saw me at the FEMA riot, to see if she reacted. She didn't, but I figured I should kill her anyway, just to be safe." She shrugged. "I knew the crackhead from the homeless shelter. It was easy to goad him to do it. He would've done anything for the promise of one more fix. But he messed it up and got himself killed in the process. Served him right. I decided that I would have to do it myself, and I would have done it, too. All I had to do was get her alone. I had it all planned out. Then Sykes showed up, and everybody went to Defcon 4. You and Eli tucked her into that Northwoods cult, and I couldn't get to her." She pinched her fingers together. "I was that close."

A chill shivered through him. "You underestimated Shiloh."

"That girl's got balls," Astrid said with something that sounded like admiration. She leaned forward intently. "I'll get her eventually. I always get what I want, in the end."

Horror tasted like rotten fruit on his tongue, like death and decay. Interrogating a sociopath was like crossing a tightrope a thousand feet in the air; the altitude was dizzying and disorienting, and one misstep would pitch you headlong into the abyss.

The memories came at him, one after another: Astrid watching the neighbor kid fall off his bike, a smile on her face, Astrid never crying, never showing empathy, only contempt and derision. She'd volunteered at the shelter to see others in pain—the homeless, drug-addicted, abused, and downtrodden. She gorged herself on misery and suffering.

Astrid sipped from the glass of water and set it down. "I should've just eliminated her back then. Problem solved. The truth is that I'd forgotten about Lily's snot-nosed kids until I heard a sound in the bedroom as I passed by. I saw her hiding, squished between the bedframe and the wall. She was so tiny. I was so powerful. What could I have to fear from a baby? I figured she was too young, it was too dark, and she didn't see anything. She was nothing. I granted her mercy. And look what she did with that mercy. She threw it back in my face."

Jackson sat back in his chair and stared at her, a thousand terrible emotions tumbling through him—dread, revulsion, loathing, and horror. He pulled himself together, forcing himself to stay calm and emotionless.

In an even voice, he said, "More chili?"

She nodded and he rose, went to the counter, and poured the remainder of the chili into her bowl, willing his hands to remain steady, making sure she didn't make a move while his back was half-turned. He brought the bowl back to the table and sat down.

She took the bowl. "Thank you," she said with impeccable manners, as if this were any given Sunday, a typical family meal when it was anything but.

He switched tactics. "How long have you known Cyrus Lee was a killer?"

She narrowed her eyes. "I didn't."

"I know you figured it out. No one else did but you."

Now she beamed. "Nine years ago. You cops are pathetic."

"How did you know?" He didn't need her to answer. He had a hunch.

She gave a careless shrug. "I found the tackle box in Cyrus Lee's garage. Right away, I realized who, and what, he was. I realized how easy it would be to kill someone and get away with it. I had the evidence to pin it on someone else right there in my hands."

"And that's when you decided."

Her left eyelid twitched. He'd hit the nail on the head.

"Why didn't you turn Cyrus Lee in when you learned what he was, what he'd done?"

"He always treated me like a queen."

"He stalked and murdered women."

She gave him a petulant look. "Not me."

"You didn't think he would hurt you?"

"I wasn't his type. I was his cover. He needed camouflage and I provided it. I gave him access to ongoing murder and assault cases. He needed me."

"Once you found out what he was, you were a greater threat to him than his need."

"That's why I stole four necklaces and put one in a safety deposit box in four different banks. I found Elice McNeely's driver's license in the bottom of the hidden compartment in that tackle box. I knew she was missing. The hair in the locket matched her hair color from her social media accounts. I put McNeely's driver's license in one of the safety deposit boxes, too. I told Cyrus what would happen if I disappeared—that I'd left a letter for my father and for you to find. I convinced him I was an ally, more useful alive than dead. Smartly, he agreed."

"He kept killing women. All that time, you knew, and did nothing."

Another dismissive shrug. "Not my problem."

Jackson stared at her, incredulous, like she'd grown three heads. The words coming out of her mouth felt incongruous as if he was in some alien dimension and couldn't find his way back to reality.

"He was discreet about it."

He tried to hide his revulsion but failed miserably.

"Don't look so horrified, Jackson. It's not like other serial killers haven't had partners. Fred and Rosemary West, Gerald and Charlene Gallego, The Lonely Hearts Killers, and The Sunset Strip Killers. It wasn't like I *participated*—" she said the word with distaste—"like those messed-up whores. I simply accepted it. It's easier than you think."

"You didn't merely accept anything. You committed a savage murder and staged the scene to look like your boyfriend's previous crimes to frame him. You knew the details because you cajoled him into telling you everything he'd done."

She shot him a smug, triumphant look. "I thought for sure he'd go down for it. He was the perfect patsy. Unfortunately, the bodies of his other victims hadn't been discovered, so the necklace didn't mean much until you used that evidence against Eli. You decided to frame your best friend instead, and everything worked out for me after all, like it was supposed to."

"What snapped in you? What made you do it that night, of all nights?"

"Lily brought it on herself. Her death was her fault. I had Cyrus Lee's necklace, which I knew I could use to protect myself if I decided to do it. I hated her, but I didn't have a plan. Not until the evening she came around pounding on our door looking for you. She didn't find you, she found me. You and Father were out on an investigation, some narcotics stakeout."

Astrid smiled that sly, cruel smile. "Father thought he had it under control, that he could keep Lily under his thumb, but I saw it in her face. She hated him, and she hated me. She'd lived with her secrets long enough, and she was gonna start talking. She threatened to tell you. She was going to destroy Father and me. So, I did something about it."

Jackson trembled with the effort to rein in his emotions. He had been blind to so many things. He wasn't blind now. He saw clearly for the first time. He saw his father's greed, his sister's cruelty, and Lily's desperation.

For someone who had professed to love Lily from afar, he had failed her miserably. He didn't think less of her, the things she'd held close and the secrets she'd kept. She had known what Jackson had refused to believe—the Alger County Sheriff was corrupt to the core, and she could not win against him. Over the years, it ate at her, until the corrosive lies had done more damage than the dangerous truth.

"And she just let you inside the house? That late at night?"

"I rang the doorbell. She came to the door in her pajamas. I told her she was right about everything, that I didn't want to live with the guilt either and would confess to it with her. It was like taking candy from a baby." Astrid's pretty features transformed into something grotesque. "She was too stupid to be afraid. She should've been afraid. But I made her fear me, in the end."

He saw the ugliness hidden beneath the beautiful mask. The accident had broken more than her legs; it had shattered something crucial inside her, and no one could put her back together again. But that was another lie, an obfuscation, a blurring of the truth.

Astrid was broken long before her accident. The wrongness in his own family that everyone had recognized but chosen to ignore, the monstrous elephant in the room.

"Father knew," he said dully. "Not the accident, but about Lily. He knows what you did."

Her beatific smile told him everything.

"And Garrett? What did he have to do with this?"

"I'm not our brother's keeper. Go ask Father. He knows."

"Did he figure it out? Is that why he left?"

She gave a small shake of her head. "You have no idea who Garrett even is, do you? You haven't a clue."

He ignored her attempt to distract him. "Then what about Mom?"

"You thought she was protecting our father." Her smile widened. "It was me. It was always me."

He thought of his parents with a mix of revulsion and pity. His whole life, he'd understood the unspoken rules of his family. A smoothing-over of reality, a softening of the rough spots, the ugly things. That ability to unsee what was right in front of them. The problem wasn't the person who committed the offense. It was the one who dared to call it out, to force the others to acknowledge the thing they couldn't bear to face—the truth, and their own culpability.

"I'm getting bored with this conversation." Astrid slid one hand beneath the table into her lap. With her other hand, she spooned up the last of the chili. "Forget we ever had this conversation. You got the truth you wanted; you should be happy now. Let the past stay in the past and die. None of it matters. This is the new world, like Father says, and we are the ones who will remake it in our image."

He stared until her form blurred and shifted, until she hardly looked human, her garish grin a caricature of humanity, a facsimile, so close to the real thing it was uncanny.

He'd had it wrong: she was no monster. She was fully human. That was the worst part.

"No, I don't think so." Jackson pulled out a pair of handcuffs and placed them on the table between them. "I'm going to arrest you and take you to a jail cell at the sheriff's office. I'll figure it out from there, but you are under arrest. You have the right to remain silent. Anything you say may be used against you in a court of law."

Astrid laughed hysterically. "A court of law? What fantasy world are you living in? No one cares!"

"I care," Jackson said quietly. "I am still the law."

Astrid shoved back her wheelchair and lurched to her feet. A glint of sharp-edged steel revealed the butcher knife in her left hand. She must have hidden the weapon in her wheelchair, beneath her legs. "I was hoping you would see reason, but since you refuse to be reasonable, I'll have to kill you, too. I'm not so crippled that I can't do what needs to be done."

She waved the knife at him. She took a lumbering step around the table. Her lips peeled back in a snarl. "Nothing personal, brother."

Jackson was ready for her. He'd expected the attack. Carefully, he stood and shoved back his chair. "It's always personal with you, Astrid."

She moved toward him. Halfway around the table she faltered, nearly falling and catching herself on the edge of the table. Her coffee cup toppled over. Her spoon rattled against the empty bowl.

Confusion flashed across her face. With her free hand, she reached for her throat. Her cheeks flushed a deep red. "What—"

"You are a sociopath, a parasite, a clear and present danger to the existence of everything good left in this world. You destroy everything you touch."

Her eyes bulged. The butcher knife slipped from her fingers. It clattered to the tile floor. "What did you do—!"

He'd considered the possibilities, weighed the options, and examined the consequences. He thought of Lily: wild, reckless, passionate Lily, who never got the chance to leave her mistakes behind and create something new.

And he thought of Shiloh. Astrid would not stop, not ever. She had tried to kill Shiloh and she would do so again at the first opportunity. As long as she lived, she was a threat, not just to Shiloh but to everything they were trying to protect.

"Right about now, your throat is closing. You're finding it hard to breathe."

Her mouth opened and closed, too shocked to speak.

He placed his hands on the table to steady himself. He had wrought this devastation; it was his duty to see it through. "I added a special ingredient to your second bowl of chili. Ground peanuts, from a Snickers bar for Shiloh. Shiloh, the girl you wanted dead. How's that for irony?"

Stunned, she gaped at him.

"I knew you were guilty, but I needed to hear you say it. I needed your confession. You gave it to me. You couldn't help it. You're so proud of yourself, so smug and arrogant. You underestimated me, like you underestimated Shiloh."

Astrid staggered for the kitchen drawer next to the fridge. Jackson withdrew an object from his pocket, which he'd surreptitiously taken while gathering the bowls. He held her EpiPen for her peanut allergy. "This what you're looking for? It's not where you left it."

She spun, half-stumbling, and held herself up against the counter. "Give me—the—Epi!"

He held it out of her reach. "There's still a chance for you, a way to save yourself. Where is Lena Easton?"

She swore at him, spitting and hissing, her eyes swelling and puffy. Her skin had gone red. "How would—I know?"

"You know. You know where she is. You know where they have Lena. You've been listening to Father's ham radio communications. You left scuff marks from your wheelchair on his office floor. You've known exactly what our father was up to."

"Screw you—"

"If you don't tell me, you die. If you do tell me, you have a chance to live, but you better start talking."

Veins popped out on her forehead. Sweat ran down her temples. Panic flashed in her eyes as her airway became more constricted. She started wheezing, her body heaving desperately for oxygen. "You cockroach—you stupid idiot—I'll kill you—"

"Tell me." He gazed at her, hard and emotionless. "This is your reckoning. A life for a life."

"You're—too late." A maniacal grin split her face. "They have Lena—they'll kill her. Too late—you're always...too late. Kill me—and you'll never find out—you can't save her—"

"You're running out of time. Tell me what I need to know."

With a shriek of outrage, his sister hurled herself at him, took two staggering steps, and her legs gave out. She tumbled to the floor with a crash. The silverware on the table clattered as her hip banged into the table leg. She sagged to her hands and knees, the wheezing higher and raspier, and scrabbled for the knife a few feet from her reach.

Even dying, she attacked him, a predator through and through.

Jackson moved closer and kicked the knife, sending it skittering across the tile and out of her reach. He held the EpiPen high so she could see it. "Start talking."

"You won't...let me—die. You don't—have it in you."

"Watch me." This was his sister, the woman he'd loved and resented his entire life. In his mind's eye, he saw her as a fat giggling baby, a five-year-old trailing devotedly after their father, and as a ten-year-old killing frogs with rocks. And then worse.

He wished the world was different, but it wasn't. The law he'd clung to and had depended upon to keep his life orderly, to keep chaos at bay—had it all been a falsehood, a mirage? Had chaos always waited for him, nestled at the beating heart of his existence?

"Tell me!" he shouted.

"A mine!" she spit out, half-choking. "On the radio...Sykes told the cartel...he took her—"

"Which mine?"

Astrid collapsed. On her back, she writhed, hands flailing. Her face was swelling up, and going bright tomato red, her lips garishly fat. A vivid rash appeared on her cheeks. Her eyes bulged in fury and fear. She mumbled something.

He leaned closer. "Which mine?"

"I don't know! On the radio...they used codes...I don't know..."

"What kind of mine?"

"C-copper. A copper mine."

He believed her for once.

She writhed on her back, clutched at her throat with one hand, reaching beseechingly for him with the other, pleading, begging him for salvation. "Give it—to me!"

He held the epinephrine in his hand. It was cool and slick in his palm.

He withheld it.

"You!" she gurgled. Her bloated features contorted in pain, disbelief, and rage. "You—have to—help me—"

"That's not going to happen."

"W—what?"

Jackson squatted beside her. He didn't give her the EpiPen.

In this new world, she would never have been taken to court to face justice, to spend the rest of her rotten life in prison.

Much as he loathed it, the only justice was this, right here, right now, in this room.

He said, "This is a mercy."

Her hands flailed helplessly at her throat, clawing for air, her puffy mouth gawping. A limpid flash of awareness in her eyes: this was the end, she was dying. Jackson was going to let her die.

An agonizing minute later, it was over.

He felt numb. For a long moment, he stared at her still form with a mix of consternation and nauseating anguish, tormented by the terrible thing he had done. He felt no sense of satisfaction, only a miserable emptiness, a tremendous ache in his chest.

And yet. He felt a stirring at the back of his neck, the soft exhale of a ghost finally put to rest. Lily, at long last, had found peace.

Whatever punishment or penance was due him for this hideous act would have to wait. The dead were buried and gone; the living could still be saved.

Steeling himself, Jackson rose to his feet and turned his back on the corpse of Lily's killer. He didn't want to leave his mother alone with a corpse, so he first radioed Fiona Smith and asked her to come sit with Dolores. He didn't want his mother or Fiona to stumble upon the corpse, so he moved the body into the laundry room and shut the door. He would deal with the body later.

Returning to the kitchen, Jackson righted the toppled chair, set the dishes in the sink, and checked his service pistol: it was locked and loaded for the battle yet to come. He radioed Eli and told him what little intel he'd discovered, praying desperately that it would be enough.

"Sykes has her in a mine, but I don't know which one. We don't have time to check them all—"

Eli said, "I know where she is."

65

LENA EASTON
DAY ONE HUNDRED AND FIVE

Lena awoke to pitch darkness.

Terror constricted her lungs. Her shoulder joints ached. Her arms were yanked behind her back and bound tight with plastic zip-ties that bit into her wrists. She tugged on her bindings, but there was no give, not even a centimeter, the plastic cutting into her skin, her flesh raw.

Pain radiated from the center of her face, dried blood caked to her lips, chin, and throat. Her nose was broken. Her ribs ached like she'd been kicked by a horse.

Gasping, she strained her ears and eyes but heard nothing, saw nothing. Her senses were blunted. There were no sounds but her pulse and her hitching breaths. No animal sounds. No birds or squirrels or insects. Total silence.

The darkness was absolute. Thick with a physical weight she could feel pressing down on her, a sensation of immense heaviness.

She felt like a mole deep beneath a mountain, deaf and dumb and blind.

She moved, shifting her spine, focusing on every sensation. Hard, lumpy rock beneath her butt, digging into her tailbone. She leaned against something smooth and square.

She took a deep breath. Damp, dank air filled her lungs. It was cold, very cold. Goosebumps prickled across her bare arms and legs. She shivered, using up precious energy.

A cave. She was in a cave.

"Hello?" she called softly.

The sound bounced back at her. It was some sort of cavern, a large one by the reverberation of the echoes.

Her memories returned, hard and fast: the big guy with the tattoos, punching her in the face and slinging her over his shoulder like a sack of potatoes as she lost consciousness.

"Help," she whispered, her throat parched. "Help me."

The sound of her voice resounded back at her in mockery. Her breath came in short, shallow gasps. Lightheadedness spun through her. She needed to check her numbers. They were skyrocketing, dangerously high. She could feel it.

How many hours had it been? She had no sense of time. It could have been days. Her stomach was concave, hunger gnawing at her insides. Her throat burned with thirst.

Lena was a prisoner, a captive locked in the dank bowels of the earth, and she had no insulin, no glucose pills, and no emergency injection—nothing. Every hour, every minute that passed dragged her closer to the precipice, to her death.

It was coming. Time was running out. She knew the symptoms: her clammy skin, the dizziness, her blood sugar rising, rising, poisoning her cells.

Distant sound echoed in the blackness: approaching footfalls. Light flashed bright and harsh against her retinas. She blinked against the glare, ducked her head, and squinted as a powerful flashlight beam lit up the cavern, approximately sixty feet by eighty feet in size, the roughhewn ceiling curving three stories above her.

Angel Flud appeared from the tunnel on the opposite end of the cavern, dressed in an oversized T-shirt over cargo pants and black combat boots, armed with a pistol and a knife, a flashlight in one hand and a lantern in the other.

The gangbanger set the Coleman lantern on one of the dozens of crates stacked along the perimeter of the cavern. Boxes on wooden pallets wrapped in plastic with labels scrawled across the sides: AbbVie, Merck, GlaxoSmithKline, Bayer, Gilead Sciences, Sanofi, and Pfizer.

The realization struck her like a gut-punch—this was the storage depot where Sykes and his crew had offloaded the stolen medications from the train.

A spark of hope flared in her chest. Insulin must be here somewhere. It had to be.

"You shot my dog," she said.

Angel gave a nonchalant shrug, barely glancing at her as he adjusted his belt buckle. He must've left the cavern to answer nature's call; she'd awakened moments before his return. "Next time I see that ugly mutt, I'll finish the job."

Fear clamped her throat with steel talons, but there was something else, something dark forming beneath the terror—a cold, crystalized anger.

Her natural affinity for nurturing and compassion became usurped by a righteous fury that burned so bright she was incandescent with it. These psychos had threatened the people she cared about. They'd murdered and plundered. They'd hurt her beloved dog.

She hated all of them but this one most of all.

Utterly indifferent, Angel perched on one of the boxes twenty feet from her location, one eye on her and the other on the passageway. He withdrew a combat knife from the sheath at his belt along with a hunk of flint and began to sharpen the blade.

"Where are we?"

"Underground."

"A cave?"

"Nope."

"An old mine, then."

The convict scuffed his blade across the sharpening stone in even passes. The lantern cast long, flickering shadows, highlighting the uneven surface of the rock, cut by hand in the eighteenth century by half-blind miners, given a single candle to work by, hundreds of feet below the surface.

"These are all medications that could save people's lives."

Angel didn't bother to answer.

"There will be insulin here in a refrigerated container. I'll die without it."

"Not my problem, lady."

"I know it's here, probably right in this cavern. Please, I need your help."

Angel ignored her.

Thinking tactically, like Eli had taught her, she checked her surroundings, searching for anything that might aid her escape. To her left, a narrow passageway cut into the rock. The network of pulleys and ropes attached to the ceiling of the main passageway looked new.

An ancient metal cart sat on rusted tracks used a hundred years ago to haul away the heavy copper ore. The slick walls were scarred with deep groves where the copper had been extracted painstakingly by hand with chisels.

There might be other openings and passageways she couldn't see. Where the light did not reach, the dense blackness lurked. This place was home to demons and wraiths, the monsters of the deep.

"Let me go," she said to keep her captor focused on her words rather than her actions as she fumbled behind her with her fingers, her movements hampered by the flex-cuffs. Unlike the movies, her captors had correctly restrained her hands behind her back.

Her fingertips brushed the slippery corner of a box sealed with plastic.

"Let me go and nothing bad has to happen to you."

Angel snorted. "Sure thing, sweetcakes. It's all been a terrible misunderstanding."

Her cuffed hands found the rough edge of the wood pallet stacked with boxes behind her. Furtively, she scooched on her butt and lowered her shoulders, until her wrists were level with the corner of the pallet.

"How did you find me?"

"Sykes has ears everywhere. We shook down the right people until we heard the right rumor. It didn't take too long to hear about Eli Pope's special lady friend, the paramedic with the big dog who lived in the lighthouse. Besides, your friends the Tiltons talked too much. The Tiltons sang your praises, telling everyone and their brother how you saved their kid. Sykes figured a first responder would come out of hiding to save a kid, especially one she'd already saved once."

And he had been right. Lena winced. The Tiltons were a means to an end, as was she. They were mere pawns in a deadly game for which there could only be one victor.

She was the lure in the trap Sykes had set for Eli; she understood that.

If she could have sacrificed herself to protect him, to save him from this, she would have done so in a heartbeat. But it was too late now—the plan was set in motion.

Eli would know this was a trap and still he would come. Of that, she had no doubt.

The only thing she could do now was to do her best to stay alive and try to help him when the time came.

Lena clenched her jaw. "Please let me go."

Angel glanced quickly behind him, then returned his attention to his knife. "Shut up. You're annoying me."

"Your boss told you to keep me alive. If my blood sugar gets too high, I'll lose consciousness and go into a diabetic coma. Once that happens, short of a hospital and intensive medical intervention, I'll die."

"You look fine to me."

"Please, I'll die without it."

"Not my orders, lady."

"If I go into a diabetic coma before Sykes springs his trap for Eli Pope, he'll be pissed. You've seen what he does to his enemies. What do you think he'll do to you?"

Angel's expression hardened. "Shut up!"

"I have a thirteen-year-old girl to take care of. Her mother is dead. I'm all she has left."

"We already know about her," Angel said with a dismissive wave of his hand. "If you don't get Sykes what he wants, he'll take her next."

Lena recoiled at the thought of Sykes touching Shiloh. She'd thought she knew fear intimately, had explored the depths of terror, but she had not even begun; there were always new levels of torment.

He smiled nastily at her fear. He enjoyed it. He wanted to hurt her, to get under her skin, to make her submissive, to make her cower, humiliated and afraid.

She longed to claw his eyes out. This seething anger was both unfamiliar to her, and yet it felt as natural as breathing. Without hesitation she would commit violence to protect Shiloh, as she had before so she would do again, in a heartbeat, as many times as it took.

Lena didn't waste energy begging for her life. Her effort to get him to see her as a person he couldn't depersonalize had failed. He was a sociopath, cruel and brutal, with no moral compass, no compassion, and no value system beyond his own twisted desires.

Exhaustion pulled at her along with pain, horror, and anguish. The muscles in her arms strained, taut and aching in protest, yet she continued to rub her wrists against that jagged point, unrelenting, her skin stinging and bloodied.

Angel sheathed his knife and glared at her. The light from the lantern cast eerie shadows beneath his sunken eyes and the hard slash of his cheekbones. "You're dead. No one cares if you die in an hour or a day. The trap for you is set. I don't know why Sykes hasn't put a bullet in you already."

She knew why. She'd seen it in Sykes' dead-fish eyes. He wasn't simply a killer; he was a sadist. A bullet was too easy, too quick, too painless. He planned to torture her in front of Eli before he killed them both.

Before she could respond, a sound came from behind them. A clatter, a pitter-patter like a pebble rolling across an uneven stone floor. The mountain of rock was settling with a groan.

Angel jerked around, his face papery pale, a flicker of apprehension sweeping across his taut features. One hand splayed across his upper shoulder, as if to protect himself from something unseen, to ward off an evil spirit.

He was afraid of the dark—or maybe he was afraid of Eli. Either way, he was definitely spooked. Maybe she could use that.

Three hundred feet below the surface, the dank, chiseled walls seemed to breathe with history, with the thousands of lives that had suffered, endured, and even died in this wretched place.

Kids as young as five had worked the copper mines. All day in the dark, they collected the chunks of copper and transported the great hunks in carts. Down here, it was easy to believe in ghosts and evil spirits, death itself creeping up behind you.

"There are ghosts down here. They've suffered, they're trapped, and they're angry."

Angel fiddled nervously with his radio, but there was no signal. "Sykes! Sykes, come in, damn it!"

Nothing but static.

"Bad mojo in this place," he muttered under his breath. "My granddad mined in this hellhole for thirty years. Fourteen hours in the dark, six days a week. He went blind doing it. I'm not scared of the dark. I'm not scared of nothing." He repeated the words like a mantra. "I'm not scared!"

Lena's fingers closed over a pebble on the ground. She tried to throw it, to create more unnatural sounds, but her bound hands were worthless. The pebble dropped from her fingers with a barely audible *clink*. "Did you hear that?"

"I said shut up!" Angel shouted. The sound bounced off rock, echoed eerily, and faded into oppressive silence. Angel's breathing came in hitching gasps, his eyes frantically darting in every direction.

She was getting to him. She didn't believe in much, but she believed in God, not ghosts haunting Hispanic gangbangers for bloody vengeance.

The lantern light wavered and sputtered.

Angel gave a little grunt of terror.

Lena made the mistake of smiling.

Angel saw it. Rage darkened his face and he lunged across the cavern, faster than she'd thought possible, seized her by her shirt, and yanked her toward him, inches from her face. His stale breath struck her cheeks. Even in the dim light, she could see the pores in his flesh, the tattoo tears scarring his skin, his glassy bloodshot eyes.

"No one said I couldn't hurt you, *señorita*," he snarled.

She swallowed the panic clawing at her throat. "I'm sorry, I'm sorry."

Angel shoved her to the ground, rose to his feet, and kicked her in the ribs.

The pain took her breath away. Flinching, she curled into a ball, protecting her internal organs, but there was no way to protect her head. If he wanted to bash her skull in, he would. "Stop! Please stop!"

"We're just getting started."

He relished her terror. She forced herself to let him see her pain, her fear. Let him get drunk on it. Her only chance was to act submissive and weak.

They saw her as prey; she'd act like prey.

She made herself beg. "Please don't hurt me!"

He kicked her again, this time half-heartedly and returned to the stack of boxes where the Coleman lantern glowed, warm and welcoming. He leaned against a crate labeled with the red looping *Lilly* emblem with a cunning, self-satisfied grin, more confident now.

Taunting her had placated him, beaten back his own depthless fears. He thought he'd conquered his demons. He thought the darkness had been tamed. It wasn't.

Lena had to stay alive until Eli came for her. He would come. Then the darkness would be the least of Angel Flud's fears.

66

ELI POPE
DAY ONE HUNDRED AND FIVE

Tension shot through Eli like a live wire.

Crouched beneath a limestone overhang, shielded by underbrush that snagged at his clothes, he focused on the target ahead through his field glasses. His mind spun with tactics and strategies, strengths and weaknesses, pros and cons.

Early that morning, Eli and Jackson had gathered the team, traveling from house to house and banging on doors. Then they'd geared up and headed for Eagle Falls Mine, located southwest of Ishpeming and north of Iron Mountain.

Though Sykes was likely to move frequently, Eli was fairly certain this was the location where he was keeping Lena. It was a perfect location to set up an ambush.

The eighty-mile, one-way trip would significantly deplete their emergency fuel. Eli feared they wouldn't have enough gas to return to Munising, but that was a problem for later.

As they drove, Jackson tensed, his knuckles white as he gripped the steering wheel. He was pale and haggard, shaken in a way Eli had never seen him. Something had happened, but when Eli pressed him, he remained distant and vague.

Jackson blinked, his gaze clearing. "I'm fine. My head is in the game. Don't worry." He hesitated. "Right now, we need to focus on Sykes."

Eli hadn't argued with him.

Now, he crouched in the dirt and reconned the target. Ahead of him, the uneven ground angled into a deep ravine between two ridges carpeted in dense jewel-colored greens of pine, spruce, and fir.

They'd positioned themselves on the opposite hill, halfway up, approximately a quarter-mile from the main entrance to the mine, holed up behind a house-sized boulder that provided solid cover and concealment.

Several team members squatted next to Jackson, who'd spread a map on the ground. Hart and Nash acted as lookouts on either side of the rock, while Nyx was nestled in a sniper hide somewhere on the hillside above them, providing overwatch. Her elevated position gave her an excellent view of the ravine, the hillside, and the mine.

Before they'd left, Jackson had rustled up history books from the library on regional copper and ore mines in the Upper Peninsula which included an old black-and-white copy of a map of Eagle Falls Mine.

Over the last hundred and fifty years, twelve billion pounds of native copper had been mined in the U.P. Although the main copper region ran along the western range from Ontonagon County up through the tip of the Keweenaw Peninsula, a smaller deposit had been discovered south of the Marquette iron range and had operated from the 1850s to the 1960s before shuttering its doors.

Jackson pointed at various points on the map. "The first four levels descend about four hundred feet. The fifth and sixth levels are flooded and extremely unstable. The main entrance is here. Out here along this dirt road is the old mining village. Follow the road a mile north to reach the main mine entrance hewn out of the hillside."

Eli lowered his field glasses for a moment to glance at the map.

Perspiration gathered beneath his armpits, beads of sweat slid down his temples, and his heart thudded like a jackrabbit in his chest. "What's this over here?"

"That's the dump site, the side tunnel where they dumped the waste—useless tons of rock they'd dug out and chucked down the mountain. It's steep as hell."

"But it leads to the main tunnels?"

Jackson nodded. "There are eight main caverns large enough to store significant supplies. It's likely Sykes is keeping Lena in one of these locations, but we can't be certain."

"That's a hell of a lot of possibilities," Antoine said.

From his vantage point, Eli eyed the side of the hill through his field glasses. The tunnel entrance stood perhaps eight feet tall by seven feet wide with a narrow ledge of rock protruding from the hillside.

The slab face was two hundred feet tall and steeply sloped at a forty-five-degree angle. Over the decades, thousands of rock chunks had been flung over the side, littering the slope like the mine had vomited up its insides. It was piled so deep the base of the hill was buried.

Jackson was right. The slope was steep but not impossible to scale with the right equipment.

"How are your mountain climbing skills?" he asked.

"Rusty," Moreno muttered.

"Anyone who climbs the side of that hill will be fully exposed," Jackson said.

"We'll have overwatch and constant radio communication," Antoine said. His injuries from the train ambush had mostly healed, at least enough that he could fight. The burn on the side of his face was still pink and a bit raw.

"Until we get inside. No signal beneath all that rock."

Eli glimpsed movement, motion in the shadows within the tunnel entrance. He stilled, peering through his binos as a distant figure poked his head out, scanned the forest below, then pulled a cigarette and lighter from his pocket and lit it.

The man stood, relaxed and casual, smoking. Clearly, he did not expect a threat to emerge from the dump site below him. The man was burly, bearded, and heavily tattooed. A rifle was slung over one shoulder, a pistol at his hip. He wore a military-style chest-rig over a T-shirt and ratty jeans.

A second sentry appeared and bummed a light off the first. The second guy was scrawny, likely from drug use, his greasy, stringy hair pulled back in a ponytail. He carried an M4 in his hands.

Eli's breathing quickened. He recognized these two from his time served in prison. The big bearded one was ex-military, not Special Forces, but he knew enough to be dangerous. A longtime member of Sykes' crew, he'd committed armed robberies, including one where he'd bashed in the homeowner's head with a crowbar. He'd be a problem.

The stringy one was a small-time drug dealer who'd earned himself a two-decade sentence behind bars after a drive-by shooting where he'd slaughtered a rival dealer and his girlfriend on the street. He didn't look like much of a threat, but he was vicious and bloodthirsty.

"I've got visual on two sentries guarding the dump site," he said into his radio. "They're definitely Sykes' guys. Sitrep, Echo Two."

Through the headset, Alexis said, "Four convicts guarding the main entrance. They switch sentry duty on top of the hour. All heavily armed. We spotted two more sentries a half-mile down at the road turnoff ensuring no one gets through. I've seen four additional guys pop in and out of the entrance. An hour ago, two convicts loaded a truck with boxes and took off."

Alexis had situated herself inside an abandoned café a mile from the mine, using the drone to get eyes on Sykes' security protocols. They'd been reconning the target site for three hours. Eli was so anxious to get inside he was about to crawl out of his skin.

Antoine frowned, a line appearing between his bushy brows. "I hate to say this, but Sykes may have already killed her, brother. If this was my op and I was the bad guy, that's what I would do."

"He won't kill her until he has me." The words were razor blades in his throat. "He made it clear he'll make me watch as he tortures Lena. It's part of his sick revenge shtick."

That wasn't entirely true. There were myriad ways a hostage could get killed. If Sykes' plan for revenge fell apart, he might shoot Lena in the head and leave her body for Eli to find.

Beside him, Jackson and Devon exchanged apprehensive glances. Darius Sykes wasn't the only threat; Lena's body was a ticking time bomb, and they all knew it.

Above them, the bruised sky loomed low, dark clouds swollen with rain. The air crackled with electrons, raising the hairs along his arms and the back of his neck. A storm was headed their way.

"Let me get this straight," Moreno said. "They have three times the manpower we do. We have no clue on their whereabouts within the labyrinth, or the weapons they've got inside. They're minions of the cartel. They have freaking missiles for all we know. We have no idea where the hostage is located within that dragon's lair, but we sure as hell can expect multiple threats to burst from every tunnel, hole, nook and cranny to pop us when we least expect it." Moreno shuddered. "And rats. I bet there'll be rats."

All Eli wanted to do was leap down the hillside and run and gun, use shock and awe and sheer force of violence to mow down the enemy and save the love of his life.

His mind raced through the tactical questions for which they had no answers. There were too many unknowns. It was a logistical nightmare. "That's about right."

He had to constantly remind himself that most of the team were small-town officers, dedicated to their jobs, fiercely brave and loyal but neither soldiers nor tier-one operators. They did not have years of experience in hostage rescue. They were not shock troops.

"I can't ask anyone to do this," Eli said. "I'm the one he's after."

"Like hell!" Jackson exploded. "You'll get creamed before you make it ten steps, and you know it. We're in this together. We're a team. We take the risk together, we take the victory together. We celebrate or mourn together. That's how it works."

"What he said," Antoine said.

"Let's go get these bastards and bring Lena home," Devon said fiercely.

Moreno shrugged. "What the hell. I'm in, rats or no rats. Just tell me where to sign."

Eli stared at them, a little stunned. He'd spent eight years trapped in a cell with monsters, solitary and alone, hunted at every turn, betrayed and abandoned. To trust again was slippery, difficult, incredibly painful. It felt foreign and unnatural.

"Okay," he said. "Okay."

"We're in," Jackson said. "But I won't lose my men to a half-cocked plan. I hate it as much as anyone, but we need better intel."

"He's right. We cannot go in there without intel. We cannot. They could have mineshafts booby-trapped with explosives. They could be lying in wait in various passages and hit us like fish in a barrel. We have no idea what we're walking into. If we go in like this, we will die—not just Lena, all of us."

Reluctantly, the others nodded.

"We're not letting her die," Devon said.

"We won't," Eli said. "But we're getting intel, one way or another."

"How?" Jackson asked grudgingly, like he didn't want to know.

Before Eli could answer, Alexis spoke into his headset. "This is Echo Two for Alpha One. I've got movement at the entrance. A red Jeep just pulled up. One suspect behind the wheel. Two more approaching the vehicle."

"Keep watching, Echo Two."

There was a moment of tense silence. Everyone waited. A black fly buzzed around Eli's face, but he ignored it. Frustration roiled through him. He was utterly blind and he hated it.

"Two suspects in the Jeep now. They're driving down the two-track toward the main drive."

His pulse accelerated. He glanced around the group and considered the moves ahead. He trusted Jackson to have his back, to fight hard in the battle to come, but Jackson was an idealist who didn't have the stomach for what needed to be done.

Eli needed someone as cold-blooded as he was.

"Let's go," Nyx said. She'd come down the hill to switch places with Antoine, who'd take the next shift on overwatch. Her blue eyes reflected a steely resolve, her jaw set. "You and me. Hurry before they're out of range."

Eli eyed the bandage wrapped around her shoulder.

She glowered at him. "It hurts like hell, but I've got full range of motion. How's *your* arm?"

"Touché." He shot her a grim smile. Nyx would do just fine. Eli rose to his feet. "We're going after the targets in the Jeep to get that intel. The rest of you keep eyes on the main target and apprise me of any changes. We'll be back as soon as we can."

Jackson gave him a disquieted look, his expression hesitant. "How are you going to obtain that intel?"

"Don't ask me that, Jackson."

Jackson's eyes were dark and conflicted. Like he wanted to stop Eli, his idealism interfering with the reality of what they must do in this world to survive.

A strained look passed between them, weighted with everything they'd left unsaid. He knew Jackson was torn between order and lawlessness, morality and survival, mercy and violence. Jackson looked tortured in a way that Eli had never seen him.

With a jolt, he realized he still cared what Jackson thought.

"These people aren't innocent," Eli said. "They're the wolves who prey on the innocent."

Jackson's mouth thinned into a bloodless line. There was a hard edge about him that Eli hadn't noticed before. Though reluctance still etched his face, he nodded. "I trust you."

Eli tucked those words away to consider later: Jackson's admission and what it meant for him and for Jackson—for their tentative, complicated relationship. Did trust mean friendship? Was that even what Eli wanted?

He pushed it out of his mind as he gestured to Nyx, weapon in hand. "Let's go."

Without a word, Nyx headed downhill. Eli followed her, jogging along a deer path that descended the steep hill through the underbrush.

He spoke into his headset. "Echo Two, keep that drone on them, don't let them out of sight!"

"Unless they drive out of range or the battery dies, I'm on it. But we're on borrowed time here."

Eli had never been more aware of the time he did not have.

67

LENA EASTON
DAY ONE HUNDRED AND FIVE

A faint sound came from the darkness. A subtle scratch, like a rat scrabbling in the darkness or fingernails scraping across rock. Or a demon crawling up from the abyss.

Alarmed, Angel leaped from his spot across the cavern. He spun and aimed the flashlight at something behind him. The beam flailed wildly over scarred stone and piles of rock.

He was agitated, his anxiety skyrocketing.

Lena was almost delirious with thirst and hunger, her belly an aching knot. Her broken nose pulsed with agony, making it difficult to think clearly. Dried blood coated her lips and her chin.

Hours ago, she'd drunk the bottle of water Angel had held to her mouth to keep her alive and conscious. Twice, he'd hauled her to a spot outside the cavern along a secondary tunnel to use a chemical toilet, pulling her pants down and watching her with a leering smile because it humiliated her and because he liked to make people small and afraid.

Anger flushed through her, but she hid her emotions and acted as he expected: weak and scared, a harmless mouse.

To her left, a small furred creature skittered behind a stack of crates. Not a mouse, but a rat. The presence of another living creature in this hellhole was bizarrely comforting. Luckily, Angel didn't see it.

"Something's out there," she said. "I heard it, too."

He cursed, then crossed himself and reached for his radio, but it only hissed static.

"What if there are ghosts down here?" Lena shuddered, acting scared as she worked her bound wrists against the edge of the pallet. "The little kids who died, begging for their mamas. What if their bodies are still trapped down here, angry and out for vengeance?"

"I said, shut up!" Angel shouted. His voice careened and bounced, distorted by the echo, almost deranged. "I know how to shut your pretty little mouth. Permanently."

He hurled threats like a boy throwing rocks at a stray cat, but his heart wasn't in it. His attention was elsewhere, his head on a swivel, the tendons standing out on his neck, his movements jittery and tense.

Lena kept half her attention on him, half on the rat. It scuttled between the crate and the cavern wall, then disappeared. She leaned closer, squinting. The shadow cast from the row of crates obscured a hole approximately two feet wide by two feet high.

Not a hole, but a human-sized tunnel.

Angel spun with a jerk, pistol up and aiming frantically at ghosts he couldn't see, the flashlight spun strobe-like across the cavern walls. Adrenaline surging, Lena straightened her spine, faced away from the tunnel, and subtly shifted her body to shield it from Angel's view.

His fear made him furious, and Lena was the closest target. He whirled on her with a vicious smile. "Sykes will carve you up in front of Pope, and then he'll do the same to him. You'll both be begging at the end, and I'll watch it all. Once he's done with you, he's gonna burn through the U.P. and slaughter anything and anyone who gets in his way. No one is coming for any of you. We can do whatever the hell we want, to whoever we want; we can

take whatever we want. It's ours. It's all ours. There's no one who
can stop us."

Lena said nothing.

"We're going to kill all your friends. Sykes is waiting for them.
He's set the trap. They won't even see it coming."

Lena didn't react. She stared at her feet, kept herself small and
still.

After a minute, Angel lost interest in taunting her without a
reaction. Instead, he messed with the silent radio, his hands shaking, his eyes half-crazed as he glared at her. "I'm going to the
surface for a signal. Don't you dare move."

Flashlight in hand, Angel stalked across the cavern into the
northern passageway and vanished from view. He left the
Coleman lantern behind.

Lena closed her eyes and listened to the echoing footfalls fade
to nothing, her breathing shallow, conserving her energy except
for the frenetic activity behind her. Her wrists bruised and bleeding, she worked feverishly.

Her vision darkened as the strength leeched from her muscles,
suckled by the rapacious cancerous force inside her, despite her
stubbornness, her willpower. You couldn't outwill biology.

Time was her enemy now, a creeping darkness slowly
consuming her bit by bit as her body betrayed her.

With one final jerk of her arms, the flex-tie snapped.

Lena's hands were free.

68

ELI POPE
DAY ONE HUNDRED AND FIVE

E li jogged down the hill at Nyx's heels.

They scrabbled down a steep deer trail through old-growth groves of hardwood and birch, hemlock and maple. A chipmunk scurried across the deer trail. Thick clouds of mosquitos swirled, biting like they would eat them to the bone.

"Tell me where we're headed, Echo Two!"

There was a moment of silence. Alexis said, "It looks like they may be headed to the old mine shaft operation. It's a collection of dilapidated buildings. The road takes a long loop around, but there's a dirt trail that cuts through the forest along the creek. You can catch up going that way."

They'd hidden their four-wheelers to the south, concealing them off the road, inside the trees, covering them with pine boughs.

Now they shoved aside the foliage, ignoring the bugs, and clambered onto the four-wheeler, Nyx behind Eli, grasping his waist with one hand and holding her pistol down at her thighs with the other hand.

"Copy that," Eli said.

"If they turn onto the main road and head east or west, I won't be able to follow them for more than a couple of miles. The drone will be out of range. We'll lose them."

"Let's hope they stay close."

They took the narrow dirt path winding through the forest, the trees crouched in close. Thorns and brambles scratched their arms and legs as they drove, low branches and twigs slapping at their faces.

Five minutes later, Echo Two verified the Jeep had indeed stopped at the old mine shaft. Eli and Nyx hid the four-wheeler behind some pine trees a half-mile out and closed the distance on foot, keeping the forest between themselves and their targets.

Every fifty yards they took a knee and paused behind a tree, boulder, or another natural concealment, intent on listening and looking for sentries, roving patrols, or booby traps.

Eli glanced up through the canopy of leaves in growing apprehension. The wind had picked up, whipping at the foliage and obscuring the sound of their movements as the sky transformed to gun-metal gray. Dense dark clouds roiled above them.

He couldn't see or hear the drone hovering several hundred feet above them. Hopefully, their targets hadn't noticed it either, or he and Nyx would be walking into a death trap.

Ahead of them, a clearing appeared. The air smelled of decay and rot. The jumble of rickety buildings was in ruins, with roofs half-caved in, and vines and ivy snaking across rotting plank walls. Dusty train tracks choked with weeds meandered through the property; mining equipment hulked here and there like bleached dinosaur skeletons.

It looked like a ghost town.

Eli pointed to the two-story building in the center, the red Jeep parked beside it. Nyx nodded, revolver in hand, her M2010 sniper rifle slung across her back.

After circling the perimeter, they approached the rear of the building. They snuck in a low crouch along the northern wall, Eli leading with his rifle as he rounded the corner of the building. Nyx was right behind him, covering his six.

They crept to the front door and each took a side. Urgency crackled through him. At least two hostiles were inside, waiting for them, maybe more.

Either way, they were going in.

On the count of three, they exploded into action. Eli whirled and kicked the doorknob. The rotted wood splintered. The door caved inward as he and Nyx breached the entryway and surged inside. Eli went low and spun left while Nyx went high and spun right.

In the center of the large space, a man knelt over a duffle bag. Startled, he turned toward the threat and reached for a weapon.

Eli had him dead to rights, his finger on the trigger but not squeezing, not yet. "Don't move!"

On the right, the second hostile raised his long gun and swung it around to shoot at Eli. Nyx fired first. The man tumbled backward, stumbling over another duffle bag, and sank onto his butt.

With a scream, he dropped the gun and grabbed at his kneecap, which was reduced to a pulpy mess. Blood bubbled from the wound and saturated his pants leg. He was damn lucky Nyx was shooting .44 special and not .44 magnum, or he wouldn't have a knee left.

Nyx aimed her revolver at his center mass. "We said don't move."

Defeated, the hostiles raised their hands. They glared at Nyx and Eli with pure malevolence.

The first man was heavy-set. In his thirties, he sported a shaved head and a handlebar mustache, like he wished he were from the Wild West and not a run-of-the-mill thug. A handgun with a suppresser was jammed into the waistband of his pants.

He'd run with Sykes in prison, roughing up anyone who dared disobey Sykes' commands. His name was Paul Macek.

"I know you," Macek growled in a raspy smoker's voice.

"Funny, I'd completely forgotten about you."

Eli recognized the guy with the blown knee. African-American and short at five feet six inches, he was lean to the point of emaciation, with prominent buck teeth and the ragged look of a deviant who'd do anything for a fix.

Kirk Thompson had once taken a swipe at Eli with a sharpened toothbrush in the mess hall. In retaliation, Eli had cracked three of his ribs and collapsed a lung with Thompson's own toothbrush.

"Radios out," Nyx commanded. "Throw them across the room. Knives and guns, too."

Slowly, furiously, the men obeyed. One of the knives skittered across the dusty plank floor and landed at Nyx's boot. She didn't look down at it but kept her gaze scanning their surroundings.

Eli ordered them to lay prone on the floor, hands forward, legs crossed so they couldn't try anything tricky. The one Nyx had shot howled in agony as he dropped to the floor on his belly.

Nyx covered Eli while he secured their hands behind their backs with zip-ties, frisked them thoroughly, and removed an ankle pistol from Thompson and a pocketknife from Macek's pocket.

Thompson kept howling. Eli needed him quiet. He put his Glock 19 against his skull. "Shut up or I'll gag you, but not before I shoot the other knee."

The whining stopped. The man's breathing was deep and ragged. He was shaking, probably from blood loss, but Eli didn't care.

While Nyx watched their prisoners, Eli swiftly cleared the building, finding nothing of interest but a pair of ratty mildewed sleeping bags in one corner, trash everywhere, and several duffle bags surrounded by footprints in one corner, the tell-tale bulge of weapons pressing against the canvas.

Sykes had used this spot as another makeshift weapons depot.

In the center of the main room, a massive support beam held up the moldy ceiling. The stale air smelled faintly of urine. Dust swirled in the dim light streaming through the broken windows. Thick layers of dust coated everything, the floors, the windows, and the walls. The equipment had been salvaged, sold, or stolen decades ago.

A minute later, Eli returned. "Everything's clear. Check the duffle bags."

Nyx bent, unzipped a few, and cursed in delight. "A whole bunch of toys! AR-15s, ammo and magazines, and better yet, a bunch of flash-bangs, smoke grenades, and hand grenades."

Eli smiled. "Perfect."

"What the hell do you want with us?" Macek snarled. "You think Sykes is gonna let this go? He'll kill you for this."

"He's planning to kill me anyway. Guess it doesn't matter what I do, does it?"

Macek blanched.

To Nyx, Eli said, "In case you feel any qualms about what we're about to do here, Thompson's a serial rapist, and Macek here gets off on beating women."

Nyx showed her teeth. "I'm plumb out of qualms."

He wondered briefly at her past, what had made her so hard. There was no time for anything but the mission at hand. He turned to their prisoners. "Where is Lena being held in the mine?"

They stared at him blankly, hate in their eyes, and violence, too. Neither man spoke.

"We need answers, and we're getting them, one way or the other."

Macek snorted in derision. He wasn't afraid yet, not nearly enough.

"Do you know why both of you are still alive?"

They didn't respond.

"So I can kill one of you to get the other one to talk."

Thompson winced. Macek's expression hardened. Thompson was the more frightened of the two, and already suffering tremendous pain. He was the weakest link. Men who preyed upon women were cowards, every last one of them.

"Your lives depend on telling us the truth. Tell us what we want to know, and we let you go. Don't tell us, we start shooting body parts."

"You're going to kill us anyway!" Thompson whined.

"We'll tie you to that load-bearing beam in the center of the room and leave you. If any of your intel comes back rotten and some of my guys get hit, we come back and do things to you that you cannot even imagine."

Macek looked dubious. Thompson's frantic gaze darted everywhere but at the gun barrel jammed in his face, his whole body twitching with terror.

"Cross my heart, hope to die," Eli said. "Or we can do things the hard way."

"I think they're asking for the hard way," Nyx said.

He angled his chin at Nyx. "Go ahead."

Nyx holstered her revolver and drew her Ka-Bar knife. She held the point of the seven-inch carbon steel blade against Thompson's thigh.

"Hey, wait—"

Nyx didn't wait. She shoved the Ka-Bar into the meaty part of his leg, careful not to hit an artery. No use in him bleeding out before they got the intel.

Thompson shrieked in agony, writhing on the floor and kicking up sprays of dust. The coppery smell of blood permeated the air. His breathing went rapid and gasping.

Nyx put her knee on his back and grabbed his hair. She put the blade against the fold in the top of his ear. A smirk twitched across her face. "I can do this all day."

"What are you using the mine for?" Eli asked. "Someone answer me, or Thompson loses an ear."

Macek had gone pale. "Sykes is using abandoned mines as black-market shipping hubs. The train offloads the cargo at various strategic locations. Then we transport supplies to regional dealers via truck, horse, four-wheeler, boat, whatever."

"You've got the meds right here," Nyx said. Eli knew she was thinking of the beta blockers her grandmother desperately needed.

It made sense. The abandoned mines offered natural refrigeration, were well-hidden, and easily defensible. "Where is Lena being held?"

"I don't know," Macek insisted.

Nyx made to shove the blade into Thompson's ear.

Thompson shrieked. "Wait! Wait!"

Nyx hesitated. "Start talking."

"Sykes has her in the mine!"

"Duh," Nyx said. "Tell us something we don't know."

"Which chamber?" Eli asked.

"The...the second one. On the second level. Where most of the meds are."

Eli didn't let his expression change. At last, they were getting somewhere. "How many guarding her?"

"O-one, as far as I know. They've got her tied up."

"And where is the insulin?"

"The...what?" Thompson looked genuinely confused.

"Insulin, you moron," Nyx said. "The elixir that keeps diabetics alive."

He shook his head, frantic. "I don't know, man. The second and third chambers on the second level are the storage levels. That's all I know."

"How many guards are inside?"

"Five," Macek said.

"Liar." Eli moved so fast Macek never saw it coming. He drew his combat blade and stabbed Macek's left knee, digging deep. The man let out a keening wail.

Eli smiled a terrible smile. A part of him hated himself for relishing this man's pain, hated that he took pleasure in hurting bad people. Another part of him accepted it.

The fury was in him, hard and humming. The darkness he couldn't control, didn't want to control. The devil inside.

He was the monster he needed to be.

Eli twisted the knife. "How many?"

"Thirty-two!" Macek screamed. "Sykes has everyone at the mine. He says he's going to take out everyone at once. The—the local cops." He was near sobbing from the pain.

Beside him, Thompson sagged, moaning softly. He was losing blood and would go into shock soon.

"I'm running out of time. And patience." Eli pressed the knife against Macek's jugular. "I don't need both of you. You want to be the first to go?"

Macek had reached the point of sufficient pain and terror. He couldn't talk fast enough. He gave them what they needed: the number of guards and their locations within the mine, the chamber where the convicts were sleeping, what tunnels were booby-trapped and where the trip alarms had been set, and the weapons they had access to—automatic weapons, grenades, smoke grenades, and one .50 M2 Browning.

In the end, Eli got everything but the exact location of the insulin, and only because these two clowns were too stupid to know what they didn't know.

"When are you supposed to check in with your superiors?" Nyx asked.

"We're out of walkie-talkie range," Macek said dully. "We don't have long-range radios. We were just supposed to gather the last load of weapons and bring them to the mine."

"I predict we've got less than an hour before the alarm bells start going off," Eli said.

"Time to jet." Nyx glared at their prisoners with bloodlust in her eyes. "Do we waste them? Tell me we get to waste them."

He thought of his promise to Jackson. Lena's face flashed in his mind. In another world, he might have softened, kept his word to Jackson, agreeing to return if their intel was solid, if the team survived the assault. Let the goons rot in prison.

That world had died. Any semblance of mercy Eli might have retained had died with it.

He didn't want to be the sort of man who condemned other men to die, but he *was* that man.

These hardened criminals thought nothing of taking from others, of destroying everything good. They were parasites who preyed upon the weak and defenseless. No more.

One less monster in the world meant one more child who slept peacefully in her bed at night. And that was a thing he refused to regret.

"Kill them," Eli said. "But don't waste ammo."

"You promised you'd let us go!" Macek howled. "You can't do that!"

They ignored him. A minute later, it was over.

Eli glanced hurriedly at his watch. Fifteen minutes had passed. The clock was ticking. If Jackson hated him for this, then so be it. He spun for the door. "Time to go."

Nyx scrambled for the duffle bags of weapons. "Right behind you."

Without a second glance, Eli and Nyx strode from the derelict building into the gloom.

The air buzzed with ozone; it had an acrid taste to it. A storm was coming, a big one.

The bleak sky darkened like a stain as if Mother Nature knew the wicked things they had done and was punishing them.

The first drops of rain began to fall.

69

ELI POPE
DAY ONE HUNDRED AND FIVE

Rain poured from the sky. It drummed against the tarp, water pelting the muddy ground as saplings bent beneath the onslaught.

Eli and the others huddled beneath a camouflaged tarp strung between a few trees, making last-minute preparations for the mission ahead, their faces hardened with determination and resolve, their gear and weapons ready.

Jackson was quiet, staring at nothing with a distant look in his eyes. Something was bothering him, but that was a problem for later. Moreno loaded magazines with intense focus, and Antoine thrummed with high nervous energy. Nyx bounced on the balls of her feet, one finger massaging the trigger guard of her M2010 sniper rifle, her jaw set.

"We go in at nightfall," Eli said grimly, "at the next sentry shift. The darkness will give us cover and the rain and clouds will help us even more."

Moreno jutted his chin at the hill across from their position. "You want us to climb that in the pouring rain, in the middle of the night, hoping we don't get shot?"

Eli gave a rueful smile. "Never promised you a rose garden."

"I'm cheap," Antoine muttered. "I'll take pasties as my heavenly reward. As many pasties as I can eat, forever and ever, amen."

Eli ignored him and turned his attention to the group. "We'll split into two six-person teams like we've trained and enter through the dumpsite. Once we're in the mine, each team must be capable of being completely independent since our comms are only line of sight inside, and we can't support each other. Each team is responsible for their wounded and getting them out. If you lose enough people, either dead or wounded, your team may become ineffective, at which point, you should exfil immediately.

"After completing your mission, you'll exit through the main entrance. Once Nyx eliminates the sentries at the dumpsite entrance, she will move to a hide overlooking the main entrance. She'll provide overwatch and will pick off any pursuers with the 300-win mag. Alexis is running the drone. I'm leaving the SAW with Devon. Between them, they'll crush any quick reaction force in pursuit, or at least slow them down, but you've got to get out of the labyrinth on your own."

Everyone nodded, listening intently.

Eli pointed at the map. "Bravo team, you'll move to the lair where Sykes' men have hunkered down, here in the fourth chamber on the second level. You should find at least eight hostiles, maybe ten or more, sleeping. A few may be awake, prepping weapons, eating, et cetera. Use the IR infrared glow sticks and IR illuminators if it's pitch dark. They'll never know what hit them. If there's ambient light, use the normal setting on your NVGs.

"You're gonna be outnumbered, so this is your biggest advantage. Do this right and most of the people you're going to kill will wake up dead. If you lose the element of surprise, use the grenades instead, and make sure you have cover when you throw them. Your primary objective is to eliminate as many of Sykes' men as you can. With prejudice. They're a plague, and they need to be wiped from the face of the Earth."

"Now that deserves an amen," Nyx said.

"Hell, yeah," Moreno said.

Eli continued, "Antoine and I will lead Alpha team, to retrieve the hostage and get her and our men out of this hellhole alive."

Distant lightning pulsed, the growl of thunder swallowed by the thrashing trees. The wind whipped the tarp with a snapping sound. Rain drummed against the canvas and battered the underbrush, turning the rocky ground slick with rivulets of muddy brown water.

"Speed, surprise, and overwhelming violence of action," Eli said. "That's our best chance at success."

He didn't say it was their only chance, that the odds of success were incredibly low, or that the odds of everyone surviving this operation were even lower.

He didn't say that he alone was going to make damn sure Sykes didn't survive. Sykes was determined to kill the people Eli loved. Therefore, he had to die, even at the cost of Eli's life.

70

LENA EASTON
DAY ONE HUNDRED AND FIVE

L ena climbed to her feet, swayed dizzily, and stumbled across the cavern, collapsing against the crate containing the insulin.

Her bruised fingertips stung as she fumbled at the heavy-duty plastic wrapping the boxes in tough impenetrable layers, attempting to scratch it open with her fingernails to no avail.

She needed a knife, anything sharp at all. Breathing hard, she bent and gnawed at the corner of the crate with her teeth. An explosion of agony radiated from her nose and jaw. Bright white stars burst in front of her eyes in dizzying shockwaves, her legs turning watery as she sagged against the crate, gasping.

Trying to bite through the thick plastic hurt so much she nearly passed out. Hunger and thirst scoured her insides. Her diabetic headache pulsed like a vise against her skull. The raw skin of her wrists burned, and her broken nose throbbed.

Groaning in pain and frustration, she splayed her palm against the *Eli Lilly* symbol emblazoned across the refrigerated container for balance. Her thoughts were fuzzy, but the irony hadn't escaped her—the name of the insulin-manufacturing company that kept her alive shared the name of her lover and her dead sister.

What a cruel, bitter joke.

Scanning the cavern, she considered her options. There were two passageways: the larger northern tunnel through which Angel had departed moments ago, which seemed like a bad idea, and the smaller passageway to the south that likely led deeper into the labyrinth of the mine.

Either option was far from safe. Even if one of Sykes' men didn't shoot her, she was liable to get lost in the warren of subterranean tunnels, alone, sick, and blind in the dark.

That left the small hole in the wall behind her. The tube, around two feet in circumference, began a foot from the cavern floor and was large enough for a slender person to squeeze through.

Where did it lead? Someone had dug it out for a purpose. Maybe it would be her salvation or maybe it would lead to her death. The unknown was terrifying. Either way, it was her only option.

Lowering herself to her hands and knees, she squeezed between the stack of crates and the cavern wall and disappeared into the black shaft. Somewhere ahead of her, she heard the almost comforting squeak and scuttle of the rat.

Rock surrounded her. She scooched on her belly, legs flat out behind her, her arms squeezed close to her body. Claustrophobia constricted her lungs. She'd never feared tight spaces before, but she'd reached an entirely new level of terror.

The rock was damp and slick beneath her fingers, a faint foul smell of things that had lived and died a hundred years ago. Hundreds of feet below the surface, a hundred million tons of rock bore down on her. The only sound her ragged breath, and the scratch and scrape of her feet and arms as she inched her way forward.

The crown of her head bumped against the rock ceiling, her arms and legs cramped in the ever-tightening space. Inch by inch, the tube narrowed, shrinking down on her, constricting her body as if she'd been swallowed by a great snake.

The dim glow from the Coleman lantern disappeared as she

crawled further into the tube. As the profound darkness enveloped her, she could no longer see her hands or anything else. She was utterly blind.

A squeak near her ear. Tiny claws pricked her hand. She swallowed a cry of alarm, half expecting small teeth to clamp down on her fingers. She went rigid as the weight of a small body scurried across her arm and shoulder, down her spine, and over her legs. She couldn't move, couldn't even recoil.

Just like that, the rat was gone, and she was once again utterly alone.

The shaft narrowed further; she could hardly push herself forward. Panic snatched at her with seeking fingers. She shuddered, trembling and dizzy from the hyperglycemia. What if she got stuck? What if—

Her outstretched hands struck rock. She felt blindly in front of her, above her head, to either side. Everywhere she touched there was more rock.

A dead end.

"No," she whispered. "Please, no."

Despair curdled in her belly. She'd accomplished nothing worthwhile with her freedom. Angel would return at any moment and bring Sykes with him. They would torture and kill her.

She could stay in the shaft and pray they didn't find her, but that was a futile hope since the shaft was twenty or thirty feet deep at most; they'd find the hole.

Her captors couldn't crawl in after her, but they didn't need to. A bullet would do the job. Her corpse would remain stuck here forever, her flesh dissolving, her clothes rotting, until she was naught but a pile of bones to be discovered a hundred years from now—if ever.

She would die in this place, mere feet from the medication she desperately needed but could not access, put down like a frantic animal caught in a snare.

A sob tore from her throat. She slumped against the rock

digging into her belly and thighs and pressed her cheek to the cold ground, tears streaming down her face, her chest heaving.

This was the end, then. No way out. She was well and truly trapped.

There was a kind of relief in acceptance, in surrendering to the inevitable, abandoning the struggle for survival. A giving up of your very self.

No, her mind whispered. No. She could not give up. It wasn't a part of her makeup. She didn't know how. She thought of Shiloh, of Eli. No, she could not quit, not ever.

If these were her last moments, then so be it. She wasn't going out without a fight. Not like this, trapped and helpless prey.

Lena lifted her head. The tears dried on her face. Through the haze of panic, she forced herself to think, to do something, anything, as long as it was action.

Her hands again felt the uneven rock face, searching for anything she might have missed in the darkness. Along the floor of the tunnel to her left, near her elbow, her thumb grazed something foreign, something that was not roughhewn rock.

She fumbled clumsily in the dark, her fingers doing the work of her eyes, feeling the object: the long skinny rail, the shallow cup holder, the hook on one side, and the sharply pointed end. It was about ten inches long and two inches wide.

She recognized it, as would any student who'd toured the historic copper mines on a field trip. During the early mining days in the 1800s, the miners used an implement called a Sticking Tommy. It was an old-fashioned candle stick, forged from iron.

On one end was a candle holder; on the other end was a long, thin spike used to drive into a wood beam or rocky crevice, to light the area where the miner worked for twelve to fourteen hours a day.

How long had this implement laid here? Had a child worker left it behind a hundred years ago, crawling into this narrow shaft to chip out a vein of copper he couldn't even see?

She didn't know, and it didn't matter—this was a gift she must not waste. Her fingers closed around the Sticking Tommy. Using her feet, pushing with her free hand, she squirmed backward, keeping her head low, her stomach scraping over stone.

The rock walls clutched at her, closing in. She fought for every inch, heart thumping and mouth dry. Her blood rushed in her ears. Two feet, four feet, then five feet. Every movement was agonizingly slow.

Distant footsteps echoed from the northern passageway.

Adrenaline shot through her veins. She wriggled backward, desperately pushing and shoving, scrabbling with her feet and her hands. Her palms were scraped and bleeding, but she barely noticed.

The footsteps grew louder.

Extricating herself from the tunnel legs first, she jerked free and dove for the crate. Leaning against it, she slumped, her legs curled beneath her and hands behind her back as if her wrists were still bound, the candle stick palmed in one hand.

Not a second later, four men burst into the room. Angel and Sykes, and two others, big muscular guys with hard faces and harder eyes; they were armed with bulky weapons, wore chest rigs with helmets, with their NVGs pushed up off their faces.

Darius Sykes crossed the cavern and squatted in front of her, about five feet away. His lips spread in a lurid smile. Terror juddered through her body. Her heart jackhammered against her ribs, threatening to beat out of her chest.

She tightened her grasp on the Sticking Tommy, keeping it carefully hidden behind her, and tried to look weak. It wasn't difficult—she *was* weak, but she was not as feeble as they thought.

If Sykes would only come a few feet closer, he'd be within range of her weapon. She would kill him if she could, to give Eli and the others a slightly better chance at surviving this hellhole. If only he would come a little closer.

Sykes licked his lips like he was anticipating a delicious meal. There was something obscene in his face, the wrongness a lurch in

Lena's gut. There was pure evil in this world. She was face-to-face with it in human form.

"Go to hell," she said softly, so he had to bend toward her to hear her words.

Sykes grinned. "Hell is empty, and all the devils are here."

"Not all of them," Lena said. "One is out there and he's coming for you."

Sykes gave a hollow, echoing laugh. "You've got some spunk in you, don't you?"

"Come closer," she whispered. "And I'll show you."

"That time is coming soon enough, don't you worry." Instead of coming closer, he rose to his feet, still just out of reach. He gazed at her hungrily, like he wanted to devour her. "Oh, I am going to enjoy this."

71

SHILOH EASTON
DAY ONE HUNDRED AND FIVE

Fear rattled through Shiloh's chest.

Thick black clouds roiled across Lake Superior from the west, coming in hard as sheets of rain pounded the wave-lashed water. There was no moon, no kaleidoscope of stars. Behind her, the trees bent beneath the onslaught.

Shiloh and Ruby lay on their bellies in the sniper hide Eli had built along the edge of the bluff, a perfect position for sentries to watch for threats attempting to infiltrate the Northwoods Inn from the water. The high bluffs were a significant obstacle for an assault, making it the least likely spot for a breach, which was the only reason Eli allowed Shiloh and Ruby to keep watch.

On the lip of the precipice, it felt like balancing on the knife edge of the world itself. Shiloh had never felt so small. Mother Nature didn't give one whit for the doings of humanity, not when the sun blasted a billion tons of plasma at Earth and not now, as the trees writhed, the great lake raged, and the wind roared.

The sheer immensity of Superior was overwhelming. It felt like an ocean, a raging sea with all the power of Poseidon behind it. Waves eight to ten feet high crashed and rolled against the cliffs below. Nature's wrath came sudden and powerful.

She blinked back the wetness and peered intently through her scope, blurry shapes materializing out of darkness: swaying trees to her left and right, the jagged ledge of the limestone cliff a few feet ahead.

The great bowl of the sky was gray as ashes. The stinging rain slashed against her head and shoulders, the wind bitterly cold as it tore at her hair and lashed wet tendrils into her face.

"We should go!" Ruby shouted beside her. "This is dangerous!"

Her face was a ghastly white oval a foot from Shiloh's, her eyes huge in her pale face, red hair a drenched pelt against her scalp. "Shiloh!"

"This is my job. I'm doing my job!"

"No boats can get near us in this storm. They'd crash against the shoals and kill themselves. We need to go inside and get warm. We're the ones in trouble!"

The fierce squalls blowing across the lake felt like being sucked into the spin cycle of a washing machine. They were powerless against it. Like the solar flares, all you could do was hold on to something and hope you made it through to the other side.

Ruby was right, of course she was right, but Shiloh did not move. Her muscles stiff and sore, her body fixed rigidly in place. If she abdicated her responsibility to keep watch, the storm would destroy everything and everyone she loved.

"You go!" she shouted.

"No way!" Ruby hesitated. "We should check on Bear!"

Ruby was trying to guilt Shiloh into leaving. Bear was going to be okay; Lori was watching him now. But for the last two days, Bear hadn't left Shiloh's side.

She had tended to his bullet wound, cleaning it, applying antiseptic, and reapplying his bandages, but it was Lena the Newfie wanted.

The dog sensed Lena's absence keenly and kept shuffling to the door, rising on his hind legs and checking the windows, whining for Lena. He'd slept beside the door to Lena's room, moaning in his sleep, his paws twitching like he was chasing her, desperately searching for her even in his dreams.

Shiloh shared his anguish. She was terrified for Lena, and for Eli. She had found her father, only to risk losing him, and there wasn't a damn thing she could do about it.

She longed to fight everything, to shoot the storm, to stab the waves, to pound the world until it retreated and gave her back what she so desperately wanted.

Shiloh couldn't explain it, this desolate feeling, the desperate ache in her chest. She felt it in her heart, in her soul—the slow drain of hope and the end of all things. There was so much brokenness, in the old world and this new one. So much wrongness: danger and fear and despair, pain and loss.

"I need to stay," she said. "I—I have to stay."

Stubbornly, Ruby shook her head. "If you stay, I stay."

Shiloh opened her mouth but nothing came out. Rain ran down her face like tears. Maybe they were tears, salty on her tongue. She was weeping and she couldn't stop, didn't know how to stop. *Santiago, Chili. Bogotá, Columbia. Brasilia, Brazil...*

Ruby took her wet, ice-cold hand in her own and squeezed hard.

Startled, almost embarrassed, Shiloh's first instinct was to pull away. She forced herself not to. Instead, she squeezed Ruby's hand right back.

Despite the chill, the cold rain soaking her to the bone, warmth seeped into her chest. This was a true friend, then: the one who stays, who refuses to let go, the one who holds our hand in the dark of night, who bears witness while we painstakingly put ourselves back together, piece by shattered piece.

The wind roared like a train bearing down on them, snatching at their clothes, tugging at their hair, threatening to hurl them over the edge as easily as tossing a doll.

They braced themselves and held on.

72

ELI POPE
DAY ONE HUNDRED AND FIVE

They moved in the rain and darkness, silent and lethal predators.

Eli climbed the steep incline, his hair plastered to his scalp beneath his helmet, water dripping down the back of his neck, pouring into his face, droplets clinging to his eyelashes as he peered through his NVGs, the world awash with an eerie alien-green light.

Jackson, Antoine, and Moreno climbed beside him. Hart and Nash remained on the ground at the base of the hill, hidden in a dense cluster of spruce, their rifles swiveling in search of targets as the teams ascended the rock-strewn hillside.

Rifles slung across their backs, weighted down with chest rigs, body armor, and battle belts loaded with spare magazines, they scrabbled up the slick bedrock, using slippery footholds and handholds, layers of unstable rocks shifting beneath their feet and hands, threatening to twist an ankle or worse.

The pouring rain made the ascent difficult, but the steady drumming obscured the noise of their climb, the rain a thick gray curtain blurring the landscape.

Above them, Nyx lay in her sniper hide across the ravine, sighting through the scope of her rifle, an M2010 enhanced sniper rifle knock-off she had built to US Army standards, chambered in 300 Winchester Magnum with a large suppressor and an AN/PVS-29 clip-on sniper night sight. It was a beautiful, lethal weapon.

She was ready to eliminate the two sentries the second they appeared so that they couldn't radio an alarm to their comrades. Those down in the mine were unreachable, but Devon had eyes on at least four sentries manning the main entrance.

Halfway up, three feet to Eli's right, Antoine balanced on one foot and reached for an outcropping to hoist himself to his next handhold. The rock he'd put his weight on wobbled. His boot slipped.

With a curse, he scrambled to regain his purchase. A dozen loosened stones skittered noisily down the hillside.

Everyone froze. The men pressed their bodies against the rock, clinging like spiders, barely breathing. Eli tensed, the stitches in his forearm burning.

Antoine turned his head to face Eli, his face a white oval in the heavy rain, eyes wide with fear. They were utterly exposed. If the sentries peered over the edge, they'd get picked off like fish in a barrel. At least thirty men armed with automatic weapons would converge on them within minutes.

"They heard something," Nyx said into their headsets. "Sentry One is moving toward the mouth of the tunnel. Sentry Two is right behind him. They both have their guns up. Come on, come on, one more step. Come out into the open..."

"Nyx," Antoine said tensely.

"I got this," Nyx said through their headsets.

"If one of them gets their hands on the radio—"

"I said I got it," Nyx said. "Shut up and watch the magic happen."

A spitting sound split the night air. A second later, another sound followed the first. Something tumbled down the rock face, bouncing and spinning past them in a dark blur.

A body.

Two seconds later, a second body followed the first.

Eli clung to the hillside and glanced down. Two corpses lay bent and broken on the piled rocks, a small round hole in the center of their foreheads, the backs of their skulls completely gone.

The 300-win mag was originally built to hunt elephants and was adopted by Army and Marine snipers alike for its superior ballistic performance at long range. Against human targets, it was devastating.

"Bull's eye!" Nyx crowed. "Don't try that at home, boys."

Relieved, Eli continued to climb. Jackson and Antoine followed, faster now but still careful of the slippery rocks, their clothes soaked through and their skin sodden. In the torrential rain, they were vague, washed-out shapes, indistinct at the edges.

He clambered over the edge onto the wide ledge that led into the mine. A barred iron gate with a rusty padlock had once kept out the lookie-loos; the lock was broken, likely by a sledgehammer or bolt cutter.

Jackson and Moreno aimed their weapons into the tunnel while Eli and Antoine crouched at the mouth and scanned the base of the hill and surrounding trees, searching for a hint of movement. Below them, Bravo Team scrabbled up the slick hillside.

Several rocks broke free and plunged down the hill, but no hostiles appeared. Once everyone had reached the ledge, Chief McCallister led Bravo team into the mine in search of the fourth chamber, intent on eliminating as many of Sykes' men as they could.

Then it was Alpha Team's turn. They entered the mouth of the tunnel, swallowed by the darkness as they crept down the throat of the mine. It felt like descending into the underworld, the house of Hades itself.

They formed a double column, Antoine and Eli in the lead, Eli on the right, Antoine on the left. Moreno and Hart stacked up behind Eli, while Jackson and Nash stacked up behind Antoine.

Eli had night vision goggles with illuminators attached to the

NVGs and IR glow sticks tucked into a pouch on his chest rig, along with several flash-bangs and five fragmentation grenades they'd stolen from Sykes' men.

IR wasn't normally used by tactical teams since hostiles with night vision could see their exact location, but in situations with zero ambient light like this damn mine, they were a necessary evil.

They each wore headsets, though their comms system only worked within line of sight underground. Each team could communicate with their teammates, but no one else.

They were cut off from the world above.

Bravo team had headed left at the first forked passageway, while Alpha team turned right. Stepping quietly, they crept through the darkened shafts. The cold, dank air smelled of sediment and rust. Their clothing and gear made soft rustling sounds, but they were otherwise silent.

Eli had memorized the blueprints of the mine but faded lines on a piece of paper and the reality of deep subterranean tunnels were very different things. A maze of larger tunnels and small tributaries branched off in various directions.

The signs of long-dormant mining activity littered the passageways: holes drilled in the rock for dynamite and rusted tools and ancient implements left behind like detritus. They stepped over strips of original rail tracks, old-fashioned drill steels, and iron candle holders.

When they approached a side tunnel, three team members entered and cleared the first twenty feet, while Antoine and Eli held their guns forward and Nash pointed to the rear to cover their six.

Once the tunnel was cleared, the three fell back into the stack, and the double column proceeded down the passageway. A long straight tunnel stretched ahead of them.

Eli motioned, and three men moved up while three remained behind the turn to provide cover. They executed the same move for every turn, every abandoned mine cart, and every tall cairn of piled rocks.

In this way, they moved cautiously from cover point to cover point.

Eli hated the claustrophobia, the feeling of exposure as they moved in the narrow tunnels. Ballistic shields would've offered significant protection in these labyrinthine corridors, but the deputies weren't trained in how to use them, and neither the rural sheriff's office nor the police department had the budget to purchase them anyway.

Ahead, the tunnel forked in two directions. The left passageway was eight feet wide by ten feet tall, with a six-foot-tall pile of rocks stacked near the entrance like a giant cairn. To the right, the shaft was low-ceilinged and narrow.

According to the intel they'd gleaned from Macek, the left passageway was booby-trapped with a trip-wired grenade just past the cairn. Eli checked and caught the gleam of the thin filament stretched across the tunnel at ankle height.

Alpha Team headed to the right and followed the tunnel straight a few hundred feet before it curved into a bend with no sightline beyond it.

At the front of the double column, Antoine and Eli stopped, took a knee, and listened hard. The men behind them did the same. No sounds of approaching hostiles were heard, only the beating of their hearts and the rustle of their breathing.

Eli was about to gesture to Antoine to move into the right branch of another forked passageway. He froze. The reddish glow of the IR illuminated a silvery thread about an inch off the ground. Another tripwire.

Eli held up a closed fist. Antoine followed his lead.

Behind them, Alpha Team halted. Eli followed the slender wire with his eyes to the grenade lodged in a crevice hidden in the shadows.

Motioning to his team, he gingerly stepped across the wire. They continued, crouched and stealthy, descending steadily into the bowels of the earth, moving silently through the labyrinth.

Repeatedly, Antoine and Eli took a knee and paused, straining their ears. Eli's laceration stung, the stitches pulling with his movements. He wasn't healed, but there was nothing for it.

Lena would pitch a fit. If that meant she was alive, he'd accept a hundred lectures.

He started to rise. Then he heard it.

Pebbles crunched underfoot.

Far ahead, a single pair of footsteps approached from around the bend. A small penlight beam appeared, sweeping back and forth across the tunnel walls.

Eli motioned to his team, then bladed himself against the wall, dropping the HK417 on its sling and drawing his combat knife. Moreno and Nash followed suit behind him while Antoine's column pressed themselves against the opposite tunnel wall.

Adrenaline spiked his veins as he tensed, waiting. A second later, the hostile appeared around the corner. Big and burly, he gazed straight ahead with his weapons holstered, his guard down. The flashlight obscured his night vision.

Eli was on him in a heartbeat. He clamped one hand over the thug's mouth and punched the tip of the knife upward into the back of the man's neck, piercing the base of his brain stem and killing him nearly instantly.

The man crumpled. Eli lowered the corpse to the ground as Alpha Team fell back into position, stepping over the body as they approached the first of the large caverns.

Eli peered around the corner, leading with his weapon. According to Macek, Sykes didn't have men stationed here. Their IR lights didn't reach the opposite side of the cavern. He sensed a vast openness; the subterranean room was immense.

He loathed the thought of crossing the exposed space, but the passage leading to Lena was located through this cavern. There was no way out but through.

Eli and Antoine led in a half-crouch, weapons up and ready, scanning ahead. The others followed. They moved through the darkness. The blood rushed in his ears. He counted off the steps. Ten. Twenty. Thirty—

A sound came from ahead of them. Before Eli could react, the first hostiles appeared.

From the opposite end of the cavern, several thugs strode into the cavern, beams of light sweeping the walls and ceiling. Startled, they halted in their tracks. Eli glimpsed seven shadowy figures carrying AR-15s and AK-47s held low, tactical flashlights affixed to their weapons.

Alpha Team reacted first. Swiftly retreating, the six-man team laid down rapid fire. Shouts and gunfire exploded as they dove for cover behind the rear tunnel wall. Rounds sprayed the ceiling.

Plucking a grenade from his pouch, Eli pulled the pin and hurled it into the cavern, ducking into the passage just as the thugs unleashed a barrage of firepower. In anticipation of the pressure blast, Eli closed his eyes and opened his mouth.

Someone shouted, "Grenade!"

A thunderous boom trembled the cavern wall, seemingly the mine itself. A cacophony of tortured screams rent the air. Even with the noise-canceling headsets, it was deafening. Eli's ears rang, sound going dim.

Unlike the movies, there was no massive fireball. The frag grenade boasted a kill radius of five meters, with casualties up to fifteen meters, approximately the size of the cavern itself.

A moment later, Alpha Team leaped up and darted into the cavern, searching for targets to eliminate. The weapon lights on the ground provided enough ambient light for the NVGs so they could see the entire chamber now.

Smoke hung heavy in the air. A thousand fragments of twisted metal scattered across the cavern floor. There were five men on the ground. Two were ripped to pieces and appeared to be dead. Three writhed on the floor, disoriented and mortally wounded, screaming in agony.

Antoine swung right and fired at two of the injured. Eli went left and put a head shot into the dead guys to ensure the dead stayed dead. Nash and Hart fanned out, each moving across a section of the cavern and eliminated two more enemy combatants.

At the far end of the cavern, one of the hostiles sat propped against the wall, his right leg a bloody wreck, but he was conscious and firing. Rounds pinged and cracked above their heads.

Nash dropped to one knee, fired twice and missed. Jackson spun and squeezed a double tap. Both rounds caught him in the face. The thug sagged against the wall, very dead. The hostiles wore ballistic vests and headgear, their NVGs pushed up. Little good it had done them.

"So much for stealth." Antoine reached down and seized an M4 from one of the corpses. An M203-grenade launcher was attached beneath the barrel of the M4. Antoine grinned like it was his birthday. "This sweet baby will do some damage!"

Jackson motioned toward the opposite tunnel. "Time to move! Let's go!"

If their presence hadn't been discovered yet, they'd surely been exposed now. Tension thrummed through Eli, his nerves raw. The seconds counted down in his blood. Lena's time was running out.

73

LENA EASTON
DAY ONE HUNDRED AND FIVE

R apid footsteps echoed from the opposite tunnel.

Lena looked up as a huge man appeared. In his thirties, he boasted big meaty hands and a muscular body writhing with tattoos; a jagged scar cut deep into his leathery right cheek. He carried an automatic rifle with a pistol stuffed into the back of his jeans.

"This better be good news, Huffman," Sykes said, his attention still on Lena.

"Garr and Reynolds didn't report in as scheduled. I sent Clayton to check on them."

Sykes went still. "Anyone else missing?"

Huffman hesitated for just a moment. "Well, Thompson and Macek should've been back twenty minutes ago, but the storm could've slowed them—"

"It's Pope!" Sykes growled.

"We don't know that," Huffman said.

Sykes rounded on him. "Of course, it's him! It's too early! How the hell did he find us?"

"I don't know—"

"That was a rhetorical question, you idiot. Rouse the men and tell them to prepare for an attack. Now!"

Again, Huffman hesitated.

"Go!" Sykes snarled. "Don't come back until those deputies are dead. Every single one of them! Hang them by their entrails from the nearest tree! Let every law officer know from here to Marquette who's in charge now, and what happens to the cockroaches dumb enough to stand in our way."

With a curt nod, Huffman vanished down the main tunnel. Sykes jutted his chin at his other men. "Guard the tunnels! No one in or out without my say so!"

As they obeyed, Sykes turned to Angel. "Pope thinks he's getting one up on us, does he? We'll start with her now. Her screams will draw him. When he sees her shattered body, he will know he's already lost. I will break him before I gut him."

Panic torqued through her. Eli was coming for her, but too late. Her vision went indistinct and hazy. Her limbs were full of lead. She was too weak to do anything, to help him or herself.

So, she did the one thing she could do; she went limp. Her muscles turned to water, her bones liquid. She slumped against the side of the crate, her arms behind her back as if bound, her face slack.

"Wake up!" Angel shouted at her.

She didn't respond.

Angel strode over to her and kicked her savagely in the ribs, knocking her onto her side. The pain was like a hot poker to her kidneys. He put his boot on her throat, cutting off her breath. Only slightly more pressure and he'd snap her neck like a twig.

It took every ounce of her self-control to remain still.

Angel removed the boot from her throat and nudged her ribs. "I said wake up!"

She didn't move. She was insubstantial as air, a wraith, a ghost.

"What's wrong with her?" Sykes demanded.

"She said she was diabetic. That she could go into a coma or something?"

Sykes cursed. "That explains why Pope ambushed the freight train. Damn it!"

"I thought she was lying."

"Check her stomach. She'll have a pump or something."

A shadow fell across her body. She sensed a figure looming over her, smelled the sour tang of Angel's sweat, that dank unwashed scent of him. He squatted, searching fingers like spiders beneath her shirt. She fought the urge to recoil from his touch.

"Uh, no pump, but she's got a weird hole thing in her side. Guess she was telling the truth. She's breathing, but she's unconscious."

Sykes cursed louder. "You worthless moron! I should've put a bullet in your belly back on the prison transport! Fix her!"

"What do you want me to do?"

For a moment, neither man spoke. There was only the sound of their ragged breathing. Lena remained utterly still, eyes closed, body limp; her right hand gripping the Sticking Tommy flopped behind her, out of view in the shadows cast by the stacked crates.

"Pope won't know the difference. He'll think I killed her. Either way, I'll rub his face in her bloody entrails." Sykes' words were calm and controlled, but fury laced his soft voice. There was a sound like the scrape of a knife sliding from its sheath. "Bring her over here, into the light. I like to see my handiwork."

Angel bent over her. His pungent breath struck her face. His clammy hands grasped her shoulders, yanking at her, pulling her up to drag her to her death.

There came another sound, much louder, a distant rumble like thunder, or the throaty growl of a dragon wakening from its slumber, deep beneath the earth.

Surely it was Eli, coming for her.

Angel jerked his head up. "What the hell—"

"Pope is here!" Sykes shouted, half enraged, half panicked. "Kill her!"

Before Angel could act, Lena's eyes popped open. She seized the gangbanger's shirt with one hand, yanking him toward her and knocking him off-balance.

He froze, bewildered that she had two hands free when she

should be bound and helpless. He was more surprised at the strange, sharp object in her hand.

With the last of her strength, Lena rose and thrust the stake into Angel Flud's tattooed throat, right below his frantically bobbing Adam's apple.

The stake sank three inches deep. His mouth gaped, eyes bulging. Blood spilled hot and wet across her chest. As he collapsed on top of her, she whispered, "That's for shooting my dog."

74

ELI POPE
DAY ONE HUNDRED AND FIVE

Eli motioned toward a passageway to their right. He and Antoine took the lead as the team fell into position behind them.

They crossed the cavern and entered the broad passage which wound to the left before straightening out. Performing a tactical reload, Eli dropped the half-used magazine into an empty pouch on his chest rig, grasped a fresh one from a different pouch, and slammed it in.

Thirty yards down the tunnel, two more hostiles appeared. Spotting them, the armed men broke into a run, firing wildly with automatic weapons.

Jackson, Nash, Hart, and Moreno dove to the ground. Eli and Antoine crouched low against opposite sides of the tunnel wall.

Adrenaline spiking, Eli fired two shots at the first assailant. He missed and both shots went high.

Rounds impacted all around them, pinging and sparking off rock. The sheer volume of firepower was deafening.

Aiming for center mass, Eli squeezed off two more rounds. They struck the first target in his groin and shattered his pelvis. As he fell, Eli fired a kill shot into his temple.

The second assailant fired rounds that zipped over Eli's head.

Before Eli could reacquire the second target, a massive boom sounded. Antoine had fired the grenade launcher beneath the barrel of his newly acquired M4. The massive tube held a buckshot round, lead pellets spraying the second hostile's vest, groin, and throat.

The result was instantaneous. The man toppled with a tortured shriek of agony. Death followed within seconds.

Simultaneously, a third man emerged from a side tunnel just behind Antoine and Eli.

He ran down the tunnel, careening toward them like a demon, bullets flying. Hart swung over Eli's shoulder and fired, hit him in the right collarbone, and fired again.

The round pierced his upper thigh. The thug tumbled backward, still firing, his finger twitching on the trigger.

"He's hit but not down!" Hart yelled.

Eli spun and put a kill shot in the center of the thug's forehead. "He sure is now."

Beside him, Jackson ejected his spent magazine and shoved in a fresh one. "Me and Moreno are gonna check the tunnel and make sure there aren't any more."

Jackson and Moreno moved into the mouth of the passageway. Nash leaned against the wall, weapon lowering as he glanced down at his leg with a curse.

"You okay, man?" Antoine asked.

In the light from the IR illuminators, Eli saw blood oozing from a hole in Nash's pants leg on the outside of his upper right thigh.

"Winged," Nash said between gritted teeth. "I'm okay. It's okay."

"Like hell, we're checking you first. Antoine, cover me." Eli squatted in front of Nash. "Pull your pants down, kid. Either that or I cut them off. This is no time for modesty."

Nash made a pained face but obeyed. Eli checked the wound. It was a graze, a bloody notch a half inch deep in the meat of his upper thigh. It'd hurt like hell, but wasn't lethal. Reaching for his

IFAK, Eli quickly wrapped it in a pressure bandage. "You sure you're okay to keep going? We can come back for you."

Nash clenched his jaw. "No way you're leaving me behind. I'm good."

Moreno and Jackson returned. "No one in the tunnel. We're good to go."

Eli rose to his feet. "We're almost there. Keep your heads on a swivel."

The team rose, resumed their loose formation, and kept going. Urgency crackled through them. They stepped over the corpses, moving fast.

Blood trickled down Eli's left arm. He'd ripped his stitches open, but the adrenaline masked the pain. He ignored it and kept moving, always moving.

A minute later, the acoustics changed. A large space opened up ahead. He strained his ears, listening to the distant voices reverberating. He inhaled the dank mineral scents of the mine mixed with the smell of kerosene.

This was it. Everything was on the line, for Lena, and for the men under his command. Eli was determined to get his team past the fatal funnel of the chamber entrance. If they didn't get this right, people would die.

Crouching, Eli and Antoine peered around the corner. Low lantern light shimmered from the entrance, light enough that they didn't need their NVGs. They pushed the goggles up on their helmets.

"I can't see Lena," Eli whispered. "No flash-bangs or grenades. When I say NOW, I want Jackson and Antoine to go in, crossing left and right. Once you get to the far corners, open up. Nash and Moreno, go in after me, one on each side, and head toward the crates in the center section, which we'll use as cover. Hart, you hold back, covering the rear."

Antoine said, "Stay frosty."

Hart gave a thumbs-up.

When Eli gave the cue through their comms, Jackson sprinted

into the second cavern, weapon up and swiveling to the left, ninety degrees from the tunnel entrance. Antoine went in fast, pointing his weapon ninety degrees to the right.

Eli, Nash, and Moreno spread out behind them in a fan pattern, moving forward to cover the perimeter of the massive chamber. Hart remained at the tunnel entrance, crouched and peering backward, covering their rear for threats.

The cavern was immense, grand and high-ceilinged as a cathedral. Stacks of large crates and boxes circled the perimeter. Lantern light wavered across the roughhewn walls.

In the center of the cavern, four armed thugs spun to face them, automatic weapons rising. Gunfire sprayed in wild arcs. Rounds impacted the cavern's walls and ceiling, chipping bedrock, and thudding into wooden crates.

Eli dove to the ground. A dozen rounds blasted over his head. Rolling hard, he came up in a combat crouch and squeezed the trigger in rapid succession, firing a zipper across the closest man's chest. The first two rounds struck body armor; the next two punched into his throat and skull.

The man slammed back against a crate and slid to the ground.

Eli swung left and fired at a thug bringing his weapon to bear. Several rounds impacted body armor, and the last one hit pay dirt. The bullet drilled into his mouth and tore off half his face as he went down with a garbled scream.

Eli was already scanning for the next target with his weapon.

"Incoming!" Moreno shouted. "On the left!"

At his nine o'clock, Nash and Moreno crouched to the side of a stack of crates. They opened fire as a half-dozen of Sykes' men poured into the cavern from a side tunnel.

They unleashed a barrage of firepower but imprecisely, muzzles bouncing with each jarring step, their aim veering wildly. Rounds thudded and thumped all around them, sparking off stone.

The hostiles were caught in their own fatal funnel. They were dropped one by one as Nash and Moreno returned fire, 5.56

rounds slamming into body parts not protected by the ceramic plates in their chest rigs.

Eli saw an opportunity. "Nash and Moreno, when I start moving, head to the boxes ahead. Antoine and Jackson pour on fire when we go."

"We got you, brother." Antoine and Jackson crept along the perimeter, shooting steady cover fire, keeping a clear line of sight from Nash and Moreno as they moved forward. When Moreno and Nash reached their cover positions, they opened up on the men crouched inside the opposite tunnel as Antoine, Jackson and Eli moved forward.

On the far right at Eli's three o'clock, a figure cowered on the ground between two crates, seeking cover from the firefight—Lena. A body lay beside her, blood spurting from its throat.

One of the thugs ran toward her, likely to put a gun to her head and use her as a hostage. Before Eli could readjust and aim, Antoine took the goon down, stitching rounds across his torso from his crotch to his throat. He crumpled ten feet from Lena.

Eli had no time to feel relief. The *rat-a-tat* of an AK-47 split the air. Rounds sprayed the walls, ricocheting off the stone.

He spun to the right, weapon swiveling.

Across the cavern, Sykes dropped his Kalashnikov rifle, the 30-round magazine run dry. He wore no plate carrier or battle belt with extra magazines.

Sykes fled through a secondary tunnel to the right. Jackson and Moreno spun and fired at him. Both shots missed. Sykes slipped between two crates and darted into the shaft, firing behind him with his pistol as he escaped.

The thunder of gunfire faded, the enemy combatants either dead or fleeing. Eli's ears rang, and his nostrils filled with the stink of gunpowder.

With the rest of Alpha Team covering the tunnels, Eli went to Lena.

Angel Flud writhed on the ground beside her. Blood gurgled

from his punctured throat, mouth gawping like a dying fish, his limbs spasming.

Without an iota of remorse, Eli shot the gangbanger between the eyes.

Lena was covered with blood. Blood spattered across her shirt, her face, and her hands. Her skin was bone-white, her eyes closed. A blood-drenched implement lay at her feet.

Fear punched his chest. For a heart-wrenching moment, he didn't know if she was alive or dead. Kneeling beside her, his rifle in one hand, he touched her cheek. "Lena!"

Her eyelids fluttered, then opened. Her eyes were the most beautiful he'd ever seen. He checked her over quickly—a broken nose, bruises, a few scrapes. Most of the blood wasn't hers.

"I knew you'd come," she said.

He was already rising to his feet. "We have to get you out of here."

"Insulin," Lena gasped.

He looked around at the hundreds of crates. "Where is it?"

She pointed weakly at a crate across the cavern. Jackson went to it and tore it open. They'd brought a syringe with them, along with her blood glucose meter. Within moments, they'd found what they needed.

He hadn't known whether Lena would be conscious or not, but before she'd been kidnapped, Lena had given both Eli and Shiloh thorough, detailed instructions on what to do if she went into a diabetic coma. Eli administered insulin in the field.

Lena was barely coherent. She tried to stand and faltered, swaying unsteadily. "I can do it."

But she couldn't. She staggered, and Jackson caught her.

Clearly, she was physically weakened, but her will had not broken. They had not broken her, and he thought his chest would explode with love and fear. He would not breathe until she was out of here, safe and sound. He would not rest until Sykes was dead.

Hart reloaded his weapon and slapped in a fresh magazine. "Let's get the hell out of here!"

Jackson put his arm around Lena and helped her to her feet. They loaded her onto the portable stretcher they'd packed in Hart's field pack. Hart and Nash carried the stretcher with Antoine and Jackson in the lead, Moreno taking up the rear. They headed for the main tunnel.

Eli did not move with them.

Jackson hesitated. He glanced back at Eli, a dark awareness in his face—he knew what Eli was going to do, what he needed to do.

Jackson nodded, not in tacit approval, but in acceptance. "I'll get her out."

Eli had no choice but to trust Jackson with her life. "I know."

"We've got her, let's go!" Antoine shouted, cursing loudly in French.

Alpha team vanished through the tunnel. Lena was too dazed to realize Eli wasn't with them, which was for the best. Their footsteps echoed faintly, then disappeared.

Eli turned and headed for the passageway through which Sykes had fled less than a minute before. He must have been winged in the firefight; a faint trail of blood glinted oil-black in the light of his IR light.

The maw of the tunnel before him was dark as a coffin. Wiping the blood leaking down his arm onto his chest rig, he entered it. Subterranean drafts whispered as if an ancient voice was speaking from the throat of the mine.

This ended now, this very hour.

Either Sykes died, or he did. One thing he knew—only one of them would walk out of here alive.

75

ELI POPE
DAY ONE HUNDRED AND FIVE

H e hunted.
If there was one thing Eli Pope was good at, it was hunting men.

Again, he entered the twisting tunnels, the oppressive darkness. The air was dank against his skin; the cold like the kiss of a ghost on the back of his neck.

It felt like a labyrinth, willingly stepping foot into the heart of darkness itself. There was a monster at the heart of the labyrinth. There was always a monster.

He could never eradicate all evil. Evil was endemic, a part of every human heart. It spread like a fungus, a disease. There was no finish, no end to it.

But this evil, this monster—Eli would end him now, one way or another.

He moved cautiously through the tunnel, straining to hear, feeling the wall with his left hand, his Glock 19 held tightly in his right, going mostly by sound and touch. Only occasionally did he switch on the illuminator to see what his hands and tentative footsteps couldn't tell him.

He searched for the scattered droplets of glistening blood, hot on Sykes' trail. His IR beam swept tunnel entrance after tunnel entrance. Impenetrable shadows lurked outside the reach of the light, stalking him, waiting to pounce.

The dank smell of water and minerals filled his nostrils. He strained his ears, listening hard, to no avail. His hearing was impaired. He would not be able to hear the padding steps if Sykes snuck up on him.

His throat closed in fear. It would be a terrible way to die, lost down here, sightless and afraid. How easy it would be to make a wrong turn at a fork, choose the wrong tunnel, twist an ankle and stumble, plunging into an abyss. The thought made his flesh crawl.

He passed a cavity carved into the wall, no larger than the size of a walk-in closet, approximately four feet wide by ten feet deep, the beginning of a tunnel offshoot from the secondary artery. It went nowhere; the copper vein the miners had followed dried up.

Similar grottos were interspersed along this shaft. They provided perfect ambush locations for Sykes to lie in wait for him. Ahead, he glimpsed another splatter of blood, fresh and glinting.

Eli had no choice but to continue on. The roof of the tunnel sank gradually lower. The walls closed in, growing narrow. Rock scraped his spine like clawed fingers.

Cold panic flushed through him. He fought it back and kept moving.

Five minutes later, he entered a larger space, the ceiling arcing forty to fifty feet above him. To the left was a narrow path, steeply angled and six feet wide. To the right, a cliff, the sheer drop-off black and bottomless as the abyss.

His imagination conjured demons and wraiths keening from the depths, slithering up the steep walls to devour those who dared trespass, the windigo hunting for human flesh to devour.

The narrow path clung to the lip of the cliff and descended along the ledge to another passageway a hundred yards distant.

If Sykes was hidden behind the bend, he'd be able to see Eli's light a long way off. With grave misgivings, he switched off his IR illuminator. He was plunged into darkness.

He would have to feel his way from here. Pausing, he stopped to listen over the dull ringing in his ears. Had he heard something? A soft step, perhaps. An expelled breath.

He stopped breathing. His muscles tensed. He waited, silent for a full minute but heard no other sounds.

Instinctively, his hand moved over his chest rig, wishing he could touch the Saint Michael's medallion beneath it for good luck, for blessings from any saints or supernatural beings who might be watching from above. He thought of the sacrifices of noble men.

Warily, his nerves raw, he again began to move. Keeping close to the wall, his palm scraped the rough rock, then felt an empty space carved into the passage: another grotto.

Pebbles crunched underfoot. The blood rushed through his veins. Absolute blackness pressed in on him. Terror stalked him in the dark.

Behind him, a pebble skittered. A whiff of body odor.

Eli started to spin—

The rock struck Eli's spine, just below the shoulder blades.

Pain exploded throughout his entire body. Knocked off his feet, Eli launched forward and smacked the wall face first, then fell on his back, his breath expelled from his lungs.

His pistol was smacked from his hand. It skidded off the ledge and tumbled over the drop-off. He never heard it hit the bottom, it was so far down.

Sykes had attacked him. Hidden in one of the grottos, he must have snuck up behind him and struck him with a rock.

Fear scythed through him. Pain like a hot poker stabbed between his shoulder blades. Gasping, he flipped onto his belly, the ground slick and uneven, angled downward toward the abyss he couldn't see, terribly aware that Sykes was somewhere, invisible and out of reach, about to attack again.

Painfully, Eli clambered to his knees. Before he could climb to his feet, a heavy form leaped onto his back. Hot breath in his ear, hands like claws on his shoulders, his throat.

Eli fumbled desperately in the darkness. He found Sykes' arm, locked it with his own, and spun him to the ground.

Something hard slammed into his forehead. Sykes had head-butted him. Forced to release his hold, Eli stumbled back, scrambling for balance. White stars swirled across his vision. His chest pounded, his lungs bursting for air.

He sensed Sykes moving backward, heard the thud of his footsteps, the sound of a blade sliding from its sheath as Sykes drew his karambit.

Simultaneously, Eli drew his combat knife. The men faced each other, knives out. Both blind, enveloped in all-encompassing blackness. Balanced on a narrow ledge, the wall to his right, the cliff to the left. A fight to the death in total darkness, hundreds of feet below the surface of the earth.

So be it.

Eli sucked in a single deep breath. He rushed Sykes and snap-kicked hard. His boot made contact with Sykes' stomach.

Sykes grunted, pained.

White-hot pain slashed across his shin. Blood gushed down his leg as Eli's boot hit the ground. Sykes had nicked him. He danced backward, attempting to stay close to the wall.

A sensation of movement, a displacement in the air molecules.

Eli braced his left forearm to protect his face and throat and slashed outward with the knife. He struck at empty air.

He spun, trying to place Sykes by sound. A grunt, a footstep. To the left? Two feet away? Three feet to the right?

He didn't even sense Sykes move. Sudden stabbing pain punched his right shoulder outside his chest rig.

Sykes had slashed downward and barely missed driving the blade under Eli's vest for a kill shot. The cut sliced his flesh from the top of his shoulder to his armpit.

Eli held out his blade, but his muscles were slow to respond. His shoulder wasn't moving right. Something was wrong. His entire arm was a white-hot flame of pain.

Eli kicked again and made contact. Sykes cursed, stumbling

backward, but fresh pain from the blow shot up Eli's leg where the karambit had knifed him.

His leg was bleeding hard, blood filling his boot. His pulse throbbed in his cut shoulder, blood spilling with every beat of his heart, soaking his T-shirt.

A breeze touched his cheek as Sykes landed another attack. The blade sliced the front of his chest rig. Eli checked the arm holding the blade while his knife hand slid across and underneath's Sykes arm to try and disarm him, to cut his hand or wrist.

But Eli's right arm was injured, too slow and pouring blood. In the darkness, he couldn't see his way. He missed.

Sykes didn't. The karambit blade sliced across Eli's left hand and cut through flesh, tendon, and bone.

With a strangled cry, Eli jerked back. His bloodied foot struck a rock. He stumbled and nearly fell. The sensation of a yawning void to his left was the only warning that he was inches from the edge.

Regaining his balance, he clenched his fists. Blood ran down his fingers in rivulets. Agony pulsed with every heartbeat.

Sykes broke free and pulled back, breathing hard.

"Death by a thousand cuts, Pope." His girlish sing-song voice echoed eerily, seeming to come from all directions at once. "As I promised you."

In the total blackness, he could hear Sykes' breathing, could smell his sour sweat and tangy adrenaline, his own coppery blood mixed with the dank air of the mine. Eli sucked in oxygen, his lungs burning, the pain throbbing through his body, weakening him beat by beat.

"I'm gonna cut you wide open and watch you bleed." Sykes' words echoed off the cavern walls and reverberated in the yawning pit. "Your girlfriend is next. She can watch me torture and kill your daughter before I do the same to her. Oh yes, we found out about Shiloh. Did you think you could hide her from me, Eli? Did you think you had a chance?"

Nausea churned in Eli's gut. He swayed, sickened and enraged.

"You think you're such a big shot, but everyone will know you failed. I'll put your head on a stake and parade it in front of your friends before I kill them, too. Admit it. You can't beat me. You'll never win. You can't win."

Eli understood what would happen, what had to happen. He refused to allow this demented psychopath to harm his daughter or the woman he loved.

The pain receded, the fear vanished, replaced with a cold resolve.

This then, was how it would end.

For Sykes, but also for Eli.

He inched to the left, away from the wall. In his mind's eye, he pinned Sykes' location based on his voice: directly ahead, five or six feet between them.

Sykes was laughing. "You're beaten. You're alone in the dark and that's how you'll die. I win, Pope, not you—"

"I don't need to win."

He felt Sykes still for an instant, confused at his words.

Eli said, "I just need you to lose."

With the last of his strength, he launched himself into darkness. He lunged not at Sykes, but past him, to the edge of the ravine. His left foot slid over the lip of the pit. His right hand brushed the outside of Sykes' arm.

Behind Sykes now, Eli spun and grabbed his hair with his left hand. With his injured right arm, he managed to shove his blade deep into Sykes' side, puncturing his kidney.

Stunned, Sykes gave a stifled cry. He struck wildly with his knife. But Eli was behind him and out of reach.

Eli pulled Sykes close, felt his body heat, smelled his sour sweat. He said into his ear, "Game over."

Wrapping Sykes in his arms, Eli flung them sidelong toward the cliff. Sykes' feet scrabbled for purchase but found none. He roared in outrage, his knife hand striking backward and down, stabbing at Eli's neck.

The knife slashed his ear, but he didn't feel the pain. Eli

shoved the knife deeper into Sykes' side. Then he pushed them both over the edge.

Sykes teetered, clawing at Eli's bloody arms. The blood made his skin slick. Sykes' hands slipped away.

Sykes screamed like a wounded demon returning to hell. He plunged into the abyss.

Eli fell with him.

As he fell, Eli managed to twist in midair. His upper half slammed into rock. His legs dangled over the pit, his chest on the ledge, his hands grasping for anything to hold him.

Dimly, he registered the thud of a body striking hard rock far below him.

His own body began to slide backward. A rock broke free and skittered down the sheer wall, dropping a hundred feet, maybe more. Pain quaked through every nerve in his body. His right arm wouldn't work correctly. The agony threatened to paralyze him, his muscles spasming as he skidded toward the abyss.

Panic bit at him. Eli clutched at blood-slick rocks, desperate to drag himself up and over the ledge. His fingers rigid like claws. His fingernails split as his hands found a shallow ridge of stone and dug in, pulling hard, muscles straining. His whole body trembled from exertion and nerve-shredding pain.

He let out a groan. The sound echoed, cruelly mocking him. He was about to fall, to pitch over the edge to his death, with no one to witness his demise but the cold, indifferent rock.

Inch by quivering inch, he hauled his upper half onto the ledge. His boots slid down the steep wall. He dropped several gut-clenching inches before catching himself.

Stinging, burning pain wracked his arm, his leg, and his ribs. Grunting, mustering all his strength, he managed to lever one leg up. Finally, he flung his left leg up and over the ledge, then the other.

Gasping in relief, he rolled away from the edge. He lay on his back, the agony like a boulder pressed upon his chest, blood leaking from a half-dozen cuts, breath rasping from his bruised lungs.

Dully, he touched his head with numb fingers. His hand came back sticky. His night vision goggles were gone. They must have been knocked off in the fight. He stared up at the black nothingness, at the white stars pinwheeling behind his eyelids.

The monster was dead.

Eli had thought he would die. He had been meant to go over the edge with Sykes. By some damned miracle he couldn't comprehend, he hadn't.

He was far from saved. He was injured, bleeding profusely, and hopelessly lost. Down in the dark, hundreds of feet below the sun, with no light to guide him home.

76

ELI POPE

DAY ONE HUNDRED AND FIVE

E li tried to rise, groping his way along the rough wall, but his legs would no longer hold his weight. His knees buckled. He sank against the tunnel wall, the rock damp against his head and spine. He exhaled an unsteady breath.

Dizziness washed through him. He'd lost a lot of blood. He was bleeding profusely from several punctures and slashes, a dozen tiny wounds, a thousand cuts.

It was okay. It was okay because he had done the thing he'd set out to do. The monster was dead. Eli had killed him. The girl and the woman he loved would be safe now, safe at the end of the world.

There was no way out of the labyrinth. If he'd had Ariadne's thread, he might have escaped certain death like Theseus, but alas, he had no string to lead him from this dark maze into precious daylight. He was no Greek hero, and this was no myth.

His movements slow and lethargic, he forced himself to reach for his IFAK kit tucked into a pouch on his chest rig, fumbling for bandages to attempt to slow the bleeding, but it was no use.

One hand clasped his stomach, his blood pulsing like a little river, sliding in rivulets over his knuckles, down his fingers, spurting in time with his heart, slowing, ever slowing.

He was dying.

Time passed. Minutes, and then hours. The silence thick and heavy, his heart turning on him, pumping his life from his inert body. He'd become the darkness, he was the darkness, the darkness was in him, would consume him.

Oh, the irony. At the end of all things, he had found his beginning, only to have it brutally stolen from him. Violence was a cruel mistress, a double-edged sword.

The sound was gradual, a distant thing, unknowable and strange and alien down here. Footsteps approached—slow and hesitant, but purposeful.

He knew he must be hallucinating. There was nothing down here but demons and devils, himself included.

A red tactical flashlight shimmered along the rock floor, reflecting off smooth puddles of water. Not water but blood, he thought dully, his blood.

And then Jackson stood in front of him. He crouched and held the flashlight beam angled down, so as not to hurt Eli's eyes.

Still, Eli squinted as if he'd been trapped in the dark for years, as though his very soul had forgotten the promise of light.

Jackson glanced around warily, pistol in hand. "Where is Sykes?"

"At the bottom of hell."

"Good."

"Lena—-" Eli croaked.

"Will be fine."

"The—the others—" he mumbled, thinking of the brave team members who'd entered the labyrinth with him.

"Don't worry about them. The battle is over. It's you we have to worry about now."

Eli nodded dully. "You came back for me."

"I did."

"Why?"

"For one, before we left, a certain thirteen-year-old hellion told me she'd cut out my tongue and feed it to me if I didn't bring you home."

"Sounds perfectly reasonable."

"She is her father's daughter."

Eli attempted a smile in the dark. It hurt. His mouth wasn't working properly.

"I came to bring you home," Jackson said. "Once they got Lena out, everyone wanted to come back for you. I've got Antoine, Devon, and Nyx a little ways back checking our six. They've got the portable stretcher. Looks like you're gonna need it."

Eli tried to say he was fine, but the words wouldn't come. He was far from fine, and Jackson knew it.

Jackson unslung his pack, squatted, and rummaged through it as he spoke. "You're bleeding pretty badly, so I'm gonna bandage you up as best I can with these Israeli trauma bandages and Quik-Clot to get the bleeding to stop. Then we'll get you out of here, okay?"

While Jackson worked on him, Eli faded for a while. Everything dim and distant. And cold, so impossibly cold. When he came to, he was shivering uncontrollably.

He mumbled, "I think I'm dying."

"You're far too irritating for that. Come on, get up. People are waiting for us."

Eli managed one word. "Who?"

"Everyone that matters," Jackson said simply.

Then Jackson's arm was around his ribs, his arm slung around Jackson's neck, his legs heavy and dragging, Jackson practically carrying him as they trudged in the near dark, shadows pressing in, ghosts breathing all around them. Each step was a grueling ordeal of pain, effort, and exhaustion.

Not today, he thought dimly. The darkness would come for him, but not today.

"How did you find me?" Eli asked.

Jackson's voice was wry and grim. "I followed the cookie crumbs."

"Crumbs?"

"Blood, you big oaf. I followed your blood."

77

ELI POPE
DAY ONE HUNDRED AND TEN

"You're awake."

Eli's eyes fluttered. He groaned and tried to sit up, but a detonation of pain throughout his whole body sent him right back down again. He was on his back in a bed, a mattress beneath him, a feather pillow propping up his head.

He was shirtless, his dog tags and St. Michael's medallion resting on thick white bandages wrapping his ribs and right shoulder. His left hand was bandaged, along with his left leg from ankle to knee, which was propped up with more pillows at the foot of the bed.

An IV bag hung from a hook attached to the bed frame, saline dripping steadily through a plastic tube into the needle taped to the inside of his forearm. The deep laceration carved into his ear was stitched; it felt like someone had pressed a hot iron to the side of his face.

It hurt everywhere. It hurt to move, to breathe.

"I'm alive," he croaked in surprise.

"You're alive," Lena confirmed. She sat in an armchair next to his bed, a pile of yarn and knitting needles in her lap, an array of medical equipment stacked on the antique dresser behind her—

bandages, gauze, topical antibiotic creams, saline bags, needles, a urinal bottle, and a bed pan.

"Barely." Shiloh sat cross-legged on an ottoman in an oversized T-shirt emblazoned with a picture of Darth Vader, the words *#1 DAD* scrawled below it. Her head was bent, and strands of black hair slipped across her face; her mouth pursed in concentration as she sharpened her knife.

Bear flopped on the floor at her feet, snoring loudly.

Eli blinked. "How am I—"

"Still breathing?" Lena asked. "Dr. Virtanen came back. Her family...didn't make it. So, she decided to return, and just in time. You lost a lot of blood. We got you patched up, but it was touch-and-go there for a bit."

"More than a bit," Shiloh said.

"You needed a blood transfusion. The hospital had none left, but we had a donor volunteer. Dr. Virtanen was a bit rusty working with a living patient. She prefers the dead since they don't talk back. You were her first live patient in a good while, but we got it done. I remembered your blood type from the time you hit your head on the boulder at Chapel Rock when we were twelve, remember?"

He did. He remembered waking up in the ER to her concerned, pretty, reproachful face leaning over him, just like now. "The donor?"

"Jackson."

Eli grunted. Jackson Cross, the man he loved and hated. "Why am I not surprised?"

"You're brothers, Eli. In spirit, if not through DNA. It's in your blood."

"Literally," Shiloh quipped.

"He came back for me."

Lena smiled. "He was determined not to leave anyone behind. If there's one thing I can say about Jackson, when he sets his mind to do a thing, he stays on it until it gets done."

"Like a pit bull."

"Or a cockroach," Shiloh said.

"Not so dissimilar to someone else I know." Lena's eyes shone with fierce affection, her chestnut hair swept over one shoulder, with the soft waves burnished bronze in the candlelight.

She was still too thin, her face swollen and bruised from her broken nose at the hands of Angel Flud, but she fairly shimmered with vitality. Her gaze was bright and alert and her cheeks flushed a healthy pink.

His heart tumbled in his chest. She was beautiful, so beautiful, for a moment he forgot the pain, forgot how to breathe.

Clearing his throat awkwardly, he forced himself to look away, to take in his surroundings, blinking blearily as he recognized the log walls and the lacy curtains, the sweet smell of wood smoke. Distant waves murmured as they lapped the shoreline.

"I'm at the lighthouse."

Shiloh rolled her eyes. "He's a genius. No lasting damage from nearly dying."

"Sykes—"

"Is dead," Lena said. "And his gang of criminals, too. Jackson saw to that. I think Nyx single-handedly took out five or six with her sniper rifle. They managed to kill all but one or two of them who snuck out, turned tail, and ran."

It was like he was swimming from a great depth, everything distant and fuzzy around the edges. The pain muddled his brain.

"What about Devon? Nyx and Antoine?"

A shadow darkened her features. "They're okay. They got out."

Eli's chest went cold. They'd lost someone—at least one. He could see it in her face. "Who?"

"The police chief, Sarah McCallister. A couple of rounds got beneath her plates and hit her in the gut. There was too much damage. We tried, but we couldn't perform the surgery she needed."

He'd barely known her, but he did know she had been tough and brave, one of the ones willing to stand in the gap, to fight against evil without pay or reward. For that, she had suffered miserably and died.

She'd been under his charge, and he'd lost her. Like Charlie Payne and David Kepford had been lost fighting to save him. Like the innocent kid in the bowels of Sawyer's yacht. He closed his eyes, remembered that Lena and Shiloh were here and safe, and that Sykes was no more.

That was something.

"And the insulin?" he asked.

"That, too. And the rest of the meds. Cartons and crates of the good stuff: antibiotics, painkillers, beta-blockers, anti-psychotics and anti-depressants, and steroids. Nyx got her beta blockers for her grandma. We have enough to start a real clinic, even reopen a small wing of the hospital maybe."

Eli nodded painfully. "What about the Tiltons? Traci and her son?"

A shadow passed across Lena's face. "Keagan is stable. He was pretty hyperglycemic, but now that he's got the insulin he needs, he's doing great, physically, at least. He and his mom are still at the Inn. They're both in shock and grieving over the death of Curtis."

"We should kick them out after what that woman did," Shiloh said. "I guess the kid can stay, but she almost got you killed!"

Lena shot Shiloh a warning look. "No one is getting kicked out, at least not right now."

"Something has to happen to her. She can't just get away with what she did!"

"We'll deal with them later," Lena said. "We've got plenty to worry about right here, right now."

Shiloh pouted, but she didn't argue for once.

"How long have I been out?" Eli asked.

Lena hesitated. "Five days."

Five days? The shock to his system made him dizzy. He groaned and tried to rise, or at least sit up. Stabs of pain throughout his entire body reminded him why he shouldn't.

"Slow your roll, cowboy." Lena leaned forward, put her hand

on his bandaged chest, and pushed him gently but firmly back. "You need to rest."

"Hurry up, though," Shiloh said. "Don't let your lazy butt lay around too long. I've been doing your chores for days, and it sucks big time."

Reluctantly, Eli obeyed. "Guess I'll be laying off the ten-mile runs for a while."

"Damn straight you will," Lena said.

"You hungry?" Shiloh asked. "We've got bear patties, bear bacon, bear chili, or bear steak."

"Sounds delicious." He offered a wry smile. The smile hurt, but it felt good. It felt...wonderful. There were still threats to contend with: desperate people, Sawyer, and the cartel. But this moment, right here, was perfection.

Lena swiped at her eyes, which had gone suddenly glossy. "I could smack you."

He frowned in confusion. "That took a hard turn."

"We almost lost you." Her voice was raw with worry, her expression a map of the fear and sorrow she'd carried. "I almost lost you."

"That goes both ways." He seized her hand. "We're right here. I'm right here."

She gave him a shy smile. "Guess we'll have to make up for lost time."

"We'd better."

She squeezed his hand. "Nobody knows how the story ends."

"What does that even mean?" Shiloh asked.

"It means I never imagined I would ever be here like this, with you and Eli. That I'd ever have a family. Despite everything terrible that has happened, there is good here, too. There is beauty, joy, and goodness."

Shiloh made a disgusted face. "Eww. Don't get cringy on me."

"Too late." Lena met Eli's gaze. "All we can do is our best, every day. It's all we have. We keep trying." She leaned in and kissed his cheek, smelling of vanilla and sunlight. Her warm lips set his skin tingling. "We don't give up on each other, not ever."

Despite the pain, Eli reached up and touched her temple, tucked a strand of silky hair behind her ear, and traced the contours of her cheek. "I know."

Shiloh watched them, her eyes widening in bewilderment. "Wait, what's happening right now?"

Bear snorted awake, lifted his head, and whined, his big head swinging in confusion from Shiloh to Eli and Lena and back to Shiloh. His bushy tail thumped happily. His fur was already growing out where he'd been unceremoniously shaved.

His wound was healing. Like the humans, it would leave a scar. The walking wounded, with scars that marked what they'd survived.

Lena smiled as she kissed Eli on the mouth. He kissed her back.

"Gross!" Shiloh cried. Horrified, she clapped her hands over her eyes. "Stop, please! What the hell is happening?"

They didn't stop. Eli kissed her harder, deeper, with every fiber of his being. Lena returned the kiss with enthusiasm, though she was cautious of her healing nose. She held his face in her hands, her hair a curtain draped around them.

With an angst-ridden groan, Shiloh leaped from the ottoman and fled the room. She shouted, "Who's paying for my therapy?!"

78

JACKSON CROSS
DAY ONE HUNDRED FOURTEEN

"I t was Astrid," Jackson said.

Lena blinked, stunned. "What?"

Shiloh's expression darkened. Her eyes burned with ferocity, the terrible understanding. "Astrid killed Lily."

Lena, Shiloh, and Jackson had hiked to Sand Point to visit the beach and marsh for foraging. Located a few miles north of town, they'd made it up the trail past several tumbling waterfalls through dense northern hardwoods of sugar and red maple, yellow birch, and hemlock. The leaves of the trees were already tinged red, orange, and yellow.

Summer had vanished as swiftly as it had appeared. The heat and humidity seeped from the earth and the chill of fall creeping in, the sky a hard enamel-blue, as unforgiving as winter when it fell upon them with vengeance.

Jackson told them everything: how he'd unraveled the mystery, thread by thread, leading to Gideon Crawford, then his father, and then ultimately, to Astrid.

He saw his sister clearly now: a wretched soul, deformed not by the scars on her legs but by the grotesque hatred she'd fed and nourished until it consumed her and anything within reach.

"She tried to have me killed," Shiloh said. "She thought I was remembering."

"She did. The thumping sound you heard helped me fit those last pieces together. It was her cane."

Shiloh nodded gravely, pride and satisfaction in her eyes. She had helped catch her mother's killer.

"Do you think your father knew Astrid killed Lily?" Lena asked.

The question still haunted him. "I think he spent his life protecting Astrid from consequences. It was about protecting *his* reputation. I kept sniffing around, asking questions, and my mother knew something. She started remembering, and Horatio saw her as a threat, so he drugged her to keep her from speaking the truth. To my father, secrets stay secrets and bodies stay buried, no matter what. The truth is more dangerous than kryptonite to someone like him. He created his own reality balanced on a precarious house of cards. If one of those cards toppled, then the whole house collapsed."

"Where is your father?" Lena asked.

"He ran. He's gone. He may have linked up with the Côté cartel. As of now, it's unknown."

"And where is Astrid now?" Shiloh asked.

A jolt of guilt speared him. "Astrid is dead."

He didn't know what he expected, but Lena simply nodded, accepting it. Her reaction surprised him. Hers was an indomitable will. Though her nature was to heal, nurture, and help, when it came to protecting those she loved, few were more dauntless.

Lena was alert and bright-eyed, quickly regaining her strength. She had years of insulin to keep her healthy and alive. Jackson loved her like family, more than family, she and Shiloh both.

"Good," Shiloh muttered. The girl shared her father's warrior spirit. She didn't blink in the face of death. Taking a life didn't seem to torment her like it did gentler spirits, like Lena's and his own.

"I killed her." Jackson stared unseeing at Lake Superior. The water shone calm and bright in the near windless day, little frothy ripples ruffling its surface. "I don't know if it was the right thing. I worry that I'm no better than a common criminal."

"It was justice," Lena said.

Fair laws, unbiased court systems, and prisons to incarcerate those who could not abide by society's rules for the betterment of all—that was the justice he'd believed in his entire life. Yet justice had always been flawed, even before the solar flares set civilization on fire.

The justice system had collapsed. He had done the most just thing he could think of to do. The world had changed. For better or worse, he was changing along with it.

Four months ago, to take another person's life would have been shocking and reprehensible. Perspective changed things. He was adjusting to the decay of the old world and the birth of something new.

Still, a thread of despair tugged at his chest. Part of him felt like he'd sacrificed his soul in the act of killing his sister. Fear gnawed at him somewhere deep down; he'd stepped across a line that could never be uncrossed.

All his life, he'd believed he knew the right thing, the moral thing. He was the good guy. And now? Now he didn't know anything.

"I have so many doubts," he said. "I have nightmares."

"Keep doubting. The second you lose that doubt and think you know everything is when you've lost your way." Lena leaned over and brushed an unruly lock of hair out of his eyes. "You haven't lost your way."

Jackson wasn't sure he believed her.

Shiloh saw the torment on his face and took his hand. "Thank you."

He hadn't realized how much he needed her absolution until that moment. Shiloh held his hand in her warm small one and looked up at him with something like affection beaming from that mischievous, elfin face, her coal-black eyes fierce and so very alive.

He knew, in his heart of hearts, that he had done what he had to do. Whether it was the right thing or the just thing, was a different matter. It was a scar he must live with.

"You're free now, Jackson," Lena said.

"What do you mean?"

Lena gave him a penetrating look. With the insulin, she was rapidly regaining her strength and vitality; her eyes were bright and alert. She'd always known him better than he knew himself. "All these years, you've been haunted by this case, by Lily. I don't believe in ghosts, but if I did, I would tell you that she's at rest. You can rest now, too."

It felt like lightness, an unburdening. He had kept the promise he'd made to Shiloh and Lena. He had followed the case to its bitter end and found some semblance of peace for Lily and himself.

That wasn't entirely true. For every mystery he solved, another lay beneath it in ever darker layers. There was a reckoning to be had, things left unfinished in a way he could not articulate.

In some ways, he'd constructed his entire life in penance to his family. There would be no redemption until he had tracked down his missing father and confronted him face to face.

And found...what? He didn't know. The burden of the Cross family, the curse that had plagued him from birth, was not finished with him yet. Nor was he finished with it.

A cold resolve filled him, to end what needed ending.

Lena touched his arm. "I am sorry about your mom."

His mother was gone, too. It still surprised him, fresh grief washing over him at unexpected moments. He'd planned to bring her to live with him at the Inn, but two days after the raid on the mine, he had found his mother stiff in her bed.

Fiona Smith had stayed the night with her but had left when Jackson arrived to remove Astrid's body and bury it in the rapidly growing graveyard. When he'd returned hours later, hands calloused and grimy with dirt, Dolores was dead.

Several empty pill bottles sat on the nightstand beside the bed alongside an empty glass. There was vomit on her nightgown. He didn't know if it was an accident or intentional; perhaps she'd found the state of the world incomprehensible and had chosen to abdicate her own life.

In truth, Jackson had hardly known her, not really. His mother had shielded her deepest emotions, wearing a pleasant mask, playing the role they'd allowed her to play because it was convenient. She had bent herself around others, to their needs and desires, never her own.

He was the only one left who would miss her, though Garrett was still out there, somewhere. In one fell swoop, he'd lost his mother and his sister; his corrupt father had vanished, and his prodigal brother was a complete mystery.

The family that defined him, guilted him, and haunted him— gone.

Shiloh looked up at him with a pensive expression as if she knew exactly what he was feeling. In many ways, she was the only one who possibly could.

"You have us," she said. "We're your family, now."

79

ELI POPE
DAY ONE HUNDRED TWENTY

"Eli," said a voice behind him.
Eli recognized Jackson's distinctive footsteps and did not turn around. Jackson approached and stood next to him. Eli leaned heavily on crutches. He was still incredibly weak, his legs rubbery, and his shoulder stiff and sore, his body betraying him at every turn.

Lena insisted that he rest, but Eli didn't have a restful bone in his body. He had to move, no matter how much it hurt. But each day, step by agonizing step, he got a little stronger.

Together, Jackson and Eli stood on the bluff and looked out over the rugged coastline. The unseasonably high temperatures had finally broken. The day was chilly, in the high sixties. The wind whipped up whitecaps across the lake.

It was already September. Winter was coming, and with it, the frigid cold, starvation, and more death.

It had been four months since the fiery northern lights lit up the skies and set half the world on fire. North America plunged into darkness, along with Canada and Mexico, Russia, Europe, and the entire UK; nearly all of Asia except for Indonesia. In total, over fifty countries, consisting of billions of people, were affected.

Everything transformed in a heartbeat. Things were still changing so rapidly that people's heads were spinning. One must adapt to new ways or die. Some people had adapted better than others.

Some had chosen to drown their sorrow in booze, prescription pills, meth or heroin, or with a bullet to the brain. Hundreds of thousands more had perished due to lack of medical care, hunger, and disease—waterborne illnesses and lack of sanitation, especially in the cities.

As for Eli, he had found his home at the lighthouse, though he feared it wasn't yet safe enough for his little family to return. Maybe it would never be safe.

He sensed Jackson's tension. "What is it?"

"Antoine just called me. A security team captured someone trying to sneak past the checkpoint on Adam's Trail out by the Pictured Rocks Golf Course, where we found the golf carts."

"What do you need me for? Moreno or Nyx can take care of it."

"Antoine says it has to be you. He thinks this clown is a spy."

Eli sucked in a breath. "For Sawyer?"

"No," Jackson said. "For the cartel."

Eli had seen firsthand the cartel's ability to lay waste to anything it touched. Scenes of war slammed through his mind: countless dead, crows picking stringy meat from corpses, flies buzzing across a horrific battlefield.

Every cell in his body thrummed in alarm. Balancing awkwardly on his crutches, he withdrew his pistol, his head on a swivel, scanning the placid scenery as if he could suss out the unseen threat slinking through the trees, coming once again for everything he loved.

In this harsh new world, there were no happy endings. The darkness was unrelenting, ruthless, and malevolent; the only thing to do was to fight, to keep fighting, in a never-ending struggle to push back the despair for a moment, for a day, for a brief respite before rising to fight again.

"They've got him talking," Jackson said. "He says the cartel is coming here, to Munising. They know we stole the meds from Sykes and killed their band of proxy soldiers. He said—" Jackson hesitated, fear on his face.

"Tell me," Eli said.

"He says they're going to burn us to the ground."

AUTHOR'S NOTE

Thank you for reading the third book in the *Lost Light* series, *The Hope We Keep*. This story clocked in at my longest yet at 130k words! I hope you enjoyed the ride! I've really enjoyed fleshing out the location of Michigan's Upper Peninsula, which is rural, wild, and filled with spectacular beauty.

This past September, my family and I visited the U.P. and toured an abandoned copper mine, which included repelling down a deep hole to 300 feet below the surface and edging across a narrow wooden bridge over a fifty-foot deep pit.

This is where I saw the sticking Tommy candle holder the miners once used; I knew instantly it was a perfect murder weapon for one of my characters. I didn't know at first that it would be Lena, but she really stepped up in this third book in the series, and I can't wait to see what she and the others do next. Can you?

Thank you so much for reading this series and following Jackson, Eli, Lena and Shiloh as they struggle not only to survive but to live with purpose even as the world unravels around them.

ACKNOWLEDGMENTS

As always, a deep heartfelt thanks to the behind-the-scenes readers who give early feedback on the raw manuscript as I shape the final story that you hold in your hands. They catch those pesky typos and watch for plot holes and make sure I have my facts right. Any errors are my own.

To my fabulous BETA readers: Ana Shaeffer, Fred Oelrich, Melva Metivier, Jim Strawn, Sally Shupe, Jose Jaime Reynoso, Randy Hasting, Annette King, Rick Phipps, Cheryl WHM, Kathy Schmitt, Cheree Castellanos, Mike Neubecker, Bavette Battern, David A. Grossman, and Courtnee McGrew. Your thoughtful critiques and enthusiasm are invaluable.

To Donna Lewis for her excellent line editing skills.

Thank you to Joanna Niederer and Jenny Avery for detailed feedback and proofreading.

And another special thank you to David Kepford for his tactical expertise and experience in everything from undercover work to paramedic gear and psychological insights into the twisted mind of a killer.

Also, a big thank you to Karen Colley Cleaver for sharing what it's like to live with type 1 diabetes.

To my husband, who takes care of the house, the kids, and the cooking when I'm under the gun with a writing deadline, even when the septic system backs into the finished basement! To my kids, who show me the true meaning of love every day and continually inspire me.

Thanks to God for His many blessings. He is with us even in the darkest times.

Thank you.

ABOUT THE AUTHOR

I spend my days writing apocalyptic and disaster survival novels, exploring all the different ways the world might end.

I love writing stories that explore how ordinary people cope with extraordinary circumstances, especially situations where the normal comforts, conveniences, and rules are stripped away.

My favorite stories to read and write deal with characters struggling with inner demons who learn to face and overcome their fears, launching their transformation into the strong, brave warrior they were meant to become.

Some of my favorite books include *The Road*, *The Passage*, *Hunger Games*, and *Ready Player One*. My favorite movies are *The Lord of the Rings* and *Gladiator*.

Give me a good story in any form, and I'm happy.

Add a cool fall evening in front of a crackling fire, nestled on the couch with a fuzzy blanket, a book in one hand and a hot mocha latte in the other. That's my heaven. I also enjoy traveling to new places, hiking, scuba diving, and the occasional rappel down a waterfall or abandoned mine shaft.

I love to hear from my readers! Find my books and chat with me via any of the channels below:

www.KylaStone.com
www.Facebook.com/KylaStoneAuthor
www.Amazon.com/author/KylaStone
Email me at KylaStone@yahoo.com

Made in the USA
Middletown, DE
21 February 2024

50085269R00288